PUNK ROCK VS. THE LIZARD PEOPLE

PUNK ROCK vs. THE LIZARD PEOPLE

JOSHUA S. PORTER

ALSO BY JOSHUA S. PORTER

The Spinal Cord Perception
The Insect
Nevada
The Joke That We Play On The World
An Edict Of Worms
Cannibals: Iambic Pentameter & The Teaching of Twelve

1st Edition
Cover illustration by Simon Lindenthaler
Jacket design by Tyler Hanns

ISBN-13: 978-0-578-48974-2

THEWORDVIRUS.COM

For Sitcom Monday.

Everybody needs love and affection,
Everybody needs two or three friends.

—The Human League

VI

PART ONE
EARTH ANALOG

"If aliens visit us, the outcome would be much as when Columbus landed in America, which didn't turn out well for the Native Americans. We only have to look at ourselves to see how intelligent life might develop into something we wouldn't want to meet."

Stephen Hawking

2

PROLOGUE
HARBINGER FROM SPACE

For reasons that will become clear around page 41, I feel it best to begin with this image: There's me, 17-year-old Danny Thomas with a towel around my waist, stepping into my room to discover a reptilian humanoid from another world.

"Conspirator," the Lizard Person said.

And he was right, only not for the reasons he thought at the time. This alien in his crimson cloak, his long tail undulating on my bedroom floor, had come to disrupt my world and forever change the lives of my friends and me one winter morning in 1987. When in a single moment one is about to begin an incredible, life-changing intergalactic adventure—an adventure that makes a Spielberg movie seem dull by comparison—one doesn't always realize the gravity of said moment.

In this case, I did.

Standing in a towel before a Lizard Person from outer space, part of me knew that all my teenage angst, romantic complications, my friends, my problems at school, all the pain of the last few years and all the punk rock spirit inside me were somehow converging on this unique moment in human history. Of course, I couldn't find the words to express all that.

So I just said, "holy shit."

MOD LOG 01
WINTER IN OREGON, 1987
[SIX DAYS LEFT ON EARTH]

If you're going to understand my story, you have to put on Lionel Richie's "Say You, Say Me." It is the first song I heard on the day that my friends and I began our quest to overthrow the Lizard People.

It's from *White Nights*—that awful drama from a couple years back. Say what you will about the flick (it blows) but "Say You, Say Me" is seriously bitchin'. Why the song isn't included on the soundtrack is absolutely beyond me. I want to take you back to the beginning of the story—it's like, my job as the author of this log—but we've got to set the mood. My friends say that confessing my affection for Lionel Richie is tantamount to relinquishing my punk rock credibility, but I say *bogus*. If anything, it's *more* punk rock to listen to Lionel Richie.

If you don't have a copy of "Say You, Say Me," you won't understand my story. Your brain will crackle and fizz from all the scientific data, absolutely. Your heart will race in frantic step with our great adventure, sure. Your nerves will tighten and cramp from all the tension, totally. The romance will make you go all warm and gooey inside, duh. But you won't *get it*. Not really, anyway. So put in the *Dancing On the Ceiling* tape (or CD if you're the fancy type) and let's party.

Got it? Wait to hit play, I'll tell you when.

In Portland, Oregon, it rains from September to April. The sun recedes behind a wet, grey haze as fall sets in and doesn't crawl back out of its soggy cave until summer descends and every pallid Oregonian hisses and shields their faces like scalded vampires. Me? I *like* the winter. I like the cold and the smell of wet concrete and groaning radiators in every house. I like falling asleep to the drum of rain on my window at night. I like drinking coffee in the morning (yes, me, 17-year-old Danny Thomas drinks coffee. I'm not trying to act all grown up. I just like it). Of course, admitting you prefer winter to summer is akin to pledging your allegiance to Satan, even in Oregon. I've resigned myself to enjoying the season silently, dreading the heat and the harsh light that will oppress us come May, disrupting my cozy little world.

So, imagine me, Danny Thomas, waking up at 6 a.m. on a Friday morning, November 19, 1987, while it was still dark out. My room is this wicked lair in my mom's attic (it's not as creepy as it sounds). When *Gremlins* came out three years ago, I was so stoked on Billy Peltzer's attic room that I *begged* my mom to let me relocate upstairs. After all we'd both been through that year she eventually gave in. You even access the attic via one of those pull-down ladder doors. It's awesome.

My twin bed is on the far end of the long, narrow chamber— either end of it nearly touching the A-frame ceiling, which I'd covered in rad posters; *Star Wars*, David Bowie, *Evil Dead*, The Ramones, *Aliens*, you name it. The long walls are lined with everything you need to survive a nuclear winter: Comic books, sci-fi novels, Dungeon Master's Guide, a wicked vinyl and cassette collection, a ton of old issues of *Starlog* and *Fangoria*. You know, that kind of stuff.

I'd managed to wire my dad's old turntable into a less-than-awesome GE 3-5635 boombox, which I'd also wired into my more-than-awesome Atari ST computer (I'm not rich, it was a gift from my grandparents on my fifteenth birthday, partly informed I'm sure, by all the grief I'd gone through the year before). All my gadgets were set up on the end of the room opposite my bed, where my tunes were rigged into my Atari ST, which was wired into my Nintendo Entertainment System. By some stroke of unbelievable luck, my mom had been offered a Radio Shack TRS-80 1200 baud modem by a friend who "knew her son liked gadgets." With some work, I'd been able to disable the lockout chip in my NES, gut the TRS-80, and transplant its brains into a hacked NES cartridge that was previously home to an extra copy of *Excite Bike*.

For all you non-tech savvy readers, that means that I can now use my Nintendo to get online.

All this is, of course, beside the point. On that fateful morning in November of 1987, I woke to those digital piano chords that open Lionel Richie's "Say You Say Me," (hit play now![1])

During winter in Portland, the sun doesn't even attempt to show up until around 8 a.m., so it was still dark out. Thin, cold sheets of rain were beading on the single, round window of my attic room, a low drone of white noise. My clock radio alarm must've gone off minutes prior, but whatever the DJ had to say about traffic or the news rebounded off my snoring subconsciousness. Lionel Richie,

---

[1] Lionel Richie, "Say You, Say Me"

on the other hand, broke right through, and I sat up slowly, flicking on my desktop lamp and filling the attic with a gentle, orange-ish glow.

The Mr. Coffee I'd scored at a garage sale made a horrible cup, but I'd snuck it into the attic anyway and kept it just out of sight beside my bed, covered by my dad's old journal, which remained by my bedside at all times for easy access.

My mom wasn't stoked about my coffee intake, but she hadn't exactly wigged out about it just yet. I mostly tried to avoid the subject. That morning, hearing that comforting percolation after I'd flicked the switch, it just seemed to synch with Lionel's ballad and the rain on the window like a match made in heaven.

It was on, man.

I sat up in bed. Rob was sitting silently at my feet, doing nothing. The "Robotic Operating Buddy" (or R.O.B.) was a sad attempt on Nintendo's part to promote the NES, which, as it turned out, wasn't even necessary. Looking like a cheap knock-off of the Number Five robot from *Short Circuit*, Rob kinda sorta interacted with a couple of crappy NES cartridges, but his purpose was questionable at best. Some dweeb of a clerk at Service Merchandise had convinced my mom that Rob was *the* Christmas gift for any Nintendo enthusiast, and there he was under our tree come December 25th. I had, of course, feigned delight and kissed her cheek, but really I was thinking, "What the hell is this thing?"

It didn't take much to modify Rob enough to respond to some simple voice commands by utilizing a few basic Kurzweil speech recognition programs I'd dug up online and some parts I managed to hack from one of those talking Worlds of Wonder Julie dolls. Rob took my voice commands about as well as he played Nintendo games: Pretty damn hit or miss. We had a sort of love/hate thing going on.

"Rob," I said, enunciating dramatically. "Boot up my computer."

"You'll rot your mind," Rob protested, servos whirring as he peered up at me, his flat, rectangular head looking like a pair of space binoculars.

"Rob," I sighed, rubbing my face, "*boot up my computer*."

This time Rob obeyed, turning and scooting across the hardwood floor on the wheels I'd given him.

"You spend too much time on that thing," he nagged.

Why, I wondered to myself, had I added that to his bank of responses?

THE hacked *Excite Bike* cartridge clicked into place inside the Nintendo, and the familiar-yet-infuriating modem static soon followed. For a moment, I saw myself reflecting in the greyish darkness of the blank computer screen. My straight, brown hair— parted to the right and constantly hanging in my face—always drove my mom crazy. I could practically hear her in my head as I ran my fingers through the obstruction, creating a line-of-sight through my stringy mop.

In a moment, the NARS login screen glowed into focus on the Atari ST monitor, asking for my username and password. Whenever possible, I kept any telling personal information away from my public NARS account. To create a profile, you practically had to give a DNA sample, so maintaining anonymity on the NARS servers was impossible. But unlike most users, I didn't even use my first name. My profile is called the Mod Log.

Much of the Mod Log appealed only to the super nerd, but I found myself weaving ambiguous threads of my life-narrative into things like a tutorial on disabling the NES blockout chip. On its best day, the Mod Log was like the very personal diary of a mad teen scientist with an affinity for pop culture and punk rock. At least I liked to think so. It has become more than my geeky way of chronicling (read, *bragging about*) all my misadventures in technological modifications, it is now the very means by which I am distributing my story—the one you're reading now.

I typed in my username and password, and the NARS welcome screen appeared before me. After a cursory read-through of the updates my friends had made to their profiles, I checked to see if anyone had read, commented on, or "liked" my latest update.

By clicking a small smiley face icon at the foot of any given post, NARS users could "smile" at said post. It was the sad, insecure currency of the NARS world: He who has the most smiles wins.

Nothing noteworthy. A couple of smiles from strangers, a friend or two letting the world know what they thought of last night's sitcoms, a banal comment—"so true"—on my recent essay about the infamous Atari 2600 E.T. game.

Okay, far be it from me to interrupt two consecutive times with hardly any break at all—but I want to point out that my thoughts on the *E.T.* cartridge were especially timely. Like every kid in America, I was given a copy of *E.T.* for Christmas in 1982, and like most of those same kids, I didn't get it. I didn't hate the thing; I just

10

couldn't get into it. The rest of the world, however, *loathed E.T.* like it was the damn plague. The entire video game industry crashed the following year, and E.T. took the brunt of the blame. There were even reports that Atari had dumped millions of unwanted copies in the desert of New Mexico, where they rest like dinosaur bones to this very day. Thing is, I don't think *E.T.* is *that* bad a game. I own games that are much worse. Have you ever played *Fire Fly* on Atari? Good God. Anyway, I have no way of proving it, but I think Atari had a rough time financially and that amidst a number of contributing factors, they declined and went kaput. Being able to blame E.T. is just more interesting, and the urban legend about millions of loathsome *E.T.* cartridges under the crust of New Mexico is an absurd yarn that gamers spin to make a boring story more interesting. Companies, even big ones, go out of business sometimes, that's all. For any of you readers in the distant future, I'm entirely confident you can confirm that to date there have been no telling Atari findings out in the Alamogordo desert. If there have, you have my permission to throw this book away right now. But there haven't. So don't.

I sat back in my chair and sipped my steaming cup of coffee from a warm Max Headroom mug that read, "Party to the Max." I stood up and stretched, my red flannel robe draped around my thin—but not *totally* wimpy—frame. I wasn't tall or buff or anything, and even though my mom said I was "the all-American boy next door," I was just sort of a typical teenager. I squirmed out of the robe and pajama pants quickly, practically shivering, and climbed into a typical day's outfit: Denim jacket, threadbare Minor Threat t-shirt, black jeans, black hi-top Chuck Taylor's.

"Rob" I semi-yelled. "What time is it?" Rob seemed to think for a moment before Cyndi Lauper's "Time After Time"[2] began playing from his dinky speakers.

"Damn it, Rob"

BARRELING down 9th Avenue, I centered my gravity on my skateboard, leaning hard, and careened on the sharp corner to Davis Street[3]. With two brisk movements, I ollied over the low curb outside of Fuller's Café, then pushed the tail down into the wet concrete to bring my ride to an abrupt, satisfyingly crunchy stop. Hopping from the deck, I stomped the tail once more and the board popped from the sidewalk and into my hands, the cold trucks wet to the touch. Without looking, I reached for the Walkman fastened to my hip like a cowboy's revolver and drove my thumb into the STOP button before Gang Green could hit the final chorus.

The sounds of the street faded into the foreground, and I was suddenly aware of the smell of wet concrete and exhaust: Portland in the morning. Through the rain-streaked windows of the café, I could see Conner, black-clad and solitary at our booth, hunched over a book.

"Church is closed on Friday, Altar Boy," I laughed settling into the booth across from Conner, who I could now see was squinting into an open Bible.

"Ah ah," Conner tisked, his gaze still fixed on the book. "The God who made the world and everything in it is the

---

[2] Cyndi Lauper, "Time After Time"
[3] Gang Green, "Skate to Hell"

Lord of heaven and earth and does not live in temples built by human hands."

"Is that you or the Holy Scriptures?" I asked.

"The Apostle Paul, retard," Conner sighed, closing the weathered tome. "Good morning."

Conner Froud: How to describe this anomaly? Conner introduced me to punk rock when I was 14 by giving me a copy of The Ramones' *Rocket to Russia.* Every cool band I listen to—The Cramps, Black Flag, Bad Brains—Conner discovered them first by befriending the clerk at Music Millennium, his favorite record shop in the city. Conner's all-time favorites were The Misfits, a bizarre outfit marked by Elvis-like crooning set to dissonant power chords and goofily morbid lyrics. Their signature emblem—The Crimson Ghost of the eponymous 1964 horror flick—was forever stitched on the breast pocket of the black leather jacket Conner wore every day, year round. Actually, he wore the same outfit entirely, every day, year round. A tattered black t-shirt, equally ratty black jeans, and black leather combat boots to compliment his coat, both of which he claimed to regret since becoming a vegetarian. His hair was a long and scraggly black mop, teased and stringy as if he'd acquired a bottle of hairspray at some point and never recovered. His black Ray Bans usually masked whatever emotion managed to eek out in conversation.

Conner's parents had all but disowned him, and he avoided being kicked out of his house by keeping to himself and staying out of trouble at school. A couple of years ago, some classmate of ours attempted to save Conner's discernably hell-bound soul by proselytizing his head off through an entire period of P.E. using some bogus speech he'd obviously been fed at his local youth group.

13

Conner had sat there quietly, either staring right at this young evangelist, or out into the gym (because of his shades, no one could tell). When the whole spiel was over, he had simply said: "Damn. Jesus is *punk rock*."

And that was it. Conner started reading a bible and digging this Jesus of Nazareth dude, whom Conner described as a poet, a revolutionary, and a criminal. Exactly Conner's type. The rest of us assumed the Jesus-phase might subside, but Conner's fandom showed no signs of waning. He had little patience for what he called "bullshit Christians," but for this Middle Eastern dude from 2,000 years ago, he had all the time in the world.

On that winter day in 1987, Conner was first to our morning meeting ritual, a cigarette smoldering in the ashtray before him.

"Good morning, Father Froud," I bowed solemnly, "You better give up the ol' cancer sticks before they revoke your preaching license."

"Pray for me," he said, extinguishing the butt and scooting the ashtray aside. "What are you listening to?" Conner looked down his nose at the Walkman as I set it atop my backpack in the booth next to me.

"Christopher Cross," I lied. "What can I say? 'Sailing' helps me get in the zone when I skate."

"Your sarcasm belies your insecurity, my friend," Conner leveled a finger at me. "What guilty pleasure lurks in thy Walkman? Tell me you're not still jamming that Cameo record."

"Cameo is not a *guilty* pleasure. You just lack the soul to fathom that gnarly bass."

"Funk is for dweebs," said Conner. "This is why you are a poser."

Before I could defend myself, a thick British accent interrupted my prepared defense of Cameo's bass lines.

"Cameo is gnarly, Conner," Jade Calegory said excitedly, settling into the booth beside me with his backpack in his lap. "You're so punk that I worry you'll narrow your listening experience to the point I reckon the only thing you'll be able to listen to is the static of that busted TV in your room."

"Hey!" Conner barked, giving Jade the same wary index finger I'd seen moments prior. "That TV works just fine."

"Dude," I scoffed. "You spend more time pounding on that lamewad TV with your fist than you do watching it."

"On this you are correct," Conner conceded. "I am not a slave to the idiot box, unlike *some* spazzoid over here."

"I'm a foreigner in this great nation," Jade said in mock defense. "I've been tasked with the burden of using the telly to lower my IQ to a more *American* standard."

Conner threw a straw at Jade while I punched him in the arm. Jade Calegory's family had moved to America from an English village called Fair Oak. He'd been a social enough guy his first year at our school but found in our little crew a shared obsession with movies, TV, video games, and music. He was loud, always full of energy, and surprisingly sentimental. Jade was so fond of our company that we could always count on him to show up and participate in our never-ending arguments.

"Surely you, Conner, owe this British lad a certain amount of respect. After all, 'tis our people who invented the punk rock of which you are so fond."

"Hold the phone, Prince Charles," Conner immediately protested. "We had The Ramones and New York Dolls before your posh Sex Pistols ever trashed a hotel room."

15

"Bollocks," Jade said. "The Dolls were just glam poofters. The Ramones are about as punk as The Monkees."

"Dude," I said. "The Monkees? What the hell are you talking about?"

"That's a thing, right?" Jade asked, turning to me as if he were asking in confidence.

"The Monkees are like, a 60's sitcom band."

"Who am I thinking of?"

"We have no idea."

"The *point* is," Conner interrupted, "that your insult is bogus, Mr. Knit Sweater."

"Oh, begging your pardon," Jade laughed. "My studded jacket is at the cleaners."

For all his knowledge of punk trivia, Jade was just an ordinary British teenager usually dressed in a loose-fitting sweater and blue jeans, his hair gelled back.

The same waitress to serve us every Friday morning for the last two years appeared, placing a steaming coffee mug in front of me before setting out a few glasses of water and promising to return with the rest.

"We're one short this morning," Conner smiled at the waitress, his commitment to manners contrasting his appearance.

"No problem, sweetie," the waitress replied absently.

"Who are we missing?" Jade asked.

"Emma's family just got back from California last night," Conner said between short sips from his glass of water. "I doubt she'll want to get up early to hang with you bozos."

Emma. My stomach undulated at the sound of her name, then sank with the realization that she wouldn't be showing up this morning. "Is she coming to school?" I asked, putting on my very best casual voice.

Conner shrugged, then nodded to the café entrance. "Here comes the rest of the band."

"I could *so* be in a band," Becky said, appearing beside me. "Sorry we're late, it's Barrett's fault."

"What the hell, Becky?" Barrett said, moving into the booth with his palms up in frustration.

"What?" Becky shot back, "I was ready at 7:30."

Barrett turned to face the rest of us as if Becky had suddenly vanished. "I waited outside her house for ten minutes."

"Oh please," Becky groaned.

"You're here now," I offered. "Thus, all is right in the world."

"All could have been right sooner," Becky mumbled.

"Yes," Barrett said coldly, his eyes back on Becky. "Yes, it could have."

Becky smiled, her freckled nose wrinkling, and sipped from a glass of water, only asking if it was for her afterward.

Rebecca Burkley, the sassy freckle-faced redhead from the Deep South, had wandered into our oddball brigade on a total whim. We had met in Chemistry and settled into an effortless rapport one seldom develops even amongst family. Becky became like a sister to me, and before anyone realized it was happening, she was grafted into our little group. She didn't care for all the nerdy things we went on about per se, but Becky was as clever as any of us and far more emotionally mature. With her endlessly fiery personality, beautiful face and figure, any of us could have fallen for Becky, but instead, she became a sister to the group, and we became brothers to her—hyper-protective brothers. I'm sure many of her gal friends wondered why she wasted so much time with us, but she was as faithful a friend as anyone could hope for, and our social circles eventually just accepted the strangeness of our connection.

"*Any*way," Becky said with cartoon exaggeration, then smiled at the table. "How is everyone?"

"No, no, no," Barrett said, stifling Becky's warm inquiry. "Let the record represent *my* reliability and *Becky's* tardiness. I want that settled before we move on."

Becky crossed her eyes. "Gag me with a spoon. I apologized a squillion times."

Barrett Stevens was a comic foil to Becky's feminine liveliness. Though he had the looks and physique to be some class of high school jock or elite, he preferred painting and arguing about movies with us. He came off gruff at first, but he was deeply loyal, and despite all his razzing, I think he just loved our company. His straightforward personality and generous sense of humor seemed to contradict his artistic bent—Barrett spent much of his spare time in a closet he had converted into a dark room for developing the photos he'd taken of the city of Portland. Like the rest of us, he was more clean cut than Conner and favored denim jackets and button ups to tattered leather, but ever since *Back to the Future* had come out a couple of years ago, he wouldn't stop wearing that same red Class-5 vest donned in the movie by Marty McFly, much as we begged him to retire it.

"Paul didn't ride with you guys?" Jade asked, drawing our attention to the absence of our final party member (other than Emma, who apparently wouldn't show this morning, major bummer).

"He's paying for parking," Barrett said absently, finally relaxing into the booth and lifting the same menu he'd seen dozens of times before this morning.

"Barrett!" Becky scolded, "You made Paul pay for parking?"

"He offered!" Barrett said.

"He always does," Conner shrugged.

A moment later, Paul Patchett strolled into the diner, a black beanie pulled over his shaved head.

"Poor baby," Becky sighed. Paul looked at her, confused.

The peacekeeper of the group, Paul specialized in thankless favors and uninvited (but undeniable) wisdom. Paul was a better friend than any of us knew how to be, and even though he was a year older, he was more laid back than the rest of the group. Happy to sit comfortably in the background, Paul's endless kindness and inability to get pissed off drew us all into silent admiration.

"What did I miss?" He asked, unzipping his grey Members Only jacket.

Jade started counting his fingers. "Either Barrett or Becky are to blame for your collective tardiness, but we'll never know whom. Before that, we deduced that Conner is too punk for Cameo's funky bass lines, even though Brits created punk and are therefore authorities on the matter."

"Also," I added, "Conner is too punk for TV, which is just as well because his ancient static box is always on the fritz."

"Did that thing finally break?" Paul asked, sipping the water that had been waiting at his seat.

"It's not broken," said Conner. "And anyway, who cares? You know the Lizard People use that stuff to brainwash us."

"Here we go," Becky sighed, rolling her eyes.

"Sorry," Conner grunted. "The *Imi*. Didn't realize 'Lizard People' was offensive at this table."

"It isn't," said Becky. "But your conspiracy theories are a little silly." She offered him a patronizing pat on the shoulder.

Our waitress appeared, as if from nowhere, and asked, "the usual?"

Conner looked around at the table, and when we'd all confirmed with a nod, spoke for the group. "Yes ma'am, that'd be righteous. Thank you."

She nodded with a half smile before disappearing again.

"Why do you drink that?" Becky sneered at the black coffee I'd been quietly enjoying.

"Danny is a mad scientist," Barrett stated in mock admiration. "Every mad scientist worth their lab coat has to have coffee jitters."

"You have jitters?" Becky asked, sounding concerned.

"I don't have jitters," I said.

"But you *are* a scientist," she insisted.

"Not sure about that one either."

"Dude," Conner interjected, "as long as you're making computers out of toasters and stuff, you should come fix my Nintendo."

"The Imi aren't controlling your mind with Nintendo?" Jade asked.

"Price worth paying," Conner shrugged.

"He can fix that NES all day, but what the hell are you going to play it on? That busted-ass TV?" Barrett goaded.

Conner raised a middle finger at Barrett without turning to face him. "Don't end sentences with prepositions, man."

"Why the sudden concern for grammar, Reverend?" I asked Conner.

"I have my moments," he said.

"Where is Emma?" Becky asked, and I felt my stomach slip again.

"Probably sleeping," Jade offered, as though he had become the authority on Emma's whereabouts. "She's only just back from holiday."

"*Vacation*, dammit," Barrett barked, banging a fist on the table. "You better straighten up and fly right, Napoleon!"

"Dude, Napoleon was French," Jade said.

Barrett raised an eyebrow and sipped slowly from his water glass. "Close enough," he finally said.

"You can watch TV at my house, Conner," Becky said, leaning over the table as if to shut the rest of us out of her invitation.

"To watch what?" Conner laughed, "reruns of *ALF*?"

Becky immediately spoke up to defend herself, but couldn't get a word in over our gloating howls and laughter. She watched *ALF* like a lonely housewife watches soap operas.

Our waitress reappeared and mechanically distributed the same dishes we ordered every Friday morning. We thanked her as she topped my mug off and warned us not to be late for school.

"*ALF* is a *good show*," Becky said defensively as if the conversation had never stalled.

"Nothing quite like an anthropomorphized wad of fur and felt to round out prime time television," Barrett said. "You're not missing much, Conner."

"That 'wad of fur and felt' is my favorite Muppet, thank you very much," said Becky. "You like Muppets, Conner. Don't act all high and mighty."

21

"I like *Muppets*, Becky. *Muppets*. ALF is not a Muppet."

Becky crossed her eyes again. "Oh my God, seriously. What is he then?"

"He's the all-American sitcom star," Jade laughed, mouth full of pancakes.

"Seriously though," Becky went on, unwilling to relent. "What's the difference?"

"The difference," I said, sipping my coffee, "is that a psychedelic hippie with a beard didn't create ALF."

"Hey!" Conner barked, pointing at me again. "I'll not have Jim Henson spoken ill of at this table."

We all groaned.

"Here we go," Paul sighed, exhausted by the Jim Henson motif.

"No, no," Conner said, "Jim Henson is punk rock."

"Ah for Christ's sake," Barrett grumbled, rubbing his temples. "We *know* about the punk rock adventures of Jim Henson, creator of the Muppets."

"He's 'fearless,'" I recited, doing my best Conner impression.

"He's 'a visionary,'" Becky added.

"Always re-inventing himself," Jade said attempting an American accent, spinning his hand in the air.

"Guys, listen to me, I actually have something *new* to contribute to this," Conner pleaded. "Now he's in *jail* for being so punk rock."

"Or for LSD," Paul laughed, stealing a bite of Conner's pancakes.

"He's not into drugs, man," Conner said.

"Why is he in jail, our resident conspiracy theorist?" Jade finally asked, taking the bait.

"Dude. For *The Dark Crystal*."

I furrowed my brow and took a long sip of my rapidly cooling coffee. A few years ago, Jim Henson—benevolent bearded creator of Muppets—had embarked on the noteworthy task of producing the world's first fully puppet-populated feature film. Rather than stocking his completely fabricated fantasy world with smiling, googly-eyed sock puppets, Henson had opted to employ complex, realistic creatures that required the combined efforts of hundreds of designers, builders, and puppeteers. More surprising still, the resulting movie, *The Dark Crystal*, was a creepy, humorless adventure featuring screeching monsters, sword fights, and genocide.

The *real* uproar over *The Dark Crystal*, however, had less to do with confused parents and more to do with implied insurrection. The antagonists of Jim Henson's surprising foray into dark fantasy bore an uncanny resemblance to the Lizard People—or, for those politically correct readers who prefer to call them by their native name, *the Imi* (pronounced *ee-mee*). Humanoid, reptilian, buzzard-like creatures garbed in royal robes and ornate jewelry. It didn't take long for someone to wonder whether Henson had some subversive parody in mind—the similarities to our alien guests were pretty glaring. Henson refused to comment on the suspicious resemblance. *The Dark Crystal* tanked at the box office, and Jim Henson disappeared from the public eye.

Which is a shame, because *The Dark Crystal* is totally wicked. You *have* to see it. Not to mention the fact that rumors had been swirling that Henson was in talks with none other than David Bowie about the possibility of some insane puppet musical. With Henson hidden away somewhere, incommunicado, his outstanding projects were put on hold, and rumors began to circulate that the not-soflattering depiction of the Imi had something to do with it. That he had been *locked up*, however, as Conner was now suggesting, seemed pretty farfetched.

"In *jail?*" Barrett said, vocalizing the apprehension we were all feeling.

"For what?" Becky asked.

"Man, that dude ain't in jail for that movie," Paul laughed, reaching for another bite of Conner's pancakes. Conner lifted his hands as if he was baffled by Paul's willingness to dismiss the conspiracy theory and yet partake of Conner's pancakes.

"Why would he be in jail for the movie?" Becky asked again.

"You think the Imi *locked him up* because he made some puppets that kinda sorta remind people of them?" I asked, making no effort to disguise my disbelief.

"I'm just saying, man," Conner shrugged. "Dude was *prolific*. Projects left and right. He was about to work with *Bowie*, dude."

"Freakin' Bowie," Jade nodded to himself. Who could argue with Bowie? Bowie was punk to his *core*.

"I just feel like no one is listening to me," Becky groaned.

"For God's sake," Barrett sighed, turning to face Becky in mock attentiveness. "Jim Henson is that guy who made up the Muppets. He operates Kermit the Frog. He made that whacked out movie with all the lizard-vulture-puppet-things we went and saw a couple of years ago."

"I didn't like that," Becky interrupted, wrinkling her freckled nose.

Barrett stared at her impatiently.

"I'm *listening*," she fussed.

"Some people think those buzzard things were meant to parody the Imi, and since they're the *bad* guys in the movie, that'd be pretty controversial. Now Jim Henson has gone mysteriously missing, so Conner over here—ever the subversive thinker—wonders if he's been locked up by the evil powers that be."

"Oh my God," Becky gasped, suddenly getting it. "They locked him up for that? Can they do that?"

"They *didn't* do that," Paul reiterated, chewing a mouthful of pancakes.

"What the hell, Paul," Conner protested. "You can't eat my pancakes and piss on my theories, man."

"Sorry sweetheart, I haven't got time for anything else," Paul quoted, doing his best to sound like Han Solo.

"That quote doesn't even work here, man," Conner said.

"So wait," Becky pleaded. "So he's *not* in jail?"

"We don't know, actually," said Jade. "Conner suspects he might be. Popular opinion likely suggests otherwise."

"Those things in the movie didn't *really* look the Lizard People," Becky thought aloud.

"Subtlety, Becky," Conner said, pointing a fork at her. "Besides, it's not like any of us hang out with Lizard People. We've never even seen them in real life."

"Who *has*?" Paul asked as if this point proved nothing. "It's not like they hang around Portland."

"Portland, no. Vancouver, yes."

Vancouver, Washington—a city just north of Portland—was home to a semi-secret research facility that was rumored to employ Imi scientists. Very few knew what went on there. It was something of an urban legend in the Pacific Northwest.

"Well then go peek in the windows of the big bad lab and let us know how subtle Jim Henson was," I said to Conner, setting my empty coffee mug down on the table.

"Get Mem'Rah's autograph while you're there," Paul added. "We can sell it."

Our waitress casually tossed the bill in the middle of the table. "We good?" She asked.

"Very," Conner smiled, as the group moved all at once to lay crinkled bills and rattling change atop the receipt, already soaking up rings of moisture from a nearby water glass.

THIS was our mini-society. Each of us cut from different cloths, different stories to tell, different rungs on the high school social ladder, and yet somehow we had found one another. There were imperfections, to be sure. Insecurities, pettiness, you know, *human* stuff. But here we were. I think all this occurred to me as we stood up from the table that morning. At least it seems that way now, looking back.

Of course, I have assigned the morning a tremendous amount of retroactive significance, given everything that followed. Even so, I can't help but meditate on these little details, the things that made us who we were. I wish that I'd thought about it more. Writing it down this way feels like one way of confessing my profound affection for this group of misfits.

I wish I could do more.

Once outside, Conner lit another cigarette and we all set to work shaming him for his disgusting habit.

"I've been given a thorn in my flesh," Conner said, the cigarette bouncing on his lips as he spoke. "A messenger of Satan, to torment me. Three times I pleaded with the Lord to take it away from me. But he said to me, 'My grace is sufficient for you, for my power is made perfect in weakness.'" Having finished his mini-speech, he flicked the butt away.

"What's that, Pastor?" Barrett asked, retrieving car keys from his Marty McFly vest.

"Once again, the Apostle Paul."

"The Apostle Paul wrote about nicotine addiction, did he?"

"No," Conner sighed, fanning away the last wisps of smoke. "Just trying to get some damn sympathy around here."

"Have a good day, Breakfast Club!" Becky smiled, putting on her coat, ignoring the spontaneous bible lesson.

We all groaned.

"When you grow up," she warned us, quoting *The Breakfast Club*, "your heart dies."

"Who cares?" I sighed.

"*I* care," she smiled, delighted that I'd acknowledged her reference.

Standing outside of Fuller's café, Jade, Conner and I stood there in the light rain, holding our skateboards by their wet trucks as Paul, Barrett, and Becky climbed into Barrett's Ford Aerostar parked just outside. Barrett rolled the window down and nodded at the three of us on the curb.

"You guys want to skitch a ride to school?"

By *skitching*, Barrett meant the seemingly awesome but actually horrifying act of riding a skateboard whilst clinging to the back of a moving vehicle.

"Dude," Conner called back, "people don't really skitch. They'd die."

"Marty McFly did it," Barrett reminded us.

"Always with the Marty McFly," I groused. "Yeah well, when you have a special effects team to help us, let me know."

"I bet he really did it," Barrett said thoughtfully as the window ascended.

MOD LOG, 02
THE GIRL

I was late.

I could hear the bell ringing over my skateboard's tail, grinding into the sidewalk as I dragged to an abrupt stop.

"Dammit," I hissed through my teeth, jogging into the glass double doors and creeping down the already empty main corridor of Wesley High. I made every effort to sneak mouse-like toward my locker, open it and place my skateboard inside as if I risked waking some flesh-eating giant. The irony, of course, was that no matter how quietly I crept about; I still had to barge into first period late. No avoiding that one now.

Looping the combination lock through the latch, I felt a presence looming over me. I turned to find none other than Mr. Clanton himself—principal of Wesley High—within an inch of my freaking face. I lunged backward, reflexively, dropping my bag and books everywhere. Mr. Clanton stood there statuesque, impervious to my shock.

"Mr. Thomas," he purred, like some movie villain having finally cornered his protagonist. "Running late, are we?"

"Woke up sick," I lied. "But I decided school was too important to miss, sir. So I finished barfing, got cleaned up, and booked it to first period."

"Newfound appreciation for your education then, Mr. Thomas?" Clanton's nose drifted upward as he spoke, observing me like a supine insect.

"More appreciative every day, sir," I nodded, turning away.

Mr. Clanton grabbed my shoulder, rotating me slowly to face him again. If I asked you, right now, to draw a suspect sketch that I described as, "failed drill sergeant turned high school principal," you'd draw Mr. Clanton. Perpetually misted by sweat, thin lips drawn over small yellow teeth, jutting chin, black-rimmed glasses and a buzz cut so precise it must've been issued with a clenched butthole. Tall, lanky with instances of muscle-turned-flab here and there, Mr. Clanton's short-sleeved button up never escaped the confines of his high-water slacks. He hated the things many authority figures hate: People below or unlike himself, ideas new or alien to his way of thinking, and teenagers. He sighed, apparently not done talking.

"So when I saw you and your gang of delinquents funneling out of Fuller's Café this morning, you had just pulled your sickly head out of a toilet long enough to grab breakfast?"

"Geez, Mr. Clanton," I stammered, running a hand through my hair. "I was okay then, yeah, I mean, sure. But something didn't agree with me, y'know?"

"I'm sure if I asked those of your misfit gang who *did* make it to class on time, they'd confirm observable signs of your impending illness."

"Oh sure, Mr. Clanton, they'd say as much."

"Why do you drag those students down, Thomas?" Clanton sighed, finally releasing my shoulder. "Mr. Stevens, Mr. Patchett... Did it ever occur to you they might prefer to *do* something with their lives besides play video games and skateboard?"

Except for Conner, most of my friends did just fine in school. They kept their heads down, their noses clean, and just did their work as to avoid the greater headache that typically proceeded rebellion.

Mr. Clanton cleared his throat, apparently expecting some answer to his dumb-ass question, but I said nothing. Just looked down and stared at my shoes like a total chump.

"And Miss Burkley? Miss Cates?" he tisked. "Not exactly your class of people, Mr. Thomas." His thin, froggy lips drew up in a smirk.

It's true that most folks had no idea why Becky or Emma spent so much time with us. With me in particular. I'd often heard of certain teachers pleading with either of them to avoid me, lest my unsavory no-goodness tainted them. Becky and Emma almost never shared those stories with me, presumably concerned for my feelings and capable of seeing through my lame attempts at emotional invincibility.

"Get out of my sight," Clanton growled, and to annoy him just a little, I moved very slowly down the hall as if unexcited by his effort to flatten my spirit. I even hummed quietly, which was probably pushing it.

STANDING outside of first period algebra, I had now come to the final moments of my ability to blissfully ignore the knowledge that, in all likelihood, Emma would be among the crowd of students to suddenly turn and follow my tardy entrance.

Emma Cates. Emz. The living embodiment of "still waters run deep." A petite little brunette, her long, flowing hair usually drawn up or over one shoulder, Emma was thin and delicate looking, fair skinned, elegant nose, soft pink lips, big blue eyes with impossibly long lashes. A unique beauty utterly unlike the bland bombshell cheerleaders or the glasses-wearing pretty-in-disguise nerd girls. She was like a would-be ballerina and teen European model hybrid. Like Becky, Emma was subject to an endless parade of crushes and admirers who could never quite figure her out and eventually threw their hands up in frustration. Emma was quiet until you got to know her, then she was outgoing, fun-loving, thoughtful, clever, and unintentionally hilarious.

She was also one of us. As long as our group had been around—our *Outsiders*, our *Goonies*, our (shudder) *Breakfast Club*—Emma had always been a part of it.

And yeah, I've been madly in love with her the whole time. So what?

You'd be surprised the lengths you can go to in order to suppress your affection for one of your closest friends. For the longest time, no one had any clue I was secretly infatuated with Emma. An engine that kept the vehicle of our gang in motion was the fact that we were strangely mismatched and yet dealt with one another as a family. There had been the makings of a juvenile love triangle once or twice, but we recovered quickly. Emma and Becky knew and related to us as guys that cared for them *without* the hassle of wanting to be their boyfriends, so fessing up to my deep dark secret was absolutely out of the question. Besides, I'd only been hiding it for a year. I was sure it'd go away any moment now. I'd often gone through mental exercises during particularly intense bouts of admiration. Picture Emma belching, picture Emma barfing, picture Emma on the toilet (gross), picture my Grandma on the toilet (worse). But all I did was pave the way to escape into my imagination with Emma—picture Emma laughing, picture Emma dancing, picture Emma in a bikini...

So on that morning in November, standing outside of first period, I fired up some stock "unappealing Emma" routines to mute my excitement over her return to Portland after a couple of weeks visiting family in California, balanced of course, with a friendly "welcome home." (Emma with rotten teeth, Emma screaming at a little old lady, Emma punching a kitten, Emma rising from the foamy waters of the Oregon coast, sun-dappled, goose-skinned, in a two-piece, swinging her wet hair...)

Dammit.

I took a deep breath, shook the image from my mind (by physically shaking my head), and opened the door. There came the immediately drawn attention, the predictably sarcastic welcome, and in the back of the classroom next to the only empty desk: Emma Cates.

Somehow, the two weeks away had made her *more* gorgeous, and I thought, "What sorcery is this?" But I managed to muster my coolest, most casual walk, and I sat down in the empty desk beside her, ignoring the tracking gaze of every lamebrain in Algebra 2 and gave Emma a devil-may-care smirk and nod of recognition—which I'm fairly certain was actually a creepy, lurching grin.

Emma smiled back, silently mouthing a hello with a look of excitement, simply happy to be reunited with a friend.

"YOU guys didn't have too much fun without me, did you?" Emma asked, making an irresistible pouty face after the bell had rung and students began to flee Algebra in a scramble.

"Duh," I scoffed. "We've exhausted the possibilities of fun. There's none left for you, I'm afraid."

"Shut up," she smiled, giving me a feeble punch in the arm. "Are we doing something tonight?"

"We?" I asked after a momentary pause, blood probably rushing to my face.

"Yeah," she said with a confused look. "Everyone. Are we hanging out?"

"Oh, right, yeah, we totally should."

"I'll tell everyone. We'll come over tonight."

"Right on," I nodded—presumably like an idiot—"See you then."

Outside the classroom, I sighed at my open locker, looking down at my skateboard and wanting more than anything to get the hell out of Wesley High. I peered down the crowded hallway and groaned at the sight of Flynn Hardey and Bradley Press as they came sauntering over like a couple of make-believe fashion models.

Flynn and Bradley were two of Wesley High's only examples of what it meant to be "NARS famous." With a few hundred thousand NARS connections between the two of them, these two deluded assholes were more convinced of their notoriety than any human had ever been in the history of time. They walked around Wesley High with their noses in the air radiating their self-approval and dressed like a couple of preppie pretty boys who had agonized over just the right button up to tuck into their tight jeans.

"The lighting wasn't right," Flynn was saying as he opened the locker just a few down from mine. "It made my hair look all wrong."

"Oh God," Bradley nodded. "I know exactly what you mean. I tried to get the perfect narsy for an hour before I just gave up altogether."

"It's like, I believe in the cause," Flynn said, forced look of sincerity on his child-like face. "But I just can't post content that's out of synch with my brand, y'know?"

"Totally, bro," Bradley nodded, eyes closed. "It's like, I appreciate that they want to, like, stop AIDS and all, I really do. But if I start posting something I don't believe in, I'm not being true to myself, man."

"Oh God," I groaned, turning to them. "You narcons are killing me. Just give me a minute to get out of earshot, so I don't have to hear another second of your narcissistic blathering."

"Oh, I'm sorry," Flynn grunted sarcastically, crossing his long arms. The guy was tall and thin and painstakingly groomed. "Did we arouse your jealousy?"

"Listen to yourselves," I said. "You're actually bragging about taking narsies as if the very concept isn't shameful. Are you not embarrassed to confess your love for taking pictures of yourself?

"*We* were both *personally* invited to an AIDS Action Committee benefit last night. Our NARS profiles are doing so much good in the world that AAC came to *us* to promote the cause."

"Yeah, yeah," I sighed, pinching the bridge of my nose as if they were giving me a migraine. "I heard all about it. You spent the evening taking pictures of yourselves, and you're not going to say anything about AIDS relief after all because your hair didn't look quite right."

"We're trying to *change the world*," Bradley sneered, leaning toward me. "What good are *you* doing? Helping people turn Atari games into cassette players?"

"FM radios."

"Either way," Flynn laughed, cinching up his backpack. "I'm sure the five people that see your NARS profile appreciate it."

"Sounds like you're one of them," I said. "Thanks for reading."

"Eat shit, loser," Bradley snarled before the two of them whirled around and strolled proudly out of sight.

"Sheesh," I whispered to myself, turning around. Then the Washington rednecks got me.

Though Washington State is a mere twenty-minute drive over a river, the class of hillbilly they grow there feels as if it belongs on another planet. Garbed in baggy stonewashed jeans and thermal underwear draped in unbuttoned flannel, these mulleted freakazoids were more fearful of anything new or unknown than even Mr. Clanton. Their only means of confronting the horrifying outside world was to fan their mullets out like defensive peacocks, then set to work hurling insults or fists, whichever was more appropriate for the situation at hand. Many had migrated to Oregon, and we now had several at Wesley High. There I was at my locker when two archetypal goons suddenly flanked me.

"Hey boy," one of them said between loud smacks of gum. "You know Rebecca Burkley, don'tcha?"

I had a whole database of sarcastic responses to this question, but today, I just wanted to make it to seventh period and get the hell out of here, so I ignored them.

"This one, here?" The other goon snorted in unbelief. "*He* knows that redhead babe with the rack? You her little faggot friend or something, boy?"

I sighed, blinking slowly.

"Hangs around with Emma Cates, too," the first redneck chuckled, giving me a shove, "ain't that right?"

"Well I'll be damned," his crony said in mock wonder. "Now that little gal is a serious piece of ass."

"Hey boy," the first one went on, "how you get in with those girls, anyway? You paint your nails together? Braid each other's hair?"

I looked around the busy hallway. I could've just walked away.

"Hey!" the other one shouted. "You deaf, faggot? You need to tell both those bitches to give *us* a call if they want—"

Before he could finish, I had wound up and hit him in the face. I could hear Conner's words in my mind, "those who take up the sword will die by the sword," and before the Conner of my imagination could gloat I was on the ground and they were wailing on me. I crossed my forearms in front of my face like a shield, and they both set to work clumsily jabbing me in the ribs, barking out threats, trying to get a shot at my face.

On my back, peering through my makeshift faceguard, I could see my skateboard teetering upright in my open locker. I drew up a knee, slammed it into the lockers, and the skateboard came down on Redneck Number One's skull with a sharp cracking sound. The Neanderthal leaped up, grappling at his burning brain case, a string of indecipherable obscenities escaping from his clinched teeth like air from the pinched spout of a balloon.

The sidekick was temporarily distracted from his hard work pummeling me.

"What the hell..." the baffled dolt said.

In one (admittedly awesome) moment, I managed to jump to my feet, shovel the toe of my Chuck Taylor hi-top beneath my skateboard, flipping it on its wheels with a swift kick. In another second, I was on the board, escape stance activated.

"I'll leave you two lovebirds to it, then," I said as I took off down the hall—the goons giving immediate chase.

I went on zooming down the polished concrete floor of the hall, weaving frantically through a maze of unsuspecting high school students, most of them yelling at me or jumping out of the way, spilling paper and textbooks in the process. I was almost to the exit, the sea of teenagers parting before me when a final obstacle suddenly appeared to block my escape.

Mr. Clanton.

I dragged the tail, grinding to a stop, and whirled around to see behind me. There was the wake of wreckage I'd left, and in the middle, the charging rednecks. I looked ahead, and there was Clanton, all waxy and sweaty under his buzz cut. At this point, anxiety was at an all time high.

Then it hit me: *Brain Drain.*

I drew my knee up to my chest and pushed forward as hard as I could, catapulting myself down the now parted sea of students looking on as if I were a gladiator in the Thunderdome. I could see flashes of gaping, awe-induced expressions as I passed, Mr. Clanton's shape growing before my very eyes as I closed in on him, his brow furrowing as if in slow motion.

There comes a moment in any crucial, fight-or-flight scenario when one must choose whether to accept or deny the reality your brain is rapidly pumping to your every extremity—the panic, the intellectual chaos, the anxiety that cripples. Those who accept the brain's message must then gather the means to govern the mind fireworks and face the moment at hand. *Or*, you can employ the *Brain*

Drain. Imagine the mind's emergency alert being siphoned out of your grey matter until all that remains is placid clarity. Instinct. Muscle memory.

I was now playing chicken with Mr. Clanton, rushing toward him at what felt like 60 miles per hour. The Brain Drain was working. I felt no panic or apprehension, didn't wander who'd budge first or if I'd be expelled when this was all said and done, I just kept cruising and didn't flinch. Clanton got down in a goalie stance, apparently bracing himself for impact. I did the same.

In the chaos of it all, I hurtled at Clanton without slowing, and just before what I was convinced was going to be impact, Clanton barked, "little butt worm!" (of all things), and then dove out of harm's way. I positioned my shoulder in front of my body and aimed at the exit's push bar. The collision hurt (badly) and I nearly flew backward off the board and on to Mr. Clanton, but the focus of my shoulder allowed the door to absorb enough of the impact that it opened, and with another push, I was outside.

The Brain Drain wore off, and three things became immediately apparent. One: That was *awesome*. Two: How the hell was I going to get out of hot water at school after this? I could always blame the rednecks, mention the fight, try to get some sympathy, say I wasn't in my right mind. Of course, it's not like I had many sympathizers at Wesley High.

The last thing that occurred to me was: My mom is going to *kill* me.

MOD LOG, 03
THE VISIT

Having worked up a sweat during my ill-planned escape from the rednecks (and unsure of what to do with myself after having returned home in the middle of the day), I decided to take a shower. By the time the steam had enveloped the bathroom in a swampy fog, I stepped out, wrapping a thick towel around my waist. Clearing the humidity from the mirror with an open palm, I examined myself for a minute or two. Yes, I flexed my virtually non-existent muscles and hunched forward until my stomach revealed a set of proto-abs waiting to happen.

Feeling a little better, I moved back down the hallway toward the extended attic stairs. My mom was at work, and the house was eerily silent. My hair dripping, I climbed up the stairs into the attic, then turned around.

There, in the middle of my room stood an *Imi*.

A Lizard Person.

A real-life alien from another world in my own personal room with my own personal skateboard in its big scaly claws, spinning a wheel and staring at it the way a baby stares at a dangling set of keys.

"Holy shit," I said.

Okay, pause. Time out.

At this point, I need you to understand the magnitude of the situation. See, although nearly every human young and old was familiar with the Imi and their worldwide presence—what they looked like, how they got here, what they were doing on earth—relatively few people *saw* them in real life. The Imi were like celebrities or recognizable politicians; always on TV and magazine covers, yet you subconsciously assume you'll never come home to discover Molly Ringwald or Ronald Reagan in your room holding your skateboard. Go ahead, imagine it. Imagine coming home and stumbling upon Molly holding your skateboard, just standing there spinning the wheel all curious. Okay, well, maybe not Molly because that'd be awesome. No, imagine Reagan instead.

So, there's an immediate avalanche of complicated emotions, right? One: This is scary. Like, home invasion scary. Two: Am I in trouble or something? Three: Is this happening? Now, double—no, *triple*—each of those reactions and more because this isn't the president or a hot actress, it's a damn *alien* from another planet. I realize that to my parent's generation, even the discovery of intelligent life elsewhere in the universe was a world-changing experience, but for folks my age, this was the only version of the world we'd ever known. You get used to spending all your time amongst other human beings. To see an Imi up close is like taking a kid to an aquarium to see an Octopus for the first time. Sure, they've seen the invertebrates in coloring books or alphabet charts, but this is something else entirely. This is weird. One might assume that they'd happen upon an Imi if they were visiting Los Angeles or Washington

D.C. or New York City, or maybe even near the secret research center in Vancouver, Washington, but even *that* was a stretch. You don't expect to find an octopus in your attic.

So with all that in mind, try and put yourself in my head as I stood there like a stupefied idiot, naked except for a towel, staring at an actual uninvited space alien lizard in my bedroom.

Get it? Okay, let's continue.

The first thing I thought to do was to grip my towel. I guess I felt that things were weird enough without accidentally flashing the alien. The second thing I did was to stammer, "uh, uh"—just like that. I assumed more was coming and surprised myself when nothing did. I couldn't help but notice that the alien was bigger than I thought they'd be. Still vaguely humanoid in shape and stance, it was about as sizable as one of our freakishly tall NBA players. It squatted there in the attic the way I imagine a bipedal dinosaur might pause for rest. And like a dinosaur, the alien had lean, muscular legs that ended in big, three-toed feet like an enormous owl, all talons and shingle-like scales. A crimson hooded robe covered most of its body, tattered and filthy. Out of the back issued a long, muscular tail undulating on the floor behind the alien. One hand gripped the skateboard with three long, spindly fingers and an opposable thumb, all of them in ornate gold rings fixed with polished stones. With the other hand, the alien flicked at the skateboard wheel with a sharp black claw like whittled graphite.

When the Imi finally turned to face me as I remained stationary—all wet and in shock—we stood in silence for what felt like an unbearable eternity (I'm pretty sure it was a few seconds). The big yellow eyes sat in sunken sockets, shadowed by boney protrusions that gave them a look of perpetual ferocity like a bird of prey. It had a long lizard snout, lips lined with broad, flat scales like a Komodo dragon. Drawn down over its muzzle was a gold chain ornamented with other dangling gold chains creating a sort of jewelry veil across the Imi's maw. Like its cloak, the jewelry appeared to have seen better days; several links had been bent or broken as if it had mostly fallen apart and the Imi had just decided to go on wearing it anyway.

"Conspirator," the Lizard Person said.

Of course, like everyone, I was well aware that the Imi spoke English, albeit somewhat garbled by a heavy alien accent—some muddling of snake-like hissing, tongue rolls, clicks, and a snore-like fluttering of the pallet. I'd seen Imi speaking on TV and in school documentaries hundreds of times, and yet the only thing more jarring than the physical presence of this alien in my room was hearing its voice, and the name it had called me. By the time you finish my story, you may assume that this accusation, "conspirator," was what cued the reaction that follows, but it wasn't. I didn't have the time or the cognitive resources to consider *what* this thing had said, let alone what it implied.

So, I screamed.

I don't mind admitting it. I screamed in several falsetto bursts as if suddenly doused with cold water. Then, one hand still on my towel, I leaped over the open attic door beneath me and ran foolishly into the corner opposite the alien, who went on standing there staring at me. Right away, I wondered what I was doing and why I hadn't just gone back down the stairs.

"Holy shit," I said—to whom I don't know. Then repeated it. "Rob!" I yelled, my voice gasping and freaked, "Rob! Call the police!"

Immediately, The Police[4] began issuing from ROB's crappy speakers.

"Conspirator," the Lizard Person said again, a hiss and gurgle tucked into the syllables. It was otherwise ignoring my panic attack. The alien tossed the skateboard aside and swung its bulk toward my corner of the attic. Its tail became animated, swimming in the air behind the. "You conspire with The Historian," it said, hissing the S like a cartoon snake.

"Every breath you take," crooned Sting from Rob's speakers.

"Uh, uh…" I stammered. "Mom!"

The Imi paused, turning an ear to the floor as if to give Mom a moment to answer. Then it turned back to me and furrowed its brow.

"What's your problem?" it asked.

That's when I realized how wigged out I was. My breathing slowed, and I felt the way one does when a friend leaps from a shadow to scare you; embarrassed by my panic.

"Oh can't you seeeeee," Sting went on singing.

"Dude," I said, not knowing how to talk to an alien lizard. "What the hell are you doing in my house? In my *room*?"

Now the Lizard Person had both hands up, fingers fanned out in a *settle down* gesture. "I'm like you," it said. "A *conspirator*."

---

[4] "Every Breath You Take," The Police

"No no no," I stammered, "I'm not a conspirator. I never conspired. I don't conspire."

The alien produced a portable computer-like device that resembled a futuristic Speak & Spell and peered down at it.

"Consistent Internet research in areas of deep space travel, the history of the SIAHD, paleontology, the facility in Vancouver…"

"I knew it," I barked. "I knew you guys were monitoring our Internet use!"

"Extensive research on Jim Henson?" The Imi cocked its head, tapping its device.

"That had to be Conner."

"…every smile you fake," sang Sting.

"Do you know who The Historian is?" The alien asked.

"The who?" I squeaked. "Rob!" I yelled, "no more music."

The song silenced.

The alien tucked its device into the satchel over its shoulder and stepped forward. "I need to show you."

The sudden movement startled me, and I let loose another falsetto gasp. The alien seemed surprised, and it raised a finger to its lips in a panicked "you have *got* to be quiet" gesture.

"Dude," I fired back, suddenly defensive. "Are you *shushing* me?"

Its hands still up, the Imi said, "I just want to talk. If anyone comes home and hears you squawking like that they'll flip out."

"*I'm* flipping out!" I whispered loudly.

"Clearly, but you should calm the hell down and let me talk."

"Why are you here?"

"I told you, I'm a conspirator. Like you."

46

The sound of the front door opening silenced us both. In perfect unison, our heads both whipped toward the open attic door, then back to one another.

"I'll hide!" said the Imi.

"What? No, don't hide. Leave!"

But the alien was already moving to the other side of the attic and attempting to cram its big body between the bed and the wall, where it tucked itself down, the red robe making it appear as though I'd covered a pile of laundry with a crimson blanket.

"Yeah," I said sarcastically. "No one will suspect a thing."

The Imi shushed me again. Before I could say anything else, I could hear Mom calling for me from downstairs.

Still wearing a towel, I scanned the attic as if I expected to find some solution in my surroundings, but there was only Rob. Mom called again, this time closer. She was making her way to the attic, looking for me.

"Rob," I whispered urgently. "Play Bad Brains at full volume!" Immediately, a barrage of chaotic, screaming punk rock exploded from Rob's dinky speakers[5], dissonant and peaking horribly. A moment later, Mom appeared at the top of the pull-down stairs, squinting into the horrible din of the attic.

"Yikes," she yelled over the music, noting that I was in a towel. "Turn Rob down for a second."

"He's screwed up," I lied. "I'm trying to fix him."

"Well come downstairs for a minute, okay?"

She disappeared before I could answer. In the corner, the conspicuous red blanket stirred and the Imi peered out from beneath its hood.

---

[5] Bad Brains, "Joshua's Song"

47

"Dude, what the hell," I yelled over Bad Brains. "You didn't even know if she was gone."

It made a sound like sucking its teeth. "I could tell," it insisted.

"Shut the hell up, Rob," I said.

The music stopped.

After running frantically downstairs, I found mom in the kitchen emptying brown paper grocery bags into the pantry and fridge.

"Got something against clothes?" She asked without looking at me. I looked down and realized I was still in the towel, still holding on to it with one hand.

"I just took a shower," I said.

"I gathered. There a reason you're home early?"

"I wasn't feeling well. They sent me home."

She eyed me suspiciously but seemed to relent. "Listen, you have plans with your posse tonight?"

A new wave of stress crashed over me as I remembered my conversation with Emma. "Uh, yeah. I guess they might be here at some point."

"Great," Mom said, still fluttering about the kitchen. "I'm going to dinner with the gals from work. You going to be okay without me?"

I'd solved one of my problems, at least for the moment. "Yeah," I said. "Sure."

"Listen, babe. I'm in a rush, so I'm going to get ready and book it. You sure you're all set for the evening?"

I smiled. "Go to dinner, dork."

"*You're* a dork," she winked at me, then turned to head upstairs.

I watched her go up, my heart hammering against my ribs as she approached the open attic door, but of course, she passed right by it. Breathing a sigh of relief and exhaling slowly through puffed cheeks, I looked down at my towel, then back up the stairs. What the hell was going on?

When I climbed back into the attic, the alien was just out in the damn open for the whole world to see, powering up the Atari ST.

"Dude," I said, exasperated. "What the hell are you doing, seriously?"

"There's something you need to see," the Imi said, effortlessly logging into my NARS account.

"Are you kidding me?" I asked in frustration, moving over to the gadget table. "You know my NARS credentials?"

"What?" the Imi asked, not listening.

I refused to let it go. "*You know my NARS credentials*," I said a second time, louder. The volume startled us both, as our heads spun around, expecting to see Mom's head appear at the attic door.

"Dude," the Imi whispered. "You seriously need to take a chill pill."

"A *chill pill*?" I whispered the way one does when they want to scream but have to be quiet. "I have got an *alien* in my room talking about conspiracies, and my mom is downstairs!"

Beneath us, Mom called up to let me know she was leaving.

"Okay, Mom," I yelled absently, my eyes on the Imi. "Have fun!"

In another moment, we heard the front door open and close. I looked at the clock.

The Imi stood. The closeness of it only occurred to me now. I began to focus in on every bizarre detail: The bird-like flick of the eyes, the undulating of the sinuses along either side of the snout, the black tongue inside the mottled green jaw, the inside lined with crowded fangs.

"I am Aye'Sayuh," the Imi said.

"Isaiah?" I asked.

"*Aye'Sayuh*," he repeated slowly. "I am an exile."

"Exiled from what?"

"From my home at the SIAHD base in Vancouver. From my people."

"Wait, you're from that research center in Washington?"

"I *was* there, yes."

"But you've been exiled?"

"Yes."

"From a research center?"

"From my people," Aye'Sayuh corrected. "Well, I ran away from home, you could say."

"Ran away?" I asked, raising an eyebrow. "What are you, six-years-old? Did your parents not get you a bike for Christmas or something?"

"I am not six, and my parents are dead."

"Well I'm sorry to hear that, but I've got my own tragic origin story, Isaiah. I don't break into stranger's houses and give them heart attacks."

"You didn't have a heart attack," he scoffed. "You just yelped like a girl for a little while. And I know you're familiar with tragedy, that's one of the reasons I'm here."

"Oh well how do you like that," I said, getting angry and loud again. "You know about my tragedy, you know where I live, you know my damn NARS login. So what are we doing here, Isaiah?"

"*Aye'Sayuh*," he corrected, matching my tone. "You have questions. Doubts about the stories you've been led to believe. I can tell you've been doing research."

"So?" I fired back. "I also wrote a whole NARS post about *Godzilla 1985*! What the hell do I know?"

He sneered. "So the hours you spent in search of answers were meaningless?"

"Uh, *yeah*, Tyrannosaurus Rex, give the Internet a browse sometime. It's a bona fide treasure trove of useless information."

"And is that what you do on there? Useless things?"

"Who, me?" I asked.

"No, numbnuts, Rob. Who the hell else would I be talking to?"

Rob lit up. "How can I be of service?"

"Shut up, Rob," we both said.

"If you're going to spend all your time on useless endeavors, I'm not sure authoring guides to modifying Nintendo consoles and Beta Maxx players are the sort of things that impress the ladies," Aye'Sayuh said.

I shrugged. "Maybe I only like nerd girls, and that's how I weed them out."

"That so? Any prospects?"

I paused, looked down. "No."

"Listen," he said. "I think you're lying. I think you have begun to suspect the truth, and there's something I want to show you…"

Suddenly, from downstairs, we heard the front door open.

"Miss Sarah?" Emma's voice called out. "Danny?"

Aye'Sayuh's eyes widened. He pointed at my towel. "Dude, you better get dressed."

"I'm up here, Emma!" I suddenly yelled back. Aye'Sayuh looked at me like I'd lost my mind.

"What was I supposed to do, ignore her?" I whispered in a panic.

"I'll hide again!" said Aye'Sayuh, moving toward the corner.

I ran after him, cutting him off. "What? Dude, no, you look like a dinosaur under a fucking blanket."

"I'll get down real low," he insisted.

"You're as big as the bed!" I shot back.

"Danny?" Emma's voice in the hallway below.

I looked around the attic in desperation. Ignoring me, Aye'Sayuh bounded over to the bed, sidled up to the wall, and settled into as low a pile as he could. The result was a distractingly bizarre shape gathered up under a crimson cloak in the corner. It looked like something I'd lure a guest toward only to snatch the drape away and reveal some invention I'd developed in secrecy.

"Danny?" Emma asked again, appearing at the attic door. "Oh!" she giggled, turning away. "Sorry, I didn't realize you weren't dressed."

I looked down at the towel for the millionth time.

"Oh! Right! Yeah! Sorry about that," I babbled awkwardly.

"I'll just wait at the bottom of the stairs, let me know when you're dressed," she said warmly, vanishing from sight.

I scrambled over to my dresser, frantically grabbing underwear, jeans, and a threadbare Bowie t-shirt. Nearly shaking, I dressed like the speed of doing so could ward off a nuclear blast. In the corner, the conspicuous red shape shuffled about, a big lizard head poking out over the edge of the bed. I made a frenzied "get down you idiot" gesture with my hands, and he narrowed his eyes like I was being unreasonable, but then tucked his head out of sight.

"Uh, okay, Emma," I stammered. "All dressed."

She climbed up the stairs smiling. "Thanks for the peep show, buster," she smiled, somehow diffusing the weirdness I felt. I laughed, and she smiled big but attempted to subdue the smile, making a cute little puckered lip face that made my head go all warm and gooey.

"Uh, are you just stopping by, or...?"

"I heard about what happened at school, so I cut class to come and see if you were okay. I think the others are on their way."

Emma moved over to where I was standing, pinching her knuckles one by one the way she often did when she was fidgety. Her back was to our hidden guest, which was a small relief, but I was still paranoid she'd turn around or that he'd suddenly stand up and start talking.

"I'm fine! I'm sure it'll all blow over."

"Listen," she said. "I still wanted to talk about, you know, the other night. Before I left for California."

"Oh, right," I nodded, feeling self-conscious.

Emma reached out and took one of my hands. "I didn't mean to, you know, complicate anything. I don't know where you're *at*, I guess."

I stood there staring, wide-eyed, heart racing. Eventually, I realized she was waiting for me to respond. I nodded dumbly.

"It doesn't have to, you know, become an ordeal or anything," she added

In the corner, Aye'Sayuh stirred, then stalled again.

"Right," I said, nodding again.

"Right?" Emma echoed as if she didn't know what that was supposed to mean.

"Yeah, I, uh, I agree."

More movement in the corner.

53

"With which part?" Emma asked patiently.

"That, you know, it doesn't have to be a thing."

"You don't want it to be a thing?" she asked, raising her eyebrows.

Aye'Sayuh's head was out and entirely visible, watching the two of us like we were a sitcom.

I went on clumsily. "No I just mean, you know, it doesn't have to be an ordeal or anything."

Emma looked at me for a moment, eyebrows lowered, then nodded slowly.

"If that's what you want," she shrugged with a sad looking smile.

Aye'Sayuh was practically standing up.

"Listen, Emma," I blurted out like a crazy person. "I hate to, like, kick you out, but do you mind if I get dressed real quick?"

She looked at my body and gestured at my clothes. "You just did," she said.

"Oh, right," I said, stretching my t-shirt out as if I were surprised to find it on my person. "I put on dirty clothes cause I was, you know, in a rush and all."

Emma seemed genuinely perplexed.

"Am I freaking you out, Danny?"

My heart was beating so hard and fast that I began to feel as if it might break my ribs. "No!" I gasped, giving her an awful start. "I just, uh, I smell."

"You're being weird," she said, and leaned forward to sniff my shirt. I caught a brief whiff of her hair and felt a warm rush of sensory memory flood my system like a drug, calming me momentarily. "You don't smell," she said.

In that moment, the only thing I could think to say was the utterly stupid, "thanks."

Emma eyed me apprehensively. "And you're not trying to kick me out because this conversation is making you uncomfortable?" She asked.

"No, seriously Emma, no, I just…"

Aye'Sayuh, now completely upright, was looking at me with a lowered brow, shaking his head like a disapproving parent.

"…I need to change."

Emma searched my eyes for a moment. Aye'Sayuh folded himself back into the corner, and Emma turned and moved down the attic stairs with what seemed to be a bit of attitude.

"Rob," I called out, "play music." Of course, Rob activated the last thing he'd been asked to play, and Bad Brains came blaring out of his nearly blown speaker.

"Volume down! Volume down!" I yelled.

Running to the corner, I leaned into Aye'Sayuh's maw and whispered furiously through clenched teeth.

"Dude, you have *got* to get the hell out of here."

"Just tell her," he scoffed, like this was the most reasonable suggestion in the world.

"Tell her what?" I asked. "That by spending hours secretly reading conspiracy theories online I've somehow invited an actual alien into my house? Go out the window! Now!"

He turned to the window, then back to me, the ornamental gold chain swinging with his big head and making little twinkling sounds.

"Fine. I'll hide in the shed out back."

"Fine, the shed, yeah whatever," I said, shooing him with my hands. "Why do you wear that thing on your face?"

"This *thing* is a talisman handed down by the matriarch of my tribe—"

"Oh my God, fine, it's an heirloom, whatever, just go to the damn shed!"

I opened the window and watched as he narrowed and flattened his bulky frame to move effortlessly through the small opening, then crawled down the side of the house, fast and spider-like.

"Okay, Emma," I called out when Aye'Sayuh had vanished from sight. "You can come back up."

Emma ascended the stairs with a slightly annoyed look on her face—something I hadn't seen before.

"You didn't change," she said, shifting her weight on to one leg, hand on her hip.

She was gorgeous. Her wavy brown hair fell carelessly around her bare shoulders, exposed by her loose-fitting grey t-shirt. I hadn't begun to think clearly yet, but the panic was slowly subsiding. The details of the conversation we'd just had were settling in my mind. What had I said?

"Listen, Emma," I began, rubbing my face like a spazz.

Beneath us, we could hear the front door swing open and several loud, animated voices wandering inside. It was the rest of the gang.

"Yo!" Conner yelled. "Miss Sarah! Danny! We bring you glad tidings of great pizza!"

A few feet away, Emma bit her lip and gave me a sad look.

01001001 00100000 01100001 01101111 01101110 01110011 01101001
01100100 01100101 01110010 00100000 01110100 01101000 01100001
01110100 00100000 01101111 01110101 01110010 00100000 01110000
01110010 01100101 01110011 01100101 01101110 01110100 00100000
01110011 01110101 01100011 01100110 01100101 01110010 01101001
01101110 01100111 01110011

THE HISTORIAN 01
THE LIZARD PEOPLE ARE COMING

For our purposes and beginning with this letter, you may refer to me as The Historian. I have something important to tell you, so bear with me.

To you (the reader), limited by your narrow 1987 vantage, the Lizard People are an ordinary bit of otherworldliness. The people of earth had been obsessed with alien life since the days of the hominids—an upright ape craning his fur-covered neck to the bright canopy of stars above him, long before the modern veil of atmospheric pollutants softened their glow. Yours is a world of Frank Herbert, of *A Princess of Mars*, of ALF.

A world of the pizza-stomping Noid.

Thus, you have been appropriately desensitized to the commonplace fusion of alien life on earth. Your widely accepted historical narrative describes the integration of human and alien life with a clinical synopsis, censored to the brink of unintelligibility. The average adolescent of 1987 will crack the weathered spine of his or her outdated and dishonest history book and will trudge through a story told and retold by their parents and grandparents since the first day that adolescent pointed at a Lizard Person with curiosity flickering in their supple brains.

And that story goes something like this:

In the winter of 1962, a group of Soviet scientists hauled the first interstellar radio message from the massive, steel bulk of their archaic transmitting array, charged with the thrum of invisible energy one grey USSR winter.

Nothing happened.

On the second day of March 1972, an American space probe christened Pioneer 10 became the first spacecraft to muster the soulless determination necessary to escape the steely bonds of our Solar System. Fastened to the adventurous little probe was the Pioneer Plaque, a metal plate showcasing two rudimentary human shapes etched in its aluminum surface. To the human's immediate left, a cryptic star-map intended to provide any little green men who might confiscate the probe with decipherable directions back to Pioneer 10's fragile blue homeworld.

Little Pioneer 10 went on his way, banked around Jupiter, and bid adieu to our Solar System in December of 1973. Before our friend the Pioneer 10 could even appreciate its spacious first-class tour of the Milky Way, it was intercepted by the exact intelligent space life that earth's scientists secretly doubted it would ever find. Utilizing fancy pants superluminal travel (owed to a technological prowess light-years ahead of humanity's) these curious aliens accepted the invitation of the Pioneer Plaque and our first visitors arrived on earth the following year—November 28, 1974—setting down in the obvious choice of global superpower: The United States of America.

Hailing from the Zen-like, peace-loving homeworld of Gaina (pronounced guy-EE-nah) billions of years our senior, these interplanetary ambassadors empathized with the plight of our violent, polluted, war-torn Earth—they'd been there themselves eons prior. Unlike us, the aliens had managed to rise above. They'd evolved. They'd corrected course. They worked things out.

They could help us do the same.

Of course, integrating what began as a small group of alien visitors into a mostly hostile, paranoid, xenophobic worldwide civilization was only step one in getting Earth from "doomed" status to "enlightened" status. Our small band of visitors became dozens, then a few thousand alien life forms arrived at Earth's doorstep. The other world governments assumed it was prime time to warm the nukes, what with space aliens hanging out at the White House and all. President Ford was understandably weirded out—a shivering wreck of a pinch-hitter president, but Jimmy Carter had time to wrap his head around the whole thing and just sort of embraced it.

The aliens had their work cut out for them: Bridging the gap between mid 70's Earth and their futuristic society made Doc Brown's attempt to get Marty McFly out of the 50's look like a cake walk. So, things changed fast for us and slow for them, and the world settled into its rhythm of incremental leaps forward in technology and political science. Achievements that would have undoubtedly evaded humanity for decades—if not centuries—became ordinary, even dull. The whole alien shock value thing waned without fading altogether, like the spectral ghost of American racism; publically reviled, privately nurtured.

There were and are conspiracy theories ranging from the slightly unlikely, to those close but off base, to the outright ludicrous. Like any celebrity or political leader, the aliens were critiqued, satirized, followed, worshipped, merchandized, studied, loathed, and adored. The 80's saw the first generation of adolescents for whom a world populated by both human and alien life was not only normal but the only world they'd ever known. Imagine though, the impression that the first group of alien ambassadors made on a reeling public in 1975.

The first headline to report on our interstellar visitors read: THE LIZARD PEOPLE ARE COMING. Because that's what they looked like. Lizard People.

Wreathed in dark, monk-like robes, the visitors stood upright in recognizable humanoid shapes, carrying long, animated, prehensile tails behind them. Saurian scaled snouts (or beaks) peaked out from beneath each crimson cowl. Long, boney, clawed digits folded thoughtfully in front of them. Sociologists described the phenomenon as "patent blindness," a marriage of the surreal and expected so flummoxing that the human mind lurches in its cranial aquarium of cerebrospinal fluid. If someone asked a science-fiction geek to illustrate that first headline— THE LIZARD PEOPLE ARE COMING—without a single glimpse of the visitors that inspired it, they might have depicted the scene with relative accuracy.

Eventually, we all adjusted to the site of the aliens among us: Slightly taller than the tallest human, each limb a bit leaner and longer, the long iguana tails, the dinosaur-like and slightly avian heads. The hide of a Lizard Person was leathery on the back and shoulders, with raised scutes like alligator armor. The mottled green skin of their bodies pulled taut over their muscular dimensions.

Eventually, we learned to refer to them by name: The Imi.

The Lizard People—or Imi—dressed in flowing robes, unisex gowns, or in grey bodysuits wired for haptic communication technology we earthlings have yet to unlock for ourselves. The suits, mapped like a circuit board with complex constellations and blinking lights, drew a predictable amount of satire—Did we really guess aliens *this* well? Because they look almost exactly like we suspected alien lizard people might look—especially if they stepped off the set of *Tron*. Any competent human citizen might learn any of this from their parents, popular culture, or grade school history.

This is, of course, not the entire truth. Not by a long shot. And this brings me to a guy called Dale Russell.

You have never heard of Dale Russell. Admit it. His voice was removed from the scientific community before it could ever find its way to popular culture. This is what we call a case of "hitting the nail too close to the head."

In 1982, Dale Russell conjectured something he called the Dinosauroid Thought Experiment. After studying the fossil remains of Troodon—a dinosaur famous for having the largest known brain of any dinosaur group relative to their body mass—Dr. Russell wondered if Troodon had not been wiped out in the Cretaceous-Paleogene extinction event some 65 million years ago, might it have evolved into an intelligent being not wholly dissimilar to humans in body plan and intellectual capacity?

Sounds wacky, but Russell noted a noteworthy and steady increase in Troodon's brain weight over geological time—

impressive considering Troodon's beefy brain was already a whopping six times bigger than other dinosaurs to begin with. So, to put things plainly, imagine an Earth-like world on a similar evolutionary trajectory as our own home sweet home. The little single-celled guys turn into tadpoles, the tadpoles turn into the fishy things, and the fishy things eventually sprout legs and crawl up out of the primordial ooze. Some further science stuff happens, and you enter something like our Mesozoic era—an interval of geological time marked by the appearance and thriving of Dinosaurs.

The Age of Reptiles.

Now, stay with me, imagine this alternate Mesozoic era on some alternate life-sustaining planet not entirely unlike our own. Imagine that unlike earth's Mesozoic era, this alternate era *wasn't* drawn to a climactic close by the impact of a colossal asteroid that eventually wiped out some three-quarters of all plant and animal species on earth. Instead, the dinosaurs go on thriving as the dominant species on the planet, and—not unlike humanity's ancestral primates—ride the evolutionary train all the way to humanoid station. Or in this case, *Dinosauroid* station.

If such an alternate Earth existed, Dr. Russell speculated, and if it had been ahead of the evolutionary curb—prime for life-developing conditions millions of years before our late-blooming earth ever got there... *Well then*.

There could very well be an advanced society of Dinosauroid *alien* life elsewhere in the vast unreachable expanse of the universe. And indeed, *if* this "hypothetical" race of sentient dinosaurs (let's call them "Lizard People") *were* to exist, and if they were indeed so far beyond our technological timeline, they may well have unlocked secrets that humanity has only been able to theorize: Artificial intelligence, teleportation, cloning, wormholes, *interstellar travel*.

It stands to reason then that if such a zany thing indeed *had* happened elsewhere in the universe, it would only be a matter of time before the aliens in question made their way to our humble little solar system and the only life-sustaining planet in it. *Especially*, he added, if we kept inviting them over.

With this, Dale Russell must have smiled knowingly, looked at his watch, then sat back at his desk awaiting the inevitable knock at his door and the Lizard People on the other side waiting to take him away.

This man is on to us.

MOD LOG, 04
ROOMMATE
[FIVE DAYS LEFT ON EARTH]

Again, neon orbs ascended the black screen to the tune of a synthesizer twinkle as the title screen for *Bubble Bobble* appeared on the TV. I let my head fall back with a dramatic sigh. Ignoring me, Aye'Sayuh nodded at my controller and grunted, "Hit start." I obliged, and when the second screen appeared he grunted a second time; "Two players." I looked over at him, staring.

"What?" he asked.

"Dude," I said. "Take a chill pill."

"I *am* chill," he said.

"Do you somehow think I've forgotten you're sitting here beside me? Do you think I don't know to select *two* players?"

"You didn't select two players on Mario."

"I keep telling you. That *was* two players. You have to take turns on Mario."

He grunted in disbelief.

"That's why we're playing *Bubble Bobble*, dummy. It's the only crappy game I have that we can play at the same time. It sucks."

"It's *your* game."

"My *grandma* gave me this game, man," I argued.

"Two players," he said again, nodding at the screen as if the last few seconds hadn't happened.

Groaning, I hit the stupid START button and two pudgy little dragons encapsulated in floating bubbles levitated on the black background. Words appeared.

Aye'Sayuh squinted at the screen and began reading aloud. "Now is the beginning of a fantastic story…"

"I can read, I can read," I interrupted him, waving a hand in front of his face. "Remember? I read that whole Historian thing you made me look at last night after everyone left."

"Don't be dismissive. We're the same: You, me, the Historian. We're all on to something. You read only one document. There are four of them."

"So why are we sitting here dying in *Bubble Bobble*? If reading these Historian posts is what it takes to get you out of my attic, then let's read them!"

Aye'Sayuh looked severe. "You aren't ready," he said.

The bubbles floated down into a room of platforms and popped, freeing our dragons to bounce about the levels, burping bubbles out at the enemies that drop from the ceiling.

"I've got him I've got him," Aye'Sayuh announced as I inched toward a blue crab-like opponent.
A new level began.

"Oh Jesus," I sighed. "I can't play any more *Bubble Bobble*. I just can't."

"Let's beat it again," Aye'Sayuh said, ignoring my disdain. "That was cool."

"We beat it, dude. It's over. We've got nothing left to prove."

Aye'Sayuh tossed his controller aside and began sorting through the mess of Nintendo cartridges scattered about the floor in front of us. I knew what he was looking for.

"No, dude! Seriously! *No* more *Marble Madness*."

Locating the cartridge, he held it up for dramatic effect and said, "The Imi thrive by confronting challenge and overcoming it."

Marble Madness: The game of guiding a rolling marble down a descending maze of pitfalls and traps.

"Challenge?" I echoed sarcastically. "I'm not sure 'challenge' is the word for it. Your thumbs are too big, man. You roll the damn marble off the ledge the minute the game starts."

"You talk to me while I'm playing. It messes me up."

"Oh, it's *me* messing you up."

"You distract me."

"You die instantly whether I say a word or not, then you flip out."

"The game cheats!" he suddenly shouted, freaking out. "Your controllers are delayed."

"Uh huh," I said, standing up and stretching. "It's the controllers. Dude, let me hold that alien Speak & Spell thing."

"I told you, it's called a Scroll, and it doesn't work for humans."

I groaned in frustration. "Listen, man. I can't spend the whole day doing this. Everyone is wondering what's up. What are you *doing* here?"

"I told you—"

"No! No more about some weird NARS account run by some jackoff who calls himself the *Historian*. I told you, I'm not who you think I am."

Aye'Sayuh eyed me carefully, then sighed. "No. I don't think you are. At least let me hide here until I've made a plan."

"Well unless your *plan* is to die at *Bubble Bobble*, you may be going about this all wrong."

The seriousness returned to Aye'Sayuh's face. "Something is coming, Danny Thomas. And when it arrives, your little world of video games and skateboards, your friends, your mother, all of it will come crashing down."

Heavy.

I'd spent the end of the previous night sneaking Aye'Sayuh back into the house if for no other reason than the paranoia that he was lurking around the yard waiting to scare my mom. I'd been an awkward tangle of anxiety; all fidgety and quiet, not laughing at a rented copy of *Short Circuit* with everyone else, not eating any pizza. Emma eyed me from across the room all night. She lowered her eyebrows and just barely pursed her lips the way she does when she catches her reflection—her way of trying to figure me out. Each expression seemed to ask, "what's going on?" My inability to soothe her misgivings made things even worse.

Unaware of the American tendency to ignore visible discomfort, Jade eventually asked point blank what was wrong with me. I could've been cryptic, but I was worried the group would press me, so I made up something about feeling sick but downplayed the whole thing. Everyone seemed to buy it except Emma, who went on watching me with quiet skepticism.

When everyone finally left, I found Aye'Sayuh in the dark shed outside hunched over the same futuristic device I'd seen him consult earlier that afternoon in my room. The device opened like a tall, thin book. Instead of pages, the inside of the book was lined with monitor screens. Unlike the convex matte blackness of the Atari ST, these screens were flat and alive with bright, vivid color. Aye'Sayuh seemed to be manipulating the screens via a small and confusing keypad below them. The whole device flashed and responded to his flickering fingertips.

"What the hell is that thing?"

He whirled around as though I'd caught him with a porno magazine, then breathed an annoyed sigh of relief at the realization that it was me.

"It's a NARS Scroll," he said, turning back to the device.

"A NARS Scroll?" I repeated, a tone in my voice to suggest this name was totally stupid, though I was already jealous of whatever it was.

"Yes, a *NARS Scroll*," he said again, mocking my mockery.

"What is it?" I asked. "Like a computer thing?"

"Not a computer *thing*," he hissed, moving the device further from my reach. "The Scroll creates a connection with NARS without need of wires or modems or your bulky, primitive personal computers."

I had a million questions. "Wait, what? How does it connect to anything without wires? How is that even possible?"

"Waves," he said, swirling a scaly finger in the air between us. "Like your wireless phones and radio antennas."

Of course, I knew how to modify Nintendos and program plastic robots, but I didn't know any of the science behind how it all worked. I saw no need to admit this to Aye'Sayuh. I moved on to something else. "And *you* have a

NARS account? Since when do Imi use NARS? I thought you guys had that whole Apop thing."

"*Apep*," he corrected me, clearly offended. "It's *Apep*. And *Apep* is not some ridiculous virtual dump for fabrications and narsies. Apep is a living network that moves through the very life of Gaina."

"Sort of like waves," I interrupted absently, peering over his shoulder to try and steal a look at the mysterious Scroll.

"Look, humans are going to get something even more impressive than Scrolls. The majority of the human population. Unless we can stop it from happening."

"Why do we need to stop humans from getting portable computer things?"

He snapped the book-shaped machine shut and looked at me with new intensity. "That's not what we're stopping."

"What *are* we stopping?"

Aye'Sayuh looked over my shoulder, through the open shed door and to the house behind it.

"Can't we go back inside?" he asked. "I want you to read the second post from The Historian."

GROUND Kontrol was empty, and I wondered aloud if it was even open to the public. "Nah," said Conner, strolling into the maze of arcade cabinets and flashing lights. Of course, shutting off the machines would mean erasing the high scores, so the arcade never slept. Conner reached behind an EMPLOYEES ONLY door and began tinkering with a tape deck until music filled the room[6], mostly smothering the low cacophony of video game sound effects.

---

[6] The Exploited, "Sex and Violence"

70

"Sometimes," Conner yawned, "The Great Powersurf will let me borrow a set of keys if I promise to stay out of trouble and lock up afterward."

The Great Powersurf was a legend in Portland. A mysterious video game expert of some kind, well known but rarely seen. He'd earned the funny nickname by becoming the only human we knew to achieve a high score in the surfing portion of an awful Nintendo cartridge called *California Games*. Not really the sort of accomplishment for which one accepts a new moniker, but the ridiculousness of it seemed to appeal to him, and somehow made him seem even more badass. Powersurf was often out of town, or else hidden away from the public eye, emerging long enough to do something like give a random punk rock teenager the keys to his arcade.

"Aren't you supposed to be in school?" Conner asked without looking at me. "Or have I corrupted you?"

"I'll leave in time to be early for next period," I lied. With everything that had happened yesterday, I had decided not to brave returning to school but needed to get out of my house for at least an hour or two. Conner, on the other hand, skipped school more often than he attended it. When he called and mentioned Ground Kontrol, I hid Aye'Sayuh as quickly as possible before I was out the door.

"Dude," I said, "how is Powersurf cool enough to give you the keys to the kingdom?"

"Every quarter counts," Conner shrugged, moving immediately to the dreaded *Dragon's Lair* machine.

"Ah for Christ's sake, dude, enough with *Dragon's Lair*,"

"Yes, my doubtful companion, I will play *for* Christ's sake, and slay that ancient serpent the Devil."

"Is the Devil even *in* Dragon's Lair?" I asked, setting

my skateboard up beside Conner's against the side of the arcade's tall cabinet.

"Who knows," Conner said, "no one can get that far."

I scanned the other cabinets. "At least entertain me," I said. "Play that new ninja game."

"*Shinobi*?" Conner asked, disdain in his tone.

"Yes, *Shinobi*," I echoed, mocking his sass. "It's awesome."

"Dude, *Shinobi* is for posers. Complete and utter historical bogusness. Who the hell has that many throwing stars? Where does he keep those things? It's like, call Stephen Hayes, man. Get a consult."

Stephen K. Hayes is an American martial artist who took a totally badass pilgrimage to Japan to find an authentic ninja master to train him. The coolest part is that he *did it*. Hayes was trained by the last living ninjitsu grandmaster, Masaaki Hatsumi. Hayes was the first American ever to do such a thing. He'd authored a ton of books about his experiences and Conner and I—enthusiasts as we were—read them all.

"Have you seen his NARS profile?" I asked Conner.

"Totally," said Conner. "I've thought about writing him, but I have no idea what I'd say."

"Yeah," I agreed excitedly. "I've already written to him."

"About what?" Conner asked, sounding surprised.

Momentarily flustered, I changed the subject. "Okay, *Shinobi* is bogus," I said. "But even if he drove a Cadillac and battled villains with a lightsaber he'd be less bogus than *Dragon's Lair*."

72

Dragon's Lair was an infuriating game powered by, of all things, a laserdisc. In it, you "control" a knight called Dirk the Daring through a complex dungeon in an attempt to save Princess Daphne from the evil dragon Singe. Unlike basically *every* arcade game *ever*, *Dragon's Lair* had decided to forego the immediate responsiveness of guiding a character, jumping, attacking, that sort of thing. Instead, the game worked by having the player stand there and view tiny animated vignettes, each of which necessitated some unpredictable response on the player's part to cue the next scene without dying.

So, Dirk the Daring wanders over a bridge—you watch it happen—and you're supposed to somehow know that you're meant to toggle the joystick left, or he abruptly falls to his death. Another, similar scenario follows, and before long you're out of quarters and baffled by what just happened.

Dragon's Lair blows.

The game's only appeal was in its vivid animation, rendered by Don Bluth, the guy responsible for *The Secret of NIMH*. So kids were drawn to the demo screen thinking, "Screw Pac-Man, I'm about to play a goddamn cartoon!"

Of course, *play* isn't exactly the word I would use to describe what you do. More like *watching* a cartoon while you dumbly clamor at the controls in the off chance something you press might affect the pre-determined laserdisc response for the good of your character, which it almost never did.

"Why the *hell* do you keep playing this game?" I groaned, looking around the empty arcade.

"Dude, you're wrecking my concentration," Conner suddenly barked. I looked over and saw the first of what I was sure would be many GAME OVER screens.

"You suck," I said.

"I only died cause you were talking to me," he said, dropping in another couple of quarters.

Did I mention that it takes *two* quarters to play this thing?

I was struck by the eeriness of the empty room, each of the dozens of machines all singing out into the total lack of customers with monophonic themes and flashing demos begging you to "insert coin" and go for the ride of your life. The room was mostly dark and utterly windowless, the glow of the flickering screens flashing on the carpet beneath us, adorned with neon geometric patterns.

I looked back at Conner.

"Go left," I said, then yelled, "no, *right!*"

"Go to class, dammit!" Conner yelped, pounding a fist down on the console as another GAME OVER lit up the display—Dirk's goofy visage suddenly shriveling to a pale corpse.

"*This,*" Conner stated emphatically, leveling both hands at the game as if it were an idol of some kind. "*This* is my white whale. Do you understand me? This is my Everest."

"Your *white whale*?" I asked, watching him deposit another 50 cents. "Dude, did you even read *Moby Dick*?"

"Of course not," he answered, his eyes flicking frantically over the animation. "But dude, I get the idiom."

"Abandon your hopeless quest and let's play *Rampage*."

"Never. Besides you've got to start shredding if you're going to be 'early to next period.' You have your own princess to save."

"The heck you say?"

He looked at me with an expression that read, *give me a break.* "What's up with you guys anyway?" Conner asked.

I reflexively played dumb, asking "who?" and immediately regretting how contrived it sounded coming out of my mouth.

"Whatever it was that happened with her," Conner continued, ignoring my little charade, "you won't resolve it by watching me die in *Dragon's Lair*."

Another GAME OVER. He swore silently through clenched teeth. "Either way, your word was 'early to next period,' and word is bond."

"Word is bond," I sighed, retrieving my board and heading for the door.

"Dude!" Conner called out, looking back over his shoulder as I opened the door and the sound of the rain mixed with the beeping cacophony of the arcade. "Don't die, man."

On the screen, Conner's character did just that. Again.

01100001 01110010 01100101 00100000 01101110 01101111 01110100
00100000 01110111 01101111 01110010 01110100 01101000 00100000
01100011 01101111 01101101 01110000 01100001 01110010 01101001
01101110 01100111

THE HISTORIAN 02
THE FERMI PARADOX

Let's say, just for the sake of argument, that Dale Russell's theory about an Earth-like planet—much older but with a similar evolutionary trajectory—somehow checked out. Well, the odds *would* seem to be in his favor. Look at it this way: If current thinking is on target, then there are 100 billion galaxies in the observable universe, each with up to 1,000 billion stars. Within those unfathomable figures, there are probably *trillions* of habitable planets in the universe. Meaning, the odds in favor of life developing and evolving are pretty damn skippy. Amongst these trillions of planets, chances are *one or two* of them might be quite like our Earth.

We call this an *Earth Analog*.

This line of thinking led Italian physicist Enrico Fermi to a valid question while enjoying lunch with some colleagues in 1950. As Fermi and company pondered the vastness of the universe and the supposed mathematical likelihood of life developing elsewhere, Fermi posed the question, "Where is everybody?"

After all, these eggheads suspect that if interstellar travel is possible, colonizing the universe might take some 50 million years. Since Earth has already celebrated more than 4 billion birthdays, shouldn't someone be here by now? There's been plenty of time. Let's break things down even further.

The Milky Way Galaxy—home to Mother Earth—is somehow storing some 400 billion stars. Amongst said stars are roughly 20 billion sun-like stars, and scientists estimate that maybe 1/5 of those 20 billion are enjoying the company of an Earth-sized planet within its habitable zone. So, get this: If just 0.1 of those planets managed to conjure up life, this means that there would be a *million* planets full of living things within our galaxy alone. A million.

But our solar system seems to have only *one*. And it gets weirder.

The Milky Way is about 13 billion years old. During the Milky Way's cosmic infancy, it probably took one or two billion years to develop some habitable planets. At this point, let me remind you that the Earth is a little over four billion years old. Meaning, there must have been *trillions* of opportunities for single cells to do their thing on other planets long before ours.

So, let us imagine that just one of those potentially life-sustaining planets has enjoyed its many eons without bringing about its swift end. It logically follows that a race of living beings billions of years our evolutionary and technological senior is happily spinning along somewhere within our galaxy. To even fathom such a civilization, Soviet astronomer Nikolai Kardashev proposed a three-fold scale, based on the amount of energy these alleged super-beings might be capable of harnessing toward communication.

A *Type I* civilization should, in theory, be capable of harnessing *all* of its planet's energy sources. To put things bluntly, humanity itself is not even a Type I civilization. A *Type II* civilization moves us further toward the world of science fiction, as such a people would be capable of harnessing the full energy of its Sun. By the time you hit *Type III*, you have a civilization *controlling* its entire galaxy and all the energy in it.

So there are millions of potentially life-sustaining planets, many of which have had billions of years to get the jump on us, and yet here we sit: Alone. Or so Fermi thought back in 1950. There are two concepts worth mentioning for those of us with ears to hear, now in 1987. The first concept has to do with previously suggested solutions to Fermi's Paradox.

One theory was pretty simple: It's really, *really* hard for life to get going on even the most hospitable planet. *So* hard in fact, that it wasn't until recently that life managed to flourish at all. If this were the case, we'd be the happy special little creatures we all imagine ourselves to be: Unique in all the world, and perhaps the first civilization to ever develop in the universe.

Others suspected a less shiny solution. These downer scientists wondered if perhaps older, life-teeming planets had indeed been all around us, but an inevitable planetary doom awaited them all—a doom just on the horizon for our young Earth.

What type of doom? It could be the obvious option of nuclear holocaust or global extinction, or perhaps the apex of technological achievement for every developed civilization concludes in the destruction of the planet that houses them.

Or, if there are indeed Type II and even Type III civilizations at large in the universe, then perhaps they watch from afar and then go about eliminating problematic developments when they deem it necessary to do so—conveniently narrowing the life total of the universe.

Any of these solutions would have answered Fermi's 1950 conversational lunch question, "Where *is* everybody?" Of course, paradoxical though it may have been, Fermi died four years after posing the question with all signs pointing to life on earth surrounded by an endless ocean of dead universe. Nobody anywhere, ever, and that's it. It took another two decades for Fermi's Paradox to reach any confirmable solution in the arrival of the Imi, and even now questions linger.

This is why, I believe, we must merge the thinking of physicist Enrico Fermi and paleontologist Dale Russell to make sense of the road ahead.

Now, in 1987, we understand that at least *one* other advanced civilization—this one capable of interstellar travel—does exist elsewhere in the universe. Dale Russell suggested that if an Earth Analog *did* exist among the trillions of potentially life-sustaining planets in our galaxy, and if one of them gave way to evolutionary conditions not completely unlike our Earth some hundreds of millions of years ago, then a species not unlike our pre-historic dinosaurs could and *would* become the dominant species on Earth Analog. Now, if Earth Analog avoided the asteroid anomaly that ended the Mesozoic era on *our* Earth, these dinosaur-like creatures would *continue* to evolve, unencumbered by the notable handicap of being dead.

With a head start like this, a civilization of sapient dinosaurs *billions* of years beyond our technological capacity would be out in space harnessing the power of their sun while we were still working out how to go from one cell to two.

But I submit that Fermi's quandary errs in its presupposition that an advanced civilization's superior knowledge would inevitably compel it to colonize the galaxy, to come looking for us, or to answer our calls.

Does it not stand to reason that such a sophisticated class of beings may have somehow surpassed humanity's certain tendency to *look before it leaps*? Think about it: The hubris of man dictates that if we *can*, we *should*. Science can, in this way, contribute to the creation of an atomic bomb, but why the hell would anyone create an atomic bomb? Mankind is typically already flying said bomb over Japan by the time anyone thinks to posit the question: *Wait, should we do this*?

With billions of years of trial and error under their belts, a higher class of intelligence needn't rush out on a galactic bridge as they build it. Indeed, such beings might be deliberate about when and if they interact with other civilizations they know to exist, and have known of a great long while. Fermi, a man of science, could not see this.

And yet, here they are: The Imi. Which leads us to an essential realization, followed immediately by an equally important question. Given that we know the Imi have been capable of interstellar travel for eons, and that they have known of earth and its measly inhabitants longer then we have, why did they ignore us for so long?

Or, put another way, why are they here *now*?

MOD LOG, 05
MOM

My mom used to work with my Dad, but now she's a waitress. They were both computer scientists, but she decided to leave the field behind. With the memory so painful, we almost never talked about their old jobs, and the only relic that seemed to have survived that era was the notebook in which my dad had chronicled his work—something I'd discovered hidden in the attic and that my mom didn't know I'd taken.

A lot of people gave my mom grief about squandering her education and experience to become a waitress—especially my grandparents—but my mom isn't the type to care. If anything, all the flack she got for becoming a waitress strengthened her resolve to stick with it, and she started calling herself "the best damn waitress in Portland," probably just to piss off her naysayers.

"You can do anything, Sarah," they'd say. "With your education and your experience... Why this... *waitressing* business?"

We'd both been through hell over the last few years, and together we felt like survivors with a secret no one else could understand. We were in a club you can't ask about joining until you're already in it. It was awful, but at least we were there together.

Since she looks like she could be Linda Hamilton's sister, dresses and talks just like Linda's character in *The Terminator*, works as a waitress, *and* her name is freaking *Sarah*, all my friends call her Sarah Connor. The joke so stuck that many of my friends even say, "Miss Connor," with no trace of humor at all anymore. She doesn't seem to mind.

But Mom is more like Sarah Connor in the last half hour of *The Terminator* than the fearful, screaming damsel at the beginning of the movie. Most of her life she'd had to make do with little money, and since my dad knocked her up and she got married so young, she was used to leering, judgmental glances. Folks sucking their teeth at her. "Poor Sarah," they'd say. "Where did she go wrong?"

She'd known tragedy and suffering. I'd seen my fair share as well. Even so, we'd had it pretty good most of the time, and we'd managed to survive together—not just us of course. We had our friends, our lives, our dreams, but we knew we were some kind of team weathering a storm.

And yet here lately, I'd been driving her insane.

On this particular Friday in November of 1987, she was *supposed* to be working a double shift, and yet, when I arrived home from Ground Kontrol Arcade in the middle of the day, there she was at our round kitchen table, soft music playing, a steaming cup of coffee in front of her.

"Afternoon cup?" she asked, not reacting to the way I'd practically fell over when her unexpected presence scared the bejeezus out of me. I gathered myself, exhaled deeply with my hand on my chest.

"Sweet merciful crap, Mom," I started to say, then paused midsentence when I realized it was Christopher

84

Cross[7] on the living room stereo. "Ah geez, mom, seriously? Isn't it too early for 'Sailing?'"

"Never," she said coolly, getting up to pour me a mug of coffee from her slightly nicer but still not-so-great Mr. Coffee machine. "Sit down and have a cup with me."

I tried playing it cool. "I had a headache, and it's no big deal if I ditch school now and then because— "

"The school called me at work a little while ago," she interrupted. Mom set the second mug in the empty chair in front of me, sat back down, took a sip, and looked up at me, smiling.

"Uh.." I stammered, "What did they say?"

Yes, writing this now, I can see this was a lame thing to ask.

"That you got in a fight yesterday, nearly assaulted your principal and made a grand exit in the middle of the day." She drank from her mug again and added, "sit down," waving a hand at the empty chair. "Don't let it get cold. It's already been sitting for a while."

"Assault?" I said. Slowly taking a seat, I awkwardly set my backpack and skateboard down on the kitchen floor. "They used the word *assault*?"

"Mm hm," my mom said, all chipper sounding.

"What is this?" I asked.

"What's what?"

"This whole disposition."

She raised an eyebrow as if my question made no sense at all. "Disposition?"

"Uh huh," I said.

---

[7] Christopher Cross, "Sailing"

"No disposition," she shrugged. "Think of me as..." she looked off thoughtfully, "as a researcher."

"A researcher."

"A researcher," she echoed. "You're a science guy. We're science people. I'm speaking your language."

"Okay," I said, drawing out the word, expecting more. There was another long pause. "I've got to admit," I finally said, "I'm confused."

"I'm doing investigative research on the perplexing mysteries wrapped up in the mind of the adolescent male."

"Mom, I—"

"Imagine this," she interrupted, silencing me with an outstretched hand. "Imagine a scenario in which an adolescent male has always had one hell of a time in high school. The kid is smart, mind you, smarter than most people even realize, but he can't seem to bite his tongue, get his work done, and behave long enough to complete this silly social charade we call high school."

"Okay, I can see where this is going—"

"Thing is," she interrupted again, finally raising her voice a bit. "This kid has been operating below his capabilities for years because high school doesn't interest him. Makes sense—he'd rather hotwire robots, play video games, and listen to cassette tapes with his friends. But this kid is intelligent enough to realize there are certain things he has to get through if he ever plans on utilizing his yet-to-be-harnessed full potential. Say, for example, *getting through high school without being expelled*."

"I doubt they'll expel me, Mom—"

"*Damn* it, Danny!" she yelled, banging a fist on the tabletop, then immediately holding up her hands in apology, eyes closed, taking a deep breath. "I *know* this isn't your thing, Danny, but you have *got* to see the bigger picture here."

"I'm sorry, mom," I pleaded, already sounding defensive. "You don't get it, though, two rednecks were wailing on me and—"

"Give me a break, Danny. You're too smart to act like you don't know how to see the bigger picture."

I considered telling mom about the Brain Drain but decided against it. She had a point here.

"Yeah," I sighed. "Yeah, I know."

Mom leaned back in her chair and closed her eyes, thinking, I guess. Finally, she sat back up and took a sip from her coffee mug.

"I'm sorry," I said again.

"They're going to suspend you, but I think in this case we should be grateful that's the worst of it."

I took my first sip of coffee and made a face. It was now lukewarm and gross.

"You know I hate this angry mom stuff, Danny," she said, looking at me with the first expression I could read since I got home: She was pleading with me. "I don't need you to be a class all-star or captain of the football team. I just need you to get through this thing so that you can go on to whatever amazing thing you're going to do. This *can't* be where you stall out. You're better than that."

I looked down at the table and nodded. It occurred to me in that moment the way my mom carried the weight of not only *her* world on her shoulders but mine as well. I felt ashamed for being so shortsighted, but I didn't know how to articulate it to her.

She took a deep breath. "You're meant for *something*, Danny. You don't have to save the world, but you have to do whatever it is you've been made to do."

"What is it?" I asked.

"I guess we'll see," she shrugged. "I hope."

"You're right, mom," I said, looking her in the eyes. A smile gradually crept up her face, and there she was in a nutshell. My mom: Tough as nails, smart, independent, and a little bit sad.

NARS was a strange black hole, and I'm not sure the world was equipped to handle it. Imagine some primitive tribal people out in the furthest reaches of the Amazon, their society suddenly inverted by the introduction of television and reruns of *Mork & Mindy*. Suddenly the hunter-gatherers can't muster the motivation to spear boars and pick berries because man, *what the hell is Mork going to get into next?* So it is with our modern world and NARS: The Network Assisted Record of Self.

At first, the novelty of recording your life to some small degree, connecting with friends and family, preserving memories and information, it all seemed like a promising development in our ability to know and relate to one another as, you know, *people*. That lasted, oh I don't know, a week or so? Before long, there were already clichés on NARS. Right and wrong ways to post. A new dialect. People you knew for a fact were not awesome were able to craft a more impressive virtual proxy of themselves.

Two NARS profiles could be "connected" or "disconnected" with the click of a button, and either decision carried with it enormous social implications. Many friendships buckled under the crushing weight of a single disconnection or were strained over time to the point of disrepair by an expected connection that never arrived.

NARS users read all sorts of paranoid meaning into who was or wasn't connecting with them or anyone else.

I hated nearly everything about NARS, but I wouldn't cancel my account, and I sacrificed hours every week on its hypnotic altar. I guess part of the reason was that, like everyone else, I was in my own way lonely and afraid and frustrated with my life. NARS distracted me. But I think the other more obvious reason was that Emma was on NARS. She wasn't a narcon, not by a long shot. Emma was one of the few people just using the network for what it was (ostensibly) created for: Sharing the occasional update, and checking in on the people in her life. Pathetically, I checked her account for updates daily.

That afternoon, after I'd talked to my mom, I went up to the attic and powered up the Atari ST, loaded my NES modem, and connected to NARS. My stomach moved between my lungs when I saw that I had a message from Emma waiting for me.

"We need to talk."

01110111 01101001 01110100 01101000 00100000 01110100 01101000
01100101 00100000 01100111 01101100 01101111 01110010 01111001
00100000 01110100 01101000 01100001 01110100 00100000 01110111
01101001 01101100 01101100 00100000 01100010 01100101 00100000
01110010 01100101 01110110 01100101 01100001 01101100 01100101
01100100 00100000 01101001 01101110 00100000 01110101 01110011
00101110

THE HISTORIAN 03
INEVITABLE DESTRUCTION

The Fermi Paradox addresses the seemingly monumental likelihood that intelligent life exists elsewhere in our galaxy, coupled with the fact that we have zero evidence of any of it. If aliens were out there, we once asked, where the hell are they? But rather than solve the paradox, the arrival of alien life on earth has further complicated it. Now, one might ask: If there has indeed been alien life elsewhere in the universe, as was most probable, and if said life was capable of colonizing the galaxy, or at *least* answering our numerous calls, why have they waited until now to arrive at the party?

It logically follows that since our alien visitors, the Imi, have long been capable of knocking on our door, they had—prior to November 28, 1974—elected *not* to do so. Humanity does not know why, other than some passing assurance that the Imi "watched and waited for the right time," whatever that means. How long the Imi "watched and waited" is also a mystery, given that life on their homeworld is millions upon millions of years our senior. How long the Imi have been technologically capable of "watching" life on earth is anyone's guess, but it may have been as far back as our earliest pre-wheel hominids, all hairy and grunting around a primitive fire.

What we know about the Imi homeworld is also in short supply. A planet called Gaina, well beyond our solar system, but within the Milky Way galaxy. Gaina developed along an evolutionary trajectory, not unlike Earth's. Like Dr. Dale Russell hypothesized, cells showed up, did their thing, then there were all those gooey bug-like water things, fish, fish with legs, gilled lizards, and so on, all the way up to Tyrannosaurus Rex and his much smaller theropod relatives, some of which continued to evolve, besting our smart, but still ape-like, humanity by a long shot.

The history books, of course, use the story of the Pioneer 10 space probe and its amazing little engraved plates to explain how the Imi wound up making their way to Earth. In this story, American scientists are the heroes, and those poor super-intelligent alien dinosaurs couldn't have made it here without the scientist's special little space invitation. It's a flimsy wash, considering that all one has to wonder is, "hey wait, these interstellar all-stars knew about us and could get here, but they needed an engraving on a space probe to finally do it?"

Before we stall out in the confusion of the further-complicated Fermi Paradox, I want to consider a few possibilities. The universe is pretty damn old. On Earth, we've had life for oh, a bit less than four billion years. We've had intelligent-ish human life for about 250,000 years, but those intelligent-ish humans have only been able to send messages into space via satellites and probes for nearly a century. Even if the Imi and humans are the only intelligent civilizations left in our galaxy, we may have just missed everyone else, as they died out before we could figure out how to contact them.

Look at it this way: 99% of all species on earth have gone extinct. When you learn this, the realization that the final 1% may be on borrowed time slowly comes into focus.

Consequently, maybe a great many alien civilizations have also been wondering, "Where the heck is everyone?" Just before we get the quarter into the phone, our neighbors go extinct, and we go on suspecting that we're alone in the universe. That might explain why only one alien civilization has answered the call.

Or, to posit a more troubling theory, consider all that is lost in translation when communicating with aliens. Though the Imi have maintained an extensive presence here on Earth, and though our technological prowess has been turbo-boosted to degrees of sophistication it may have taken us centuries to achieve on our own, how much do we know about the Imi, *really*?

Take, for example, the nature of Imi technological integration via SIAHD (The Society of Imi-Assisted Human Development). An Imi innovator named Mem'Rah—perhaps the most famous and well-liked Imi public figure on earth—founded the SIAHD. Mem'Rah worked his way into public consciousness via seemingly endless patience with Earth's xenophobia, his brand of disarming self-effacing humor, constant flattery of human achievement, and carefully worded concern for the future of Earth. By the time the SIAHD was actually introduced to the world, most people would have happily accepted just about any idea at all so long as Mem'Rah was behind it.

Mem'Rah was an innovator. A humanitarian. A philanthropist. A philosopher. Mem'Rah was super space Gandhi.

We came to understand that the Imi have access to an Olympic-size swimming pool worth of knowledge and information, but Earth has only a water balloon to accommodate it. Thus, the Imi must drip the data at a rate so slow that the balloon itself grows without exploding. The SIAHD is said to act as that drip.

We have no idea what's in the Olympic-size pool. We can't even fathom it. We're too busy losing our minds over a computer simulation called NARS that allows us to share photos of ourselves or present false representations of our lives to strangers who don't care. At this rate, we're so distracted that we'll never find out what's in the pool. And would we want to know?

The premise of the SIAHD is of course, based on the god-like benevolence that, surprisingly, developed in an advanced civilization. The Imi have managed to avoid extinction long enough to evolve from self-preservation to concern for the rest of the universe. But if it *weren't* benevolence that compelled the SIAHD, what would motivate the Imi's patience? Their ongoing labor to integrate their way of life into human society?

Before the arrival of the Imi in 1974, one solution to the Fermi Paradox was *inevitable destruction*. Perhaps, given the time and space to spread our megalomaniacal wings, every intelligent civilization self-destructs; Nuclear war, genocide, technological hubris, germ warfare, pop music, *whatever*. Or, if there were a Type II or Type III civilization elsewhere in the universe, perhaps most of our alien neighbors have been wiped out for one reason or another, leaving earthlings in their lonely spin around the sun for a quarter-million years.

Consider the premise of the Factory Farm. In a Factory Farm, tens of thousands of animals are stripped from their mothers, crammed into filthy sheds, immersed in their excrement amongst the corpses of their peers, pumped full of unfathomable drugs that cause defects and deformities, and all this *before* they are beaten, bludgeoned, and hacked to pieces often while still alive. Put plainly; this is the softened, G-rated version of what happens in a Factory Farm. Now, why the hell would human beings treat other intelligent living things this way?

Because we think of ourselves as superior and therefore deem ourselves worthy of exploiting any resources the animals have to offer.

When we obliterate the rain forests, dump toxic sludge into the ocean, or force-feed a shackled duck until it dies just so we can eat its liver, few humans do these things because they hate rain forests, the ocean, and ducks. They do these things because they lack compassion, desire resources, and do not think—let alone *care*—about other living things. Humanity exploits nature because we *can* and because we want to, that's about it. Humans manipulate animals to harm and destroy them just because humans *want* to satisfy appetites. Is this essential or even necessary to our survival as a species? Of course not. Could humanity thrive without torturing animals? Sure. But we don't want to do things that way.

Humans even manipulate *other humans* to harm and destroy them just because humans want to—human trafficking, sweatshops, slave labor, child abuse, and on and on the list goes.

"We are human; we are god."

Now, imagine a civilization of alien life millions of years further developed, potentially hardened in their narcissism and the means by which they abuse the universe. Imagine such a civilization, like humanity, hungry for resources they don't even need, their own planet ravaged to the brink of death, their technological expertise and manipulative capabilities matched only by their cruelty and selfishness. Such a civilization would spend even *less* time contemplating the ethics of exploiting a planet like Earth and the beings therein.

Like the vast majority of humans, these aliens would not stare down at a plate of bacon wondering if it were "ethical" to treat a living thing with abject cruelty and then kill it, just for an optional meal that is horrible for your body. They wouldn't pause in the aisle of some cooperate retail chain wondering if the slaves who sewed the garment they were about to buy were treated with dignity, they'd just eat the bacon and buy the garment, despite the fact that they don't need it and could employ their funds elsewhere for the sake of compassion.

By and large, humanity doesn't care and is—on a wide enough scale—culturally sociopathic. How much worse would we be with a few million more years under our belt?

MOD LOG, 06
A STRANGE MESSAGE
[FOUR DAYS LEFT ON EARTH]

"Let this be my exit music[8]," Aye'Sayuh announced, pressing a finger to the screen of his NARS scroll and somehow activating my stereo.

"Don't be dramatic," I sighed. "And how did you do that?"

"Oh the things you could know but won't, Danny Thomas," he answered, closing the scroll.

"Yeah, well, best of luck gathering troops to overthrow an advanced alien race and all of their subservient drones." I flicked him a lazy salute.

Aye'Sayuh opened the attic window, and perching for a moment, turned to say, "I'll be in the shed until dark, and then I will leave."

"Fine. My friends will be here any minute. Just… stay out of trouble."

Aye'Sayuh peered out the window and drew a deep breath. It was dusk, abnormally rainless under a dark, overcast sky, the backyard's grass encrusted with frost. "I've opened the final Historian letter on your computer." Aye'Sayuh said. "My final request is this: Read it."

"So dramatic," I said.

---

[8] New Order, "Your Silent Face"

97

"Will you just *read* the damned thing?"
"Fine! Yes! I'll read it, geez."

BECKY was the first to show up to the attic that night.
She'd come over directly from dance class, her hair drawn
up in a ponytail on one side, dressed in a Wesley High
pullover and matching shorts.

"Reading your dad's notebook again?" She asked.

I put the book down and changed the subject.

"Aren't you cold?" I asked.

"I've been dancing for two hours," she answered
without looking at me, plopping down on the long couch,
grabbing the remote, and switching on the TV. "It warms a
girl up."

I was at my tech desk, my chair turned to face Becky as
I crunched loudly from a big bag of Crunch Tator chips and
sipped obnoxiously from a small box of Ecto-Cooler Hi-C,
obviously trying to bother her.

"Really?" She asked, cocking her head at me. "Hey,
what else do you have to drink?"

I lazily kicked open the mini fridge at my feet,
revealing several further cases of shrink-wrapped Ecto-
Cooler and a six pack of New Coke.

> While it's true that the average teenager cannot
> afford a mini-fridge, I was able to bypass that small
> technicality thanks to my mom, who, upon quitting
> her job, outright *stole* the fridge from her former
> office. Yes, my mom is sometimes punk rock.

"Diet Pepsi?" She whined, pursing her full lips into
complete pouty face.

"Nope," I said decisively. "But New Coke is equally disgusting. Your taste buds will never know the difference."

Becky groaned and turned back to face *Jeapordy!,* cranking up the volume to compete with the rain now beating down on the nearby window. "I *hate* New Coke."

"Yeah, it's gross," I agreed, locking a can into Rob's claw-like grip. "Rob, take this to Becky!"

Rob rolled in Becky's general direction, servos whirring loudly.

"No, Rob!" Becky yelled, drawing her knee up and away as if Rob were a misbehaving dog. "Becky doesn't want New Coke! No!"

"Why do you refer to yourself in the third person when you talk to Rob?" I asked, opening a can for myself.

"I don't know," Becky barked defensively, waving the little robot off. "Does it understand personal pronouns?"

"Not really," I shrugged. "Why is *Jeopardy!* on?"

"They're re-running Tuesday's ALF next, and I didn't get to see it yet."

"Oh for God's sake, Becky."

"What?" she griped. "You didn't even have the TV on, *Daniel*," she said, emphasizing my name as if it validated her point.

"Rob," I yelled, his head slowly turning to face me. "Tell Becky that ALF is lame."

"Becky…" Rob's synthetic voice began.

"No, *Rob*," Becky yelled over him, his message still in progress. "I don't want to hear it!"

"Where is everyone?" I asked.

Becky grabbed a pack of Shark Bites fruit snacks from the table beside the couch and put her feet up. "I'm sure they're coming. Everyone wants to know what happened after your little fiasco at school on Thursday."

I rolled my eyes. "It wasn't a *fiasco*," I said. "It was a momentary lapse in judgment."

"What happened?" Becky said, looking suddenly concerned. "Like, what did they say? Did they call your mom?"

"Yeah," I sighed.

"Oh my gosh," she leaned forward. "Are you in big trouble? They aren't going to expel you are they?"

"No, no, sheesh," I assured her, waving my hands as if to calm her down. "I just got suspended is all."

"That's *all*?" Becky echoed sarcastically. "Smooth move, ex-lax. If you keep this up, you won't be able to graduate this summer, and you'll be stuck at Wesley High with Principal Clanton *all over again*."

"Becky, calm the hell down," I insisted. "I didn't get expelled. They aren't holding me back."

Becky could be so maternal. She got frustrated with us when she felt like we were unnecessarily reckless. She narrowed her eyes at me, popped another Shark Bite, and turned back to the TV.

The attic's pull-down door suddenly collapsed, the creaking stairs unfolding, and in a moment Conner appeared, his hair and weathered black jacket beaded with rain. Stepping over to my gadget table, Conner set a big key down on the table and said, "don't let me forget this."

"What is it?"

"The key to the arcade."

"Just keep it in your pocket."

"Dude," he said, ignoring me and rubbing his damp hands together. "It's *heinous* out there. Seriously cold."

Becky turned the attic's small space heater toward Conner without taking her eyes off the TV, the glow of the hot coils turning his face orange.

"Rob!" Conner yelled, leaning down in front of the heater. "Get Conner an Ecto-Cooler!"

Rob rolled noisily toward the mini fridge.

"Why does everyone keep referring to themselves in the third person when they talk to the robot?" I asked, crunching on a mouthful of potato chips.

Coke in claw, Rob rolled clumsily past Becky—who drew her feet up as if the robot were a passing rat—and stopped just short of colliding with Conner's shin.

"Thanks, Rob," said Conner, popping the Coke's tab with a fizzy hiss. "Becky, tell me you're not waiting on *ALF*."

"Shush," Becky said immediately without looking at him, then, talking to *Jeopardy!*, "What is a sonnet?"

"What is a sonnet?" the *Jeopardy!* contestant answered.

"That's correct," said an emotionless Alex Trebek. Becky looked down at Conner with raised eyebrows and sassy pursed lips. Conner sucked his teeth and turned back to the heater.

"Is anyone else coming?" I asked.

"Dude, you mean is *Emma* coming," said Conner.

"What the hell," I protested.

"That's what you meant," Becky agreed, eyes still on the TV.

"Rob," I said, "go pinch Becky."

Rob rolled in Becky's general direction, and she tucked her legs up again, barking at him. I have no clue what he planned on doing—I've never taught him to pinch anyone.

The attic ladder dropped again, and after a few loud steps, Paul appeared with Barrett and Jade right behind him.

"Why is *Jeopardy!* on?" Paul asked, plopping down on the couch beside Becky.

Becky shushed him.

Barrett was at the mini fridge, staring as if he expected something new to appear. "Well great," he grunted. "If I wanted a gross version of Coke or something a grade schooler packs in his lunch I'd be all set."

"You don't like Ecto-Cooler?" Jade fired back in shock.

"I'm an adult," Barrett said.

"Does the adult want some Crunch Tators?" I asked, extending the bag to him. Barrett eyed the potato chip bag for a moment, squinting at the cartoon alligator in a cowboy hat. He raised his eyebrows and nodded thoughtfully.

"Yes," he finally said, taking the bag.

Conner was over by the bed, looking out the window. "It's been raining for like, a month," he said.

"Welcome to Portland," Paul called out.

Conner sneered and echoed Paul's sarcastic quip in a mocking marble-mouth voice.

Beside the bed, my discount Mr. Coffee machine beeped loudly, and Rob instinctively rolled after it. There was some clanging, an audible spill or two, and Rob emerged from behind the bed with my Max Headroom mug now full of piping hot joe.

"How much of that crap can you drink in a day?" Jade asked without disguising his disgust at the thought of someone drinking coffee, let alone multiple cups in a 24-hour period.

"Whatever feels right," I shrugged, taking the mug and patting Rob on the head before I joined the others on the couch.

"He's an adult," Barrett said, crunching the potato chips loudly as he moved toward the computer. "I'm just going to check my NARS."

The attic door dropped a fourth time, and with it, my stomach. This was either my mom—who never climbed up without asking—or it was Emma, and I didn't hear my mom's voice. Everyone seemed to be looking at me, so I tried my best to affect indifference, which probably looked jittery and nervous. Then, there was Emma: Her rain-misted hair and shoulders. Her bright blue eyes and subtle smile. I'm certain I was staring.

"Sorry I'm late," Emma said, running to the couch to join the others. "Did it start already?"

"Did *what* start?" Barrett asked, seemingly concerned.

Becky ignored him and leaned forward, speaking over Paul and Barrett to Emma on the other end of the couch. "Nope! Any second now."

As if on cue, the ALF theme began; a painfully lame, jazzy sitcom tune set to footage of the hairy puppet's point of view as he wanders around filming his adoptive family with a camcorder.

"Wait," Jade said, squinting at the TV. "ALF is trying to film the mom in the shower?"

"He's a pervert," said Paul, chewing a mouthful of fruit snacks.

"He's *not* a pervert," Beck snapped back, sounding wounded.

"It just occurred to me," Barrett said, pointing at the TV, "that ALF's nose and cheeks are shaped like a penis."

"And *who* did you say was a pervert, lame brain?" Becky said. "Can we possibly watch this without you guys interrupting a squillion times?"

"I'm thinking about it like this," Jade said as if no other conversations were happening. "If ALF can stroll into the loo with a camcorder while the mum is nude, and she hardly seems annoyed or surprised, this can't be all that unusual."

"ALF knows what he's doing," Barrett agreed.

"ALF," I said, "you *dog*."

"He's not a dog," Emma argued. "He's an alien."

Barrett put his face in his hands. "Oh for God's sake. This show is making us all dumber." He turned his chair to face the Atari ST monitor. The modem flashed its red lights from within the *Excite Bike* cartridge. The Atari's processor crunched loudly. A minute or two passed before Barrett spoke up, his voice serious.

"Danny... Have you read this thing on your computer?

Having forgotten about Aye'Sayuh's dramatic "final request," I stepped toward the glowing monitor. There was the fourth and final post from The Historian. Conner appeared over my shoulder and scared the hell out of me.

"What's all this?" he asked, pointing at the monitor.

I tried not to let on how frazzled I was. "I don't know. Some NARS wacko I stumbled upon earlier today."

Jade was already making his way over. "What's this about a wacko?" he was asking, his eyes moving over the letter as soon as he could see the screen.

"Okay look, everyone," I snapped. "I'm sure it's nothing but some guy who posts a bunch of freaky essays about Imi conspiracy theories."

The rest of the group was crowding around my computer now. "Dude," Conner whispered, "this is this kind of stuff that got Jim Henson locked up, I bet."

Becky rolled her eyes at Conner, but then put her hand on my shoulder. "I'm sure it's just some dweeb, but you may as well keep this kind of thing off your computer, so you don't get in trouble for some lame reason."

No one moved as we all read the final message in silence. The letter was a bunch of feverish rambling about the development of the Internet and theories about addiction. There was mostly silence as the seven of us read, save the occasional "what the hell," or "this is getting weirder."

We seemed to arrive at the final line simultaneously when Barrett said "that doesn't seem good" just as I was thinking it.

"So what?" Emma asked, clearly shaken. "It's just a prank. Someone is messing with Danny."

"Scroll back up," Paul said, skepticism in his voice as he squinted at the computer.

"What does this mean?" Barrett asked.

I shrugged.

"I don't like it," Emma said.

"I don't either," Becky agreed. "I think you should report it to the NARS admins."

"I think it's *rad*," said Conner. Everyone turned to look at him. "Dude, this is *so* punk rock. What if it's all true? Did you ever consider that? You'd be like Luke freaking Skywalker, man."

"Well, not exactly," Barrett interrupted. We all turned to look at him. He was silent for a moment, then said, "in the message Leia sends via R2-D2, she asks for Obi-Wan's help, not Luke's."

It was silent again. Everyone turned back to Conner.

"What I mean is that this could be awesome for you," Conner said. "You could be leaving the moisture farm behind. You could be like Alex Rogan saying goodbye to the trailer park. You could be like Marty McFly gearing up for a late night rendezvous with Doc!"

Becky scrunched her nose. "That doesn't sound right," she said to herself.

"If it *is* some prank," Paul spoke up, ever the voice of reason, "it could look bad if you get caught with it."

"Why do we keep talking like we live in some insane police state?" I asked. "Urban legends about Jim Henson aside, it's not like people *really* get locked up for just *reading* anti-Imi posts on NARS."

We all looked at each other, not knowing what we thought about any of it.

"We're all wigged out," I said, breaking the silence. "We need to relax and not overthink it." I shut down the computer with everyone still gathered around it. The attic seemed quiet except for the TV, where ALF was dressed in a red sweater, riding on a train with Willie.

"Just, you know, don't ignore it, Danny," Becky said, going back to the couch.

"No way," Conner agreed. "I'm dying to know what that's all about."

In a moment, only Emma remained by my side. She reached out and put a hand on my shoulder.

"You freaked?" She asked.

I looked up at her from where I sat, and there she stood, a sympathetic look in her big blue eyes. She was biting her pink lip.

"I'm cool," I said. "It's just weird. That's all."

"Listen," Emma whispered, leaning in close to me. "Do you want to talk later? I mean, when everyone isn't around."

"About the weird posts?"

"About..." she scanned the room to make sure no one was listening. "About us?"

My stomach flipped.

"Oh," I managed to say, doing everything in my power to keep my voice from cracking. "Oh, right. Yeah, totally. Right on."

Right on? What the hell was I saying? It didn't seem to faze Emma. She smiled, squeezing my shoulder with a subtle nod before she went back to the couch. The channel had been changed over to ABC as *Full House* began the TGIF lineup. I rotated my chair to face the now dormant Atari ST monitor. In the darkness of the monitor, I could see the lingering burn of the Historian's final post as it slowly faded.

Beyond it, my reflection.

01110100 01101000 01100101 00100000 01100011 01110010 01100101
01100001 01110100 01101001 01101111 01101110 00100000 01110111
01100001 01101001 01110100 01110011 00100000 01101001 01101110
00100000 01100101 01100001 01101111 01100101 01110010 00100000
01100101 01111000 01110000 01100101 01100011 01110100 01100001
01110100 01101001 01101111 01101110 00100000 01100110 01101111
01110010 00100000 01110100 01101000 01100101 00100000 01100011
01101000 01101001 01101100 01100100 01110010 01100101 01101110
00100000 01101111 01100110 00100000 01000111 01101111 01100100
00100000 01110100 01101111 00100000 01100010 01100101
00100000 01110010 01100101 01110110 01100101 01100001 01101100
01100101 01100100 00100110

THE HISTORIAN 04
IMPENDING REVOLT

Why was the SIAHD's first order of business creating and implementing a primitive version of Apep here on Earth? Mem'Rah—the beloved Imi founder of the SIAHD—had insisted that an Apep of our own would be the first step in staving off human extinction.

Consider how little we actually know about *Apep*. According to Imi history/mythology, Apep is the name of a biomechanical system that acts as a connective network for all Imi technology, making possible the exchange of data and information from one system to another on a planet-wide level.

On Earth, we had foreseen the possibility of networked computers to the same ends but had yet to crack the question of *how*. In the late 1960s, a group of American scientists conceived of a proto-network called the ARPANET, which was for all intents and purposes, little more than a means by which the enormous mainframe computers of yesteryear might actually *share* their substantial processing power with other such mainframes. Meanwhile, across the pond, British scientists at the National Physical Laboratory were working out the means by which data is disassembled on one computer, sails through a network to be then reassembled in another computer on the receiving end.

Now that computers could talk to one another, the next dilemma to be resolved was the fact that respective networks could gab amongst themselves all day but had no means by which to talk to *other* networks. It wasn't until 1972 that network users became capable of sharing electronic correspondence (called "e-mail"), and in 1975, multiple networks were communicating with one another.

In 1976, we were mostly using this newly chatty community of networks—called the *Internet*—to send and receive e-mails. Sharing of information was exclusively text-based and visually simplistic to say the least. But in the early 1980s, the English computer scientist Timothy Berners-Lee began developing a means by which The European Organization for Nuclear Research (called CERN) might better share their information with clarity and ease. Of course, it's no secret that Berners-Lee became the first human employed by the SIAHD.

The progress Berners-Lee had made by 1980 was given a cosmic upgrade by the newly formed SIAHD, and building upon the human infrastructures already established, the Imi employed a rudimentary interpretation of the principles that power Apep— at least to the degree that Earth could handle them.

In another few years, the Internet moved from the private rooms of sophisticated labs and into the homes of ordinary citizens, as phone companies invested in the idea of digital communication, e-mail became readily accessible to the masses, and the concept of networked information via personal computers became as commonplace as cordless phones.

Of course, the crown jewel of what Timothy Berners-Lee called "the world wide web," was NARS, the Network Assisted Record of Self—the world's first "social network." Thanks to NARS, human beings all over the world could share complex information—text, photographs, even music and video—via user-friendly interfaces called *browsers*. By uploading personal information to the Internet, it is widely held that humanity becomes more interconnected than ever before, that the sharing and resourcing of knowledge and information becomes a greater reality, and that our mounting awareness of other humans will combat our inherent tendencies toward narcissism and xenophobia—replacing them with empathy.

In the early 80s, SIAHD began incorporating NARS in readily available government assistance programs. So great was the Imi emphasis on the use of NARS that just about anyone could fill out some simple paperwork, meet with a caseworker, and be issued a very basic modem with a NARS-ready personal computer. A bright new dawn awaited the Earth of the 80s.

Of course, in 1987 NARS has become less a platform for humanitarian awareness and more of a means for already self-obsessed earthlings to obsess over themselves to a degree we never thought possible. With NARS, humans accomplish this under the guise of progress, and they do so over the Internet. Use of the NARS quickly bred limitless subcultures and isolated havens of depravity. Every generation X kid with access to a computer is able to retreat into their own delusions of grandeur with enough digital assistance to last a lifetime, or if they'd rather, play more video games, view pornography, or chat with drug dealers and pedophiles.

Mounting apprehension with NARS worked its way from largely ignored conservative groups of the early 80s and into the conversations of sociologists worldwide. According to the SIAHD, earth's Internet could, in theory, "reach Apep" at some point in the next few decades, assuming the slow drip of Imi technology into Earth's delicate water balloon receptacle doesn't result in the great *pop*.

So, researchers began to wonder: On the road from World Wide Web to Apep, is some level of social downfall inevitable? After all, the communicative and technological possibilities unlocked by the Imi's rapid development of our primitive computer networks have yielded results undeniably fortuitous for mankind.

According to a study conducted in 1986, authentic *addiction* to NARS is now a real-life, diagnosable disorder. The expeditious updating of information—new posts, new messages, new smiles—via the NARS interface is believed to activate the neurotransmission of dopamine, the very chemical responsible for feelings of love and compassion.

Human beings *love* this social network.

And since the dopamine fix offered by NARS is faster, simpler, and easier to acquire than say, a similar chemical reaction by way of human interaction or the arts, most humans have no problem rushing to the arms of NARS rather than a loved one, a novel, or Mozart. These same chemically dependent Internet users inflate their addiction with a false sense of purpose, i.e., they claim to use the NARS to contribute to society in some way, as if self-portraits and a carefully curated but wholly inauthentic presentation of their lives were humanitarian work.

Scientists once assumed that addiction was created by simple exposure to addictive agents. The thinking went: Allow someone to take heroin a few times, and they will become addicted to heroin. But in the late 70s, Canadian psychologist Bruce K. Alexander put this mode of thinking to the test with his famous *Rat Park* experiments. In it, Dr. Alexander challenged typical studies on addiction conducted by offering a rat water laced with morphine alongside plain drinking water. In every typical study, the rat in question chugged dope-water until he was addicted, and eventually dead. Scientists thus concluded that the availability and use of drugs create addiction and all of its subsequent fallout.

But in Rat Park, Bruce Alexander wondered if the same results could be produced in a radically different setting. Rather than isolating a single rat in a cold, sterile cage, Alexander created a luxurious rat fun world 200 times the floor area of a standard laboratory cage. Rat Park was populated with all manner of rats, as well as comfortable places to sleep, play, and have rat sex. And, in Rat Park, there were two water sources: One laced with morphine, and one laced with nothing.

What Alexander discovered is that in Rat Park, very few rats *ever* sampled the dope water. None of the rats used the dope water compulsively, and not a single rat overdosed. Rat Park seemed to demonstrate that exposure to—and even use of— addictive substances did not create addiction in and of themselves. Instead, the *cages* our subjects are placed in create the necessary conditions for addiction to occur. Many life forms possess the innate need to bond and connect with other life forms. When said life forms are healthy and given the ability to bond and connect with other life forms around them, they will do so. If life forms are cut off or distracted from their ability to bond with other life forms, they seek to bond with something that promises a reprieve from the pain created by lack of bonding, and on the cycle goes.

All along, the Imi remind us that not unlike evil resulting from free will, some level of social decline is expected in the face of progress, conveniently sidestepping the question of digital addiction. Addiction to the very thing by which progress is allegedly achieved. Bear in mind that creating a NARS account involves more than merely posting self-portraits and bragging about your make-believe awesomeness—each NARS account requires personal information fed directly to the SIAHD, not to mention the steady feed of voluntary updates that follow via each NARS profile. Every member of the Network Assisted Record of Self receives regular required reading from the SIAHD, delivered directly to your inbox, suspending account activity until opened and archived. These bulletins range from simple updates on NARS' functionality, to lengthy and cryptic pieces on progressive Imi ideology—stuff any thinking person could easily classify as propaganda.

A message arrives, and you *have* to open it before using NARS for anything else. You *have* to scroll through the whole thing, and you *have* to confirm your understanding of the message by clicking an icon that communicates as much. Of course, very few people outside of conspiracy theorists and elderly users paranoid about their identity being stolen actually read these things, but they're being exposed to them for a brief period one way or the other.

I want you to think about everything I've mentioned in my previous three posts: The mystery surrounding the arrival of

114

alien life on earth, the smoke screen that shrouds this arrival in inexplicable deceit, and the lingering question of the Imi's origin as well as their future goals. Now I want you to think about NARS, the very means by which these messages appear on your computer screen.

The Imi have all but guaranteed worldwide use of their very own information hub, asking for access to our personal records, homes, and even our psychological profiles via our NARS accounts. We now know that human beings are developing chemical addictions to the means by which the Imi disseminate their information and absorb ours. We not only agree to this, *we line up for it.*

By nature of our utterly unprecedented circumstances, things are moving at such an outrageous pace that very few have had even a single moment to draw their head out of the information flood and ask, "Hey, what the hell is going on here?" Any attempt at reasonable inquiry is clouded by the easily dismissed voices of the paranoid and delusional. "The Imi are actually gods!" "The Imi are the Antichrist!" "The Imi have the ark of the covenant!"

At the rate we're exchanging information and the number of voices that have been given a platform—for better or for worse—very few ideas that may challenge the status quo can find their bearings in a virtual tsunami of data and communication.

It is for these reasons that—over the last few years—I began to seek answers not by engaging the rules of the very machine that enslaves us, but by stepping out and subversively working *against* the machine *from the inside.* I have collected several years' worth of information that will change the world forever,

115

and I have conceived of a plan to do exactly that—to save the human race and to expose the alien threat hiding in plain sight.

Their task is simple: *Enslave the lesser life forms. Absorb them into Apep. Take what they do not deserve away from them.*

Now that I have initiated this final correspondence, time will be limited, as will the means by which our dangerous mission might be carried out. Make no mistake, the road ahead is a frightening one: To bring Mem'Rah down from his seat of power and to overthrow the Lizard People.

I need your help, Danny Thomas.

The Historian
November 19, 1987

MOD LOG, 07
THE TALK WITH EMMA

By the time everyone else had left, Emma and I were
sitting on my couch sharing an Oreo Big Stuf and watching
Who's The Boss. Emma had her legs drawn up on the couch
and was taking a small bite of the giant Oreo. She was
wearing her floral jeans—white with a pattern of orange
blossoms and green leaves—and this baggy grey off the
shoulder top that made my palms sweaty. Her dark brown
hair pulled up in a long ponytail, Emma looked through the
TV thoughtfully, took a bite, and asked me if I ever thought
about my dad.

"All the time," I admitted, feeling incapable of
pretense.

Emma looked at me—looked *into* me, and without
saying anything, seemed to understand. She didn't pry. She
didn't go all awkward and overly sympathetic the way most
people did when they talked to me about my dad. She
looked at me with a sad, understanding little smile, touched
my arm, and nodded.

"Why?" I finally asked.

"I was thinking about you today," she said. "I wonder
how you can be so strong. Or Becky for that matter. I know
it's totally different, what you guys have been through, but
you're so strong. I'm not sure I could do that."

Becky went through hell a year prior when her mom suffered some sort of breakdown and left her, her sister, brother, and dad behind for a life of wanderlust and depravity. Rebecca Burkley, not unlike Emma, is a tough girl. But having your mom abandon your family out of nowhere will break even the most resilient teenager. At school, people looked at her sideways, as if she somehow had something to do with the ruinous state in which her family had been left. They stepped around her as if a gentle breeze would make her crumble, and the majority of her allegedly close friends vanished.

Not us. Amongst a group she could have never assembled if she tried, Becky found a new family willing to be pissed at her mom, and to grieve her loss in the next breath. We knew Becky wasn't tainted; her mom left because her mom was a moron, but that didn't mean Becky didn't want her to come home. I think we got that, in our own way.

"Having you guys helps," I shrugged, looking back at the TV, breathing slowly.

Emma took another bite of the Oreo. "I haven't even been through anything really gnarly, and I already feel like you guys keep me sane."

"Or *in*sane," I laughed.

Emma looked at me and smiled. "I think I like that better."

This moment of electricity passed between us and I became incredibly aware of the empty space between our bodies—how small it was, and how close we were. There was so much of her simultaneously clear and mysterious in my peripheral vision; the welcome, soul-piercing kindness of her blue eyes, the soft glisten on her glossy pink lips, the fair, soft-looking skin of her shoulders, the swell of her chest, even her red-tipped fingernails as she pinched the Oreo.

And there we were, just sitting there staring at each other while the laugh track from *Who's The Boss* played gently in the background. My heart was hammering so violently in my ribcage that I felt like it was audible. While I'm sitting there, obsessing over whether or not she can hear my pulse and if she's judging me for it, Emma extended a hand and touched my face. She cupped her soft palm around my cheek and chin like we were in a movie. Before I had could wrap my head around this development, she leaned forward, and we started kissing.

> I should tell you at this point that I've only kinda sorta kissed one other girl. It was Heather Salzwedel in junior high, and it wasn't pretty. I think Heather expected a quick peck while I fully anticipated we were about to have the make out of our lives, so the end result was... messy. I was so embarrassed I stopped returning her calls, and her brother Alex threatened to beat me up. This kiss— with Emma—wasn't like that.

People always talk about these momentary highs when they experience wild abandon during a performance or stunt or competition. They only realize much later they may not have been as incredible as they *felt* they had been in the moment. I guess that could have been what was happening here, but I really doubt it. I think I was awesome and she was even more awesome. Or maybe it was only good because of her, I have no idea.

The point is: It was awesome.

I was grateful not to be alone in the attic that night. There are nights when being alone is just what you need, and there are nights when it's the last thing you need. This particular night was the latter.

Later, I watched Emma drive away. I was smiling from ear to ear, invigorated with resolve. Something was clicking into place. I remembered what my mom had said about purpose, and it suddenly hit me. I had to get to Aye'Sayuh before he left.

PART TWO
THE EXILE

"To survive a war, you gotta become war."

John Rambo,
Rambo: First Blood II

MOD LOG, 08
RETURN OF THE ROOMMATE
[THREE DAYS LEFT ON EARTH]

Swearing under my breath, I rummaged through the fridge gathering up any loose produce I could find; Some celery hearts, baby carrots, half a tomato, a shrink-wrapped head of lettuce. I arranged the groceries on a He-Man TV tray my mom had given me a few years prior. When I'd asked why, she'd shrugged and said, "to eat while you watch TV, *doi.*"

Ascending the attic's steep ladder with one hand balancing the packed tray was no simple undertaking, and I'd lost the half of tomato in the process, its wet open face was now speckled with carpet fuzz and an anonymous long, red hair.

"Becky," I sighed, using my index finger and thumb like tweezers to clinically remove the offending hair.

Having found Aye'Sayuh still in my shed late that night, convincing him to stay was relatively easy. Now he was back at *Marble Madness*. Given that the game involved guiding a marble down a system of steep ramps and around geometric obstacles, I never understood the grand appeal. For whatever reason, Aye'Sayuh sucked absolute balls at *Marble Madness*. Before I had the chance to clear my throat, his marble rolled over a ledge to its death, and

Aye'Sayuh grabbed his head as though he'd just received word that a loved one had been killed.

"Dude, play something else."

Aye'Sayuh went on clutching his frustrated skull. "Did you get food?"

"Yes, your majesty," I said, plopping the tray down next to the TV where, on the screen, another marble plummeted to its death. "Remind me why I've just gathered a small salad bar for you?"

"Humans," he began, picking through the options with a curious claw, "are one of the only evolved species in the galaxy that happily opt for the suffering of another intelligent creature for the sake of appetite."

"What the hell, man. I've just presented you with a platter of every vegetable in the house, and you're *judging* me? How am I supposed to tell my mom I had a craving for celery, carrots, lettuce, and half a tomato?"

"Tell her you made a salad, lame brain," he said, crunching loudly on a baby carrot. "And you can put that fuzzy tomato back." He gave it a disgusted flick.

"What are we doing?" I asked. "Why are you here, dude? I'm finally listening. What is your big plan?"

Aye'Sayuh rose to his feet, impressing upon me our difference in height. He was dressed the same as before; a crimson cloak and cowl, veil of dangling gold chains across his reptilian snout.

"You," Aye'Sayuh began, voice thick with Imi accent. "You are prepared to conspire with The Historian, yes?"

I shrugged. "I wouldn't call it *conspiring*. I read his messages."

"I conspire with The Historian as well."

A pregnant silence passed between us.

"Well great," I shrugged again. "So here we are; A couple of conspirators. What now?"

"We act."

"On what?"

"Against the *Esk Hahr o' Mek*."

Another pause.

"The esk har amek?"

Aye'Sayuh nodded.

"I don't know what that means," I said.

"The Esk Hahr o' Mek is an Imi conquest scroll. It means, *The Final Heresy*."

"What does it say?"

"It details the plot against the lesser worlds. Against Earth."

I went on staring at him for a moment. Then raised my eyebrows and shook my head as if to say, *well, go on*.

Aye'Sayuh reached up and drew his cloak up over one shoulder, revealing a thin but muscled green arm. There was a canvas satchel drawn around his shoulder. He retrieved the book-like computer device from within the bag. Closed, the device looked like a small tablet of grey marble. With his dragonesque index finger, Aye'Sayuh drew an invisible design on the outer surface of the closed device, and a simple melody sounded from inside—three notes played on something that sounded like a vibraphone. With hands on either side of the tablet, Aye'Sayuh opened the computer—the soft glow from within bathing his green face in dull white.

Again, he manipulated the device with a single finger— sweeping, curved strokes, then button-mashing jabs. Extending the open tablet to me, I looked down over the screen to find a series of indecipherable Imi glyphs. In another moment, a holographic projection appeared hovering over the surface of the outstretched screen; A star map of some kind, a large moon or planet rotating at its center. A synthetic voice played over the image.

"Their task is simple: *Enslave the lesser life forms. Absorb them into Apep. Take what they do not deserve away from them.* Now that I have initiated this correspondence, time will be limited, as will the means by which our dangerous mission might be carried out. Make no mistake, the road ahead is a frightening one: To bring Mem'Rah down from his seat of power and to overthrow the Lizard People."

Then the voice fell silent, the image flickered out of sight, and Aye'Sayuh closed the tablet.

"It's from the last letter," I said. "The last letter from The Historian."

"I think he speaks of the Final Heresy."

"The esc-hairy-mek thing?" I asked.

"It's the *Esk Hahr o' Mek,* and yes," Aye'Sayuh said. "I happen to know for sure that the SIAHD has compiled several large fragments of the document and is using them in their plot against Earth."

"So?"

"So we find it. Expose them."

"Wait, wait," I said. "We show people some old crusty alien papyrus, and suddenly they'll believe in our wild conspiracy theory?"

Aye-Sayuh shrugged. "It's enough to begin the revolt, but it isn't enough to complete it."

"So what good is *that*? If this Historian character is planning some kind of revolution what good is a start without a way to finish it?"

"There are two problems," Aye'Sayuh said, stepping closer, his tone suddenly more severe. "The first problem is that Esk Hahr o'Mek must be read by human eyes to expose the truth, but no human has ever successfully read the document."

"What, like we can't read Imi?"

"Humans are capable of reading the Imi language, but the few humans who have read from Esk Hahr o' Mek have all died."

"Reading it killed them?"

"Sort of," Aye'Sayuh shrugged. "Ten years ago two human SIAHD scientists stumbled upon several pages of Esk Hahr o' Mek while attempting to debug encrypted lines of NARS code. The first scientist completed the reading, then walked quietly to the twelfth story window and hurled himself headlong on to the pavement."

"Damn," I said.

"The second scientist had it worse. He wandered straight down to the mechanical engineering floor, leaned over in front of an industrial drill press and brought it down on his own temple."

"Damn," I said, more emphatically this time. "Hasn't anyone else attempted to read it?"

"One other SIAHD scientist. A guy called Stewart Raffill was employed for his expertise in tracking the origins and sources of complex codes, transmissions, and even ancient texts. Raffill was involuntarily entered in a clinical trial that—among other decoy tests—involved reading short passages of Esk Hahr o' Mek aloud in a containment room. No way out and nothing inside he could use to kill himself."

"So what happened to him?"

"He's nuts now. They keep him locked up at the center in Vancouver. I heard that he could never make it through a full reading without screeching and flinging his body at the wall or punching himself or something. They kept it up for months until his mind was essentially tapioca pudding. The guy is catatonic."

"Okay well, so much for this Historian guy's big plan, right? If the whole thing hinges on a human reading a book that kills humans, I'd call that checkmate."

"These were earth scientists. Untrained. Unprepared. They had no idea what they had stumbled upon or how to understand its implications."

"So you give some humans a pep talk and an instruction manual and hope for the best?" I asked.

"Not a pep talk, we teach them to read with *Imi* eyes. And not an instruction manual, but *training*. We draw them out of their human context and into an Imi context and prepare them to guide their minds. To prepare for the impending revolt."

"And how exactly do you get these imaginary human volunteers in an Imi context?"

Aye'Sayuh smiled; A long, slow-spreading grin that revealed dozens of curved fangs. "That's the second problem. To train, we must go to Gaina."

"*Guy-ee-nuh*?" I pronounced dramatically. "You want to take them to a planet somewhere on the outskirts of the galaxy just to read a damn paper?"

"Not to read, to *train*. On Gaina, they will be trained for revolution."

"So what? Even if someone trains for revolution, we've still got no one to read this mysterious murder book."

"I'm still working on that part," Aye'Sayuh admitted. "At least they will be prepared for what follows when we figure out the Esk Hahr o' Mek."

128

"What's all this *they will be* talk, huh, Aye'Sayuh? You're hiding in a teenager's attic, eating all his damn lettuce, man. I don't see any recruits."

"You said you were listening. Well listen to this, Danny Thomas: You think you know tragedy? You and everyone you've ever loved will soon know tragedy you cannot yet *fathom*. This is it. No Luke Skywalker is coming to sort this out. Either we do something, or we sit back and wait for the end to come."

I thought for a moment. "If you think about it," I said calmly. "*I'm* kind of like Luke in this story. Just an ordinary moisture farmer invited by a mysterious stranger to join a rebellion."

"Dude," Aye'Sayuh countered, "that's like, a *million* stories."

"Still. It's pretty punk rock."

"You and I aren't enough. We need the others."

"What others? My friends? Maybe we can get one or two them to listen to us, but most of those guys will never believe a word of this. I'm not sure *I* believe it."

"Well, at least one of them will," Aye'Sayuh insisted.

"What? Who?"

He looked over my shoulder and acknowledged something behind me. When I turned around, I could see the look of fearful shock on Emma's face, her head peering into the attic.

MOD LOG, 09
ACCOMPLICES

I was standing behind the locked door to Ground
Kontrol Arcade, peering through the dark window out at
the empty street in the middle of the night.[9]

"It's 3 a.m.," Emma said, placing a gentle hand on my
shoulder. "No one's out there."

I turned to look at her. Her brown hair was drawn up in
a high ponytail. Her eyes more thoughtful than usual. Her
lips a reassuring smile. The arcade was lit only by the glow
of streetlamps and moonlight from outside, the only noise a
few cabinets still beeping away. Before I could say
anything, there came a frantic pounding on the door that
made us both lurch backward as if the door was about to be
kicked in. Outside the window, Becky was shivering,
tapping her foot impatiently.

"It's freezing out here!" She shouted.

Emma and I both looked at one another and took a deep
breath. I opened the door, and Becky hurried inside.

"Is anyone else here?" she asked, arms folded, her
posture hunched.

"Not yet," I said. "Okay, Becky, listen…"

---

[9] Joy Division, "Atmosphere"

"You guys are *freaking* me out," she whined. "You can't just call me in the middle of the night and get me out of bed to come meet at an empty video game place."

"Video game place?" I asked.

"Whatever it's called!" she fired back. "Why is it so dark? Where is everyone else? What happened? Is everyone okay?"

"Becky, calm the hell down," I said. "Remember those weird NARS posts we read earlier?"

"Oh my God," she said. "Did something happen? Are you in trouble? Are we *all* in trouble?"

I looked at Emma. She sort of shrugged. I turned back to Becky. "We're not in trouble," I finally said. "But there's something I think everyone should see."

Becky shuffled backward as if I'd just told her the room was full of spiders. "What is it?" she whispered.

I looked around the mostly dark arcade. "It's, uh, playing video games, I think."

Becky leaned forward apprehensively, then bolted upright as if from an electric shock at the sound of another knock on the door. I dashed to the entrance, unlatched the lock, and opened the door for Conner, Barrett, Paul, and Jade, who had all filed out of Barrett's Ford Aerostar minivan.

"This is awesome!" Jade said as he stepped inside.

"What is?" I asked.

"Sneaking into Ground Kontrol in the middle of the night! Does Powersurf know?"

I looked over at Conner, who just shrugged, seemingly half asleep. "He gave the keys to Conner," I finally said.

"Gnarly," Jade said quietly, peering around the room. "Let's play *Shinobi*."

"Shinobi is bogus," Conner said, yawning.

"Oh my God," Barrett groaned, rubbing his face. "Here we go with the ninja historical authenticity lessons. Weren't we all *just* together? Must we convene in the middle of the night?"

"Dude," said Conner. "*Shinobi* is not historically accurate. Ninja didn't roam the streets fighting mobs of gunmen with shuriken."

"Oh, so you were there?" Barrett asked.

"What's a shuriken?" Jade asked.

"I read about it, man," Conner said to Barrett.

"Shuriken are those things people call throwing stars," I said to Jade.

"What the *hell* are you boys talking about?" Becky suddenly shouted. "He drags us all out of bed, into the cold, in the middle of the night, to some dark video game place, and you're arguing about *ninjas*?"

It was quiet for a moment, then someone whispered, "video game place?"

"Look, listen okay," I said, shushing everyone. "You guys remember those weird NARS posts we read? By someone called The Historian?"

They all stared at me in attention.

"Okay, well, someone reached out to me about it— someone who has been talking to this Historian person. Apparently, the situation is pretty… dire."

"How dire?" Paul asked.

I took a deep breath. "Total end of the world shit."

It was quiet for a moment. "Bummer," said Paul.

"But this dude—the one who reached out to me—has a plan. He sort of needs us for it. All of us."

"Oh God," Becky said. "I'm going to be sick."

"What in the world?" Barrett said in frustration. "*What* guy? *What* plan? We still don't know anything, and Becky is already getting sick. Enough with all the Obi-Wan shit, man. Are you sure this guy isn't just some NARS nerd screwing around with you?"

"Pretty sure," I nodded.

"How?"

As if on cue, Aye'Sayuh stepped out from the shadows behind me, eliciting a predictable gasp from the group.

"Ah hell," Barrett said. "They're about to lock us up, aren't they?"

"No," Aye'Sayuh spoke up, giving the group another start. "We're going to lock *them* up."

I squinted at Aye'Sayuh's lame threat.

He shook his head. "Well, not literally. But we're going to do something."

We all stood there in silence.

"Why isn't anyone saying anything?" Aye'Sayuh asked.

"Is that real?" Becky whispered, her voice thick with panic.

"You asked *us* here, man," I said to Aye'Sayuh, embarrassed. "Tell them everything. Tell *us* what we're supposed to do."

"I will," said Aye'Sayuh, popping his knuckles one by one. "But first, do any of you guys have any quarters?"

I rubbed my face and sighed again.

"For what?" Conner asked.

"*Dragon's Lair*," Aye'Sayuh answered, lifting his chin.

"Waste of quarters," Conner said, shaking his head. "May as well pick something else. It can't be won."

"Oh yeah?"

"Pretty much."

Aye'Sayuh grinned. "I can *beat Dragon's Lair*, mother fucker."

134

Everyone was silent for a moment, until Conner whispered, "wicked."

THE two coins dropped one after the other—that familiar clink of metal on plastic—and Aye'Sayuh's play of *Dragon's Lair* began. We'd all gathered around the cabinet as best as we could in the soft neon glow of the dark arcade. Aye'Sayuh's physical dimensions made it tough for everyone to see, so Becky, Emma, and Paul were all standing on plastic chairs behind us. On the screen, the game's dopey protagonist, Dirk, strode into an ominous castle, presumably the eponymous lair of the dragon.

The game begins with immediate peril. No instructions of any kind. The player has no idea how to identify the actual gameplay. As I mentioned earlier, the visuals are generated by a laserdisc, so the game itself looks like any other animated movie with high production values and nothing at all like the games on either side of the *Dragon's Lair* cabinet; *Shinobi* and *Centipede*. So, you drop a quarter in, assume you're watching an animated intro, but then Dirk falls into a pit as he attempts to cross the castle's threshold. One of your lives has been expended. Before you can process what's happened, the whole ten-second debacle has begun again, and you're about to die a second time.

The game progresses based on the intuition (or ESP) of the player, who is rapidly choosing between three controls: Joystick, Jump, and Sword. As the cartoon plays, furry monsters approach, and you'd better start mashing that Sword button like your life depends on it. Maybe Dirk will swing, but probably you were too slow, and here it comes, GAME OVER. Much of the game's frustration is born from the assumption that there must be *some* way to actually succeed in the unforgiving lair of the dragon. If there weren't, why would the game exist? "To get our quarters," I'd often told Conner.

So there we were, in a mostly darkened arcade in the middle of a cold night in November. There was an honest-to-God space alien at the controls of *Dragon's Lair*. All of us crowded around him as though whatever transpired here would reveal what was to become of this bizarre chapter in our lives—this strange visitor and all his cryptic talk about conspiracy and revolt and the end of human civilization as we knew it. Well, guess what, I'd endured some heinous things in my time and I was still here. And yeah, I know lots of people have endured worse, but I am at the limit of my own narrow experience, and it seems that experience has led me here, for whatever reason.

Emma had taken the whole story with much more composure than I had. She'd freaked out, to be sure, but she recovered quickly. After fleeing down the attic stairs when she'd first seen Aye'Sayuh earlier that night, I'd chased her to the living room yelling, "Emma wait," like a movie cliché. In a wild, inarticulate ramble, I did my best to explain to Emma what had transpired during the last day. It was a relief to explain why I'd been so weirdly aloof the afternoon prior, though I can tell she was disappointed to have stumbled upon the truth via happenstance rather than my honesty.

"I was freaked," I said with a shrug.

She smiled, leaned forward and kissed my cheek. This sent a jolt through my central nervous system more intense than discovering an alien in my room.

I'm sure you've gathered by now that it was Emma who suggested we get everyone together that night. Upon hearing everything from both me and then an awkward retelling from Aye'Sayuh, she'd said we needed to tell the others.

"It doesn't sound like he's leaving until we hear him out," she'd said, pointing to Aye'Sayuh, who then nodded with a shrug.

"I'll never get *everyone* up into the attic in the middle of the day without my mom asking why. If she pokes her head up here and sees him, she'll wig out."

"Well, we'll never sneak into my house without getting caught either. Is there anywhere we can go that's private and empty? Maybe at night while our parents are asleep?"

Over her shoulder, I caught a glimpse of a big key—the one Conner had predictably left behind a couple of days ago.

"I've got an idea," I said.

Not long after that, there we all were, gathered around Aye'Sayuh as he loomed over the *Dragon's Lair* cabinet with laser focus.

"Think he can really beat it?" I heard Conner whisper from somewhere in the group.

"No," Barrett—who was taking all of this rather calmly—answered.

Dirk attempted to cross the castle's drawbridge, and as always, collapsed through the wood. Hanging on for dear life, a purple monster rose out of the moat, and Aye'Sayuh gave the joystick a nearly imperceptible flick, to which Dirk responded with a swish of his sword, fighting the monster off and leaping out of the danger zone.

"Big deal," Barrett said. "Even I can get past the first thing."

"I can't," Paul admitted with a whisper.

"Is he playing?" Becky asked. "Is this the game?"

"For Christ's sake, Becky," Barrett groaned.

"Okay, well I'm sorry I'm not Miss Video Game master."

"Yes, he's playing," Jade said. "This is the game. But he's about to die."

Dirk ran down the castle's first chamber, arriving at three doors as the room around him began to shake. Another flash of Aye'Sayuh's wrist and Dirk sprang to the right of the screen and through a new door that opened there.

Connor and I looked at one another cautiously.

"Whoa," Jade said.

We all watched as Aye'Sayuh avoided a collapsing wall and a flaming floor, then navigated the treacherous subterranean waters of the castle while riding in a barrel. He outraced a pursuing boulder (Indiana Jones style), destroyed a wraith, and battled a hoard of floating ghost weapons, all without looking at his controls. After taking on another host of baddies and racing his way over a crumbling bridge, Dirk bested a black night, navigated a maze, surfed a falling platform, swung from a flaming rope, and took flight on an iron horse.

"What the hell," Barrett whispered.

"He's incredible," Connor agreed.

"I'm talking about the game," Barrett said. "What the hell *is* this nonsense? How could anyone ever learn to get through this mess?"

"*He's* figured it out," Paul reminded us.

Aye'Sayuh reacted to nothing. His gaze was cold and unchanging, his movement subtle and confident. A legion of cackling skulls surrounded his player. Dirk dismissed them with a wave of his sword. Boney specters set in on him and met the same fate at his blade.

"He's doing it," said Conner, rubbing his eyes in childlike disbelief.

"So this is the whole game?" Becky asked again, shifting her weight to one hip.

"Damn it, Becky," Barrett groaned in frustration.

"Oh shut up, Barrett," Becky said, giving him a shove.

Dirk escaped an electrified cage and a wall of blue flames, fought off a lizard knight, collected a treasure, and decapitated several giant snakes.

"How long is this thing, anyway?" Paul whispered.

We all stood there, eyes wide, as Aye'Sayuh avoided dozens of pitfalls, navigated even more complicated tunnels and doorways. Eventually, to our sustained disbelief, his player entered the chamber of the dragon. A sexy-in-a-cartoony-sort-of-way princess sat encased in a crystal orb guarded by the snoozing dragon of the game's title. Scantily clad and talking like a fantasy bimbo, the princess directed Dirk to a magic sword. Aye'Sayuh was as cool and unshakable as ever as his gnarled talons snapped the joystick to the left and right, avoiding the dragon as it gave chase.

"This is it," Jade pointed out.

"What is?" Becky asked, leaning toward Jade without taking her eyes off the game.

"He's going to freaking beat it," I whispered in awe.

After an exciting chase, Aye'Sayuh's knight seized the magic sword, skewered the big green beast through the heart, and rescued the busty damsel from her prison. She leaped into Dirk's arms, cartoony breasts pressed to his chest, and nuzzled his neck in thankful adoration. Dirk grinned, and the game faded to black.

For the first time since the quarters had dropped, Aye'Sayuh loosed his grip from the controls and stepped silently from the cabinet.

"Holy *shit*," said Conner.

It was quiet for a few moments before Paul finally asked, "What do we do now?"

There was another stark silence. Eventually, Paul answered his question with another one.

"Pizza?"

WE sat on the cold floor in a tight circle, music filling the air around us[10] as the girls complained about the dirt until we found a towel to lay out for them. I'd ordered a veggie pizza for Aye'Sayuh after his little "only inferior humans eat meat" speech, but he insisted that pizza was "not sustenance" anyway.

"Why?" Paul asked.

"Yeah," Jade joined in. "Like, you *can't* eat it, or you just don't want to?"

"Imi have billions of years of digestive evolution on humanity. I *can* eat it. I don't want to."

"Bullshit," Barrett said, covering the comment with a fake cough.

"Try it," Paul said, lifting a slice to Aye'Sayuh.

"Yeah," I said, "all the cool kids are doing it."

A chant broke out: *Peet-zuh! Peet-zuh!*

Aye'Sayuh raised his hands in resignation—long, clawed digits in the air—and forfeiting, took a slice. He removed the ornate chain from around his nose, his reptilian mannerisms on full display as lifted his head, bird-

---

[10] David Bowie, "Cat People"

like, and the slice vanished with two predatory chomps. He shook his head, his gullet undulating as the pizza was carried down his long esophagus.

"Happy?" Aye'Sayuh asked, black tongue moving over his chops.

"I am," Jade nodded.

I laughed at the ridiculousness of the moment. Was everyone deliriously tired or had we all adjusted to the insanity this quickly? It's true that Aye'Sayuh himself was pretty disarming. His physical presence was intimidating, sure, but as I said, we'd all seen images and video of Imi thousands of times before, heard the weird accents, seen the robes and jewelry and all. Aye'Sayuh seemed more than adjusted to the social and behavioral norms of American humans. So much so, even, that I began to wonder.

"How long have you been here, dude?"

"I came with you, remember? I was made to hide under a blanket in the back of your mom's car."

"No, man, 'here' as in *Earth*. How long have you been on Earth?"

"It's almost the anniversary of my arrival here," Aye'Sayuh said, lifting a second slice of pizza. "In a few days, it'll have been thirteen years."

Emma was the first to do the math and make a connection. "You were one of the first."

Aye'Sayuh swallowed another slice of pizza and nodded. "I was small then. Just an apprentice. The student of a scientist—gifted. I was brought to learn under the leadership of the small and newly formed SIAHD. You have to understand; I was like you guys then. Space aliens, adventure on another world… It all seemed too incredible for a young apprentice to pass up. I had no idea what was truly at stake. In his posts, The Historian spoke of the

Fermi Paradox and Type I, Type II, and Type III civilizations. He was right to wonder whether a civilization would evolve in their collective cruelty just as they evolved biologically. The truth is that they do."

"But civilizations aren't collectively cruel," Paul interrupted. "They can be cruel, sure, but they're also capable of a lot of good."

Aye'Sayuh shook his head. "Good is an exception to the rule. Your Jesus of Nazareth. Your Mahatma Gandhi. Your Martin Luther King, Jr. All of them exceptional, and you killed them. These no more represent the common character of the human race than an albino hunchback dwarf represents your physicality."

"Well, damn," someone whispered. "That sounds bad."

"The more technologically sophisticated a civilization becomes, the more it creates a consumerist need that few natural habitats can actually sustain. Fast food requires animals to be born and bred into abject cruelty, shot full of mutating drugs, only to create processed poison that makes humans fat, lazy, and diseased. Fast fashion and digital addiction yields factory pollutants, human trafficking, child slavery, rampant narcissism, and eventually crowded landfills as people buy things they don't need just to throw them away."

"Yeah, that's bad," Jade said.

"And it's not just that humans don't *care*," Aye'Sayuh continued. "They don't *want* to care. Humans will do *anything* to avoid disrupting their comfort, even when their comfort is killing them. Sure, this pair of jeans supports the destruction of the planet and the enslavement of children, but I *want* the jeans. Sure, this hamburger is the accumulation of unimaginable torture and toxicity, but it *tastes* good. And so evolves the human race."

142

"So the Imi aren't here to help?" Conner asked. "What? They want to secretly wipe us out because we suck so bad?"

"Because *they* suck so bad," Aye'Sayuh corrected. "The Imi surpassed the collective sociopathic disposition of humanity a million years ago. We are a Type III civilization."

"The Historian said a Type III civilization was determined by that civilization's ability to harness the power of its *entire galaxy*," I interjected.

"That's right."

"So, I don't see us running into Imi satellites or some energy-sapping Imi structure built around Milky Way's sun."

"The Imi are not from the Milky Way galaxy."

"What about that probe?" Emma asked. "The Pioneer 10. Isn't that how you found us? We aren't capable of sending probes beyond our galaxy."

"We knew about the probe and the crude little engraving on its plates long before it got lost somewhere around Jupiter. The Imi civilization can monitor much of what transpires within the observable universe. The probe and its plates were just a way to show up without crashing the party."

"Like a bunch of damn vampires," Conner said, shaking his head. "Can't come in unless we invite them."

"It still makes no sense," Emma said. "If the entire Imi agenda is just a veneer disguising some evil scheme, then why the SIAHD? Why NARS?"

Aye'Sayuh seemed to think for a moment. "Dr. Harry Harlow was an American scientist famous for his experiments on reses monkeys. To track the correlation between companionship and cognitive development,

Harlow developed sophisticated ways to torture primates. He would banish newborn monkeys to isolation chambers for the first two years of their lives to verify the predictable hypothesis that those same monkeys would emerge emotionally and mentally disturbed. Harlow forced screaming monkeys into mating scenarios by way of a device he called the 'Rape Rack.' Unsatisfied with his initial isolation chamber research, Dr. Harlow developed a device he christened the 'Pit of Despair,' in which newborn monkeys were left alone in total darkness for up to a full year."

"Zero times," Becky interrupted. "He gets an F. I *hate* this guy."

"He's dead," Aye'Sayuh shrugged. "Died in 81 as a somewhat respected, somewhat controversial figure."

"Why the hell did you just go on about this guy?" Barrett spoke up, clearly frustrated by this doctor we'd never heard of moments before, but now uniformly despised.

Aye'Sayuh went on. "The point is that ideas like oppression, cruelty, even the cleansing of an entire world population mean little when the powerful become convinced of their superiority. To think of the Imi as evil and insane isn't helpful—it's dismissive. From what we can tell, Dr. Harlow never empathized with the monkeys he tormented because they were a means to an end. Perhaps some small part of him found their suffering regrettable, but to not carry on with his experiments? Absurd! After all, the presumed suffering of a lesser species is certainly a necessary evil in light of the greater good."

"What I don't get," said Paul, "is how advancing our technology and getting us all into NARS is going to help the Imi overthrow planet Earth."

"The plan unfolds in strategic phases," Aye'Sayuh said, leaning into the circle. "The Imi could have shown up and obliterated life on earth in one fell swoop, but their idea isn't destruction, it's *conquest*."

"They want to colonize earth," said Jade.

Aye'Sayuh gave Jade a slow nod.

"And they accomplish this with a web site?" Becky asked.

"The sophistication of Imi weaponry outgrew clubs and projectiles millennia ago. Our weapons are weapons of enslavement, not weapons of death."

"Well great," Barrett shrugged. "NARS is a phenomenon, for sure, but there are still millions of people on the planet who don't even use it. Who don't have computers at all."

"Not yet," Aye'Sayuh said, slowly reaching a long green arm into his robes. "But that's changing soon."

Aye'Sayuh drew his arm out from within his robes and revealed what looked like a small, thin, rectangular slab of transparent glass. The slab in the palm of his hand, Aye'Sayuh extended the strange artifact into the center of the circle, all of us looking on in silence.

Becky broke the silence when she asked, "they're going to take over the world with a coaster?"

Aye'Sayuh touched a fingertip to the slab and seemed to draw invisible shapes on its surface. Immediately, the slab came alive with brightly illuminated digital imagery more sophisticated and vibrant than any Arcade game I'd ever seen. He continued moving his finger about the surface of the slab, which I now gathered was a kind of screen, and in another few moments, we all seemed to simultaneously realize that Aye'Sayuh's fingertip seemed to be interacting with, even *manipulating* the actual graphics interface of the glass surface.

"What the hell?" Barrett said, the first to voice what we were all thinking.

Aye'Sayuh finished whatever he was doing, then turned the little rectangle toward us, revealing what appeared to be a new, fancier version of the NARS login screen lit up on the slab's little surface.

"Is that… *NARS*? On *that* little thing?"

"This is the NARS-Slate," Aye'Sayuh announced, nodding down at the rectangle. "With it, NARS users can access an updated version of the network without needing either a computer or even a modem."

"How does it get a phone connection?" Paul asked, squinting at the device.

"It doesn't. It connects to Apep."

"Apep?" Jade asked. "Isn't that what sustains the Internet on the Imi planet? The thing our network connection is based on?"

"Apep is a living network," Aye'Sayuh said. "It connects *life* through a system of organic vibrations in the atmosphere."

"That makes no sense," Barrett said blankly.

"I think I get it," Jade said thoughtfully, sounding very British in that moment. "I know some stuff."

"You don't freaking get it," Conner sighed, shaking his head.

"It's like radio waves!" Jade fired back. "Y'know? In the air, and all that."

"That's not entirely off," Aye'Sayuh said.

"Forget how the damn thing *works*," I demanded.

"Right," Aye'Sayuh agreed. "The point is that when the SIAHD distributes NARS-Slates on a worldwide level—the

Internet activity, geographic whereabouts, private communication, and photographic record of most human beings on earth will soon be fed directly back to the SIAHD, who will in turn maintain a direct and constant line of information dissemination with the majority of the planet."

"Then what?" Conner asked.

"Neurological addiction," Aye'Sayuh went on. "The constant flow of digital information releases in the human brain a strong but brief dopamine fix. With enough time, the Imi have created a world population of digitally addicted drones hopelessly tethered to the very thing by which the Imi will ultimately puppeteer them."

"So what?" Paul asked. "They get people addicted to the little coaster thing. Then they use it to tell us what to do?"

"It's not that simple," Aye'Sayuh said. "The SIAHD won't simply 'tell you what to do.' They are slowly shaping the collective consciousness of the human race. They don't have to flash *obey* messages on your screens, they *shift* herd thinking through social influence via NARS. Make people aware of the same things. Get people thinking the same things. Seeking after the same approval. Craving the same fix. Envying the same lifestyles. Before long, they not only have the world in the palm of their hand, we *want* to be there, and we don't even realize what's happened."

"Damn," Conner said after a brief silence. "That's some *They Live* level shit."

"Okay, great, fine," Barrett said, squinting and pinching the bridge of his nose. "What the hell are we supposed to do about any of that? How do a bunch of teenagers eating pizza in an arcade possibly thwart an alien conspiracy to enslave the minds of the human race?"

Aye'Sayuh turned to Barrett with a look of cool intensity, all of us observing his sincerity in one quiet moment before he spoke a single word that summarized his plan.

"Revolution," he said, fastening the golden chain around his snout again.

I guess he'd had enough pizza.

MOD LOG 10
BECKY'S FEAR

We panicked when we realized it was almost 6 a.m. After returning home, then leading Aye'Sayuh to his hiding place in the shed out back, I moved silently inside and back up the stairs, not thinking of much beyond a short nap. My room seemed abnormally quiet other than the music drifting quietly from the hi-fi[11].

"Rob," I said, sitting down on my bed. "Turn everything off."

Immediately the red lights of Rob's eyes went dark, his servos falling silent.

"Damn it, Rob" I sighed.

On the other end of the attic, Becky's red hair slowly appeared at the top of the stairs.

"Hey," she said.

"Hey," I said back.

"Listen," she said, moving slowly to the center of the room. "I just, um…"

She froze there, shifting her weight on to one leg, hands resting on her hips. She wrinkled her freckled nose and took a deep breath.

"Are you about to cry?" I asked.

"Only a little," she said.

---

[11] The Cars, "Drive"

She seemed to gather herself. The room was quiet for a while except for the sound of rain on the window. Without saying anything, Becky walked over and sat next to me on the bed, really close, and looked me in the eyes.

"I'm afraid you're going to die," she said.

This might've have been the last thing I was expecting her to say. "Me? Why would I be the one dying? Why can't Conner or Jade die?"

"Why did *you* get mentioned by that Historian person?" she asked, raising her voice a little. "Why did an alien show up at *your* house?"

I shrugged. "I guess I thought the second thing was because of the first thing."

"But why *either* thing in the first place?" She shot back. "We're all here because of *you*. We're here for *you*. All of this craziness came to *you*."

Becky sighed, fell silent for a moment. I had no idea what to say. I guess I hadn't thought of any of that before she brought it up. She closed her eyes and seemed to think quietly to herself. Her red hair spilled down her neck and moved against her shoulder blades as she breathed. I watched the way she pursed her full lips as she sat there. I wondered what she was thinking.

Then she nestled up against me, laid her head on my shoulder, and spoke up again. This time she wasn't much louder than a whisper.

"Remember when my mom left?"

"Yeah."

"After that awful year of teetering back and forth between threatening to leave and barely being there at all even when she was still home. One day she wasn't there. We knew. My sister, my brother, my dad and me. We knew she was really gone that time. That she'd abandoned us."

"I remember."

"Do you remember what you said? That first night without her at home I couldn't sleep. I crawled up into this attic."

"I remember."

"What did you tell me?"

"I said, 'I wish this wasn't happening to you.'"

Becky didn't say anything else, but she reached up to touch my face. It could have been an affectionate type of thing, but when I replay that night in my mind, I think she was making sure that I was still there.

Really there, I mean.

MOD LOG 11
TOURIST
[TWO DAYS LEFT ON EARTH]

"This is a stupid idea," Jade complained. With his head down, he pulled his hat low over his eyes in a lame effort to disguise himself.

"Would you quit skulking around like a sexual deviant? You look more suspicious than any of us." Emma was getting frustrated.

"I'm blending in," said Jade, without looking up. "Psychological studies show that the average person overlooks a passerby whose face they don't see."

"For God's sake," Paul sighed. "What psychological studies? You read something on NARS, and now you're a master of disguise?"

"I know some stuff," Jade fired back.

"You're about to know about walking into a street lamp if you don't watch where you're going," I warned, putting a hand out to keep him from colliding with the nearest pole.

"I saw it," Jade lied.

"How the hell did we get talked into this?" Barrett asked. Everyone looked at me.

"What?" I asked, sounding defensive. "Barrett was the one who went on about trying pizza, and now the alien is some kind of fiend."

"I'm not a *fiend*," Aye'Sayuh said, whirling around to us and nearly losing his cloak. "And don't call me 'the alien.'"

"Ah crap dude," Conner groaned, stepping over to rearrange the oversized coat in such a way that Aye'Sayuh almost looked vaguely human.

Sort of.

"Look, man, I mean, at least wear the damn disguise correctly."

"What *disguise*?" Barrett shouted, opening his hands in front of the scene before him as if he couldn't imagine anything more absurd. "It's just an alien in a jacket!"

"There's also a hat," Jade offered.

"This is nothing compared to the work ahead of us," Aye'Sayuh reminded everyone in an ominous voice and looking ridiculous as Conner fussed with his hood like a mom fixing a little kid's hair.

"That's not good news," Paul murmured.

Aye'Sayuh shoved Conner away. "How can we hope to save the galaxy if we can't sneak down the street for a slice of pizza?"

"Let us get it *for* you," Emma pleaded.

"I've been in secret labs my entire time on earth. I want to experience an authentic moment of Earth culture at least once before the plan begins."

"Put him, y'know, like in the *middle* of the group," Paul suggested. "There are eight of us. We can hide *one* alien."

"Just walk, damn it," Conner thundered, waving for us all to head down 23rd Avenue.

"Robert Smith over here stands out as much as I do," Aye'Sayuh argued, nodding at Conner.

"Yeah," Conner grunted, "hairspray and a lizard face. That's the same."

154

First of all, Aye'Sayuh was freakishly tall, and though his posture was mostly humanoid, he seemed to maintain something of a dinosaur hunch. His head was a problem, as it was thoroughly alien. Conner had covered it with an oversized plaid fedora, and the turned up the collar of a baggy trench coat—both items stolen from Conner's parent's closet. The tail was the real problem, as it was just folded awkwardly up into the coat, making Aye'Sayuh's already stooped back look grotesque and lumpy.

"You have *got* to stop moving your tail," Becky scolded him.

"Yeah, you look like a wet Mogwai," I agreed.

"A what?" Becky asked as if I'd spoken another language.

"From *Gremlins*."

"I just don't like it when we have to know all the movies just to talk."

"What are we *doing*?" Barrett groaned again.

"Walking," I said in a casual sing-song sort of voice. "Just walking."

In Portland, 23rd Avenue is often active, but on this particular night, it was a madhouse. Blitz, new wavers, Hessians, goths, punks, yuppies, preps, and wannabe boho lamewads littered the sidewalks and restaurants. The aspiring narcons were out as well. You could spot them by the Polaroid cameras slung around their necks like a badge of honor. NARS enthusiasts had long ago conceded the inferiority of traditional film cameras for their incapability of yielding immediate narsies. With a Polaroid, these NARS-obsessed phlegm wads could drain several rolls of film in an evening, convert them to digital images with their expensive photo scanners, and update their NARS profiles with more pictures of their own leering, vacuous expression all in a single evening.

They looked like they came off an assembly line, these jack-offs and their all-but-matching outfits, haircuts, and identical Polaroid Land Cameras. It's like someone may have been slightly original at one point, but all we had left were copies of copies of copies of copies.

"Dude," Jade said quietly as we walked. "I doubt anyone will pay any attention to us after all. There are too many people out here."

"And the narcons seem to have their attention devoted elsewhere," I observed, nodding across the street where three different teenagers were posing behind their own outstretched arms—taking pictures of themselves—the flashes from their Polaroids lighting the street like a Hollywood premiere.

"Oh for the love of…" Barrett groaned. A fan of photography and a talented photographer himself, Barrett was often more perturbed by the NARS crowd than any of us. "Put the cameras *down*."

"Let them take their freakin' narsies," Jade hissed through his teeth. "That's fewer people worried about us walking an *alien* down 23rd."

We could hear the music booming from inside Escape From New York Pizza long before we made it to the door. Post-punkers and goth kids staffed this infamous dive, and you could hardly hear yourself think over all the Bauhaus and Alien Sex Fiend.

"Listen," I yelled over the growling vocals blasting inside[12]. "Everyone be casual, be quick with your orders, and don't act nervous or panicked."

---

[12] Skinny Puppy, "Smothered Hope"

Becky made a sort of squeaking sound.

"What was that?" I asked.

"It's sort of exciting, isn't it?" She whispered, suddenly smiling. "We're like, on a secret mission."

"Operation: Get An Alien Pizza," Barrett sighed, rolling his eyes.

"Oh well I'm so sorry it's not a bank heist or a high-speed chase," Becky said sarcastically.

"Just go in and get the damn pizza," Conner said in a frantic voice.

"It doesn't really feel like an authentic Earth experience when it's so hasty," Aye'Sayuh complained.

"You're lucky we're doing this at all," Emma said, sounding very stern. "This whole big plan of yours to save the world could fall through in a few minutes if you get spotted eating pizza on the sidewalk by a bunch of narcons."

"Look," I yelled, "just go in and get the pizza and let's get back outside. We can walk while we eat. We do that every time anyway."

With that, the eight of us shuffled into the tiny cramped restaurant and lined up at the counter. Aye'Sayuh and I stood in line Behind Emma and Jade (who was still attempting to hide beneath the bill of his hat), and I leaned over to Aye'Sayuh, standing on my toes to be able to whisper into where I assumed his ear must be.

"Just say, 'one slice of cheese, please.' That's all you have to do. Got it?"

"What if I don't want cheese?"

"Do you not want cheese?"

"No, I want cheese."

"You *do* want cheese?"

"I want cheese."

157

"What the hell is wrong with you?"

From behind the counter: "What'll it be?"

Aye'Sayuh, head down and concealed by the ridiculous looking fedora: "I want cheese."

"Easy, detective," the goth kid behind the counter sneered.

"He was talking to me," I fake-laughed, sounding audibly nervous and getting even more nervous hearing myself sound nervous.

"What?" the goth kid asked.

"I just mean, he was being short with me, not you."

"Do you want pizza or not?"

"Cheese," Aye'Sayuh said, sounding suddenly casual.

The goth kid paused, furrowed his brow, stared at the big hat with the thick accent, then at me. I smiled like an idiot. The goth kid shook his head and moved a slice of cheese pizza into the oven.

We moved down the line.

Emma and Jade had shuffled awkwardly outside with their slices when I approached the register, five dollar bill already extended to the clerk.

"Two slices," I yelled just as the song on the stereo came to an end and the word "slices" rang out through the temporarily silent restaurant. "Two slices," I repeated quietly as if this somehow erased the previous moment. The clerk eyed me before the music started up again[13], then silently snatched the bill from my hand. Aye'Sayuh and I moved through the crowd and joined the others on the sidewalk outside.

---

[13] Ministry, "We Believe"

"Is saving the world going to be *that* nerve-wracking?" Jade giggled, a contagious laugh spreading throughout the group.

"Much worse," Aye'Sayuh said, his mouth already full of pizza. "And we could die."

The thought seized everyone. We stared off unhappily into space.

"Yeah," Paul shrugged. "There's that, I guess."

It was Conner who snapped me out of contemplating my mortality.

"Ah *dammit*," he hissed. "It's Flynn Hardey and Bradley Press."

I whirled around in time to see the two of Wesley High's worst narcons moving toward us with a ridiculous strut. The two of them had been mercifully absent from my mind since our last exchange on the day I was suspended.

"The misfit breakfast club is out on the town!" Flynn chuckled, shaping his hair with both hands.

"Hey, Rebecca," Bradley crooned, lifting his Polaroid camera as if it were some impressive artifact. "We should get a quick narsy together."

"Zero times," Becky grumbled.

"Did you get my NARS message, Emma?" said Flynn, stepping toward her as if the rest of us had vanished.

"No," Emma said calmly with a shrug.

"I sent it yesterday," Flynn added.

"I don't get on NARS every day," Emma said.

"Seriously?" Bradley asked, genuinely shocked. "You have, like, ten thousand NARS connections and you don't even check your account?"

Flynn joined in advising her. "Ten thousand isn't a ton, but it's a decent start. If you put a little more into your

NARS profile and the content you generate you could get some serious traction."

"Yeah," Bradley agreed. "I bet that ten thousand is just because you're hot. Build out your brand, and I bet you'd really catch on."

"My *brand?*" Emma echoed, one eyebrow raised.

"You're such a dweeb, Hardey," Becky groaned.

"*You* could get a hundred thousand followers with some bikini shots," Bradley said to Becky, winking. "Let me know when you need a photographer."

"Gag me," said Becky.

"Careful what you wish for, sweetie," Flynn giggled.

Becky seemed ready to slap him when he drew our attention to something we'd all forgotten.

"What's up with Carmen Sandiego over there?" Flynn asked, lifting his chin to eye our suspiciously large incognito friend.

"Get bent," Barrett answered them. "You guys better get all the narsies you can before the street lamps shut off."

"Our Polaroids have flashes, asshole," Flynn fired back. "Check it out, Becky."

He assumed a stupid little pose, one eye tightly closed, mouth agape as he peered through his camera's viewfinder. Becky shifter her weight to one leg and lifted a middle finger.

"Real sexy," Bradley said sarcastically and took the picture anyway. The flash was surprisingly bright, and Aye'Sayuh finally broke his statuesque illusion as he peered up from under his hat in a panic. The fedora went floating down to the wet sidewalk, and Aye'Sayuh stood exposed, looking around the group for some sign of what to do next. We were starting to freak out. Barrett was the only one who kept it together. The tallest of the group, he moved toward Bradley and Flynn, who were visibly intimidated by his sudden approach.

"Hey back off, dude," Bradley whined. "I can take photos in a public space if I want."

"You guys have got more important things to worry about than ruining our night. You just wasted one photo on us. That's one less narsy for your profile. What will those hundred thousand connections do without another photo of your face?"

"You're just jealous, Stevens," Flynn snorted. "No one is liking all those tired shots of bridges and evergreen trees."

They wouldn't shut up, but they were apparently afraid of Barrett and were slowly moving away from us. Happy to be rid of them, no one chanced another remark.

"Let me know about those bikini shots, Busty Becky," Bradley called out over his shoulder as he walked away.

"Oh not even," Becky fumed.

"Just let it go," I said quickly.

"Do not answer a fool according to his folly," Conner grumbled, "or you yourself will be just like him."

"Is that the Bible?" Becky said. "You're using the *Bible* against *me* in this situation?"

"Not *against* you. *For* you."

"Well someone needs to tell these two *geeks*," Becky said, raising her voice with every word, "that no one *actually* cares about their sad, stupid little staged photos of contrived moments created to market their fabricated lives to strangers who don't give a shit."

The two narcons froze.

"Here we go," Paul sighed.

"Becky said *shit*!" Conner whispered.

Neither Flynn nor Bradley could let something so accurate go without comment. They both whirled around and began talking over one another.

"We are changing the *world*, Rebecca."

"What do *you* ever do?"

"Sorry, *you* don't have as many connections as *we* do."

"You're just jealous that we live our lives on *purpose*."

"I get more comments in an hour than you have on your entire profile."

"I have followers in a dozen different countries, do you even *know* anyone outside of Oregon?"

And all kinds of asinine posturing. I'm not sure any of us were listening carefully, as we all went rigid just waiting for one of them to finally notice that amongst the group of eight standing in front of them, one of us was clearly an alien.

Then, of course, they noticed.

"People without purpose are always jealous of— "

Flynn suddenly froze, his eyes wide, locked on Aye'Sayuh and his accusing finger still extended toward Becky. Bradley went on talking beside him.

"You don't even *have* a brand!"

Then he saw it too.

Flynn seemed to float toward us, his eyes glazed over with purpose as he sidled up beside Aye'Sayuh, extended his camera-wielding arm out in front of himself, and before any of us realized what was happening, he had taken a narsy of them both.

"That's probably bad," Conner said.

Then, before I could process what had just happened or what should be done about it, Bradley and Flynn both ran off in the other direction and disappeared down the crowded street. We could hear them talking as they went, "that's seriously going to be my default picture, dude."

Bradley and Flynn vanished into the crowd as we stood there stupidly, the ambiance of the people and music slowly filling the space around us.

"Well," Paul sighed. "I doubt anyone was expecting *that* to happen."

MOD LOG 12
CELEBRITY
[FINAL DAY ON EARTH]

"We should go inside," Becky was saying, shivering, her arms crossed and the hood of her Wesley High sweatshirt drawn up over her head. "Why are you guys just skateboarding in the street at a time like this?"

It was dusk. The sun had made a feeble attempt to peer through the impenetrable grey dome of the Northwest sky and was forfeiting to a pinkish glow. Pushing off the sidewalk on my skateboard, I attempted to ollie over a manhole cover, but the street was still slick with rain, and my landing ended in a clumsy stumble as the board slid away from me and up to Emma's feet. She was looking at me with her big, blue eyes. Her mouth slightly open the way it often was when she was thinking.

"What?" I asked stupidly. "Aye'Sayuh's up in the attic adjusting the plan."

"I can't sit in the attic any more watching his big lizard face next to Flynn Hardy's moronic expression on every single channel."

"So turn off the TV," Becky shrugged. "I just don't know how you guys aren't freaking out."

"Skateboarding clears the mind, Rebecca," Conner sighed before attempting the same jump as me and falling the same way.

"But you guys suck at it, apparently," Becky observed. "Can we at *least* turn off the music?"[14]

"Hell yes," Jade said, reaching for the boombox propped up next to Barrett.

"What's the matter Sid Vicious," Barrett asked, slapping his hand away. "Not man enough for Deniece Williams?"

"You got us into this mess, *Busty Becky*," said Conner, lying on his back in the damp street as his skateboard slowly rolled away.

"I can't help that I have boobs, Conner," she argued, squinting angrily at him.

"Stop being so busty all the time," said Barrett rising to his feet, the first to effortlessly ollie over the manhole cover. He stopped to take a bow. "I'd like to thank Deniece Williams for that smooth landing. Sing it, girl!"

"*Emma* drew those two dweebs over in the first place, remember?" Becky reminded us. "If she didn't look like a European model they would have never bothered us!"

"You're both to blame," I sighed. "Stupid sexy friends."

Both girls laughed for the first time that day, and for a moment, things seemed normal. Behind me, I heard Becky murmur to Emma, "that baby could not handle me in a bikini. I'll tell you that much right now." To which Emma replied, pointing to herself, "*this* baby couldn't handle another moment of his stupid face." They both laughed again.

"Why don't you stand up and skate, Jade," Barrett demanded, sounding winded.

"I don't have a helmet," said Jade.

---

[14] Deniece Williams, "Let's Hear It for the Boy"

"You don't need a helmet, poser," Barrett snorted. "You just need the *Brain Drain*."

"The Brain Drain is a myth," Jade yawned.

"No way, dude," I interrupted. "The Brain Drain is as real as you and me."

"Yeah," Conner laughed. "The Brain Drain lives in your heart. One has only to believe."

"You guys just don't know how to do it," I said, stretching.

Then Conner, still lying in the street, pointed up and said, "that can't be good." All of us looked at Conner, who seemed to be staring up at the roof of my house. As if on cue, we all drew our attention up to match Conner's gaze, and a simultaneous gasp came from both girls. Aye'Sayuh was perched on the roof, peering out into the distance through what looked like a spyglass.

"Um," I said, "Aye'Sayuh. Dude. What's going on, man?"

"I can see it," he yelled back without looking at us.

"Awesome," I said. "What the hell are you looking at?"

"The SIAHD facility to the north."

Barrett and I looked at each other, then back up to the rooftop. Conner rose slowly, looking around for his wayward skateboard.

"Cool," I said. "But hey, being on the roof is a stupid idea, probably."

Aye'Sayuh said nothing but went on looking into Washington State with his little alien telescope.

"Well great," said Barrett, throwing his hands up in frustration. "It's only a matter of time before aliens or the FBI show up to take us in to get probed."

"That's happening either way," Becky said.

"Aye'Sayuh, dude," I went on. "I doubt we'll ever get anywhere with this plan of yours if we're locked up in an Imi prison somewhere. So unless you want your friends at that secret facility to show up here with an unmarked van in ten minutes, maybe you should climb down so that the neighbors don't see an alien on my roof and freak out."

"When does your mom get home?" Paul asked, sounding nervous.

"She'll be a while," I shrugged. "Went in late."

With all of us watching, Aye'Sayuh suddenly scrambled down the steep incline of the roof and the vertical face of the house. He slithered out into the lawn on all fours, then erected himself in an instant, taking up his humanoid posture once again as if he hadn't been entirely animalistic a moment prior.

"Now that we're pressed for time, we need to act sooner," Aye'Sayuh said, approaching the group.

"Dude, come on," Conner groaned, pointing at Aye'Sayuh's loose-fitting and mostly open trench coat. "It's like, is this even a disguise anymore? You're just a lizard in a big jacket."

"Were you looking at the secret lab?" Paul asked Aye'Sayuh.

"The SIAHD facility," Aye'Sayuh went on. "The facility has the closest harbor, and there's not much time before they come looking for us here."

"Remind me *why* it is that we don't have much time," Barrett piped up. "Who antagonized the narcons that got us into this mess?"

Becky elbowed him.

"Harbor?" Jade asked. "Does that word mean something different on your planet? Unless that facility is out in the open on the river, I'm afraid it's most likely harborless."

"Not for boats, nimrod," Aye'Sayuh said, sneering at Jade. "It's a port of passage—one of only a very few. A door to *Gaina*."

"To guy-*ee*-nuh?" Becky drawled, over-enunciating the planet's weird name. "As in, the *planet*? A door to a *planet*?"

"What, do you want another detailed presentation?" Aye'Sayuh sighed impatiently. "My original plan involved a formal vessel. It would be safer and easier to operate, but we don't have time to get to it or to take the journey the slow way. Now we need a harbor. I don't have time to describe quantum physics to your primitive earth minds."

"Oh well *excuse* me for living," Becky said, rolling her eyes.

"The harbor is something like a controlled and localized wormhole—by folding space-time, the wormhole brings two widely separated points together, making infinite distances traversable by simply moving from one harbor to another."

"We know what a damn wormhole is," I lied. Conner gave me a look that seemed to ask, 'really?' I shook my head at him privately and turned back to Aye'Sayuh.

"It's good news, right?" Paul asked, looking around the group. "Vancouver is a ten-minute drive from here. That's easy."

"Can we go inside, *please*?" Becky asked again. Emma gave her a side hug and sort of rubbed her arms in a kind of halfhearted gesture to acknowledge Becky was cold.

"Can you sneak us in?" Emma asked Aye'Sayuh.

"*Sneak* you in?" Aye'Sayuh echoed sarcastically.

"Do you have a space car or something?"

"A space car?" Conner repeated, squinting at Emma, who raised her eyebrows and shrugged.

"No, look, you guys are all missing the point. I'm *owl*."

We all stood there silently for a moment.

"You're *owl*?" I finally asked.

"As in, I abandoned my post without permission. I'm owl."

"You're not an owl," Jade said calmly. "On account of that's a bird."

"Does he mean AWOL?" Barrett asked quietly.

I was pinching the bridge of my nose. "Aye'Sayuh, you want a different word, look, it doesn't matter, can we get to the new plan?"

Aye'Sayuh scratched his chin, confused, mumbling the word "owl" to himself as if to double-check its accuracy. Eventually, he snapped out of it and spoke up. "We'll have to break in."

"Of course we will," Becky groaned, throwing her hands up in exasperation.

AYE'SAYUH was still on virtually every news broadcast, as were nauseating interviews with Bradley Press and Flynn Hardey. Over the course of three programs, their story blossomed from slight exaggeration to outright fantasy. At first, they had recounted the story with some accuracy, conveniently excluding every incriminating detail that might reveal their collective assholeishness while insinuating that they were close personal friends with "the alien." In the second interview, they had been out on the town with an important Imi politician and scientist. And finally, they had both been personally invited by the SIAHD to become advisors on upcoming NARS projects.

170

"It's a bad idea," Aye'Sayuh shrugged, seemingly unfazed by the infuriating lies of these two jack-offs.

"You think?" Paul asked, frustrated. "How long can it possibly take everyone to find you? I'm shocked they aren't here already."

"No, I mean it's a bad idea for *them*," Aye'Sayuh went on, stepping away from the TV, gathering various items from around the attic and stockpiling them on my bed. "They seem like ideal candidates for the Feed Camps on Gaina."

"The Feed Camps?" Conner asked, turning from the TV.

"Horrible places," Aye'Sayuh said without looking up. "Filled with poor souls like those two."

"Yeah, yeah, poor little butt-bags. Listen," Barrett said. "Paul is making an excellent point here. What the hell is going on? How are we not already bound and gagged and being fed to a giant alien lizard? These two morons could hand this address to any single reporter that asks."

"And direct all the attention to the people who *actually* know the alien?" Emma spoke up. "They'd effectively remove themselves from the spotlight."

"Right!" Conner exclaimed, laughing. "Those two will do anything to cling to the superficial limelight. I'll bet they're inadvertently drawing people *away* from us."

"Either way," Aye'Sayuh said, "we have to leave tonight."

"Tonight?" Becky yelled.

Then, something strange happened.

Paul stood up and took a deep breath. We all turned to look at him, but not in a panicked sort of way, almost like we knew he had something important to tell us and this was our time to hear it. Someone had put on Bowie's *Heroes*, and the title track[15] was playing beneath Paul's words as if masterfully planned. It seemed as though Paul—the voice of reason in our group—needed this time. Whatever it was he was about to say was for this particular moment, one rainy November night in 1987.

"I've been thinking. We've all been through stuff. I can't shake this feeling that we're meant to do this together, y'know? Like all of our hurting has brought us to one place so that we could be together and face *this*. Being a teenager is a difficult, often miserable ordeal, and it hasn't been easy on any of us. Because of you guys, I've been spared the ordeal of facing my pain alone. Now, I think it's time to do this. Together."

Surprisingly, Becky was first to speak. "I think so too," she said, her voice shaking. "I have this… this *sense*."

"That's the Holy Spirit, dude," Conner said.

Beck smiled at him. "Whatever it is, I feel it."

Barrett laughed, putting his arm around Becky. "Just like that, you're in?"

Becky leaned into his shoulder. "I was always in."

Emma stepped over and hugged them both. "Me too."

Jade looked at Paul and said, "Not bad, Paul Patchett."

"I have my moments," Paul said, sitting down.

Conner looked out the window and said to no one in particular: "I consider that our present sufferings are not worth comparing with the glory that will be revealed in us."

"Amen," I said, nodding.

"A-freaking-men," Paul agreed.

"There's a poem in my head," Conner continued. "An ancient Hebrew song. Psalm Number 148, I think. Anyway,

---

[15] "Heroes," David Bowie

it makes me think of what's beautiful about the world. A world worth saving. Together."

Aye'Sayuh, who had watched us quietly this whole time, finally broke his silence.

"Okay, I've got a plan."

We all gathered around. I took a deep breath, looked at Conner, and asked, "still got those keys to Ground Kontrol?"

MOD LOG, 13
LAST NIGHT ON EARTH

I could hardly hear anything with New Order[16] thrumming through my head. The otherwise empty arcade was alive with laser lights, fog machines, and strobes.

"Why does The Great Powersurf have this place set up like a discotheque?" I yelled over the synth-pop issuing from the powerful speakers mounted in every corner of the arcade's ceiling.

"He's a party animal, dude," Conner yelled back.

"What?"

"I said Powersurf loves to party, man."

I couldn't really hear him but nodded anyway.

Squinting into the scene around me, it looked like someone had set up a bunch of video games on the set of *Soul Train*. Unfazed, Paul was stationed in front of a *Rampage* cabinet, Barrett as his audience, sipping a bottle of Orange Crush. Jade was perched next to Aye'Sayuh on the counter where refreshments would normally be sold, both of them studying holographic diagrams projected from Aye'Sayuh's NARS-Slate. They were going over the plan again.

I could hear Jade saying, "and when we get to the harbor, you'll be able to take us to this base?"

---

[16] "Bizarre Love Triangle," New Order

I was trying to figure out exactly what they were looking at when Becky took my hands. "Dance with me!" she yelled, already gyrating in the haze of green light and lingering water vapor.

"At least play Joy Division," Conner yelled. "New Order is so bubblegum."

"Oh shut up and dance, punk rock boy," Becky said, grabbing Conner's wrist as she went on twirling. Conner laughed as he gave in, dancing playfully with Becky to the song he claimed to hate but secretly loved.

"Does this make me punk rock?" Becky asked him, hugging his neck.

Conner rolled his eyes. "I'm going to go wait outside for the pizza guy," he shouted, blushing as he wriggled free of Becky's grip.

"Looks like it's just you and me," Becky said. She lifted both arms over her head and shimmied in a little circle. "It might be our last night on earth, Danny. We might as well dance."

Well, when she put it like that…

As the song carried on, I was lost in a beautiful distraction with Becky. We both laughed at our shared inability to find any similar rhythm or science to each other's movements. Our arms playfully wrapped around one another or else swimming through the air as we skipped aimlessly in little circles, singing whichever random line we happened to remember.

I'm not sure what this could mean
I don't think you're what you seem

To think of it now, I can see that I recorded those few minutes in vivid detail on the canvas of my memory. After everything that happened, my mind continues to bring it to bear, often unexpectedly. It plays like a montage in my head, and I see the way Becky was laughing and twirling and how the lights made her freckled cheekbones seem to change colors, her long red hair moving around her head like a weightless ribbon.

When the song was over, I told her she could easily become a *Solid Gold* dancer. "Duh," she said, rolling her eyes. "They should be so lucky." She kissed my cheek, smiled at me and added, "I love you, Danny."

For a moment all that we'd been through seemed to hang in the air between us; her mom, my dad, all the suffering. I think she felt it too, and I searched my mind for some way to articulate what I was feeling, but every option seemed to fall hopelessly short. The only thing I could think to say was, "I love you too, Becky."

I guess that had to be enough.

Then Conner was yelling for us to turn the music down as he carried a small stack of pizza boxes up to the counter.

Honestly, I don't remember a great many specifics about that night. When it plays in my head like a video, I can't make the dialogue out—it's just all of us in there laughing together, eating pizza, forgetting if only for a moment what was to come. Even Aye'Sayuh seemed less like this strange intruder who had so shaken our lives and more like a dorky exchange student we had accepted as our own.

When the conversation finally lulled for a few seconds, someone noticed what had been playing in the background[17].

---

[17] Foreigner, "I Want to Know What Love Is"

"Ah, Jesus," Barrett groaned. "Is this Becky's mixtape?"

Becky threw up her hands. "Don't look at me."

"Embrace it, Bare-Bare," Emma said, squinting at Barrett, wrinkling her nose.

We all groaned.

"This song is your mixtape's last chance, Emma," Conner warned. "If the next song doesn't redeem it, we're going to feed it to Aye'Sayuh."

"Oh, sure," Aye'Sayuh scoffed. "Because I eat plastic cassette tapes.

"Not with *that* attitude," said Barrett.

The song gradually faded to a dull decrescendo, and we all sat there, eyebrows raised, waiting. Suddenly, a familiar drum machine fired up[18].

"*There* it is," Barrett said, immediately setting to work dancing in place with only his arms and shoulders.

"That won't cut it, bubs," Becky sassed. "On your feet."

As the entire crew, one by one, seemed to file out into the arcade, laughing, Conner reached for the lighting controls behind the counter.

"Isn't it *more* punk rock to dance to Whitney Houston, since so few punk rockers would do it?"

"Definitely," I yelled over the music, dancing my way out into the group.

Conner nodded, flipping the switches. The room went dark then came to life with the spiraling flickers reflecting off a disco ball none of us realized was hanging overhead.

"Damn," Jade said. "The Great Powersurf *does* know how to party."

---

[18] Whitney Houston, "I Wanna Dance With Somebody (Who Loves Me)"

So we danced.

Even Aye'Sayuh joined in the fun, uninhibited, and no one laughed at him until much later when we remembered the evening together. We had to keep dodging his big, lumbering tail, but we just went on singing as if even this was an ordinary part of any given dance party.

"*This*, my friends," Jade shouted over the steady thump of the bass. "*This* is how you prepare to save the world."

"If the people of Earth could see us now," Becky yelled, her arms over her head as she spun around in a circle, "I doubt they'd be all that optimistic about our chances."

"Speak for yourself," Conner rebutted—even he had become fully invested in the dance party. "I'm going to be an absolute Stephen Hayes against the Lizard People."

"Don't get them started about that ninja guy," Emma warned Becky.

"That ninja guy?" I repeated, clearly wounded. "Excuse me, ma'am. Stephen Hayes was the first—"

"The first American to be trained by a living ninja grandmaster in the hills of Kyoto, Japan. We know."

"Damn skippy," said Conner. "I'm going to go full Stephen Hayes on the Lizard People.

I made my way to Emma, who maintained a controlled little smile in spite of herself. My hands on her hips and hers over my shoulders, we swayed and bounced about, hopelessly unsophisticated and without any sense of intention or choreography. Our voices lifting with each chorus, I couldn't help but think that Whitney was really on to something. I too wanted to dance with somebody who loved me.

And there we were, doing just that.

Emma leaned in and whispered something I'll never forget: "I need to know you're on my team, okay?"

I looked at her wet eyes and then nodded slowly, understanding her then without the words to explain it now.

No one saw him get it, but we noticed Barrett had managed to sneak a slice of pizza into the dance party, eating as he grooved.

Aye'Sayuh, still dancing in his weird way, nodded to the slice and said, "I'll warn you all now: There is no pizza on Gaina."

"Not with *that* attitude," said Barrett.

MOD LOG, 14
HOW TO PACK FOR INTERSTELLAR TRAVEL

Outside, the streets of Portland were a ghost town. With several days to go before Thanksgiving, the lampposts were already wrapped in spiraling Christmas lights, archways of local businesses festooned with tinsel garlands. Barrett climbed into the minivan and turned the ignition, the exhaust billowing into the cold air in a thick, dense plume of dark grey.

Barrett cranked the stereo[19] before turning to address his passengers, which seemed weird because we could hardly hear him.

"Okay, here's the plan: I'll take you guys home so you can get what you need. Everyone be back at Danny's in an hour."

Paul turned to Jade sitting beside him. "I'm not going to be much help saving the world on little to no sleep."

"Rob can make us coffee?" Jade wondered aloud.

"Rob can barely turn on the damn lights," Conner said, leaning back, eyes closed.

"Dude, can *you* program a Nintendo robot butler?" I asked, sounding more sensitive than I'd intended.

"Apparently neither of us can," Conner said, eyes still closed.

---

[19] John Parr, "St. Elmo's Fire (Man in Motion)"

WHEN the girls finally returned—long after all the boys had found their way back to the attic—we swore they were going to wake my mom with the awful racket it took hoisting their ridiculous luggage up the stairs.

"Damn it, girls," Barrett whisper-yelled. "How are we supposed to infiltrate a top-secret government facility with all this crap?" He gestured at Becky's three pink suitcases, and Emma's two enormous orange ones. Both girls looked down at their luggage as if they hadn't thought of this until that moment.

"We're going to a different *planet*," Becky said defensively. "I have no idea what I'll need."

"Nothing," Aye'Sayuh offered casually. "We have all your base human needs covered on Gaina."

"What kind of electrical outlets do you have?" Jade asked. "I brought European adapters."

"Of course you did," said Paul in a mock English accent that was shaky at best.

"We have places to plug in earth electronics where we've barracked the earth rebels."

"Wait," Paul spoke up. "There are already humans on Gaina?"

"Sure," Aye'Sayuh shrugged.

"Human *rebels*," Paul added. "As in, on *our* side?"

Aye'Sayuh nodded as though he couldn't see how this question was at all relevant.

"Well, what the hell do you need *us* for?"

This seemed like an entirely valid question. The seven of us all froze and looked to Aye'Sayuh.

"We have scientists," he said in a tone that seemed to imply this should be obvious enough. "Artists. Sages. No trained warriors. Well, only one, but he's there to train others."

The attic was filled with a thick silence.

"What the *hell* are you talking about, dude?" Conner asked. "Do *we* look like 'trained warriors' to you? None of us have even been in a fight, man. And I'm a pacifist!"

Aye'Sayuh rolled his eyes, frustrated. "You're not warriors, *yet*. Duh."

We all stood there waiting.

"But…" Becky spoke up, moving her hand through the air as if urging Aye'Sayuh to complete his cryptic sentence.

"But you *will* be," Aye'Sayuh said, again sounding like we were all idiots for missing this obvious fact. He waved Becky away dismissively, adding, "you'll be trained, and you'll be given everything you need. There's no need to pack everything you've ever owned." He gestured at the collection of suitcases.

I looked over at Paul, who looked back at me and made a face that seemed to say, "makes sense, I guess."

"So what *do* we need?" Emma was asking, flicking open the latches on her suitcase.

"There's a small inorganic material transport next to the harbor. But it won't accommodate those big suitcases. And you can't go through the harbor wearing clothes. Nothing inorganic."

"What?" the girls asked in unison.

"No clothes," Aye'Sayuh repeated.

"We go through… Naked?" Becky asked suspiciously, raising an eyebrow.

"Yes," Aye'Sayuh nodded. "You can put your clothes and a small bundle of inorganic items through the transport first. Then you follow them through the wormhole by using the harbor. Your clothes and select items should be there on Gaina waiting for you when you arrive an instant later."

"*Should* be?" Paul asked.

Aye'Sayuh shrugged again. "There's always a risk of being disintegrated.

"*Disintegrated*?" Conner asked. "The clothes or us?"

"Either one," Aye'Sayuh confessed. "But neither is likely."

"Neither is likely," Barrett repeated slowly, his voice bitter with sarcasm. "That's bad news. Becky, you'll have to go through first."

"Actually," Aye'Sayuh interjected. "You'll have to go through all at once if you want to arrive at the same place at the same time. Otherwise, someone could end up at the wrong harbor."

"So we're all getting in this thing... *naked*?" Barrett asked.

"Well, yeah," Aye'Sayuh said. "What? Is it embarrassing or something? Just close your eyes, I guess."

"You all *better* close your eyes," Emma said.

"Don't flatter yourself, Miss," I jeered. "You just keep your eyes off of these specimens." I nodded at the rest of the guys, who were all looking at me as if I were only making an awkward situation worse.

Ignoring our weird human squabble over being naked, Aye'Sayuh spoke up. "The inorganic transport is about this big," he said, holding his hands apart to indicate a space of about two feet.

"What are we supposed to do when we all show up on Gaina without clothes?" Emma asked.

"You've got to stop saying it like that," Barrett told her.

"Like what?"

"*Guy*-ee-nuh."

"Isn't that how you say it?"

"It's Guy-*ee*-nuh. With the accent on the second syllable."

"What difference does it make?"

"It's just not how you say it."

Paul interrupted them. "Oh for God's sake, Aye'Sayuh, if we can bring a small bundle of items, what should we prioritize?"

"What about our *clothes*?" Emma asked. "Hello? It wasn't a stupid question."

"We have clothes for you on Gaina," Aye'Sayuh assured her.

"But are they even cute?" Emma asked, sounding very serious.

"Good grief," Barrett sighed.

"Well excuse me, Marty McFly," Emma fired back dramatically. "You can't bring your vest. What if they have you in some kind of outfit from *The Jetsons*?

"I'll look cool," Barrett said. He looked at Aye'Sayuh and asked quietly, "do the clothes look like something from *The Jetsons*?"

"Not really," Aye'Sayuh answered.

"But do we even need underwear?" Becky went on as if this premise was still entirely unbelievable. "I can't be on an alien planet with no bra."

Emma put her hands over her chest as if the thought had only now occurred to her. "No way," she agreed.

"Put the bras through the organic teleporter thing," Jade suggested.

"Inorganic transport," Aye'Sayuh corrected.

"That one," Jade nodded.

"Okay well, so far this packing list doesn't sound very promising," Becky complained, reaching into one of her open suitcases. "A bra and a Walkman, I guess," she said, lifting both. "Can this really be all we need on an alien planet?"

"Technically," Aye'Sayuh insisted, "you don't *need* either one. It's whatever you *want* to bring."

"I *want* music and support" Becky responded.

"Go nuts," Aye'Sayuh shrugged.

I took a deep breath and looked down at Rob as he wheeled up to my ankles. "I want *you*, Rob."

The funky opening notes of Marvin Gaye's "I Want You" began issuing from Rob's lo-fi speakers.

"Never mind," I said.

MOD LOG, 15
HEIST

"I seriously can't see anything," Emma whispered.

The SIAHD center was hidden within a wooded area of southern Vancouver along the Columbia River. Emma was right. The darkness was virtually impenetrable.

Peering through a dense layer of greenery, we could see the facility glowing orange in the distance. It looked like a yuppie's mid-century condo, only bigger. As big as a hospital.

"How do we get in?" Paul whispered.

"The entrances are all genetically coded to open for Imi," Aye'Sayuh said.

"So just any alien can wander right in the front door?" I asked.

"Every Imi commissioned for work on earth undergoes rigorous training and psychological conditioning. We spent all our time securing ourselves against humans. An Imi traitor is unprecedented."

"Until you came along, huh?" said Jade.

"Fuckin' A," Aye'Sayuh said quietly, his eyes on the facility.

We'd managed to combine our shared inventory of necessities into four small backpacks that Aye'Sayuh assured us would (more than likely) survive their ride through an interstellar wormhole. In the end, this is what we packed:

Seven different mixtapes (after it became abundantly clear we would never agree on anything). Three Walkmans and a boom box. Conner's leather jacket, Barrett's red vest, Paul's beanie, my denim coat, and three bras (Becky insisted on bringing two of her own despite being assured there existed a means of doing laundry on Gaina). A totally outdated issue of *Videogaming Illustrated* with E.T. on the cover because Paul "never got around to reading it." A paperback copy of *Dune* because *Dune* is totally badass. VHS copies of *Short Circuit* (just in case) and *Gremlins* (for Christmas time). Two pillows (in case the pillows on Gaina suck). Three skateboards. And a single toothbrush.

We realized later that we forgot to pack toothpaste.

Crouched in the shrubs some 100 yards from the facility—Barrett, Paul, and myself with the backpacks, a skateboard tucked beneath each of them—Jade said what was on everyone's mind.

"I'm sort of scared."

Everyone nodded silently.

"Remember the plan," Aye'Sayuh said coolly. "We just have to get what we came for then get to the harbor. Everything is going to be fine. This is going to work."

"Maybe Conner should say a prayer?" Paul suggested, his voice sincere.

We all looked to Conner as if this sounded like as good an idea as any. With his gaze locked on the facility, Conner prayed:

"God is our dad, and he is very good. Make the world the way it should be. Provide for us the things we need. Forgive us for screwing up as we forgive other screw-ups. Keep us safe from the evil one."

It was quiet for a moment.

"Amen," I said.

"Amen," everyone echoed.

"Did you make that up?" Paul asked Conner.

"No, Jesus did," Conner whispered.

"Wicked."

"Let's go," Aye'Sayuh told us. "It's time."

There was no turning back now.

ONCE inside the facility, we were hit by an immediate sense of security. The place was as white and sterile as any hospital, lit up with fluorescent bulbs and as quiet as outer space (which I'm told is very quiet).

The entrance opened into a bright white extended corridor. I felt vulnerable creeping in, but also somewhat comforted by the apparent isolation.

"Where is everyone?" Emma whispered.

"I told you," Aye'Sayuh whispered back. "Limited personnel. The staff all live onsite. They have to sleep sometime."

"Is *everyone* asleep?" Becky asked.

"How should I know?" Aye'Sayuh hissed, sounding nervous.

"Where are all the guards?" Barrett said. "Where's the security around this place?"

"What security?" Aye'Sayuh responded. "Every single checkpoint is genetically responsive. Only Imi can move through the facility or humans with Imi chaperones."

"It's the damn honor system," said Paul.

"Yeah," Aye'Sayuh said as the group approached the end of the corridor. "Not working out so great for them."

I came to a gradual stop behind Aye'Sayuh and took a moment to survey our surroundings. The architecture of the place was as minimalistic as possible; the halls, ceiling, and walls all a marbled white, the tall doors nearly invisible except for their thin seams as if cut into the wall itself. With no knobs or hinges, I had no idea how anyone got in or out of any of the rooms. Innumerable doors lined the hall with perfect spacing and symmetry, but it didn't matter. The plan was to follow Aye'Sayuh, who had warned us that the facility used no visual indicators of any kind to guide its inhabitants throughout its complicated infrastructure. SIAHD workers were all trained to memorize and navigate the labyrinth long before stepping foot on the premises. In the unlikely event that an intruder managed to find their way inside, they'd be hopelessly lost with no way to pass between checkpoints long before they managed to cause any trouble.

We were all crouched in a line, leaning against the wall as Aye'Sayuh peered around the first corner. Behind me, the group looked like a worried conga line. Against our stark surroundings, everyone looked absurdly flashy. Becky with her pink and purple jacket. Emma's neon sweater. The deep red of Barrett's vest. Even Conner stood out in his typical ratty black uniform.

"This way," Aye'Sayuh whispered, creeping around the corner. No one spoke as we followed Aye'Sayuh through the maze of identical corridors for what felt like an hour. After a while, I began to suspect Aye'Sayuh himself had lost his way but couldn't muster the courage to admit it. I was feeling pretty scared, and the idea that we might abandon the mission suddenly seemed like a good one—a notion I was almost certain the rest of the group would readily affirm. Just as I was about to suggest as much, we came to a stop in front of a random door (or a door-like shape cut into the wall) indistinguishable from the dozens we had passed on our way. Fanning his three long fingers and an equally long opposable thumb, Aye'Sayuh pressed his palm into the unmarked center of the door. A gentle chime resonated from the door's surface, as a green panel illuminated beneath Aye'Sayuh's hand. The rectangular space that seemed to indicate a door in the wall moved silently away from Aye'Sayuh's outstretched arm, then quickly disappeared to the right as if on a track we couldn't see.

Beyond the door was thick darkness. Before anyone could mention it, another relaxing chime sounded as the room was flooded with white light. Inside was an empty chamber of white except for a small island situated in the center of the room made from the same material as everything around it.

Following behind Aye'Sayuh, the seven of us wandered slowly into the open room, where Aye'Sayuh approached the island, his hand outstretched.

"The door closed behind us," Becky whispered.

I looked behind us and observed that she was right. Everything up until now had felt insanely dangerous. Somehow the closed door and the privacy of the room provided a sense of safety.

Aye'Sayuh set about punching in a series of entry codes by tapping what looked to us like arbitrary points on the island's surface, each of them chiming and responding with a quick blink of green light. There was another chime, some synthetic-sounding words spoken in Imi, then the entire surface of the island became transparent as if made from glass.

Inside, what looked like an ancient scroll was suspended in midair.

"Is that...?" I whispered.

"Yep," Aye'Sayuh answered quietly. "Esk Hahr o' Mek."

"The final heresy," said Jade.

"Oh crap," said Emma, shielding her eyes as if the scroll were playing a horror movie. "We shouldn't read it, right?"

"You *can't* read it, dork," I reminded her, smiling. "Unless you know how to read Imi and didn't tell us."

Emma squinted at me. "Maybe I do, buster."

As the group cautiously approached the scroll, I moved silently away from them to the control panel Aye'Sayuh had used to open the island chamber. The interface lit up on the island's clear surface, and I discovered the interactive keyboard still visible. The keys, however, were all marked with unreadable Imi glyphs. I touched one of them, and the series of keys immediately reoriented themselves into the keyboard format with which I was accustomed, the glyphs becoming the letters of the English alphabet. Quickly, I began typing a name I'd read hundreds of times in my dad's journal. I looked around nervously—the others were still scheming a few feet away, my deviation from the group unnoticed. My search inquiry produced a series of archived documents, the first of which I was able to quickly forward to my own NARS account by following a series of user-friendly command prompts. I then stepped casually to the other side of the island to rejoin the group. No one had seemed to notice.

Aye'Sayuh went on staring at the scroll in silence.

"Dude," Conner whispered to Aye'Sayuh. "What are you doing? Get it out. That's the plan, right?"

"Also," Becky interrupted, "do we need to keep whispering?"

"They've changed something," Aye'Sayuh observed, pointing to some inscriptions frosted on the glass-like surface of the island housing the scroll. "I don't get it."

"Can you get it out or not?" Paul asked impatiently.

"It says something about…" Aye'Sayuh squinted at the text as if it must be mistaken. "Something about a prisoner."

"That's not good news," Barrett whispered.

"They're going to take us prisoner?" Becky asked urgently.

"No, you dweeb," Barrett answered. "You think they wrote about us before we got here?"

"Oh like *you* know," Becky said, rolling her eyes.

"The SIAHD doesn't normally take or keep *prisoners*," Aye'Sayuh told us. "It doesn't make any sense." He set about punching in a new set of commands slowly as if reading them from the strange inscription he had discovered.

When what must have been the final key to whatever combination Aye'Sayuh was entering was pressed, one entire wall of the square room chimed, glowed momentarily green, then faded from opaque to clear in an instant just as the island had done. Beyond the wall was a second rectangular room. The area was made up like small living quarters. There was a sink, a toilet, some stacks of papers and pens, and a small mattress where a thin, black man with a white beard sat.

Startled by what must have been an unexpected visit, the man turned toward us and rose slowly from the bed. He was dressed in what must have been a SIAHD uniform—something like white hospital scrubs—and both his beard and what was left of the hair on his mostly bald head were cut neatly short. He didn't look much like a prisoner.

The seven of us went rigid, but Aye'Sayuh seemed more confused than worried. "Who are you?" he asked plainly. "Are you a prisoner here?"

Then the man seemed to take note of our posse. He looked suddenly apprehensive.

"Did you kids wander away from the tour? You shouldn't be in here. You need to leave."

He kept looking from Aye'Sayuh to the rest of as if he couldn't make sense of our partnership and who was here for what.

"Tour?" Aye'Sayuh asked, cocking his head. "What tour? Are you being kept here against your will?"

Then the man seemed to realize that the island in our room had been opened, the scroll visible inside.

"No," he said, clearly panicked. "I told you, I can't help with that damned text. You're wasting your time."

"He seems upset," Jade said, still whispering.

Aye'Sayuh looked to the scroll, then to the man, then back to the scroll again until I tapped him impatiently.

"What are we doing, man?" I asked. "Are we getting this thing or not?"

Aye'Sayuh looked into the small chamber as if something had just clicked. "We can get you out of here," he said. "You can help us."

Without waiting for a reply, Aye'Sayuh punched in a new code, causing a new door to appear and open in the wall dividing the strange man's room from ours. The man stepped out of his cell immediately, like he hadn't much thought of what he'd do next but may as well get out of there while he had the chance.

Aye'Sayuh went back to typing on the clear glass, and a small opening appeared before the scroll. He snatched it from the case without delicacy, rolled it up and tucked it under his arm.

"Let's go," he said to the man. Then, turning to us, added, "New plan. We need this guy's help."

"Who the hell is this guy?" Conner asked.

Aye'Sayuh whirled around to face the man, who was moving slowly toward us. "You've read from the Esk Hahr o' Mek, haven't you?"

The man nodded slowly.

"You're Stewart Raffill." Aye'Sayuh concluded. "They told us you were a vegetable. Catatonic."

"I'm not," the man said.

"No duh," Becky whispered.

Aye'Sayuh took a step toward the man, who held his ground. "We're leaving," Aye'Sayuh said firmly. "We're taking the harbor to the rebel base on Gaina."

The man slowly lifted a hand and pointed at Aye'Sayuh as if something was only now occurring to him. "You... You're SIAHD?"

"I was," Aye'Sayuh nodded.

"Then it's true. The revolution the Historian spoke of is coming."

"It is."

The man seemed to focus, seized by some sudden urgency. "Who?" he asked, closing the distance between Aye'Sayuh and himself. "Who did the Historian gather? The SIAHD thinks he's recruiting warriors."

"They do?" I asked quietly, sounding nervous.

Aye'Sayuh turned to look at the seven of us. No one said anything. Conner turned around to see if he was looking at someone behind us.

The man scratched his beard and sighed. He leaned over to Aye'Sayuh and whispered, "Is the Breakfast Club here really the best we could do?"

Becky squealed, delighted with this label. "Did you hear him?" she whispered excitedly, all of us shushing her.

WE were running now—the effort of keeping up with Aye'Sayuh without dropping my backpack or skateboard becoming increasingly difficult as we tore through every new blank corridor.

"How big *is* this place," Paul asked, panting.

"I'm convinced we're just doing laps," Jade wheezed.

"Apparently we should have also packed sports bras," Emma added, though no one had a chance to get what she meant before we all crashed into each other when Aye'Sayuh came to an unexpected halt.

"Aye'Sayuh!" I yelled, staggering backward after colliding violently with his lifted tail. As soon as I'd braced myself, Becky came crashing into my back, then Emma behind her, and on down the line until Paul collided with Barrett. Somewhere in the pileup, someone must have barreled into whoever had the boombox, which somehow came to life within one of the backpacks[20].

"What the hell, dude?" I yelled at Aye'Sayuh over the music.

Then I realized why we'd stopped.

About twenty feet down the long corridor stood, of all people, Flynn Hardey, Bradley Press, and a human SIAHD scientist. Bradley and Flynn were fixed with visitor badges, both of them clutching their very own NARS-Slates.

---

[20] Misfits, "Hybrid Moments"

196

"The tour," the bearded prisoner man whispered, startling me when I remembered he had joined our party.

Without a single word, both Flynn and Bradley lifted their little devices in the air, pointing them at us, and began tapping at them furiously. For a moment, I expected we'd be zapped with a laser or something, but instead there was just the incessant sound of a camera shutter.

"Should we run?" I gasped.

"Brain Drain!" Paul shouted.

"My bladder is about to drain,"[21] Jade called out.

"Run!" Aye'Sayuh shouted, taking off *in* the direction of the unexpected bystanders, the rest of us following behind with no time to consider how stupid this seemed. The caravan whizzed past the three bystanders—Flynn and Bradley keeping their NARS-Slates aimed at us as we passed, the snapping camera shutters sounding off. The scientist guy seemed to be stupefied.

"What the hell was that?" Barrett yelled as we ran, the music still booming from inside someone's backpack. "Were they trying to shoot us with those things?"

"They were taking our picture," Aye'Sayuh yelled back. "We have to hurry. There's not much time left."

We came to another screeching halt, all of us steadying ourselves on one another to avoid a complete catastrophe. Aye'Sayuh went to work punching in another code, only this time when he finished nothing seemed to happen. He stood there for a moment, staring at the blank white panel, then attempted the code a second time.

Nothing.

"Uh, Aye'Sayuh," I said slowly. At the farthest end of the corridor, a group of Imi appeared, moving toward us.

---

[21] Tiffany, "I Think We're Alone Now"

"That's not good news," Barrett said.

"Can we at least turn off the damn stereo?" Jade yelled.

Paul shrugged. "It sort of goes."

The chorus rang out around us:

I think we're alone now

There doesn't seem to be anyone around

"How the hell does *this* go?" Conner shouted.

"What are those two assholes doing here?" Barrett asked, still annoyed at having seen Bradley and Flynn.

"The SIAHD are giving a tour of the facility and a new device they've developed to prestigious NARS users," the bearded man called out from somewhere in the group. "The first guinea pigs."

The SIAHD Imi were closer now, three or four of them, stalking like menacing dinosaurs and dressed in weird looking *Tron* unitards.

"The codes have changed," the bearded man exclaimed. "They have to be completed in *his* name."

Aye'Sayuh spun around and gave the man what seemed to me, in that moment, to be an expression of horrible panic.

"Whose name?" Becky yelled.

Ignoring her, Aye'Sayuh's eyes widened. "Mem'Rah," he whispered.

Turning back to the door, Aye'Sayuh began entering a new set of key codes. This time the door opened. We scrambled into the dark room, the door closing behind us with a sound like escaping steam. White light flooded the room as if emanating from every surface. This room, like the others, was sleek and bare except for a large, rectangular glass enclosure in the center, and a small, transparent pillar about three feet tall situated next to it.

Aye'Sayuh moved quickly to the pillar, and after entering a combination of touches, was able to open it like a Pez dispenser. He crammed the scroll into the pillar's open chamber, closed it, and entered another code. There was a chime, the pillar made a brief humming sound, and the scroll looked like it had suddenly turned to ash before being hit by a powerful gust of wind. In another moment, there was nothing left, and the pillar was empty.

"The bags," Aye'Sayuh said, gesturing for our luggage. "Put them in the transport."

One by one, the items were placed in the transport only to be eradicated in an instant. When everything was gone, Aye'Sayuh took a deep breath and gave the group a knowing glance. "Okay," he said. "This is it."

The seven of us all looked around at one another. "Well," I said, pulling off my shirt. "No one can say we're not close friends after this one."

"How does this work?" Jade asked, stalling.

"What do you mean, 'how does it work?'" Aye'Sayuh asked, exasperated. "You undress, you enter the harbor, you are disassembled and then carried through the wormhole to Gaina where you will be reassembled."

"Disassembled?" Emma mumbled.

"Does it hurt?" Paul asked.

"We can't wear any clothes at all?" Jade wondered.

"Let me try and impress upon you the significance of our situation," Aye'Sayuh said. "Every room in this facility is sound-proof. So you can't hear them at the moment, but there are armed members of the SIAHD outside the door as we speak, working one decrypting the locking code I entered that will buy us a minute or two tops."

"*Armed* guards?" Emma asked.

"Heavily," Aye'Sayuh nodded solemnly. "And when they discover our plans on this," he said, reveling his NARS-Slate, "I'm not sure we'll care for what follows."

"Do we have to get in the teleporter thing with the stranger?" Emma asked, pointing to the bearded prisoner. Some of us gave her an incredulous look, and she mouthed the word, "what?" as if the stranger couldn't see her.

"Don't be racist," said Barrett.

Before Emma could defend herself, Aye'Sayuh spoke up. "He's not going where you're going. And none of us are going anywhere if you don't get in there now."

"Don't flatter yourself," the bearded man—Stewart Raffill—said, before turning to face the wall and give us some privacy.

Everyone seemed to be looking at me.

"Hey, my shirt is already off," I shrugged. "I'm waiting for you guys to catch up."

From where we entered the room we heard the familiar chime that typically followed Aye'Sayuh having entered a proper code, followed immediately by a sort of sad buzz, like answering a trivia question incorrectly on a game show.

"They've almost cracked my code," Aye'Sayuh said, unable to disguise the distress in his voice.

With no one moving, my sense of purpose was clear. If I didn't lead the charge, no one would. With speedy efficiency I removed each of my Converse, stripped both feet of their socks, climbed out of my jeans, and with one hand covering my business as best as I could manage, I pulled my briefs down to my ankles and stepped out of them. I looked up, expecting to see everyone following suit. Instead, they all seemed to have paused to observe the spectacle.

"Dude," Jade giggled. "We can all see your butt."

I tried to turn around and somehow evade their leering glances, but every way I turned, I just seemed to expose myself in a new way.

"Aw," said Becky, cocking her head. "It's okay. It's a cute butt."

"It really is," Emma agreed, nodding thoughtfully.

"Do you guys want to die?" I yelled.

Everyone snapped out of their butt trance and set to work frantically undressing.

"Everyone keep their eyes to themselves," Emma yelled.

"Alright you perverts," Barrett called back, fumbling with his belt. "We all know you've just been waiting for some opportunity to sneak a peek but mind your own damn business!"

"Get in the harbor!" Aye'Sayuh started shouting repeatedly, and we all ran in an awkward shuffle toward an opening that appeared in the middle of the glass-like chamber. Crowding inside, each of us attempting to cover ourselves, the five guys naturally shifted to one end of the rectangular harbor, the two girls on the other, like a junior high dance. In my state of agitated dread, I couldn't help but look around like a parrot, my heart hammering against my ribs. I caught a glimpse of the girls a few feet away, and Emma yelled, "Hey! Eyes on your own paper!"

Aye'Sayuh was on the other side of the harbor wall, tapping some command into the invisible keypad when a torrent of hot water suddenly poured out from above us, followed immediately by what felt like hurricane force winds. The transparent walls of the harbor were briefly obscured, and when the mist (or whatever it was) dissipated, I could see the door behind Aye'Sayuh sliding open. Several militarized looking Imi were stepping into the room. I pounded on the inside of the harbor, yelling to warn Aye'Sayuh. I hadn't even realized I'd left my nakedness uncovered until I heard snickering behind me, and Conner's voice saying, "we can totally see your wiener, dude."

A sound erupted from inside my head like that horrible grating buzz when you accidentally touch the metal edges on Operation.

Then everything went black.

PART THREE
APPRENTICES

"This book must be given to the pupil. I then become the master. I am not worthy, but there is no one else here."

–Jerry, *Enemy Mine*

MOD LOG, 16
WELCOME TO GAINA
[7 DAYS UNTIL ALL HELL BREAKS LOOSE]

I woke up feeling like I'd nearly drowned and then washed up on an alien beach. My head was throbbing, my body felt like it'd been hit by a truck, and my tongue felt thick and uncooperative in my dry mouth. And that wasn't the full extent of how biology had betrayed me.

Drifting slowly from the gelatinous quagmire of instantaneous space travel, I could hear one of the girls' voices as they went from muffled to audible, saying, "Geez, someone pinch Danny. Apparently, he's having a particularly good dream."

Then I was being hoisted to my feet, and I could hear Conner's voice saying, "Give him a break. It's biological. Happens virtually every time you sleep."

Struggling to stand upright—though other parts of me seemed to have no such trouble—I did my best to steady myself, fumbling clumsily at my body in an effort to cover my shame.

"What happened?" I was trying to say, but it sounded like I was fighting against a mouth full of peanut butter.

"I think we're in the other harbor," Paul was saying, apparently making sense of my mush mouth. "No one got disintegrated."

"But we still don't have *clothes*," Becky yelled out to whoever was listening. "Not all of us are as excited about it as Danny seems to be."

I attempted a sophisticated defense, but the word "biology"—sloppily enunciated—was all that came. The harbor's door suddenly slid open with a gentle hum, giving the whole group an awful start, and we all froze for a moment, not sure what to expect.

My vision restored to me now, I wasn't sure we'd gone anywhere at all. This room seemed identical to the one before. Or had the jump scrambled my memory of what had just happened?

I started to speak up. "What should we—"

Before I could get the slow, pained words out, the door to the room slid open, and an Imi garbed in a uniform we'd never seen stepped in. The seven of us inched backward, all driven by the same reflex, but when the Imi spoke, it was Aye'Sayuh's voice.

"Is everyone, y'know, alive?"

"Barely," I said.

"Alive but naked," Emma fussed.

"Oh, right," Aye'Sayuh said, scratching his head. "I guess we didn't put the clothes you were *wearing* through the transport, did we?"

The realization hit us all simultaneously.

"What the hell, Aye'Sayuh?" Barrett said. "I hope your whole planet is a nudist colony."

"We did send, uh…" Aye'Sayuh began slowly, finding the words. "What did you call them? Bras?"

"Oh well great," Emma groaned. "My naked rear end will be exposed for all of Gaina, but hey, I'll have a bra."

"Would you relax," Aye'Sayuh huffed. "We *have* clothes, I told you. Lots of them."

"Well, where are they?" I yelled, losing my patience.

"On the base," Aye'Sayuh said.

"Is that not where we are?" Paul spoke up, confused.

"Not yet," Aye'Sayuh said, suddenly looking all around as if only now remembering where he'd been standing. "We're in the Feed Camp. We have to escape without notice, then make our way to the base."

The naked humans looked at one another, baffled.

"Aye'Sayuh, dude," Conner began calmly, having given up on the whole discretion thing and no longer covering himself at all. "Is this real? Are you serious? Let's just have everyone calm down, and please tell us exactly what's going on."

The display seemed lost on Aye'Sayuh, who only repeated what he'd just said.

"Dude," Jade whispered to Conner. "Cover that thing up, man." Conner rolled his eyes theatrically but obliged Jade's request.

"Don't feel threatened, man," Conner said.

"Escaping the Feed Camp will be easy," Aye'Sayuh said. "I've stolen a guard's uniform." He gestured at his strange outfit, looking very proud, then seemed to be waiting on a reaction of some kind.

"Looks, uh… Looks nice," Paul finally said.

This satisfied Aye'Sayuh, who nodded in agreement.

"But are there *clothes* here?" Becky interrupted, clearly frustrated.

"Not here," Aye'Sayuh confessed. "But once we get out of the Camp and to the transport, we'll be at the base in no time."

"So we just have to sneak out of another facility, only this time: *Naked*," said Barrett.

"It'll be easy," Aye'Sayuh promised.

Though we were grateful we'd thought to bring a few jackets and that they were big enough to cover most of the girls' nakedness, we were all still pissed at ourselves for leaving our clothes on the ground in the SIAHD center.

"Don't be so dramatic," Becky sighed, zipping my denim jacket, her long freckled legs the only thing uncovered. "At least it's easier for you guys to hide your stuff. Our hands weren't doing us much good."

"It's true," Conner shrugged. "I saw everything."

Emma punched him in the arm, looking simultaneously hilarious and painfully attractive in Barrett's puffy red vest, which fit her like an enormous life jacket.

"At least it's not cold," I suggested half-heartedly, but no one seemed comforted by the power of positive thinking.

"No one warned me we'd be getting all wet," Emma complained, wringing her hair out.

"Are you guys done complaining about the nudity?" Aye'Sayuh grumbled, approaching the door. "I swear, the only mammals that wear clothes and you act like you're so special for it."

"Easy for you to say," Becky countered. "Mr. Fancy Uniform over here."

Aye'Sayuh examined his outfit as if seeing it for the first time, saying quietly to himself, "I guess it *is* fancy."

"Are we doing this?" Barrett yelled.

"Alright," Aye'Sayuh said, a hand up to shush Barrett. "Here's the plan: You guys are Feed Camp prisoners. Follow me and... I don't know, act like prisoners I guess."

"What the hell is a Feed Camp prisoner, anyway?" Conner asked, all of us whirling around to face him, then turning just as quickly to face Aye'Sayuh, awaiting an answer to this very valid question no one had thought to ask.

"This is where the NAR-Slab was created and is tested on human participants."

"Wait," Jade began. "So there are humans here just sitting around using that little computer thing?"

"Yeah," Aye'Sayuh nodded as if no further explanation was necessary.

"I'm sorry," Becky snorted. "And how is this a scary prisoner-type situation?"

"You'll see," Aye'Sayuh said dismissively, fanning his clawed hand and placing it on the door's shining white surface.

I expected to hear the approving chime I'd become familiar with over the last few hours, but instead, there was an ear-splitting explosion of white noise from behind us. Huddling together instinctively, we all turned to see the previously empty harbor in the room's center now frosted with steam and illuminated from within with dozens of snaking electric filaments.

"Your butt is on my leg," someone said impatiently.

"Dude, watch out, you're totally backing into my crotch," someone else warned.

One of the girls yelped. "Aye'Sayuh! Watch your tail!"

The thick, grey vapor dissipated as if drained by an exhaust fan, revealing two crumpled, naked figures within the harbor. All of us leaning forward nervously, the inorganic transport stationed beside the harbor suddenly hummed to life, and with a blast of white light revealed a hastily crumpled pile of clothes.

"Ah *shit*," Barrett hissed. "It's Bradley Press and Flynn Hardey."

The entire group leaned out even further, squinting in disbelief.

"Whoa!" Emma exclaimed. "Seriously, Aye'Sayuh, watch the tail!"

"It was an accident, don't flatter yourself," Aye'Sayuh scoffed.

The human shapes within the harbor—both of them pale, soaking wet, face down on the smooth white surface—slowly stirred to life, staggering to their feet like newborn fawns.

"Ah geez," Becky said, covering her eyes. "Both of them?"

"Biology," Conner reminded her.

Bradley and Flynn seemed to realize where they'd arrived quickly enough, and lurched toward the harbor door, which slid open for them like an automatic entrance at a grocery store. No one spoke as they went straight for the transport, retrieved their wadded outfits and slowly dressed themselves like a couple of drunks.

It was Barrett who broke the bizarre silence.

"What the hell are you two doing here?"

They turned to his voice, shocked, apparently unaware of our group until that moment.

"Nice try!" Flynn slurred, pulling a fashionable little button up over his arms. "We saw you guys adventuring and knew we couldn't let an opportunity like this be completely wasted by a bunch of geeks with no NARS connections."

"Dude, that reminds me," Bradley said to Flynn as he buttoned his perfect little stonewashed jeans. "We should get a narsy before we forget."

"Coolness," Flynn replied.

In one synchronized motion they both reached into their pockets and retrieved their NARS-Slates, extending them out at arms' length, smiling moronically. The synthetic camera shutter sound repeatedly erupted from both devices.

"Sweet merciful crap," Paul sighed.

"You have to go back," I declared. "You two lame brains have no clue what's going on here. We're not here for NARS pictures."

"Not pictures that anyone is going to *see*, anyway," Flynn sniggered.

"I'm serious, dammit," I said. "Get back in the harbor." I turned to Aye'Sayuh. "We may have to force them. Can you, y'know, dial in the coordinates, or whatever?"

"It doesn't work that way," Aye'Sayuh said. "These harbors only go in one direction."

"What?" Becky gasped. "So how are *we* supposed to get home?"

"A different harbor," Aye'Sayuh said, turning to her. "I told you, these harbors utilize wormholes. There's only so much we can do to manipulate such a phenomenon. We can't exactly jump back and forth at will. There's planning that goes into it—timing, specific harbor coordination. That sort of thing."

"Well great," Barrett declared. "What do we do with these twits?"

Neither Bradley nor Flynn took any notice of our conversation. They were both too busy moving about the harbor room, taking turns posing for photos then meticulously reviewing the results, making thoughtful sounding grunts and saying things like, "I don't like my hair in that one," and "let me try that one again."

"They have to come with us," Aye'Sayuh admitted, sighing deeply. "There's another harbor somewhere in the camp, but I can't find it without intelligence from the rebel base."

There was a collective groan from the group.

"We're wasting time," Aye'Sayuh snapped. "We need to go. Now."

Jade clapped his hands, apparently popping whatever bubble in which these two were operating. "Alright you narcissistic jackasses, come on. We've got to get out of here."

"So get out," Flynn shrugged, not taking his eyes off his precious little device. "Hey Brad, how wicked is this? I'm checking my NARS from another planet, dude."

"This is a prisoner camp," Aye'Sayuh announced. "If they catch you here without us they'll lock you up and torture you."

"*Who* will?" Bradley asked, his voice quivering.

"You guys are lying," Flynn insisted. "They're lying," he whispered to Bradley.

"Bye," said Aye'Sayuh, punching in a code that opened the door. "Best of luck, jack-offs."

"We'll go with you guys," Flynn said as if the decision had been entirely his, "but we're going to need to stop for pictures. You guys might not care about making a difference, but we want to change the world."

"Oh for the love of…" said Barrett, still standing there naked, cupping his unmentionables. "At least give us some of your clothes."

"What?" Flynn balked, recoiling. "No way, get your own threads, bro."

"Are you kidding me?" Barrett asked, matching Flynn's noteworthy height. "We've got nothing, and the girls have nothing but jackets."

"No kidding?" Bradley sneered, eyeing Becky and Emma with a lecherous grin. "Nice."

Barrett leaned forward, his voice calm and even.

"That's your one strike," he informed them, a finger raised.

They both fell silent.

STEPPING out into the Feed Camp, I was immediately seized by the depth of the area beyond the harbor room. Not unlike the SIAHD center, the facility was arranged with perfect symmetry, but the chamber itself must have been several hundred thousand square feet. The entire place was covered in the same opulent white material, the outer perimeter of the chamber something like an open walkway. The room's center consisted of hundreds of rows of humans seated in futuristic-looking white chairs shaped to accommodate their reclining bodies. Each of what I assumed was the camp's prisoners were hooked to an IV that disappeared into the ground beneath them, every single one of them utterly engrossed in a NARS-Slate. No one seemed to notice our strange parade of mostly naked humans even though everyone else was dressed in matching white scrubs like we'd seen on Stewart Raffill, the mysterious prisoner at the SIAHD center.

"Aye'Sayuh," Emma whispered as we moved slowly along the wall, the first row of prisoners only ten feet away. "What's happening in here?"

"Every 'prisoner' in the Feed Camp remains voluntarily committed, though only ostensibly so." He gestured at one specimen as we passed, a teenager with his gaze fixed on the Slate in a near-catatonic trance, his mouth slack and drooling.

"Each NARS-Slate connects to your earth Internet and our Apep using electromagnetic radiation—same idea as

213

radio waves. Several stationary transmitters emit pulses of invisible dome-like signals that the Slates recognize and decode."

"So it's just the Internet without a modem?" Jade whispered, our bizarre naked line moving carefully along.

"Sort of," Aye'Sayuh answered, though his tone suggested Jade was way off. "Remember, your World Wide Web is just a synthesized version of Apep, so we have to find ways to recreate natural phenomenon with electronics."

"And Apep is like Gaina's super-planetary-mother-brain-thing?" Becky asked, sounding sincere.

Aye'Sayuh turned and looked at her as if she had just suggested gerbils powered the entire thing.

"What?" she asked defensively. "It *is*, right?"

"Yeah, Becky," I sighed. "It's basically Mother Brain from *Metroid*. That's how the Internet works here."

"What's *Metroid*?" Becky mumbled to no one in particular.

"Apep is a sentient being that communicates to Imi via invisible wavelengths. Imi have developed technology that recognizes and transmits invisible data—words, images, sounds—using the same scientific principles as Apep."

"Huh," Becky nodded, her mouth open.

Aye'Sayuh pointed to the prisoners. "The rapid dissemination of new data to NARS-Slates offers the user a well of information with a bottom that can never be reached. We call this a *feed*. The more the user cycles through the feed, the more their brains begin to understand the updating of the feed as something like a reward."

"Like training lab rats," Conner observed.

"Eventually, the subject will sever bonds to other humans and the outside world in favor of the easier, faster endorphin release that the feed offers. Once this new bond with the machine is complete, the subject becomes addicted."

"Addicted?" Barrett asked skeptically. "To a computer?"

"When the subject achieves full dependence, we designate them *hupot'asso*, which is an Imi word that means they have been driven to submission."

Paul giggled. "Heh heh… *Ass-o*."

"Then what?" I asked.

"When the number of prisoners designated hupot'asso outnumber the *periphania*—those unlikely to submit—the acquisition of earth can begin."

"Damn," said Barrett, less doubtful now. "We wouldn't even realize it was happening."

Aye'Sayuh looked out on the sea of NARS zombies. "They don't," he said. He then paused before an unremarkable space on the blank white wall and unlocked a new door. We stepped into a narrow corridor concluding in a dead end. Relieved, we crowded behind Aye'Sayuh, who seemed suspiciously silent all of a sudden. When we reached the end of the hallway, another code was entered, summoning another door.

Aye'Sayuh exhaled, sounding relieved. "I wasn't sure that would work," he said.

"What do you mean?" I asked. "The code for the door?"

"No dude," he chuckled. "Getting out of here. There was a good chance that sentries would be stationed in the Feed Hall. We would have been screwed."

Before I could voice my outrage, the door was open, and I felt an immediate swell of surprisingly warm air swirl around my naked body.

"Whoa," I gasped. "I just remembered I'm naked."

"We haven't forgotten," Conner called from somewhere behind me. "Been forced to stare at your butt this whole time."

"Still cute," Emma assured.

We moved outside, amber-colored light flooding our vision, forcing everyone but Aye'Sayuh to squint and shield their eyes. We were surrounded by endless desert. We'd arrived on what looked like a marble platform extending out a few feet from the Feed Camp, which looked like another yuppie mid-century home. The whole thing was surrounded by orange sand.

"So… Gaina is basically Arrakis?" I asked, not impressed.

"Or Tatooine?" Jade suggested.

"Good grief," said Emma. "It's hot out here."

"So lose the vest," Bradley suggested, reminding us all of his insufferable presence.

Barrett leaned toward him. "What did I tell you earlier, you little dipshit?"

Bradley shielded himself with his hands as if he expected to be pummeled. "I was just trying to help! Don't be such a spazz."

"I don't see them," Aye'Sayuh said to no one in particular, surveying the rolling dunes that stretched out as far as the eye could see.

"See who?" I asked.

"Our ride," said Aye'Sayuh.

"How the hell would anyone know to pick us up out here?"

My sentence trailed off as several figures appeared on the horizon; dark blots distorted by the thick haze of hot air.

"What is that?" Becky asked, her hand shading her eyes. "Are those... *ostriches*?"

The group shuffled forward on the platform to get a better look. Becky was right; it looked like ostriches.

"There they are," Aye'Sayuh sighed, relieved.

"What?" Becky asked, spinning around to face him. "Our *ride*?"

Aye'Sayuh smiled.

"We're *riding* those?"

"Dude," Jade spoke up. "You realize we're all still naked, right?"

"*We're* not," Flynn reminded us.

"Shut the hell up, nimrod," Jade told him.

As the creatures came closer, running with the same gait as an ostrich or emu, we realized they were something else entirely. To begin, they were far too big to be ostriches. They were weirder as well; rather than wings, they had arms and clawed hands. The plumage was an ornate tapestry of bright blue, yellow, and emerald green, a long fan of red feathers running down the middle of their heads.

"Cool," Conner said. "They've got mohawks."

"Are they... dinosaurs?" Paul asked anyone listening.

"Well, we don't call them that here, but yeah," Aye'Sayuh answered. "Something like what your scientists call *ornithomimosaurs*. We call them *gaulish*."

"*Gawl*-ish?" Becky echoed, pronouncing the word dramatically.

"Yes, Becky, that's what he said," Barrett pointed out, losing his patience.

"Well I don't speak this language, *Barrett*," Becky shot back. "And I'm not exactly thrilled about riding one with no pants or underwear."

"They have saddles," I pointed out as the gaulish slowed to a stop in front of the platform. The animals seemed enormous, maybe seven feet tall and ten feet long, feathered except for their scaly hands and feet. Their movements were sharp and agile, like birds, but their jaws were lined with protruding fangs, giving them a strangely lizard-like appearance. Each animal was fitted with a saddle that I assumed was fashioned to accommodate Imi anatomy.

"There's five of them," Paul noticed. "Are we doubling up or something?"

"With everyone mostly naked?" Jade reminded.

Barrett gave Flynn and Bradley a look that said, "don't even think about opening your stupid mouths."

"Can we use those blankets?" Conner asked, pointing to the elaborately woven coverings draped over each animal's back between their feathers and saddle.

"Just don't piss them off when you take them," Aye'Sayuh warned. "The ride is something like two of your Earth hours, though they don't exactly pass the same way here, what with the different sun and all. Once we leave, it's best if we don't stop. The base is well-hidden, and we don't want to give anyone the opportunity to track us."

I braced myself against a strong gust of hot wind, still covering my privates with both hands. Looking around at the group, the guys were all posed like me, the girls in their oversized coats and those two dickhead stowaways fully dressed and looking down at their little portable computers. Certainly, this alien planet had nothing more interesting to offer than whatever was going on with their NARS profiles.

We all looked fucking stupid.

Readying the caravan for departure was an elaborate undertaking. Aye'Sayuh assisted with the removing of saddle blankets, but anyone willing to help had to 1) uncover their nakedness in order to use their hands, and 2) behave as though we weren't all terrified of these gaulish things. The girls mostly stood back and squealed, clearly watching, while Barrett and I pulled at the blankets and yelled, "stop looking, dammit!"

"How are we supposed to share five blankets with seven people?" Emma called out from the platform just as I retrieved the last covering.

"Why do *you* guys need anything?" Jade asked, his voice incredulous.

"Hello?" Becky replied, emphasizing the second syllable. "In case you boys have forgotten, we don't exactly have underoos under these jackets."

"Are we supposed to plant our bare bottoms on those alien saddles?" Emma piped in.

Barrett and I looked at each other. They had a point, I guess. I didn't know a ton about girl anatomy but from what I did know the idea of having your bare butt on a hard alien saddle with sand blowing around everywhere seemed like something of a bummer. Before either of us could suggest anything, Aye'Sayuh appeared, reaching for one of the gaulish' saddles and revealing a hidden sheath and a menacing looking knife inside. The handle was made from something like ivory, with jewels fixed on either side of the cross guard. With surprising efficiency, Aye'Sayuh drew the blade and moved it effortlessly through the length of one of the blankets, producing three sizable strips.

"Alright," I yelled. "Everyone come put on their loincloths."

"I don't have loins," Becky reminded me, reaching for one of the strips.

IF I thought we looked stupid before, our appearance as we were riding these things was abject ridiculousness. The girls shared a gaulish, using the bras they'd insisted on bringing as masks to keep from breathing in the sand swirling over the dunes. Of course, the guys had no such protection, so we just sat there in our little multicolored diapers, squinting and cringing at the relentless gusts of hot air and pebbles. We were grunting and spitting constantly, the girls laughing at our plight and us laughing at their bra masks and getting a mouthful of sand every time. Sand worked its way beneath the backpack straps cutting into my bare shoulders, and the damn skateboard tucked beneath the pack was rubbing my back raw with every step.

I rode with Conner, Jade with Paul, Barrett with Aye'Sayuh, and the two tag-along dickweeds sat together, each of them falling from their gaulish several times because they wouldn't let go of their damn NARS-Slates and hold on. Other than the occasional mockery, the coughing and spitting, and the shouting at Flynn and Bradley, we mostly kept quiet and let the animals follow behind Aye'Sayuh. There were no reigns, and though it seemed likely the gaulish could really haul ass, we mostly trotted along at a moderate pace doing our best to balance without losing our crudely fashioned undergarments in the process.

Moving over the endless dunes toward a horizon we could never seem to reach, I thought I had begun to hallucinate.

"Aye'Sayuh," I said, my voice hoarse, "do you have weird alien turkey birds on Gaina?"

Aye'Sayuh turned to where I was pointing and observed a group of small bird-like animals bobbing along the dunes nearby.

"On Earth, you call their fossil remains *khaan*."

The animals' bodies weren't unlike the gaulish—more or less ostrich shaped, but much smaller, about half the height of an adult human and about five feet long from head to tail. Unlike the gaulish, the khaan had long, brightly colored fanning tail feathers and two puny wings that ended in long bony talons. Rather than long narrow snouts, the khaan had round little heads and broad, flat beaks. With flashy, spiky plumage of emerald green and peacock blue running up their long S-shaped necks, the little dinosaurs looked otherworldly against the barren desert landscape.

"What do they call them here?" Paul asked.

"We also call them khaan," Aye'Sayuh said. "On your planet, the name is a Mongolian word for *lord*."

It was quiet for a moment; the wind whistling over the sand. Paul looked annoyed that he had to keep asking clarifying questions. "Well what the hell does it mean *here*?" he finally asked.

"Something like *really painful bite*," Aye'Sayuh said. "It's a coincidence."

"Should they be this close?" Becky asked, apprehension in her voice.

"They won't bother us," Aye'Sayuh said, sounding so unconcerned that I felt momentarily calmed. "And anyway, they're not the ones we have to worry about out here."

"Well great," said Barrett.

With no way to track the time, I began to suspect the desert might never end. Before I could complain, I caught sight of what looked like some shrubs and small plants somewhere on the horizon where the dunes finally leveled out. No one asked if we were almost there, afraid to hear we weren't even close. As we approached the flat terrain, the sand became hardened and cracked, and the swirling hot air cooled rapidly.

"Is it getting colder?" Paul asked, staring up at a sun that never seemed to move.

"We're nearing Chi'on," Aye'Sayuh answered without slowing. "It's much colder there."

"What's *chee-own*?" Becky yelled, her voice muffled beneath her makeshift mask.

"It's a region within Siegot—where we are at the moment. Sort of like unique cities within a county, or something like that."

As Aye'Sayuh was saying this, I noticed a single snowflake flutter slowly past, then another, then several more.

"Exactly how much colder *is* Chi'on?" I asked.

"A lot. Tons of snow," Aye'Sayuh said.

I watched Barrett turn to look behind us as if to confirm we had indeed been in a desert this whole time. "How is that possible?" he asked.

"Weather modification," Aye'Sayuh explained. "A long time ago, the Chi'onian elders attempted to make certain regions of the desert more habitable by bringing the temperature down, increasing precipitation, that sort of thing."

"How exactly does one go about that?" I asked.

"I guess I don't know, because it didn't work," Aye'Sayuh admitted, gesturing to the increasing density of snowfall all around us. "Or it worked too well. You seed the clouds with silver iodide—stuff like that—but the results are unpredictable, and they eventually screwed things up to the point of irreversibility, creating a small frozen wasteland in the middle of the desert. It's mostly just an embarrassment now, which makes it a great place to hide."

"And why are *we* wandering into the frozen wasteland?" I pressed.

Aye'Sayuh turned around for the first time, smiling. "That's where the rebel base is."

THE rebel base, unlike the SIAHD facilities, did not look like a cool, designer yuppie condo. It looked like a dump. Sort of like the Antarctic research center from John Carpenter's *The Thing*. The base was all cold grey steel, exposed industrial ductwork, and bright orange floodlights. It was a good thing the lights were there, by the way, because the snowfall became so intense that seeing virtually anything was damn near impossible—the whole world swallowed in a cold cloud of white.

The building itself was a pretty big square in the middle of the snow—about the size of a department store with a low roof. Aye'Sayuh must have known what we were thinking, and as our brigade of riders all slowed to a stop, taking in the sight before us, he informed the group: "Most of it is underground."

"Can we *please* go inside?" Becky moaned, her teeth chattering.

The change in temperature had been rapid, and though we might have only been in the snowy region of Chi'on for a few minutes, all of us were nearing the end of our tolerance for the cold.

"I'm freezing," Flynn whined. "And my NARS-Slate isn't working right in the cold."

"I swear to God," Barrett warned, giving Flynn a menacing scowl.

Aye'Sayuh moved forward, and our team of gaulish followed along instinctively. As we arrived at a huge garage door stenciled in Imi script, Aye'Sayuh climbed off his animal and flattened his palm on a blank yellow panel set in the wall, snow gathering on his arm while he waited.

There was no chime this time, just a low buzz and a sound like grinding metal as the door slowly elevated. Aye'Sayuh ducked under it, leading his gaulish by the saddle. The rest of the animals moved carefully inside, and Aye'Sayuh went to work assisting each of us in our dismounts.

Inside, the facility was disappointingly just as I'd expected: A dark, grey corridor of iron, cement, pipes, and dull floodlights. Lining the hallway on either side were a dozen or so small doors, the walkway eventually concluding in what looked like an open freight elevator.

At least it was warm.

"Fancy," said Barrett.

Aye'Sayuh had a weird smirk on his face. "These are the barracks," he said, sounding like a tour guide. "They're all the same, and everything you need is inside. Each door should respond to your touch." He pointed to a panel beside the first door. Emma approached it, her hand outstretched, and touched the flat, yellow surface. The door responded instantaneously, disappearing into the wall and revealing a small living space inside. We all crowded our heads around the door as Emma stepped into the room. There were bunk beds, a small shower, and toilet, and a closet full of industrial coveralls in various sizes like the crew of the Nostromo wore in *Alien*. Emma opened the first of three drawers lining the bottom of the bunk bed, revealing a collection of packaged toiletries and underwear, including bras.

When Paul saw the bras, he tisked knowingly.

"We still needed them," Becky insisted, narrowing her eyes. "For the sand and all."

"And these are ruined now anyway," Emma pointed out, pulling the tangled thing over her head and releasing a cloud of orange dust with a snap of elastic.

"Okay, great," Becky announced, clapping her hands. "Everyone out of my way, I'm going to take a shower and get dressed."

Everyone murmured their approval, scattering toward the other doors and activating the entrance panels.

"Clean up, get dressed, then meet me below," Aye'Sayuh shouted over the commotion. We all turned to find him still wearing his strange grin. "I've got a surprise for everyone. A few of them."

MOD LOG, 17
TABLE OF INSURRECTION

The shower was perhaps the best I'd ever taken in my life. The enormous showerhead was fixed to the ceiling, producing a circumference of hot water that encapsulated my body. After what seemed like an hour, I'd had enough. Clearing the steam from the mirror with the palm of my hand, I eyed my tired looking face and stringy wet hair in the water-beaded mirror. For the first time since we'd left my attic, I thought about what was going on. I wondered what our parents were thinking; if they suspected anything was amiss just yet. Pained by the idea of worrying so many people, I pushed the thought away, assuring myself of the greater good.

My skin red and pruned, I shuffled over to the drawers beneath my bed and retrieved a pair of briefs, a toothbrush, and an unlabeled tube I assumed was toothpaste. Standing over the small sink, I opened the tube and sniffed it warily. It smelled minty. Even so, I couldn't keep myself from scrunching my face, gingerly touching the tip of my tongue to the glistening white smudge on my toothbrush, worried alien toothpaste might taste like cheese or bleach.

It didn't. It tasted like toothpaste. That's almost weirder, I thought.

After two rejected prospects, I found a set of grey coveralls that fit nicely. The only text on the garments was written in Imi, so I had no idea what they said or what they were made of, but it felt like cotton. I wouldn't say so out loud, but I looked sort of cool. Even so, I'd feel better with my own jacket and shoes.

Batting the excess sand and melted slush from my backpack, I retrieved my Converse from inside, then remembered I'd given my jacket to Becky. I sat on the edge of the bottom bunk for a moment, suddenly realizing that the rest of Aye'Sayuh's plan was about to be set in motion. We would be trained here, prepared for the insanity that would follow when we revealed the truth about the death scroll—which we'd officially stolen from the SIAHD. I wondered what Aye'Sayuh had been talking about when he mentioned a surprise.

I half expected to find everyone in the hallway waiting on me, but the corridor was empty. Approaching the room I'd seen Becky enter earlier, I knocked and called for her a couple of times without hearing any response. Were these things soundproof? Had she fallen asleep in there? Covering my eyes, just in case, I set my hand in the entrance panel and let the door open before me.

"Hey, Becky?" I said cautiously. "You decent?"

"Oh please," I heard her say a few feet away. "Like you didn't see everything already. Yes, I'm dressed you dork."

"I didn't see anything," I lied, stepping into the room. "Can I get my jacket?"

She nodded at the sink, where the jacket was draped on the countertop looking slightly damp. "I tried cleaning the sand off for you. Thanks for letting me borrow it." She leaned over and kissed my cheek. "How do I look?"

Her hair still wet, Becky had selected an appropriately formfitting uniform.

"Yeah," I stammered, awkwardly. "Space babe."

"Total space babe," she agreed. "Is anyone else ready?"

Becky and I went about gathering the others with the same cautionary method I'd used to avoid intruding on her. We were bummed to find Flynn and Bradley first, both of them in one room posing for NARS-Slate pictures.

"Are you guys' slates weird in this place?" Flynn asked without looking at us. "Mine is acting slow."

"Mine isn't working at all," Bradley whined. "This is completely bogus."

"We don't have those stupid things you little dummy," I said. "We're going downstairs."

The others all seemed to have either just finished getting ready or else wanted five more minutes to brush their teeth. Emma's was the last door to get opened by process of elimination, and when she squealed as the door opened, we assumed she wasn't quite ready. With everyone else gathered in the hallway, I took an inventory of the group.

Conner, who didn't seem to have showered, looked bizarre in his coveralls. If he hadn't put his leather jacket on over them, he'd have barely been recognizable at all. Jade was cleaning his glasses on his uniform. Paul was adjusting his beanie. Barrett gestured at Emma's door.

"Is she not ready? I need my vest."

"Please," Becky rolled her eyes. "*Need* might be a bit of an exaggeration."

"Look, *Becky*," Barrett said. "You brought the bras. I brought the vest. Must we fight?"

"Not in space," Becky relented, hugging him.

"All right, all right," said Barrett. "Let's not get carried away here."

"We're not really in space, are we?" Jade pointed out, smiling like a dork. "Not any more than when we're on Earth."

"Are you an astrologer?" Paul pressed him, cocking his head.

"Well no, because those guys write horoscopes and stuff. I think you meant to say astronomer."

"I think you meant to say you're not either one," Paul concluded, poking Jade in the collarbone. Jade swatted his hand away.

"Emma!" Barrett yelled. "We all want to find out if Aye'Sayuh's big surprise is actually just him finally eating us."

"I think our rooms are soundproof," I said.

"Wait, who is eating us?" Becky asked quietly, sounding genuinely worried.

"You get Emma," Jade proposed, tapping my shoulder as if to appoint me to the task. "She's your girlfriend and all."

"She's not my girlfriend," I said, embarrassed.

"Either way," he shrugged. "You get her. If you see blood in the elevator, steal a gaulish and make a run for it."

"Why are you guys talking like this?" Becky asked.

"Come on, Becky," Barrett said, steering her toward the elevator. "Let's go face our destiny."

"They *better* not eat me," Becky warned anyone listening, her voice disappearing down the elevator shaft with the others.

Covering my eyes again, I opened Emma's door a second time. "I'm not looking!" I announced hastily. "Are you ready to head downstairs yet?"

Peering through my fingers, I saw Emma dressed, wiping the last bits of dust from Barrett's red vest. She looked like a comic book vixen in her perfectly shaped rebel uniform.

"I'm ready," she answered coolly, folding the vest over her arm and eyeing me thoughtfully. "Have you had any time to be scared?"

"A little," I nodded. "Mostly I worried about what our parents are thinking."

Emma laughed. "I didn't exactly tell them I was going to travel naked through space with a bunch of boys."

"I tell my mom that very thing every time I leave home. Just in case."

She was closer now, smiling up at me. "It was kind of you to prepare her for a time like this."

I shrugged as she put her arms over my shoulders. "I'm nothing if not thoughtful."

"I've noticed," she smiled. "It seems to me the only reason we're all here together is because of you."

"I'm not sure that's a good thing," I admitted, suddenly realizing the gravity of it.

"I'm convinced it is, Danny Thomas," she said, just before she kissed me.

THE freight elevator was huge. You could park several cars on it. Maybe that's what they did, I thought, as Emma and I descended further and further with no idea of when we'd ever stop. Like the doors to our room, the elevator had only a single touch panel with no other buttons or controls at all. Holding my hand in the middle of this huge contraption, Emma sidled up next to me, presumably as wary as I was about the strange journey down.

Before I could fret any further, the distant sound of music[22] below us drifted in over the roar of the elevator. Emma and I looked at one another, confused, as the wall before us opened into a vast chamber, the elevator finally slowing to a stop.

"No *way*," I whispered, in total awe of the scene unfolding before me. We stepped out on a raised wooden platform overlooking the incredible sight.

The elevator opened into an enormous garage-like area that had been transformed into easily the most badass dwelling I'd ever seen. A light fog hung in the air catching flashes of neon and the flickering glow of the countless arcade cabinets scattered throughout the room. There were pool tables, ski ball, air hockey, and those frustrating games where you try to see how many basketball goals you can achieve on a timer. One area of the garage had been made into a skate park, the ramps covered in bright graffiti. Another area looked like a strangely placed pizzeria, with round booths upholstered in cracked red leather.

"Dude!" A voice called from below us. Conner was at the foot of the platform, his face urgent. "Let's go get the skateboards!"

"What is this place?" I said, quickly descending the platform stairs. "Where is everyone? What's going on?"

Conner seemed frantic, his eyes bulging. "It's incredible, dude. Are you seeing this? They have everything."

"Why?" I asked, fighting back the adrenaline rush long enough to question things. "Why in the world is this place set up this way?"

---

[22] Run D.M.C., "It's Tricky"

"They let me design it," said a voice behind me. I spun around, stumbling backward into Conner.

"Holy shit," I said again.

"The Great Powersurf," Conner whispered reverently.

There he stood, his trademark shaved head and muscular physique fit into a black t-shirt and blue jeans. This legendary six-foot black man looking like Wesley Snipes, approaching two scrawny punk teenagers on another planet.

"Did you lock the arcade before you left Portland?" Powersurf asked, pointing at Conner and sounding suddenly stern.

Conner nodded.

"Great!" Powersurf said happily, clapping his hands together. "Can you believe this place? When we first started planning it was just an empty warehouse."

"How the hell did all this get here?" I asked.

Powersurf looked around the room. "Inorganic transports, mostly. Some of it we built with Gaina materials. The Imi have a rich culture of carpentry, electronics, and engineering, and they're so damn big and strong that making something like a pool table is no big deal."

"How many people are here?"

"People?" Powersurf repeated, understanding my inference and passing judgment on it. "The only *Earthlings* here are you guys, me, and a few other brains that have been here since day one. You'll meet everyone tonight."

"And the assholes upstairs," Conner grumbled.

"Right," Powersurf sighed, shaking his head. "I heard about those two."

"Then why all this?" I asked desperately, gesturing to the amazingness surrounding us.

"Why are you questioning it, dude?" Conner pleaded. "This is Kingdom of God level stuff right here."

Powersurf laughed. "The training is going to be a bitch. I was brought on to balance the torture with some fun."

"Is the training *that* bad? This is a lot of fun for just seven people."

"Not to bum anyone out," said Powersurf, "but originally we planned for more than just the seven of you. And hell, I did get a little carried away."

"Are more people coming?" Conner asked.

"I'm afraid not," Powersurf said. "Plans change."

We stood there a moment thinking this over.

"We're screwed aren't we?" I said flatly.

"Far from it, my friend," Powersurf said, gripping my shoulder. "Even so, the training is still going to be a bitch. Like, really brutal."

"Well geez," Emma spoke up, startling all three of us. "You're sort of scaring me away, here."

"Don't worry," Powersurf smiled. "You'll have help."

WHEN Aye'Sayuh found us talking to Powersurf, he insisted that no one worry about retrieving their skateboards just yet, leading the group through the endlessly compelling wonders of Powersurf's ultimate creation. I noticed a *Dragon's Lair* machine as we moved past the arcade games.

"Dude," I said urgently, elbowing Aye'Sayuh. "Is this where you got good at *Dragon's Lair*?"

"Fuckin' A," he said.

We walked through the pizzeria and the skate park, arriving at a large door that Aye'Sayuh moved aside by gripping a handle on one end and walking the heavy thing from one to side to the other. The door rolling shut behind us, we stepped into a new area that looked alarmingly like something from an insane asylum.

Or a slaughterhouse.

"It looks bad," Aye'Sayuh admitted. "But it isn't. We perfected the procedure a long time ago, but we haven't exactly renovated the facilities."

"Procedure?" Becky asked in disbelief.

"Minimally invasive," said a painfully cool sounding British accent as a new figure sauntered into the room through a door no one had noticed. "You won't even have to go under."

"No," Conner gasped.

There, in that same creepy room with us, stood none other than *David Bowie* himself. Garbed in the same generic coveralls as the rest of us, he smiled with his hands on his hips, a glint in his mismatched eyes—one pupil forever bigger than the other. Bowie smiled beneath his teased dirty blonde mullet and nodded an informal hello.

"David Bowie," I said, astonished.

"Well done," Barrett said, slapping my back, clearly embarrassed.

"Each of you will be fitted with one of these," Bowie continued, unfazed by our adoration. He lifted his hand revealing a soft-looking pink cube. "It's called a mo'ach."

"We're going to be fit with a piece of Bubblicious?" Paul asked, unimpressed.

"Actually, it's a bit like an Internet connection for your brain, Paul," Bowie laughed, Conner and I gasping, already jealous that David Bowie somehow knew Paul's name. Bowie pointed at the pink cube and continued. "With this, your brain can engage data directly from Apep. This, I'm afraid, is our only hope to complete your training within our very small window of time."

235

"Excuse me, Mr. Bowie," I said awkwardly, "but what are you doing here? Not that we're not happy to meet you or anything."

Aye'Sayuh did the explaining. "David Bowie has been one of our scientists for longer than any of you would believe."

"So all that space alien stuff wasn't *entirely* an act," Barrett pointed out, nodding slowly in realization.

"Not an act at all, I'm afraid," Bowie answered cheerfully. "I was destined to become an Imi rebel, you see. Our elders never cared for the—shall we call it—not-so-subtle public persona."

"No way," Conner whispered. "Makes so much sense."

"Wait a minute," I said, squinting and pinching the bridge of my nose. "Didn't the Imi arrive in the seventies? I thought you were born in 47."

"How right you are," Bowie conceded. "It is indeed a matter of public record. But I suspect that by now you all have become well aware of the fact that things are not often as they seem to be."

"How has no one asked the obvious question, yet?" said Barrett, looking around the group. "Why the hell does he not look like a lizard?"

"It's not an unfair question," Bowie confessed. "But you see, I was the first success in a long series of failed attempts at engineering something quite like a human using the genetic building blocks of the Imi."

"So you're both?" Becky asked, lowering her eyebrows.

"Bit of both, yes," Bowie nodded. "But as you can see," he gestured to himself, "I appear quite human."

"*Entirely* human," Jade observed.

"Now now," Bowie chuckled, "let's not be mean. While it's true that Aye'Sayuh and I can no longer pass for brothers, there was a time—believe it or not—when distant cousins was a bit more realistic."

"What happened?" I wondered aloud after a moment of silence.

"Years of my youth in Imi labs," Bowie sighed with a sad smile. "Terribly unpleasant, you see."

"Everything is becoming clear," Conner said quietly. "My eyes are open."

"So what," Paul spoke up, pointing to the pink device in Bowie's hand. "We get the Bubblicious in our brains, and we'll just know anything we need to know?"

"Not exactly," said Aye'Sayuh. "But the mo'ach *can* trick your brain into thinking that you have, say, mastered the piano by connecting the necessary data directly from Apep. If your brain knows how to do it, your body will follow suit."

"Whoa," said Jade. "I've always wanted to learn piano."

"Forget the piano," Aye'Sayuh insisted. "Playing the piano isn't exactly crucial to this mission."

"But it could be," Jade suggested.

"But it isn't," Aye'Sayuh insisted. "There are other skills you will need, and we don't have time for you to master them. The mo'ach is how we're going to cheat."

"So why was Powersurf going on about how brutal the training was going to be?" I asked. "Just give us the Bubblicious, and we'll be ready to rock, right?"

"I'm afraid not, Danny," said Bowie, making my heart drop by using my name. "The process is effective, but... How do I put this? A bit... *untidy*." He wobbled his hand in the air with the last word, the universal sign for 'so-so.'

Bowie continued: "The mo'ach will give your brain the indication that amongst its library of knowledge exists any and all expertise cultivated over years of training in the disciplines necessary to complete your mission."

"Righteous," I whispered reverently.

"The *catch*, I'm afraid," Bowie continued, with a sly grin. "Is that your brain will tell your body that you're ready to, say, do a backflip, or wield a weapon. Your body will obey your brain, but will rapidly discover it hasn't put in the work, so to speak."

"If our brains have expertise in backflips, won't they just tell our bodies how to do a backflip?" Jade asked, not comprehending the problem.

"Your brain will get you *most* of the way," Bowie assured him. "But you will need a certain amount of physical conditioning to avoid exhaustion or injury."

"I can't believe I'm going to do a backflip," Becky giggled.

"Yeah," Paul spoke up, as if suddenly realizing something. "Was the backflip just an example, or will we *actually* do backflips."

Bowie laughed. "I'm happy to say that though they are indeed included in your upcoming neural downloads, backflips will be perhaps least impressive amongst your new abilities."

"Coolness," Paul said slowly.

"So is no one worried about having those things put in our *brains*?" Becky asked.

"Hey, yeah, wait," Jade said, considering the implications. "You never mentioned necessary neurosurgery, Aye'Sayuh."

"The mo'achs don't go *inside* your head," Aye'Sayuh explained. "Everyone mellow out."

"Aye'Sayuh is quite right," Bowie agreed, turning his head to reveal a small bracket fastened behind his right ear. "The mo'ach is installed beneath a protective casing, where a sophisticated sensor relays data to the brain, causing synaptic firing. As long as you wear the device, it communicates with your brain, and your brain will have no idea that it isn't doing all the heavy lifting on its own accord."

Conner looked around the room. "If it's all so easy, why does this room look like a torture chamber for mental patients?"

"We found it this way," came another voice as the large door rolled open behind us. In stepped a tall, bearded man. Lanky and thin, his long mop of hair going grey. The man approached our group, hands in the pockets of his slacks. "We didn't exactly have our pick of secret hideouts," the man chuckled warmly.

"Why does this guy sound like Kermit the Frog?" Becky whispered in my ear.

"Because," I whispered back, my eyes wide and my mouth hanging open. "It *is* Kermit the Frog. That's Jim Henson."

"Everyone," Bowie announced happily. "This is my friend, Jim. He and I became fugitives together."

Jim laughed. "It was only a matter of time I suppose."

"My God," said Conner. "You're Jim Henson!"

"I'm afraid so," Jim shrugged, hands still in his pockets.

"So you *did* get into trouble for making *The Dark Crystal*!" Conner declared, clearly feeling vindicated. "I *told* you guys."

"Well, yes and no," said Jim. "Dark Crystal attracted a lot of necessary attention from all the wrong characters. But it was the work David and I were involved in that led to my capture."

"Capture?" Emma asked.

"Of course *they* didn't call it that," Bowie said. "Something like conscription, they said. Drafted into the SIAHD, monitored and made to work on Imi projects, imposed with living conditions not unlike prison."

"So the rumors about you guys working together were true?" Jade asked.

"Very much so," Bowie nodded. "Two characters terribly disliked by the Imi, conspiring together with puppets and rock and roll. A dangerous combination if ever there was such a thing."

"Bitchin'," said Conner. Then, turning to Aye'Sayuh, added, "this is incredible, dude. Who else do you have out here?"

"The operation really is a small one," Aye'Sayuh assured him. "I wish it wasn't so. But we do have at least one more surprise for you guys."

Everyone looked around expecting some other extraordinary personality to walk in.

"Later," Aye'Sayuh said. "Should've mentioned that."

"So if you guys were locked up together, how did you both end up here?" said Paul.

"An enterprising young SIAHD employee willing to question the status quo," Jim declared, nodding at Aye'Sayuh. "When he'd seen the depth of the Imi conspiracy, Aye'Sayuh came to the only friends a traitor in hostile territory could find. Before we knew it, David and I were traveling through a wormhole."

"Totally," I said, pouncing immediately on the opportunity to relate to these two living legends. "It's a gnarly ride, for sure."

"Gnarly indeed," Bowie agreed. "And the ride is poised to become more gnarly still, my friends." He lifted the mo'ach once more. "Who wants to go first?"

MOD LOG, 18
THE TRIALS OF PANIC

As promised, the mo'ach installation required no
sedation, but it didn't mean the process wasn't disorienting.
Protected by some local anesthetic, each of us was fitted
with our very own soft pink brain booster, held in place by
a small casing which was secured by long screws drilled
into our skulls.

Yes, you read that correctly. *Drilled into our skulls.*

Even with David Bowie overseeing the installation
process, few of us were thrilled by the notion. Barrett was
willing to break the ice by going first, and he assured us
throughout the short process that he felt little more than
"pressure," which somehow seemed more horrifying. The
mo'ach installed, Bowie informed Barrett that the device
would then be activated, and for a few moments afterward,
Barrett behaved as though he were working his way out of
a drug-induced sleep. Jim Henson and Aye'Sayuh helped
him down off the creepy looking medical table where he'd
been laid, and walked him to a chair where he was asked to
"give it a minute."

Embarrassed that I'd been the one to get everyone into
this mess and let Barrett act as the guinea pig, I stepped
forward to be next in line. I was able to verify Barrett's
testimony—there was no pain at all—and as long as I drew

my mind away from the image of a drill bit boring into my skull, I was mostly pretty calm.

"All right then," I remember Bowie chirping. "Here's the activation then."

My tongue feeling swollen in my mouth, I "woke up" with a body made of rubber.

"Hope we didn't accidentally erase any phone numbers," Bowie joked, patting my back.

I took a seat next to Barrett, who leaned over and asked, "Does your tongue feel weird?"

Not trusting myself to speak, I nodded without looking at him, still prodding my cheeks with my tongue and blinking slowly.

"Okay, are we *all* going to look like mental patients afterward?" I heard Becky ask.

"The effect is quite temporary," Bowie assured her.

"I bet Barrett is already shrugging it off," Aye'Sayuh said. "Isn't that right, buddy?"

"I'm out," Barrett groaned. "No saving the world for me."

"Not with *that* attitude," said Aye'Sayuh.

"Hey," Barrett said, tapping me. "Aside from the tongue thing, do you feel any different?"

I thought about it for a second.

"Not really," I said. "Do you?"

He put his hands out in the air in front of him and wiggled his fingers. "Nope. Still don't know how to play piano."

ASSURED of another great reveal, Aye'Sayuh led the group—all of us fitted with our amazing brain enhancers—to a room beyond the grim medical garage. Aside from a strange taste in my mouth, I felt restored to normalcy, whatever that means.

"Aye'Sayuh, dude," Paul groaned. "Can we freaking *sleep*, man? If you hadn't noticed, the day has been on the eventful side."

"Stop touching them, dammit," Aye'Sayuh scolded the group. None of us could keep from exploring the devices with our fingertips, tapping the bolts that secured them in place and the numb flesh surrounding them.

"You're going to screw around and not be able to remember your address. And we can't sleep, not just yet."

"What's with all the memory jokes?" Becky asked, sounding concerned. "Are we really going to forget something if we bump these things too hard?"

"Don't bump then and we won't have to find out," Aye'Sayuh told her.

This new room looked like an enormous padded cell. Nothing in it but white rubberized surfaces and a door on either end, we were unimpressed.

"Is this where you put the people whose brain thingys go bad?" Becky asked. "Oh my God, is that what's happening to us?"

"You guys need to get Powersurf in here to remodel the rest of the hideout," Conner suggested. "That one area is aces. These other spots leave much to be desired."

"It does complete the insanity ward chic," Barrett admired sarcastically.

Before Aye'Sayuh could reply, the door opposite us slid open, and someone stepped into the room. An ordinary looking man in his late thirties—brown, balding hair and a bushy beard—walked casually toward the group dressed in a black robe.

"What?" Emma whispered, panicked by the way I was gripping her arm. "What's wrong?"

"It's him," I said. "It's *him*."

Conner was also shocked. "Is it…" he started to ask.

"It's *him*," I said again.

"What in the world are you two going on about?" Emma asked, annoyed.

The man paused a few feet from us, and smiling, took a respectful bow.

"Welcome students," he said.

"It's Stephen fucking Hayes," Conner whispered.

It's true. It was.

"To truly master the art of Taijutsu and the ancient shadow technique of the ninja takes a great many years," said Stephen Hayes, as if delivering a lecture. "We don't have years."

"Well duh," said Becky. "I mean, there are fifteen black belts, even though only ten are *formally* recognized, since, you know, the tenth one has five levels within it and all."

Everyone looked at her as if she'd recited the lyrics to "Rapper's Delight" in Swahili, then immediately looked away, realizing something strange.

"There it is then," came Bowie's voice from beside us. I turned to see him leaning against the padded white wall, arms crossed. He gave a sly wink.

"What we *do* have," Stephen Hayes went on, "is a few days and some help from brain upgrades."

I searched the archives of my mind. What was going on? I already knew a ton about Taijitsu and Stephen K. Hayes and the ancient art of Ninjitsu from reading books, but something felt strange as if someone had gone into my mental office and moved things around. I now recalled things I had learned as erroneous when weighed against more reliable data that I discovered in the faculties of my mind. I had what could only be described as *memories*, of explicit teachings and detailed techniques, even training. I looked around the group. Everyone was staring at the ground, concentrating, looking as though they were attempting to do long division in their heads.

"Up here," Hayes said, pointing to his temple, "You're all fifteenth-degree black belts. My job is to make sure your body recognizes what your mind already knows."

"Is this really happening?" Paul asked no one in particular.

"So," Hayes said, "let's have one of you come forward."

We all looked at one another, eyebrows raised. Apprehensive as I was, the initiation seemed familiar. Routine, even. Conner and I stared at one another for a moment before he shrugged and moved toward Hayes.

"Great!" said Hayes as Conner approached.

Waiting for some formal instruction, the rest of us stood by nervously then shared a collective flinch when Conner suddenly assumed the ichimonji no kamae combat stance before he burst into an apparent assault on Hayes. Standing calm and upright, Hayes maneuvered effortlessly away from Conner's attack, seizing Conner by the wrist as he went, using the momentum of Conner's attack to guide him to the ground. Before any of us could laugh at Conner's wipeout, we watched in shock as Conner absorbed his fall by tumbling deliberately on one shoulder and wheeling over into a somersault.

No, not a somersault. A *zenpo kaiten*.

Still crouched, Conner whirled around and drove his knee into the back of Hayes' legs, causing them to buckle.

Hayes tumbled backward over Conner's body, helpless as Conner extended his leg to strike Hayes' chest as he fell.

"What the *hell*," said Barrett.

Hayes rose to his feet, unfazed. Conner, on the other hand, was panting wildly, already breaking a sweat.

"Good," Hayes told him. "That's good. How do you feel?"

"Beat," Conner wheezed.

"Exactly," said Hayes. He reached down to help Conner up, then turned to address the group. "The days ahead won't be easy, but when we're done you'll all be as capable as any ninja master."

Becky tapped the device behind her ear. "Do they make these for, like, ballet? Or for speaking French?"

"Neither of those is exactly crucial for your mission," Aye'Sayuh reminded her.

"I've always wanted to speak French," Becky said quietly, apparently unimpressed by the magnitude of our situation.

BRUISED and sweating, we all sat on a thick rug next to a tall half-pipe watching Barrett skate[23].

"What are we listening to?" Becky whined, making a face like white noise was issuing from the speakers.

"*My* tape!" Conner said triumphantly. "Thanks for encouraging me to pack it, Becky."

"Was he always this good?" I asked, pointing up at Barrett. My voice was slow and tired. "I don't remember him being this good."

"Part of the package," Powersurf said happily, taking a spot on the rug next to me. He tapped the space behind his

---

[23] Ramones, "Rockaway Beach"

ear and explained, "additional programming by request of the Great Powersurf. What's the point of all this fun if you can't enjoy it?"

"Whoa," Conner said, sitting up quickly. "Are we all the most mondo skaters ever now?"

"Sorry, no," Powersurf clarified. "Just *better*. They asked for suggestions at the last minute. With the time crunch, they were more concerned with survival skills than skateboard tricks."

"One in the same, homie," Conner said.

I turned to face Conner. "Dude, we should see if they can put the Brain Drain on these things."

"I'm so sure," Conner scoffed. "The Brain Drain cannot be programmed or taught."

"So true," I agreed. "The Brain Drain is my ally."

"And a powerful ally it is," Conner added.

"That's enough from you two," Emma said slowly, stretching. "Someone rub my shoulders."

"Someone put their elbow in my shoulder and work out these knots," said Becky.

"I'll rub everyone's shoulders if they rub mine first," I promised. "Go ahead, line up."

"Not even," Becky said without looking at me. "Not falling for it, buster."

"She's good," I whispered to Emma. "I was totally lying."

Emma punched my arm. It hurt.

"I no longer like Stephen K. Hayes," Conner announced. "He put me through so much pain after I spent all day traveling through space and riding naked through the desert on a dinosaur."

"Yeah," Paul said. "Screw Hayes."

"Really?" Emma asked, genuinely surprised. "That's the last we'll hear of the fanboy admiration?"

"No way," Paul answered immediately. "I was bluffing. Hayes rules all."

"So awesome," I agreed.

In front of us, Barrett finally gave out and tumbled lazily over on the half-pipe's wooden surface, his skateboard continuing up the incline without him.

"Can someone program my brain chip to make me feel like I've slept for three days?" Barrett yelled, splayed out like a starfish.

"Can I just really sleep for three days, period?" Becky asked.

"I'm afraid one night will have to do," Powersurf confessed, standing up. "We don't have much time."

Paul looked up at him. "Not much time as in here in the facility? Or here on Gaina?"

"Not much time for Earth," Powersurf said, looking suddenly very serious. "Once we reveal the truth of the Final Heresy, we'll have to figure out a way to bring the whole SIAHD down. It won't be without a fight. A lot is riding on you guys."

"Well *that's* reassuring," Conner groaned.

"Dude," Jade said to Powersurf. "Do people tell you that you look like Wesley Snipes?"

"Hey," Paul interrupted, suddenly looking in every direction. "Where are those two NARS jerks?"

"Who the hell cares," said Barrett, still lying flat on the half-pipe.

MOD LOG, 19
RISE OF THE SHADOW WARRIOR
[6 DAYS UNTIL ALL HELL BREAKS LOOSE]

Honestly, sometimes Hayes bummed us out when he talked about ninjas. For example, he broke our hearts by informing us that though stealth and disguise were trademarks of the ninja, they were not typically accomplished via badass black outfits and doing acrobatics in the shadows. Instead, the ninja did things like feigning illness at the gates of a castle in order to be invited inside. Or maybe they'd dress as a priest to gain the confidence of locals harboring vital information. According to Hayes, ninja used flattery as a weapon more than they used throwing stars. In fact, according to the *Shōninki*—a medieval ninja manual—equipment has little value without the ability to deceive the enemy using charm, disguise, or a clever ruse.

Rather than an awesome black mask, the *Shōninki* suggests packing a straw hat, which hides the ninja's face while enabling them to see others. Rather than nunchaku (what is often pronounced *nunchucks*), the manual recommends carrying a pencil for taking notes and marking buildings. The only comfort we could take from this frustrating old document was that it *does* mention the use of grappling hooks and a sword. That was the *least* it could do.

The fact that we were all sitting lotus position in a big circle was the only thing keeping me from begging Hayes to stop ruining my illusions about backflipping black-clad warriors.

"They *were* warriors," Hayes rebutted. "The ninja were *shadow warriors*. Poor farmers who operated in secrecy to rebel against the tyrannical ruling class of the Samurai."

"So what? We're going to learn how to wear rice hats and do impressions?" Barrett asked.

"No," Hayes sighed. "You are going to learn to fight. But what I am teaching you is not the same thing as the ninjitsu of feudal Japan. It is a modern adaptation of many of the same principles and ideas that first compelled the earliest ninja."

"I have a question," Becky interrupted, raising her hand. "This is so cool and all, but why ninja stuff? If this mission is so important, is being a ninja really the best way to go about it?"

"The Historian," Hayes answered. "Whoever it is, it was the Historian who uncovered the Imi plot, and it was the Historian who reached out to me."

"So we're *not* doing the stealth thing?" Conner asked.

"Stealth is crucial," Hayes assured him. "But the stealth you will need for your mission isn't the same as pretending you have a stomach ache so that you'll be invited into a castle."

"I feel like I know all this already," Emma said, sounding as if she were wondering whether or not it was true. "Yeah, I for sure know this already."

"Matters of historical significance are included in your training," Hayes said, pointing to Emma's mo'ach implant. "But that data is like any other learned thing; your interest in it determines the significance that your mind attaches to the information. Seeing as how I've gathered from this group that backflips are far more interesting than scrolls from the 15th century, I thought it necessary to have this little discussion."

"Totally," Conner nodded. "So, we *can* do backflips, right?"

Hayes sighed. "Stand up," he said.

I had already forgotten most of our lesson on ancient Japan when I went limping to my room that night.

"Your back still hurt?" Emma asked, walking beside me.

"Only a little," I lied. "It's a frustrating thing to be capable of an excellent backflip and have your showmanship thwarted by one of your friends kicking you in midair."

"Barrett sure thought it was funny," Emma said. "And anyway, I still think you're more of a ninja than any of us."

For a moment, I felt a surge of pride that quickly subsided when I realized I had no idea what Emma meant.

"I'm sure you're right," I said, still grasping at my charm. "But how do you figure?"

Emma stopped in front of the door to her room. She looked at me, cocking her head to the side, then reached out and touched my chest with her index finger. "Secrets," she said.

"Secrets?" I repeated, genuinely confused and slightly panicked.

Emma took a deep breath. "I'm never quite sure what's going on in that head of yours, Mr. Thomas."

I didn't know what to say. A silence filled the air.

Emma smiled. "Sometimes I'd just like to know is all," she said.

"I'm okay with that," I said.

Emma leaned in and kissed me goodnight.

A voice from down the hall shattered the moment.

"It's awful looking," Conner said as he approached. "Like two calves awkwardly trying to eat the same apple."

Emma blushed and gave Conner a playfully angry squint. "How do you even see in here with those shades on, Conner?" she asked.

"The Holy Spirit," Conner said, tapping the corner of his Ray Bans.

Emma stepped into her open room. She waved with her fingers as the door closed.

"Space make-out," Conner said at the closed door, nodding. "Nice."

"Tired?" I asked, changing the subject.

Conner sighed. "Constantly. Hayes is an unforgiving master."

"All those books that showed him training out in the Japanese countryside made this seem more fun and less painful."

"Apprenticeship is often a painful thing," Conner agreed, rubbing his chin.

"You're an authority on apprenticeship?" I asked.

"Something like that," Conner answered. "You know, another way of understanding the word *disciple* is by exchanging it with the word *apprentice*."

"We're talking about Jesus now?"

"Apprenticeship to Jesus makes ninja training with brain implants look like a walk in the park."

"Can't you just say a prayer, read your Bible, and go to heaven or something?" I laughed, stretching.

"Oh how little you understand the way of the Nazarene," Conner said, shaking his head. "Dude, saying a prayer and reading a book won't complete your apprenticeship any more than reciting a haiku and reading a paperback about Hayes will make you a black belt. It takes a lifetime of training the body and the mind. It takes practiced self-denial and the reformation of the mind and the spirit."

"But do you get a cool black mask if you apprentice Jesus?" I asked.

Conner thought for a minute. "Actually, the idea is to take the mask *off*."

MOD LOG, 20
PREPARING FOR DEATH
[5 DAYS UNTIL ALL HELL BREAKS LOOSE]

All of us in our cool rebel coveralls, we sat in a straight line as Jim Henson handed out NARS-Slates.

"Aren't these bad?" Emma asked.

"Yeah," Conner piped in. "Isn't this how they're going to take over the world and stuff?"

"These particular devices," Jim answered gently, "have been drastically altered. They can't access NARS, or the World Wide Web."

"Great," said Barrett, handling the sleek flat tablet like it was a turd. "So what do they do?"

"They can communicate with one another," Jim said. "And they can send and receive data from the rebel uplink."

"They're just fancy Walkie-Talkies?" I asked.

"More than that, but not less," said David Bowie, who was leaning against the wall with his arms crossed.

Aye'Sayuh had gathered the seven of us at an hour that felt very early, though none of us had any sense of time on Gaina. After we'd showered and changed our underwear we were herded into a mess hall of some kind where Powersurf served us trays of what looked like boiled kale and pineapple.

"Zero times," Becky said immediately. "No alien salad for me, thanks."

"It's perfectly edible," Powersurf assured us. "We've had people here long enough to figure out which Gainian crops agree with the human stomach. There's only so much pizza we can transport to another planet."

"Guy-EE-nee-an?" Becky pronounced slowly. Barrett scowled at her. "What?" she asked defensively. "I'm making sure I say things correctly, geez."

"And what Gainian crops are these exactly?" Paul asked. "Because it looks like booty."

"Barf me out," Jade groaned. "It looks like seaweed and lemons."

Barrett was already chewing. "It's not bad," he said plainly.

I skewered a green leaf with my fork, expecting it to hang limp when I lifted it from my plate. Instead, it held its rigid shape, like a stiffened collard green. Folding the vegetable over my tongue cautiously, a strong sweet taste like honey flooded my mouth. The leaf crunched between my teeth, a pleasant tasting viscous liquid erupting from it as I chewed.

"The green stuff tastes like a piece of Freshen-up," I said.

Paul looked down the table at me skeptically. "That gum with the liquid center?"

I nodded, still chewing loudly.

Paul shrugged, took a bite, chewed thoughtfully for a moment, then nodded to himself and went on eating.

Before long, everyone had eaten most of the green *ye'rek*, but not quite as much of the yellow *pa'ra*, which sort of tasted like a mix between grapefruit and beets. Only

Barrett ate all of it, though he admitted the yellow stuff was "kind of weird."

Gainian water was also surprisingly sweet, but not dissimilar to Earth water. Even Becky, who had refused to eat "that weird kale stuff," celebrated the alien H_2O, saying it "sort of reminded her of Tab Clear without the bubbles."

Eventually, Aye'Sayuh returned to the mess hall with David Bowie and Jim Henson, the latter opening a black case and retrieving our new NARS-Slates one by one from inside.

"You can talk to one another with the Slate," Bowie explained, stepping forward. "And you can relay useful information—maps, coordinates, codes, even photos, and videos."

"With *this*?" Becky asked, lifting the small device in disbelief.

"Indeed," Bowie nodded.

"If these things are doomsday devices," Jade asked, "what are *you* guys doing with them?"

"These Slates were stolen from the facility in Vancouver," Aye'Sayuh told us. "They were sent through the inorganic transport, quickly cleared of all SIAHD software and reprogrammed for our purposes."

"Who stole them?" I asked.

Aye'Sayuh looked at me as though this were a stupid question.

"Badass lizard," Conner said, nodding. He and Aye'Sayuh exchanged a high five.

"And you totally broke them open and did mondo modifications?" I asked, suddenly very excited to identify with Aye'Sayuh in this way.

"No," he said immediately, deflating my excitement.

"So who knows how to reprogram these things then?" Emma wondered.

"Guilty," said Powersurf, raising a hand. "It took some figuring out, but there it is."

"We'll teach you to use the Slates," Jim Henson informed us in his gentle way. "Together, with the mo'ach implants, you'll have an excellent chance at completing the mission."

"A *chance*?" Becky echoed.

"But it isn't up to technology in the end, is it?" David Bowie asked. "It's up to you five blokes, you two ladies, and one fantastically reckless young lizard."

Aye'Sayuh smiled. Not even he was immune to the amazing gratification of being affirmed by David Bowie.

"David is right, of course," Jim continued. "We're doing everything we can to send you into this fight prepared, but to succeed you'll have to rely on your wits, your training, and most of all each other."

It was quiet for a moment, then Conner looked down the line of chairs at us and cautiously raised his hand like a student before a teacher.

"Yes, Mr. Froud?" Jim asked.

Conner let his hand slip slowly down, then asked, "why us?"

"You responded to the Historian," Aye'Sayuh said. "You were all willing to fight together."

"Well great," Barrett laughed. "So we were just in the wrong place at the wrong time."

David Bowie and Jim Henson looked at one another for a moment before Bowie smiled and answered. "You were all in the right place at the right time."

I was beginning to like Stephen K. Hayes less and less.

"Remind me how this makes me more ninja or whatever?" Becky yelled, perched on the half-pipe's coping. Her red hair was sticking to her glistening forehead, her helmet a size too big.

"Every student of the Bujinkan tradition must learn what it means to truly sense the intention around them," Hayes called out over the din of loud music[24] from the other end of the half-pipe. Barrett stood next to Hayes, also sweating, the wooden staff gripped in both hands.

"You know this," Hayes reminded her, tapping the spot behind his ear where a mo'ach implant would rest. "The same sensation you experience when you walk into a room that has just known hostility, and you sense that something isn't right. It's more than picking up on body language or mannerisms. It's the ability to *sense* the intention of one who means to do you harm."

"And why do we have to do it on a skateboard thing?" Becky asked, unconvinced. "And why with *big sticks*?" She brandished the staff as if Hayes might have forgotten.

"Almost every human being has the ability to sense the intentionality of others," Hayes explained. "An untapped ability clouded by emotion and distraction. But the *ninja* knows self-mastery. And anyway, you have a helmet. Let's go."

Becky shook her head, readying herself to drop in, exhaling deeply through puckered lips. "Stupid legendary ninja guy," she mumbled to herself before leaning over and moving swiftly down the ramp's vertical drop.

Barrett watched Becky transition from either end of the ramp for several passes, smiling at her as she went.

---

[24] Cock Sparrer, "Take 'Em All"

261

"*What* are you doing?" Becky shouted. "Stop being an ass, Barrett."

Still smiling, Barrett shrugged and dropped in. The rest of us watched as the two of them moved impressively along the half-pipe, passing each other at near-perfect intersecting intervals.

"Riding this thing is hard enough," Becky protested. "Are we going to do this or what?"

"That's what *she* said," Barrett chuckled.

"Who?" Conner asked.

"I can't freaking believe Becky is riding this half-pipe," said Paul, clearly astonished. "She's better than I was."

"*Was* is right, my friend," Powersurf agreed, pointing at Paul's mo'ach.

"Doesn't seem fair, does it?" Conner asked.

"What?" I asked.

"I mean, look at this," he said, moving his hand across the scene unfolding on the half-pipe. "Do you know how many times I wiped out learning to drop in?"

"Mondo head injuries," I said, opening a can of Tab and taking a sip.

"*Mondo*," Conner said. "Look at Becky! She drops in vert her *first try!*"

"What do you expect, dude? She's got that Bubblicious thing telling her brain to tell her body how to move and balance and all that."

Conner turned to Powersurf. "How did you program these things for skateboarding, anyway?"

"I'd spent a lot of time tracking movements and patterns for a video game I've been writing," Powersurf answered. "I think I'm going to add this to the game," he added, pointing to Becky and Barrett.

"What? Just two dorks riding a half-pipe at the same time?"

"With big-ass sticks," Powersurf nodded. "Like a joust, man."

"Wicked," said Conner.

As Becky and Barrett prepared to pass one another, Becky readied her staff. Anticipating the strike with ease, Barrett ducked beneath her swing and passed without incident.

"Just *fall*," Becky scolded him. "Are you honestly going to hit me with that thing?"

"We're going to be up against something more intense than a skateboarding joust, Becky," Barrett insisted, laughing as he passed. "It's no good taking the exercise lightly."

As Barrett rounded the coping and descended the vert, Becky did likewise from the opposite end. The song changed[25], setting a sinister tone. As soon as she had turned, Becky loosed her staff like a spear, which soared with perfect accuracy into Barrett's helmet, just above his forehead. Though his skateboard continued to travel, Barrett himself was forced backward where he was flattened on the ramp's vertical surface before drifting down slowly like a bug splattered on a windshield. The rest of us went nuts.

Becky reached the coping, accomplished what looked like an effortless dismount, removed her helmet, and gave Stephen Hayes a high five. In retrospect, the high five seemed a bit like gloating, but we were all so caught up in the moment that we hardly noticed.

---

[25] Bauhaus, "Dark Entries"

"Let's all just settle down," Barrett said, recovering as gracefully as possible. "Can we all just acknowledge that Becky didn't play by the rules, here?"

"What rules?" Hayes asked. "You were asked to free yourself from the distraction of the noise, the music, your peers, even the effort necessary to navigate the half-pipe and to *sense* the intention of your opponent. In this case, your opponent's intention was amplified to a degree that sensing it should have been an unusually accommodating feat. Instead, you allowed yourself to become completely obscured by distraction."

"Sure, yeah," Barrett agreed. "Or *maybe* I was so tuned in that I knew what was coming and chose to sacrifice myself to avoid having to strike a girl."

"Oh *please*," Becky groaned, rolling her eyes.

"Righteous non-violence," Conner called out, raising a single fist.

THE seven of us seated around a large circular table in the pizzeria; Conner was already complaining about Emma's mixtape[26].

"I mean, seriously, Emma. Were you preparing the soundtrack for our funerals?"

"I think it's pretty appropriate," Emma said, wrapping her lips around a flex straw. "Hoping for the best, but expecting the worst."

"Bad omen," said Paul, lifting his third slice from a tray at the table's center.

"Besides," Emma went on after a long sip, "isn't that sort of what we're doing out here?"

"Providing a soundtrack for our funerals?" I asked.

---

[26] Alphaville, "Forever Young"

264

"Sort of," she shrugged. "Preparing for death."

"Well bummer," said Barrett.

"Not the *inevitability* of death," Emma clarified. "But the *possibility* of it. Isn't it more real now than it's ever been for us?" She looked at me thoughtfully. "For some of us, anyway, I guess."

"I don't need to be on another planet to remember that I'm going to die," Conner said, staring off into the recreation center that Powersurf had designed for us. He sounded calm, almost casual, but not unserious. "It's coming for us. Either way."

Everyone seemed to consider this for a moment.

"It's a drag," Paul pointed out. "Knowing death has the final word."

"No way," Conner countered happily. "Death is an intruder in the goodness of the created order, my friend. The last enemy to be destroyed is death."

"Is that another Jesus thing?" Paul asked.

"I'm afraid so," said Conner, slapping him on the back. "I've got to tell you guys: Between Jesus of Nazareth and Stephen K. Hayes, I'm not sure how much more self-mastery I can handle."

WITH the entire group back in the mess hall, we sat in another goofy row before Powersurf, Aye'Sayuh, Jim Henson, and David Bowie. On the table in front of us where our NARS-Slates, only, y'know, without the NARS.

Powersurf guided us through the functionality of the Slate, which, despite being a weapon of mass destruction was also pretty damn cool. The little 5-ounce machine was about 6 inches tall and three inches wide, and only a few millimeters thick. Despite its insignificant size, it was somehow equipped with a processor infinitely superior to my Atari ST computer, and that made my Nintendo seem like a game of Pong designed by Neanderthals. With no keyboard or joystick, the device was operated by touching the screen, which made up the entire surface of whichever side was facing up. Responsive in ways that boggled our minds, images on the display could be clicked by a fingertip, dragged or resized by pinching, even projected as three-dimensional holograms by flicking the Slab like you were tossing the image into the air.

With the connection to both NARS and the World Wide Web severed, the devices existed in a sort of shared virtual space in which data on every Slate was readily accessible at any given moment by all seven of us. We could talk to one another (sort of like Walkie-Talkies), type short messages that were delivered in an instant, even send photos and videos taken by a camera built into the Slate itself.

"Sweet Jesus," I gasped. "No wonder this thing is going to enslave the human race."

"This is the first version," Powersurf told us. "The SIAHD plans to release a new model annually, each with significant technological upgrades."

"What?" Becky asked in disbelief. "How do you upgrade from *this*?"

"Remember the plot," Aye'Sayuh said. "Enslave the lesser life forms. Absorb them into Apep. Take what they do not deserve away from them."

The Slate tutorials were boring. The mo'ach implants had made us all feel as though we knew everything there was to know about using the machines, but our teachers insisted that we go through the motions to ensure there were no gaps in our understanding of these incredible little tablets.

266

"Pay attention!" Aye'Sayuh shouted, noticing that I'd been daydreaming.

"I'm listening, dude!" I lied.

I doubted anyone was *really* listening, anyway.

WIND. Stephen K. Hayes kept going on about wind.

"I'm so close, she can't catch me," he said, inviting Emma to attack him.

Emma rushed in, lifting a leg, ready to drive her foot into Hayes' sternum. In one seamless, fluid movement, Hayes darted to the left of Emma's foot, crouching so that his knee moved beneath Emma's extended leg, compromising her balance. She stumbled backward on the trap he'd set, and as she did, he caught her in his arms, using the momentum of her fall to turn her around and bring her down, trapped in a painful looking grip.

"It all seems like a lot of work," Emma said, wincing.

Barrett rushed in with another kick, apparently committed to having *someone* land an effective blow this way. Again, Hayes moved efficiently away from the kick, then lifted his own foot, using it to guide the momentum of Barrett's leg further than Barrett had intended, compromising his balance until Barrett was splayed out in a sort of involuntary split.

I was thinking, now's my chance! I came at Hayes with what had become a very effective punch over the last few days. Somehow, Hayes seized my wrist and locked my attacking arm between his folded elbow and his ribs, twisting me in a painful hold. Before I could utilize my free arm, Hayes rotated on his feet, wrenching my stolen arm until I collapsed. Now recovered from his forced split, Barrett returned to his feet and attempted to use his significant height and reach to get a hold of Hayes' shoulder, rearing back for a debilitating punch. Hayes moved away from the danger zone as the punch launched forward. Pivoting around Barrett's clenched fist until he was parallel with Barrett's extended arm, Hayes then drove a vicious-looking blow into Barrett's ribs, and Barrett's grip loosened on Hayes' shoulder as Barrett crumbled to the padded floor.

Both of us breathing heavily, lying on our backs, I said to Barrett, "you're really bad at this."

"You totally suck at it," he rebutted.

"Get up, both of you," Hayes instructed us. "I'm afraid we no longer have time for slowed down techniques and concern for personal safety."

"So we can *really* go for it now?" Barrett asked as he stood.

Hayes laughed. "We're beyond the point of basic demonstrations. Everyone select a weapon."

CROUCHED beside an arcade cabinet, I lifted the NARS-Slate to my ear and whispered, "I'm hiding beside *Out Run*."

Becky's voice answered, "I can hardly hear you because of these stupid masks and Conner's awful racket[27]."

"We endure *your* mixtape, Becky, you can handle his for the duration of this exercise," I tell her. "And these masks are *awesome*."

"Oh you poor babies," Becky says. I can almost hear her crossing her eyes. "Do you see them or not?"

"I see them."

---

[27] Minor Threat, "Betray"

To visualize the exercise, you need to understand
the layout of the rec room. The arcade cabinets
are mostly relegated to the left side of the floor
plan in an intentionally complicated maze-like
format. At first, I thought Powersurf was just
impractical.

"Hey!" I told Becky, interrupting myself. "Do you think
Powersurf arranged the games in a maze on purpose for the
sake of these practice missions?"

Becky was quiet for a moment, then said, "Are you
serious? That's only just occurring to you?"

"Yeah," I admitted, suddenly embarrassed. "I had a sort
of internal monologue going over here."

The arcade maze was a chaotic environment. The entire
area was dimly lit, mostly illuminated by low-watt neon
bulbs and the flicker from dozens of screens. Becky was
right, hearing was a challenge; Conner's tape was blaring
over the rec room's PA, and the tangled cacophony of the
many games added another layer of beeps, boops, and
monophonic video game melody. All this is distracting
enough without the lingering fog perpetually pumped into
the arcade, suspended over the ground like dry ice vapor.

Though Hayes insisted that the *shinobi shozōku*—that
totally awesome black outfit and mask you always see
ninjas wear in movies—was unnecessary and not entirely
historically accurate, we'd convinced him they were
necessary for our success. Ever the party-poopers, Emma,
Becky, and Barrett had opted to go in their coveralls and
some protective gear with no ninja outfits at all. Hayes
seemed determined to reframe our ninja fanboy paradigms.

"Many ninja may not have even thought of themselves
as ninja," he told us earlier. "They called themselves Iga no

Mono, which means, 'men of Iga.' Or they called themselves rappa, which means 'grassroots.'"

"DIY," Conner nodded. "Punk rock."

All this was replaying in my head as I breathed into my black mask, crouched beside the arcade games.

"Do you *see* them, Danny?" Becky repeated.

"I see Barrett and Paul," I whispered.

"What about the hostage?"

"For God's sake, Becky, it's not a hostage. It's a stuffed ALF doll."

"We're supposed to take this seriously, Danny."

"Looking at this ALF doll isn't helping."

"It helps *me*," said Becky. "I want to save ALF."

A third voice suddenly came from my NARS-Slate. "I don't know why I have to hide in the pizzeria," Emma complained. "There's no one here. It's boring."

"Just cover your post," I insisted. "Remember what Hayes said; deception is a powerful tool at the ninja's disposal."

"Yeah, sort of," Emma conceded. "But wasn't he going on about appearing to be what people expect to see? Then you become invisible, right?"

"So become a pizza," I said, leaning out from behind the arcade game and observing Paul and Barrett in the distance.

"Get bent," said Emma.

"What do they have?" Becky asked.

"Paul has a pair of sai," I told her. "Like Raphael from that *Teenage Mutant Ninja Turtle* comic book."

"Which one is Raphael?" Emma asked.

"The one with the sai," I answered. "How the hell else can you tell them apart? It's just a comic book, and they all look identical."

"They should, like, make them different colors or something," Jade's voice said. I spun around to find that he'd joined me crouching behind the *Out Run* cabinet.

"That would look so stupid," I told him.

"It must be just exhausting to keep finding new ways to identify each of them in that comic book," he continued.

"How would different colors help? The comic is black and white."

"Well if they ever did it in color," Jade said. "Or made a cartoon of it or something."

"Yeah," I snorted. "A cartoon where swearing mutant turtles kill ninjas with swords. Sounds perfect for Saturday morning."

"Who are you talking to?" Becky asked over the Slate.

"Jade is here."

"Why didn't he stay at his post by the skate park?" Emma asked, clearly frustrated.

Overhearing her, Jade answered, "It was so boring. Nothing was happening over there."

"That's it," Emma said. "I'm leaving."

"No!" I hiss into the Slate. "Everyone stay put! We have to listen to Hayes."

"Didn't you say they're right there?" Becky asked. "There's two of you. Just go get the hostage."

"But where's Conner?" I asked. "And where is Aye'Sayuh? This seems too easy."

"They're not just going to form a circle around the hostage and stand there," Jade scoffed. "I bet the other two are out looking for us. Hayes said to split up, remember?"

"Yes, I remember," I barked at him. "Which is why I told you to stay at the skate park, numbnuts."

"Just get the hostage!" Becky told us.

"All I've got are a bunch of shuriken," Jade lamented, revealing a handful of sharp, dart-like implements. "Danny has a katana!"

"It's not a katana!" I said, defensively. "The shinobi-gatana is basically a straight slab of heavy steel with a single ground edge. And it's for more than just fighting. It's a useful tool."

Jade stared back at me blankly.

"Barrett has a staff!" I added.

"Do you want me to come rescue ALF?" Becky asked.

"No, no, no," I answered immediately. "I'll get the stupid doll, dammit."

"Whoa," said Emma. "Who changed the music?[28]"

"I found the tape deck," said Becky.

"This does not bode well," I whispered.

My sword sheathed and strapped to my back, I crawled between the walls of arcade games, through the cover of fog toward Paul and Barrett. With a quick move of my knee, I was able to rob Paul of his balance by striking the back of his leg and seized him in a hold. Rather than defend his teammate, Barrett took ALF in his arms and leaped to the nearest arcade control panel, then to the top of the machines. Dodging the sudden onslaught of Jade's shuriken, Barrett gripped his staff and called down from his perch. One shuriken shattered a *Double Dragon* screen releasing a shower of bright sparks.

"The British have horrible aim!" I yelled.

"How dare you!" Jade shouted back.

I'd moved past the momentarily indisposed Paul, attempting to somehow sneak behind Barrett without his noticing.

---

[28] Irene Clara, "Flashdance... What a Feeling"

"It all sounds exhilarating," came Emma's voice emanating from the Slate fastened to my hip. "I bet you wish I weren't sitting here in the pizzeria twiddling my thumbs."

"You're not *actually* twiddling your thumbs are you?" Becky asked.

"I'm trying," said Emma. "It's sort of hard."

"You guys are seriously killing me," I whispered.

"What?" Becky asked loudly. "I can barely hear you over Flashdance."

Before I could say anything further, I was leveled by a sharp blow to my back and suddenly caught in Barrett's grip.

"I had the high ground, dude," Barrett reminded me. Taunting me, he brandished the ALF doll, squeezing it to activate one of its pre-recorded phrases.

"How 'bout a hug for the ol' ALFer?" the doll said.

"You're going to break my arm, dude," I admitted.

"That sort of thing won't work on the hostile aliens," Barrett told me, refusing to loosen his grip.

Just as these words were leaving his mouth, something shot out of the dark haze of the arcade and struck Barrett's hand with an awful thud.

"What the *hell*," he screamed.

"For ALF!" Becky shouted, stepping out of the fog wielding something called a kusarigama. The weapon was made up of a small hand-held sickle with a significant length of chain attached to the handle. The chain itself ended with a small iron weight, which had been used to loosen Barrett's grip on the doll. Becky retrieved the chain with the flick of a wrist, wrapping it around her arm and spinning the weight like a lasso.

Barrett's hold broken, I snatched ALF from the ground and made off down the maze of video games with Becky running after me.

"I can't fight aliens with a broken hand!" Barrett shouted behind us.

"You'll be fine!" Becky assured him without turning around.

We'd almost reached the end of the arcade maze when Aye'Sayuh appeared before us. Wearing a kind of shinobi shozōku himself (only tailored to fit his lizard-like frame), Aye'Sayuh looked horrifying standing there with an exposed shinobi-gatana of his own.

"Ah dammit," I said after coming to an abrupt stop, Becky slamming into my back.

"You have a sword too," she reminded me, urging me forward.

"Yeah but he's way bigger than I am," I argued. "And he looks way scarier."

"You have the cool mask!" she patronized.

"Hayes was right!" I confessed. "The mask is worthless!"

Forcing the apprehension away, I rushed forward, relying on the painful trials I'd endured at the hands of Master Hayes over the last few days and the years of rigorous training wired directly into my brain by a miraculous piece of bubblegum.

For the ninja, wielding a sword isn't like fencing. The sword itself becomes an extension of the warrior's body. With my blade raised over my head and Aye'Sayuh's lowered before him, I brought the sword down, threatening a blow that could effectively end our little skirmish before it began. As my sword descended, Aye'Sayuh's rose with a movement that not only deflected but also used the momentum of my swing to spin my sword away from me with a big circular movement. Aye'Sayuh brought his blade down over me, stopping just short of my neck.

"Never his mind on where he was," Aye'Sayuh grinned.

"Yoda?" I said, his blade still at my neck. "Dude, this is nothing like Empire."

"A sore loser you are."

Aye'Sayuh reached for the ALF doll but nearly dropped his sword when the iron weight of Becky's kusarigama struck the blade with a loud clang.

"Seriously, Becky?" I yell into the fog of the arcade games. "My face is *right* here."

"You forget," she says, "that I am a master of the mini-scythe-whipping-ball-and-chain."

"It's called a kusarigama," I shouted, leaping out of the way just before Becky began to spin the weapon's chain in a circle creating a protective field around her. Aye'Sayuh moved just beyond the chain's reach, looking for an opening. Before he could find one, Becky's chain lunged forward, wrapping itself around the blade of Aye'Sayuh's sword like Indiana Jones' whip. Becky yanked her weapon backward, and Aye'Sayuh's blade was stripped from him.

"And *I* am a master of the *sword-stick*!" Emma's voice declared as she appeared behind Aye'Sayuh. Gripped in both hands was something called a *naginata*; A long wooden pole ending in a deadly curved blade.

"You know," Aye'Sayuh sighed, "spinning it around like that serves no practical purpose at all."

"I beg to differ," Emma said, clearly showing off like a gymnast with a baton. "It looks totally radical."

From Aye'Sayuh's grip, the ALF doll announced: "Here kitty, kitty, kitty."

"Who is watching the California Raisin?" I shouted.

"He's fine!" Emma assured us. "I hid him."

"Are you kidding me with this soundtrack[29]?" Aye'Sayuh complained. "Did you plan this?"

"No, actually," Becky claimed. "But it's working out pretty nicely."

Above us, two shapes moved swiftly across the tops of the arcade games.

"Don't give them ALF!" Barrett shouted down to Aye'Sayuh.

"We're going to get the Raisin!" Paul added.

"Fantastic," I groaned, eyeing the furry brown alien in Aye'Sayuh's clutches. "Becky, use your chain! Get the hostage!"

"I don't want to hurt ALF!" she said, looking serious.

"It's not the *real* ALF," Emma assured her.

"The real ALF is a fucking puppet!" I screamed.

"Well sheesh, Mr. Swear Words," said Becky. "If ALF is supposed to be a hostage, I can't exactly throw a dangerous weapon at him.

"You're a *master* of that thing, remember?"

"Oh my God, you're right," Becky said, her eyes wide. She turned to face Aye'Sayuh, spun the weighted chain around a single time, then loosed it before her where the iron weight struck Aye'Sayuh in the chest causing him to stumble backward, dropping ALF. I dove forward in time to catch the little doll, which landed perfectly in my open hands and declared, "no problem!"

"Protect the Raisin!" I screamed. "Everyone protect the Raisin!"

---

[29] Cyndi Lauper, "Girls Just Want to Have Fun"

"I see them!" I heard Jade say through the Slate as I ran toward the pizzeria in time to catch Barrett crawling beneath the tables in search of our hostage. Not far from him, Paul was making his way behind the counter, toward the kitchen, when a quick burst of shuriken whizzed by his face, making him leap backward.

"Good grief!" Paul protested. "Are you serious, Jade? You're a ninja master now! You can't aim shuriken at my face."

"You're a ninja master, too!" Jade called out from his nearby perch. "You can dodge them!"

Paul seemed to consider this a moment, then jutted his chin and nodded proudly as if this was a pleasant bit of news.

"We don't know what to defend, Emma!" I said. "Where did you hide the Raisin?"

Emma appeared beside me, looking outrageously sexy in her complimenting uniform and wielding what could only be described as a very cool weapon. Her forehead beaded with sweat, she shrugged and said, "They're not even close."

"How do we end the exercise?" Jade asked urgently.

"We deliver ALF to Hayes," I said.

Becky, Jade, Emma and I stared at one another for a moment, then looked down at the furry doll in my hand before we took off toward the half-pipe.

"Where is Aye'Sayuh?" Paul screamed as we went.

As if on cue, Aye'Sayuh suddenly appeared from the fog of the arcade, his short sword gripped in both hands. All of us looked to Becky, who nodded, urging everyone to step back. Becky again began to swing the weighted chain in a wide circle over her head, creating a defensive perimeter. Aye'Sayuh moved cautiously outside the chain's

277

wide swing with his sword lifted overhead. Becky repeated her previously effective attack by snaring Aye'Sayuh's sword and snatching it from his grip. As the sword left his hands, Aye'Sayuh reached to his hip and suddenly drew a second sword none of us realized he'd been hiding. Half of Becky's weapon now tangled around the first sword, Aye'Sayuh rushed forward prepared to remove Becky from the fight. As the sword moved down, Becky lifted the sickle end of her kusarigama in time to block the attack as she simultaneously veered out of the danger zone. Allowing the sword to continue its trajectory, Becky used the sickle to guide it down and away, eventually breaking its connection to her weapon, which she then raised over her head and brought down on Aye'Sayuh's neck, stopping before she'd seriously injured him.

"Whoa," Aye'Sayuh said, panting. "That was seriously awesome."

"Totally," Becky agreed, also panting.

I ran with Jade and Emma to the half-pipe where we found Hayes sitting in a lotus position on the ramp's coping next to the California Raisin doll, which had been cutely posed the same way. Jade and I looked at Emma.

"I told you they weren't even close," she said.

I presented Hayes with ALF. Upon being delivered, the doll happily exclaimed, "I think *you're* out of this world!"

MOD LOG, 21
ALL WE HAVE IS EACH OTHER
[2 DAYS UNTIL ALL HELL BREAKS LOOSE]

"Seriously, Emma?" Barrett groaned[30].

Emma lowered her eyebrows and drank from a box of Ecto-Cooler Hi-C, her cheeks drawing in as the green fluid traveled up her straw. "We *never* listen to my tape," she said. "I can have a turn too, Bare-Bare."

"Not if this keeps up," I said, looking at the boom box next to me. "You've got two more strikes."

Seven human teenagers and one big lizard-like alien were all sitting in a circle on the floor in the hallway outside our rooms. Everyone was in their pajamas—the boys in their matching grey boxers, the girls in their matching grey boy shorts, everyone in white t-shirts. Even Aye'Sayuh was wearing a kind of grey robe that made him seem as if he could be lounging about a suburban home smoking a pipe.

"Remind me why we're eating on the floor of the barracks rather than the pizzeria?" Aye'Sayuh asked, gesturing at the open pizza boxes in the front of us.

"It's delivery," Paul said, taking a big bite. Then, with his mouthful, he repeated, "*delivery*," more emphatic this time.

---

[30] Stephen Bishop, "It Might Be You"

279

"How is this delivery?" Aye'Sayuh asked, reaching for a slice. "I just walked it from the recreation chamber back to the barracks."

"You *delivered* it, dude," Conner said, brandishing a slice at Aye'Sayuh. "Don't wreck the illusion."

"Aye'Sayuh," Barrett said, taking a deep breath. "You're not from Earth, so we won't hold it against you. But you have to understand; having a pizza delivered late at night is one of the great joys of life."

"Easy for you to say, Mr. Gold Doubloons," said Jade. "Not all of us have fancy grocery store jobs."

Aye'Sayuh looked at Barrett, confused.

"Jade is jealous of my prestigious employment at the local grocery store," Barrett said. "A job that affords me many a pizza delivery." He paused, something occurring to him. "I've got to be fired by now—leaving the planet without telling anyone and not showing up for work and all that."

"You had a good run," Paul said.

"Strike two, Emma," Conner said[31].

"I actually like this one," Jade shrugged.

"You would," said Conner, narrowing his eyes at Jade.

"Can we get back to pizza delivery?" Barrett said. "I just feel like one of our greatest Earth customs isn't being appreciated around this circle tonight."

"We went along with the act, didn't we?" said Becky. "I even tipped Aye'Sayuh."

Aye'Sayuh looked down at the neon pink slap bracelet he was pinching between two big talons.

---

[31] Echo & The Bunnymen, "Bring On the Dancing Horses"

"Like this, dude," I said, taking the bracelet and drawing it down over his wrist where it snapped into a circle around his scaly arm.

"Ouch," Aye'Sayuh said. "It's pinching me."

"Fine," said Becky. "Reject my tip. You know I don't handle rejection well because of my mom and all."

"Yes, we know," Barrett sighed. "Forget it. You guys don't know how to respect the beauty of pizza delivery."

I was distracted, thinking to myself. I looked up, breaking my trance, and said, "I guess all we have is each other."

Everyone looked at me.

"I mean, here we are. Who else can we depend on to save the world or to go with us into danger?"

Everyone looked at each other.

"I guess what I'm saying is that I'm glad it's you guys," I said after a moment of silence. "That's all."

No one said anything, but I think they understood what I meant. I think they felt the same way.

"You guys are great and all," Barrett finally said, "but if we make it through this alive I'm asking that girl Jackie on a date."

"Jackie Prewitt? From Algebra 1?" Jade asked, sounding like this was a ridiculous idea. "That girl is out of your league."

"Speak for yourself, British Airways," Barrett shot back. "I'm about to get some sweet, sweet pizza delivery with that girl."

"I'm about to get some sweet, sweet shower," Emma said, standing and stretching. "By all means, everyone continue to enjoy what is obviously the best mixtape on Gaina."

281

Everyone groaned as Emma made her way back to her room.

"I'm about to get some sweet, sweet sleep," said Paul, taking one last bite of pizza. "On Gaina I need about ten hours just to function."

"Good grief," Jade said. "How do you sleep so long? I can barely fall asleep at all. Knowing I'm light-years from home freaks me out."

"I have the super-human ability to sleep anywhere," Paul bragged. "I just need lots of it. Eight hours and I can struggle through the day. Ten and I'm pretty sharp. Twelve hours? Shoot, I'm all yours."

"Hey, Aye'Sayuh," I said, wanting to catch him before he disappeared down the elevator shaft. "Didn't you say that there'd be no pizza on Gaina?"

Just before the elevator doors closed, Aye'Sayuh said, "not with *that* attitude."

"That's our cue," Barrett said. "A running gag means it's time to go to sleep before this becomes *The Muppet Show*."

"I'm a vampire," Conner said, yawning. "A creature of the night, just like out of a comic book. I require no sleep."

"You crack me up in those pajamas," Becky giggled.

"Yeah, well, I can see your butt."

"Why don't you take a picture? It'll last longer."

"Girls, girls," Barrett said, walking away, "remember the power of pizza delivery. Look always to the delivery."

I had been sitting there, still thinking, feeling a bit strange, when I looked up to see that everyone had left the hallway except Becky. She was sitting just a few feet away looking at me thoughtfully, a subtle smile on her face.

"I knew what you meant," she said. "About us only having each other. I knew what you meant."

I smiled back at Becky, and she smiled bigger, her red hair falling in her face. I crawled over to where she sat and leaned against the steel wall next to her, gasping at how cold it felt.

"It warms up in a second," she said.

I had something more to say in mind, but at that moment it slipped from my consciousness, and I realized that my bare leg was touching Becky's bare leg, soft and warm. As soon as I noticed this, I realized I was staring at our legs, the ones that were touching, I mean. I tried to appear casual but looked away too quickly. Suddenly, I became aware of Becky's hair tickling my neck—she was sitting so close—and my own blood thrumming through my veins.

As the next song on the tape began[32], it all seemed so bizarrely staged that I attempted a laugh, but could only muster a nervous grunt in my throat. What was happening? With great effort, I brought myself to look at Becky and was startled to find her already looking at me, that same gentle smile still on her face. Her eyes were wide and wet and blue, and then we were kissing.

> I feel an urge to defend myself here, but I'm not sure that I can. In retrospect, I'm reasonably certain that it was me that initiated the kissing. Things escalated quickly. Listen, it's hard to explain what was going on in my head. I won't bother you with biology and angst and all that, but being a teenager is a complicated thing.

Becky pulled away from me, and we were both sitting there breathing heavily with this big space between us,

---

[32] Dan Hill, "Sometimes When We Touch"

metaphorically and literally. My mind was scrambling to find some words, some perfect sentence to bring a sense of comfort to what felt like an impossibly complex moment.

Mostly, I saw Emma's face in my head.

"Sorry about that," I said, instantly hating each word as it almost involuntarily escaped my mouth.

Becky looked at me, her eyes slightly narrowed as if she too thought that this could have been one of the stupidest things to say. My mind was reeling—scouring every corner of my most clever archives—but I just went on staring at her, unsure of what sort of face I was making. I could tell that I was disappointing her with every passing moment, and that stupid song just went on playing over the moment as if Dan Hill were mocking me or also disappointed or both.

Then one of the room doors opened, and Emma wandered out, her hair wrapped up in a towel.

"What're you guys doing?" she asked innocently, a smile on her face.

"Still listening to your tape," I said, nodding down at the boom box, feeling Becky's eyes on me.

"Do you mind if I steal it?" Emma asked. "It helps me sleep. I'm like Jade, being on another planet weirds me out at night." She looked at Becky. "Does it make you feel weird?"

Becky shook her head. "Listen," she said, "this whole place is starting to weird me out."

284

MOD LOG, 22
UNSETTLING DREAMS

The room I'd holed up in aboard the rebel base seemed unusually cold and isolated that night. I kept waking up covered in sweat, waiting for my eyes to adjust to the darkness and confirm that I was still on the base, still on Gaina, that the fate of the world was still at stake.

At some point in the night, I sat upright for what felt like the tenth time and discovered I was no longer alone in my room.

Standing about three feet tall, a stubby figure covered in dark hair was draped in the shadows just beyond my bed. I was too horrified to say anything, and before I could devise a plan, I instinctively reached for the small lamp next to my bunk and flicking it on, filled the room with a dull, yellow glow.

It was ALF. ALF was in my room.

"Would it kill you to decorate?" he asked, looking around at the drab grey walls. "Some flowers? Perhaps a nice potted plant."

"Am I dreaming?" I asked.

"If you were," said ALF, "would I be able to tell you? I'm an alien figment of your imagination."

"Totally," I said. "But you know how you have those dreams where you realize you're dreaming and then you can't wake up, but then you do?"

"Not really," said ALF, advancing toward my bed. "I mostly dream about cats, but maybe that's just me." ALF hoisted his small body up on the edge of the bunk and sat with his legs dangling. "It's not exactly the Ritz, is it?" he asked.

"Hey, listen… ALF," I said awkwardly. "I just call you ALF, right?"

"You know, my real name is Gordon Shumway," ALF said thoughtfully. "But who wants to watch a sitcom about an alien called *Gordon*."

"It's not as catchy. I'll give you that. But are you in the right dream, I mean, no offense or anything but I think Becky is a bigger fan."

"Becky's dreams have been booked solid by Matthew Broderick. It's like a Ferris Bueller marathon over there. And frankly, Danny, I'm surprised at you bringing Becky up as if nothing is going on."

I cringed. "You know about that?"

"I'm afraid so," ALF nodded.

"Did you come to tell me what to do?" I asked.

"Not about *that*," ALF said, stressing the last word as if the thing in question were too heinous to mention.

"Well, what then?" I asked. "Something else on your mind?"

ALF turned to face me better. "You know, Danny, I'm not sure you've been completely honest with yourself about this whole 'mission to save the world' thing."

"How do you figure?"

"You remind me of my cousin, Prettyboy Shumway. He grew up on the south side of Melmac, the baddest part of the planet. If he didn't like your shoes?" ALF pointed his finger and made a machine gun sound.

286

"You mean he'd *shoot* a person just because he didn't like their shoes?"

"No. He'd just point at them and make that noise."

"Is this what you came here to talk about, ALF?" I asked.

"Not exactly," he went on. "My point is that you've been behaving as though you're too tough to grieve, Danny."

"Grieve?" I asked. "Grieve what?"

"That your dad died," he said.

It was quiet for a long time. A sense of dread filled my stomach, that thick lump rising in my throat.

"I don't know how," I whispered.

"Few humans do," ALF mused with a shrug, lifting his big furry hands in resignation. "They don't exactly have a class on it. Melmac, on the other hand, *does* have a class on it."

"Is this something a lot of you have to deal with?"

"Not really," ALF admitted. "I'm not sure why we have a class on it. Listen, what I'm getting at, Danny, is that you have to ask yourself what you're doing here and if it can be done."

"I thought we were trying to save Earth from a sinister alien takeover."

"Well, in a sense, you are," said ALF. "But I think if you're honest, saving Earth is also about saving your dad."

"I don't know what you mean," I said.

"You're not alone, either. For Becky, saving Earth is about her inability to keep her mom from abandoning their family. For Conner, it's a way to prove to his parents that he's more than a mistake and a disappointment. For Barrett, it's a way to make sense of a world in which his parents are divorced. For Paul, it's about finding his place in life at a

287

time when so many others know exactly what they want to do, but he still doesn't. For Jade, it's about wanting to be known and loved. And for Emma, saving the world is really about getting some sense of control in a chaotic world."

"Why can't saving the world be about saving the world?"

"You tell me!"

"You're the one who showed up here to accuse us all of ulterior motives."

"They're not ulterior motives, Danny. They're more like subconscious ones. See, when your dad was killed, you had no way to make sense of so profound a tragedy, so you were sad for a while, and then you went on with things. And I think you and I both know that you haven't been entirely honest with your friends."

"What else was I supposed to do?" I asked, getting defensive. "Lock myself in a room and cry forever?"

"Hell if I know," ALF shrugged. "But from what I'm told, human beings are emotionally complex creatures, and grief itself encompasses a whole spectrum of emotion."

"I *did* grieve," I said, unable to keep my voice from quivering.

"Maybe some," said ALF. "But part of you is still there in that moment when you first learned your dad had been killed. Part of Becky is still looking out the window of her living room as her mom drove away."

"So what? Maybe there's nothing we can do about that."

"Maybe you're right. Because saving the world won't bring your dad back."

I felt as though someone had punched me in my stomach.

"I know that," I said.

"Not really, you don't," ALF disagreed. "But you will, when it's all said and done. You know, that Conner character you hang around with is on to something. You should listen to him more often."

"About what?"

"There's a poem he brought up that last night in your attic…"

"Psalm 148," I said, remembering this for the first time.

"Bingo," said ALF.

With that word, I was suddenly watching a scene unfold before me like a movie. I saw the vastness of space and there came a resounding choral arrangement in what should have been a soundless vacuum. Celestial bodies spun and spit fire, purple nebulas swirling with balletic grace, this indescribable symphonic extravaganza seemingly emitting from everything. There was something like hands—great, majestic hands wielding a maestro's baton and ordering all the infinite complexity of the universe with effortless panache. From there the vision sped like a comet barreling to the Earth's surface where I saw erupting volcanoes, shifting tectonic plates, the tropics, the tundra, the desert. I saw undulating colossal squid moving through the deepest fathoms of the sea, crawling trilobites and roving prehistoric marine life. I saw massive redwoods erupt from infinitesimal seeds in time-lapse, exotic birds resting in their branches, ape-like hominids swinging and dancing about its trunk. I saw the great empires of the world and all their achievements spooling out from an elaborate tapestry that itself became the source of this incredible song that seemed to reach the ends of the outer space and the lowest trench of the ocean floor.

And all along this echoing refrain: *Hallelu Yah.*

Then, with a shudder and a gasp, I was back in my bed.

289

"Really something, isn't it?" ALF asked, still perched on the edge of the mattress.

I nodded. "I don't think it's fair."

"What's that?"

"Grief. How should I know how to do it? I'm just a kid."

"I agree," ALF said sympathetically. "But you're being made to go through it whether we think it's fair or not. You see, Danny, the world is often a random, cruel place. But I think you and I can agree that there's some goodness there too."

Still shaken by my vision, I nodded again.

ALF went on. "Even if you're all fighting for the things you've lost, you just might save the world in the process."

"That's true," I said, taking this in.

"But hey, you also might not. And maybe I'm just a dumb alien, but it seems like a shame to go from one great loss to another without understanding either one."

"I wish I could get some sleep," I said. "I'm so tired of all the nightmares. I want a peaceful night's sleep."

"Well," ALF sighed, "maybe grieving will give you that. And anyway, it's almost Christmas. The world is always more peaceful at Christmas."

"What do you mean?" I asked.

Before ALF could answer, I woke up—alone in my room once again. The air around me was completely silent.

01100100 01101111 00100000 01101110 01101111 01110100 00100000
01100111 01110010 01101001 01100101 01110110 01100101 00100000
01101100 01101001 01101011 01100101 00100000 01110100 01101000
01100101 00100000 01110010 01100101 01110011 01110100 00100000
01101111 01100110 00100000 01101101 01100001 01101110 01101011
01101001 01101110 01100100 00101100 00100000 01111011 01101000
01101111 00100000 01101000 01100001 01101110 01100101 00100000
01101110 01101111 00100000 01101000 01101111 01110000 01100101

THE HISTORIAN 05
THE TRAITOR TO MEM'RAH

What follows is a detailed account of the events I witnessed on November 20, 1983.

I chose to keep this account private, having convinced myself of the greater good. I can no longer hide the truth about what happened to William Thomas, my co-worker at the SIAHD. He was also my friend.

Both gifted computer scientists, William and his wife Sarah were recruited to work at the Vancouver SIAHD facility when the organization made initial inquiries into the credentials of local professionals. For his unique role in collaborating with the scientists at CERN to develop the World Wide Web, William Thomas was awarded special attention from Mem'Rah himself.

Mem'Rah, the messiah-like figure at the head of the SIAHD, was not generous with affirmation or praise. When issued, Mem'Rah's approval could elicit profoundly unwavering obedience in his subjects. Mem'Rah balanced the tension between keeping his employees desperate for his attention and yet awarding it only to an elite class of his selection.

William Thomas was not immune to Mem'Rah's charm and was promptly tucked beneath Mem'Rah's figurative wing, where he was given the sort of deep SIAHD insight few scientists will ever know.

The friendship, however, was to be short-lived. William Thomas began to suspect a sinister plot concealed by the SIAHD in the fall of 1983 when tasked with coding into the SIAHD database translated fragments of a document known as Esk Hahr o' Mek. The fragments were ambiguous at best but gave Thomas enough pause to seek the counsel of his mentor, Mem'Rah. Thomas was assured that the fragments were merely "ancient religious texts" from Gaina's history that no longer held any significance beyond historic preservation.

Thomas was relieved of those particular duties but was unable to shake the sense of something nefarious at work within the organization. In early November of 1983, he confided to me that he had begun to fear for the safety of his wife Sarah and their thirteen-year-old son.

Two weeks later, the SIAHD announced that William Thomas had suffered an accidental death as a result of faulty equipment while working. Thomas' wife Sarah resigned her position.

Seized by shock and outrage, I began to use my high clearance access to move about the SIAHD facility under the guise of necessary safety checks in light of the recent accident.

In my unauthorized exploration of the facility, I eventually discovered an empty room except for a small island situated in the center of the chamber. The island itself was a storage unit protected by a series of lockout codes. With my security clearance and a bit of ingenuity, I was able to activate the unit, which became entirely transparent. Suspended within: All known fragments of the document called Esk Hahr o' Mek.

On the chamber's transparent surface, the interactive user interface revealed a series of logs, each of them dated at various intervals from November 18 to November 20.

Loading the most recent entry, a display expanded on the chamber's glass-like surface revealing video taken in the same room. William Thomas was visible, though the image itself was a somewhat lower resolution, and the large chamber containing the broken scroll obscured some of the action.

Strapped to a chair, Thomas was restrained and made to face the scroll; his eyes pried open by a speculum for the eyelids. Mem'Rah stood next to Thomas, goading him.

"Continue reading," Mem'Rah was saying. Savage and unhinged, Thomas thrashed against his restraints to no avail, eventually exhausting himself.

After an agonizing period had passed, Mem'Rah again implored Thomas to read from the scroll suspended in the chamber. There was a long silence, and Thomas complied. (I will not document here the words spoken before Thomas was killed.)

Bleeding from his mouth and hanging limply in the horrible contraption, Thomas twitched and sputtered for a few moments before becoming completely motionless. Mem'Rah watched all this patiently before accessing the controls on the chamber's surface, and the video log disappeared from the screen before me, leaving me alone in this haunted chamber with the horrible scroll that killed William Thomas.

MOD LOG, 23
A RELUCTANT RESCUE
[1 DAY UNTIL ALL HELL BREAKS LOOSE]

I'd gone outside for the first time since arriving at the facility. Becky found me.

"Geez," she said, approaching slowly from behind. "Didn't feel like throwing some pants on before you wandered out here?"

I looked down and realized I was in my underwear.

"Who sleeps in a t-shirt and no pants?" She asked, tugging on the sleeve of my white undershirt. "Aren't you freezing?"

Looking out into what appeared to be endless white on all sides, I sighed and said, "I got another message from... Uh, from the Historian. It came to my NARS-Slate while I was sleeping."

"We got it too," Becky said. I turned to face her and saw that her eyes were wet with tears. "I'm sorry, Danny," she said. The complications of the previous night seemed to have been put aside, at least momentarily. Or maybe it was the complications that had compelled Becky to step out into the snow and check on me. I'm still not sure.

Loving Becky very much in that moment, I realized I didn't know what to feel, let alone how to describe it or what to say, so I hugged her. Standing in the snow in my underwear, embracing my friend. It seemed like something more profound than medication or escapism. For a moment, I felt as though I might be grieving.

"Did you go for a walk with someone?" Becky asked.

I pulled away and looked at her, confused. Becky pointed behind me, and I turned to notice two sets of footprints disappearing into the snow. Becky and I looked at one another for a moment before we both realized what had happened.

WE found the others in the mess hall—the seven of us as well as Aye'Sayuh, Powersurf, Jim Henson, David Bowie, and Stephen K. Hayes.

"Flynn Hardey and Bradley Press are gone," I said, rushing into the room.

Bowie furrowed his brow. "Do tell, Danny."

We explained about the tracks.

Jim Henson casually retrieved his NARS-Slate from a sweater pocket and began poking at it, all of us watching his strange behavior with anticipation.

"Every NARS slate is equipped with a precise Global Positioning System," said Jim. "The great thing about being a rebel militia is that we develop crafty little bits of mischief like tracking software that can locate nearby NARS-Slates and retrieve their GPS coordinates."

"Dude," Conner said. "Jim Henson is seriously badass."

Bowie was looking down his nose at his own Slate. "It would appear they've set out for the Feed Camp," he said.

"Those two numbskulls are trying to get to the harbor." Said Barrett.

"I doubt that very much," Bowie sighed. "If I were to guess, I might wonder if they've gone out in search of fully functional Slates."

"Oh, right," Powersurf said, snapping his fingers. "We disabled both of their devices the day you arrived. A precaution really, but it was pretty funny to watch them wander around in here for days looking for 'better Apep connection.'" He laughed at the thought of this for a bit, all of us staring at him. "Anyway," he sighed, wiping a single tear from his eye. "They had already entered into the early stages of addiction. I wouldn't be at all surprised if they were stammering around in the snow moaning, 'NARS... NARS...'"

"Well great," Barrett barked. "What the hell are we supposed to do about them now?"

"Let them go!" Jade insisted. "They'll be happier. We'll be happier. It's a win-win."

"Not if they tell the SIAHD about the rebel base, James Bond," Barrett fired back.

"I hadn't thought of that," said Jade.

"Seems to be a recurring motif," Paul said to Jade.

"I know some stuff," Jade said.

"Be that as it may," Stephen Hayes said, "I'm afraid the mission is now changing."

Everyone locked eyes on Hayes, terrified of what he was going to say next.

He went on. "We are going to retrieve these two from the Feed Camp and then begin the journey to Earth."

"Now?" Becky asked, outraged. "We still had days of training before we were supposed to be sent out!"

Bowie spoke calmly. "I'm afraid our two friends have fast-tracked those plans."

"You are ready," said Hayes. "We can train out here for months. At some point, the mission must begin. We'd thought the fighting would begin after we reveal the Final Heresy, but it looks like it begins today."

"And you think we can handle it?" Jade asked.

"I think you've cheated your way to becoming some of the most impressive black belts I've ever trained," Hayes said, tapping the space behind his ear.

"Dude," I whispered to Conner. "Stephen K. Hayes just said I'm one of the most impressive black belts he's ever trained."

"Me too, dude," Conner whispered back.

"I'm freaking out over here," Emma told the room. "Like, when is this all beginning? I'm trying to wrap my head around what's going on here."

Bowie looked at her and nodded. "Suit up, my dear," he said in his totally awesome David Bowie voice.

SUITING up meant donning our mission apparel for the first time. Some kind of blended alien carbon fiber, leather, and latex, the suits were form-fitting and flexible. The knuckles, knees, and elbows all had a light but durable protective shell, and the rest mostly looked like a more durable version of the grey coveralls we'd been wearing all along.

Once dressed, I tightened the strap that held my sheathed gatana sword over my shoulder and stepped awkwardly outside of my room. The hallway was quiet, with only Barrett waiting for me. Like me, he seemed a tad unsure of himself in the suit, but he'd at least put his denim jacket on over it. His staff had been collapsed into a smaller rod that was threaded through a leather harness he wore on his back.

"You're wearing your jacket too?"

He shrugged.

"Can we do that?"

He shrugged again.

"I'm going back to get my jacket."

Just as I'd turned to re-enter my room, a door across the hall opened, and Emma stepped out. Unlike Barrett and I—who looked like a tailor had transformed our trucker outfits into futuristic Ghostbuster uniforms—Emma looked as though her coveralls had been converted into a factory working pixie version of a super heroine's catsuit.

"Whoa," I said.

"I feel stupid," she said, lifting her arms and examining her outfit as if she'd been unwillingly dressed by machines.

"I like it," said Becky, striding confidently from her room. "Wow, girl," Becky said to Emma. "We are going to distract these boys so much they won't be able to save the world." She gestured to Emma and then to herself. "Serious sex appeal."

"Yeah, alright," I said, seeing no option but to concede. "You guys look totally rad."

It was true. They were both very distracting.

"And look," Becky said, "David Bowie and Jim Henson made me a new sickle-chain thing."

She retrieved a black rod—about two feet long—that had been fastened to her hip. With a flick of her wrist, a menacing blade—as long as the rod itself—extended from the device like a switchblade. Becky gave the weapon another flick, and the bottom was loosed from the rod, connected by a length of chain that dangled for a moment before being drawn up into the rod in an instant.

"Yikes," Emma said.

"Totally," Becky agreed.

"Do you guys like your suits?" Conner said, looking down at his outfit as he joined the group. "I wish they had a black one." Like Barrett, he'd donned his leather jacket over his world-saving getup.

299

"You're wearing your jacket too?" I asked, sounding almost panicked. "Hang on. I'm getting mine."

When I'd returned from my room with my worn out and faithful denim jacket I felt slightly less insecure. Paul and Jade had arrived, everyone sizing up the person next to them.

"Where's your trademark?" Paul asked Jade.

"What trademark?"

"Everyone is wearing something from their trademark outfit, man."

"Where's *your* trademark?"

Paul pointed at his black beanie. "Duh."

"The girls don't have trademarks," said Jade.

"Yeah, huh," Emma said, turning her head. "This is my all-time favorite scrunchie." She pointed at the neon pink band of fabric that secured her side ponytail.

"And these are my favorite bracelets," said Becky, shaking her wrists at Jade and clinking a half-dozen brightly colored plastic bangles on each arm.

"Well my glasses are my trademark, then," Jade argued.

"Bogus," Conner said. "You *have* to have those to see, dude."

"Ergo, I wear them daily. Trademark."

"Still no weapon, Jesus Boy?" Barrett asked Conner.

Conner shook his head. "Going to overcome evil with good and all that."

"And you're not going to be offended by all our sophisticated ninja weapons?" I asked. "Have you seen Becky's? It's terrifying."

Becky tilted her head and nodded.

"What business is it of mine to judge those outside the church?" Conner said.

At the end of the hall, the massive freight elevator doors slid open revealing Aye'Sayuh inside. Garbed in an outfit like ours in every way other than the necessary differences in proportions, Aye'Sayuh was holding the tall naginata in his scaly talons, and his tail was flicking behind him the way it often did when he was excited. I think we were all acknowledging to ourselves that he looked ridiculously awesome.

"Hey," Emma complained, "That's *my* sword-stick."

"Dude," Jade said. "You look ridiculously awesome."

I was *just* thinking that, I thought to myself.

THE final mess hall briefing wasn't an encouraging one. Though we could use our Slates to track Flynn and Bradley, the GPS only confirmed what we already knew: They'd found their way back to the Feed Camp and stayed there.

"So what if they're just hooked up to some station like the hundreds of other junkies?" Barrett asked.

"They'd be the newest patients," Jim Henson reminded us. "They'll be more likely to respond or react to your presence."

"It's one huge open area filled with little drug stations," said Paul. "What are we supposed to do? Just wander in and make a ruckus?"

"Yeah," Jade said, suddenly realizing something. "If those two wank stains are already there, then they've probably told someone about this place."

"Yes, that's right," David Bowie said. "In a bit of a hurry, I'm afraid."

"Remember your training," said Stephen Hayes. "You're masters of deception. Shadow warriors."

Jim Henson spoke up again. "Remember, the mo'achs are upgrades. They don't always work with perfect seamlessness."

"Wait," I said, "what does *that* mean?"

"It means," Powersurf answered, "that often the mo'ach integrates knowledge and muscle memory completely unbeknownst to you. Other times, you may have to sort of clear your minds to fool your brain into accessing the data on the mo'ach as if it were any other information in the mind."

"Done," Paul said.

"The gaulish will take us back to the camp," Aye'Sayuh said, standing up.

"Those ostrich things?" Becky asked.

"You realize they're dinosaurs, right?" Barrett asked Becky, who seemed genuinely taken aback.

"They are?" She whispered.

"Once we get there," Aye'Sayuh went on. "There's no turning back."

"The mission? Like, the whole thing?" I asked.

Aye'Sayuh nodded. "We're about to see some serious shit."

WE were only five minutes into the blizzard when it suddenly occurred to me how much more pleasant this particular journey seemed compared to the last one.

"You know what's nice about this?" Jade said, apparently reading my mind.

"Not being naked?" I asked.

"Speak for yourself," Conner called out from somewhere in the caravan. "What situation isn't bettered by nudity?"

"Football," Paul said immediately.

"Sliding down a banister," Jade said.

"Okay, fine, there are one or two things," Conner conceded.

"Hugging your grandma," Barrett said immediately.

"The suits are so warm!" I said happily.

"We can barely understand you with the mask on," Barret pointed out.

Once again, he and the girls had been too cool (or practical) to don the shinobi shozōku masks, but Paul, Conner, Jade and myself had all assured one another of their importance.

"To keep warm," we'd all said; as if this was the real reason. Hayes had shaken his head and sighed, but then helped us put on the masks.

The gaulish were comfortable this time around, but it could have been by comparison only. With seven animals available, everyone was given their own personal dinosaur to ride, and we led them using a set of leather reins attached to an ornamental headpiece. We'd consolidated every tool that wasn't fixed to our person into two small satchels and brought along two of the skateboards just in case.

"You know," Aye'Sayuh said, "you can't have that music[33] blasting when we get close to the camp."

We'd also brought the boom box.

"Isn't it funny?" Becky giggled. "This song playing right now. Isn't it funny?"

"Not especially," Barrett answered dryly. "This isn't Africa."

"Don't be an ass," Becky warned him.

We joked amongst ourselves and kept the music playing as we wandered throughout the manufactured

---

[33] Toto, "Africa"

tundra, but there was a palpable sense that what we were really doing was disguising our collective fear. I couldn't help but retreat into my thoughts, losing track of the music and conversation around me. I'd close my eyes and try to feel the mo'ach communicating with my mind, but it was impossible.

There were all sorts of deeply familiar facts in my memory—the secret fighting art developed by oppressed farmers, not to mention a whole wealth of knowledge and experience in the functionality and mechanics of the small tablet-shaped machine strapped to the leg of my combat uniform. Strangely, there were no memories of ever acquiring any of said expertise. It was like trying to remember the precise moment you'd fallen asleep after waking up.

It was almost like the familiarity with which I could recall my mom's face, or Emma's voice, or how to recite *Indiana Jones and the Temple of Doom* from memory, or how to complete the first dungeon in *The Legend of Zelda*. I don't remember setting out to commit those things to memory; I just sort of discovered that I *had* at some point.

I knew how important it was for the ninja to dispense with any fear. I knew the mental and spiritual exercises with which a ninja did just that, but I still felt afraid. I found myself surprised to realize that even an accomplished black belt was not immune to small failure, and as soon as this occurred to me, it logically followed that we were similarly vulnerable to massive failure as well. At the end of it all, despite everything we'd been through and everything at stake, we were still just kids who had been estranged from our families, our lives, even our planet to attempt something that could very well kill us.

I felt guilty.

Eventually, the blizzard let up and the snow beneath us went from several feet deep to several inches deep. In a few more strides, the tundra had become a barren, rock-hard desert terrain. The song changed[34], setting an ominous tone.

"I bet you could shred on this stuff," Conner said, tapping the skateboard strapped to his gaulish.

"Go ahead," Paul said. "Skitch the gaulish."

"Marty McFly did it," Barrett reminded us.

The air around us now swirling with heat, I found that my suit had transitioned from keeping me warm to keeping me cool.

"This thing is amazing," I said, looking down at my body.

"What, the suit?" Jade asked. "I know! I was toasty, and now I'm breezy. How's it doing that?"

Aye'Sayuh answered. "The material reacts to what your body is doing. If your body indicates that it's attempting to warm itself, the fibers constrict, containing your body's warmth as a natural heater. If your body says it's overheating, the fibers loosen, and the suit breathes."

"Plus forget a bra, this thing is the best support ever," Emma added.

"How's that thick, black, cotton mask, boys?" Becky asked. "Does it have magical fibers as well?"

"It has the power of looking awesome," Paul said.

"Hey, Aye'Sayuh," Conner said warily, interrupting our laughter. "What about those guys? Nothing to worry about?"

We all followed Conner's gaze to the left, where, on the horizon, we could make out the silhouettes of two large bipedal dinosaurs.

---

[34] Wire, "Ahead"

"That's not good," Aye'Sayuh said.

"Not good as in we should run?" Emma asked.

"I think so, yeah."

"Are those T-rexes?" Barrett said, the slight panic in his voice betraying his calm demeanor.

"On Earth, they call them *Tarbosauruses*. Part of the tyrannosaur family. Here we call them bata'ar."

The animals looked a lot like t-rexes. Maybe forty feet long from head to toe with crocodilian scutes and leathery plating all down the back of their mottled brown backs. They moved along the horizon like enormous, slow birds.

"If we run, won't they just see us and chase us?" I asked.

"Maybe," Aye'Sayuh said, not taking his nervous eyes off the bata'ar some fifty yards away.

"Dude," said Conner. "Are you serious? We can't get eaten on our way *to* the mission."

"Dammit, you're right," Aye'Sayuh sighed.

As the words left his mouth, one of the bata'ar's heads suddenly snapped in our direction. Its eyes on us, the animal began panting and emitting a low, breathy growl.

"That's a drag," said Aye'Sayuh.

Flicking his gaulish's reigns, Aye'Sayuh's animal began to gallop across the desert terrain, the rest of us following suit. The two bata'ar took flight, pursuing us like great plodding lizards, moving horrifically fast for reptiles.

"Turn off the music![35]" I yelled. "We'll never lose them!"

"I'm trying!" Paul shouted back, fumbling at the boom box hanging from his gaulish's satchel. "I can barely hold on to this crazy thing!"

---

[35] Huey Lewis & The News, "The Power of Love"

I watched as just a few feet to my left, Paul was thrown from his gaulish's back and went tumbling over the flat, hard terrain, his satchel and supplies exploding around him. I instantly drew my reigns back and my gaulish performed a violent 180 degree turn, nearly bucking me from my saddle.

"What the hell are you doing?" Conner yelled as he watched me turn.

"Paul!" I screamed. "We lost Paul!"

Now heading directly toward the two enormous, charging bata'ar—Paul rising to his feet between us—I suddenly wondered what would happen if I lost control of my bladder and peed in the suit. Paul looked behind him and saw the bata'ar gaining, both of them making an awful sound like a lion mixed with a baby elephant. Looking around him, Paul set to work frantically gathering some of the items that had been strewn about in his crash—his sai, skateboard, and the amazingly durable boom box that hadn't given up on the music.

Knowing we'd stand a better chance without slowing to a stop, I passed Paul and made a wide arch just outside of the bata'ar's biting range. Now moving toward both Paul and the others in the distance, I shouted over the music for him to take my hand as I passed. Paul readied himself and reached out, seizing my wrist with one arm as my gaulish galloped by, his other arm gripping the skateboard and stereo. Struggling to pull himself up against the momentum of the running animal, Paul grimaced, his feet dragging painfully against the rock-hard ground below.

"Drop the skateboard and give me your other hand!" I screamed.

"But what if we need to shred?" he yelled back.

"Then drop the boombox!"

"But what if we want to jam?" Paul shouted over the gaulish's thundering gait. "This soundtrack is strangely fitting!"

"Drop it, you idiot!"

The boom box went first, tumbling along behind us before being destroyed beneath the bata'ar as if taken under the wheels of a semi truck. A moment's reluctance flickered on Paul's face before he released the skateboard, which miraculously caught beneath his dragging feet. For a moment I thought we'd both be pulled from the gaulish, but Paul managed to steady himself on the board.

"Dude!" I screamed, "You're skitching the gaulish!"

"Bitchin!" Paul shouted, his expression shifting from horrified to exuberant. Then, as quickly as this incredible moment had unfolded, there was a focus-shattering roar, and we both looked up to realize the pursuing bata'ar were only a few feet behind.

"Shit, shit, shit," Paul stammered in a panic, his balance beginning to compromise.

Then it hit me: *The Brain Drain.*

Everything seemed to go silent. "Paul!" I shouted, his terrified expression gazing up at me. The words came out of me like a movie playing in slow motion: "The Braaain Draaain!"

Paul stared up, the horror on his face melting away slowly, replaced by a calm serenity as if he was prepared to let go and give himself over to his destiny as lunch for two vicious Tarbosauruses. Instead, his grip on my arm tightened, his knees bowed, and Paul performed the most impressive ollie Gaina has ever known: Speeding along a petrified terrain at nearly forty miles per hour, the open jaws of a giant dinosaur snapping closed a moment short of making Paul a meal.

Paul's miracle ollie became a fluid dismount onto the back of the gaulish, and the disappointed bata'ar finally relented, fading into the distance before they turned and stomped away.

As the two of us rejoined the group, our exhausted animals slowing to a stop, everyone leaped from their gaulish and came around the two of us, hugging and cheering.

Barrett looked Paul in the eye. "I *told* you it could be done."

THE remaining journey through the desert seemed wonderfully dull after that. The beacon unknowingly emitting from both Flynn and Bradley's NARS-Slates continued to lead directly to the Feed Camp. Eventually, the facility appeared in the distance—a single modern structure erected in the center of what seemed to be endless miles of orange sand.

Paul took a deep breath. "There it is."

"What is this?" Barrett said, "the most cliché movie ever? Obviously, that's it."

"I wish I didn't lose the stereo," Paul said.

"It's just as well," said Jade. "Aye'Sayuh wouldn't let us listen to it this close anyway."

"Are you guys ready?" Aye'Sayuh asked, ignoring our banter. There was a nervous murmuring amongst the group that sounded like a reluctant acknowledgment of our collective readiness. We abandoned our gaulish and moved toward the facility. The open landscape offered nothing in the way of cover, so we were forced to convene at the building's only entrance.

"I don't feel like a ninja," Becky said as Aye'Sayuh keyed in an entry code on the door's interactive panel. "Do you guys?"

Everyone shook their heads, no.

"Hey, Aye'Sayuh," Paul said. "Didn't you mention last time that there might have been guards in the entrance corridor?"

"Yeah," Aye'Sayuh said.

"Do you think they'll be there this time?"

"I hope not."

"Ah, geez, are we about to get into a fight in a cramped hallway right when we walk in?" Conner asked the group.

"You better use some of that 'wind' Hayes was always going on about," I said.

"I'm still not sure what that meant," Barrett admitted. "It's just fighting someone up close?"

"I think so," I said.

"How is that wind?" Barrett asked.

"If you have to ask," Aye'Sayuh told us, "you'll never know."

Everyone drew his or her weapons as the door slid open with a soft sound like escaping steam. The hallway was once again empty. We crept silently down the white corridor toward the portal we knew led to the sea of zombified prisoners. Presumably somewhere in their ranks sat Bradley Press and Flynn Hardey, and we had to find them somehow and get to the harbor without being stopped, or by fighting off whoever stopped us. As Aye'Sayuh entered the second set of entry keys, I took a deep breath and closed my eyes until the doors opened before us.

The chamber was the same as we'd left it; a sea of humans wired into electronic stations, all of them holding NARS-Slates, their thumbs moving over the touchscreens like little hummingbirds. The entire space was filled with the ambiance of heavy breathing, grunts, sniffs, the sound of bodies shifting in their chairs—like a crowded cafeteria with no one talking. There was no sign of any guards or SIAHD scientists anywhere.

"Why is there still no one here?" I whispered to Aye'Sayuh.

"Look at this place," he said. "Would you want to stay here all the time?"

"How are we supposed to find Larry and Balki?" Barrett asked. "How do we even know they're mixed in with everyone?"

"We don't," Aye'Sayuh admitted. "Split up and search. If you locate either one of them, move to the nearest spot on the outer perimeter. If at any point you see someone from our party has moved out of the maze of prisoners, go to them."

Without another word, the group fanned out into the prisoners. Moving silently in a crouched position so that my head would not be visible to someone on the outer perimeter, I crept up the aisles between prisoner stations. Reclined in their white chairs, most of the prisoners took no notice of me whatsoever. Those that did barely flicked their eyes at me as if they'd noticed a fly but didn't care. Every prisoner I saw was either navigating NARS or exploring a gallery of narsies. Some of the prisoners were posing for narsies as they sat in their chairs, then they'd immediately set to work getting the photos uploaded to their NARS profiles. The prisoners—most of them teenagers—were all dressed in something like white hospital gowns and had a sickly, sallow look to them. Overgrown fingernails and dark circles under their eyes, they'd lick their dry lips and then switch to a screen on their NARS-Slates that I gathered was regulating their fluid intake via the IV poles fastened to their chairs. Aside from the IVs, no prisoner seemed actually to be shackled or restrained in any way. Unless you count the NARS-Slates.

After scanning more than a dozen rows, I caught sight of Emma standing against a wall in the distance with her hands in the air. She'd found them.

"They're on this row," Emma said when I reached her. "About halfway down."

Aye'Sayuh had joined us. "Danny, let's go get them. Emma, when the others get here, everyone take cover between the stations here and wait for us."

Aye'Sayuh was hardly able to conceal himself as effectively as I could due to his exaggerated height but attempted a crouching posture as we moved quickly down the long row of prisoners. Before long, we found them sitting there dressed in white gowns like everyone else, wired into the ground and thumbing away at their stupid little toys. Though they both seemed slightly less malnourished than the other prisoners, the short time they'd been gone had already taken a visible toll on them.

"Hardey!" I whispered urgently. "Press! Hey, it's us. We've come to get you guys out of here."

Neither of them reacted. None of the nearby prisoners did for that matter.

"Dude," I hissed, slapping at Flynn's arm. "Snap out of it."

Flynn seemed shocked to have been touched, and slowly drew his attention over to me, scowling as if already outraged with whatever it was that just broke his concentration on the Slate.

"Thomas?" he said, sounding disgusted. "You better get out of here, man. This place is seriously invite-only."

"You're a prisoner, dummy," I whispered. "Look at this place! You guys are a bunch of diseased lab rats."

"God, you're jealous," Flynn said, rolling his eyes. "Look, man, I don't have a lot of space in my life for negativity right now. I want to tell stories, create content, and inspire people."

I looked at Flynn, then around the room in which we were both trapped, then back to Flynn again.

"What the hell is wrong with you, dude?"

Aye'Sayuh suddenly lunged forward and seized Flynn by the arm, hauling him up out of his station. Immediately Flynn began to flail and screech like a toddler, stirring up enough commotion to attract the attention of a few nearby prisoners.

"Get the other one!" Aye'Sayuh yelled over Flynn's tantrum. "We have to go!"

I moved to the next station and snatched the IV from Bradley's arm, effectively ending his stupor and inviting a high-pitched yelp. Bradley lost his grip on his Slate, and it tumbled to the floor where it landed with a loud cracking sound, the screen visibly shattered in an instant. Then, to my utter horror, Bradley began to weep. Like, heaving sobs and a mewling whine and everything.

"He's crying!" I yelled to Aye'Sayuh, who was still wrestling with a flailing Flynn Hardey.

"Get him!" Aye'Sayuh shouted impatiently.

Around us, the prisoners had begun to lift their NARS-Slates and snap photos of the unfolding scene. I wasn't sure exactly what that meant for us at the moment, but it didn't seem promising.

"B-b-b-broken!" Bradley sobbed. "My S-s-s-s-slate!"

I drew back and thrust my arm forward, delivering a focused blow to Bradley's head. His whine tapered off, and he went limp as I hoisted his body up on to my shoulders. Aye'Sayuh had restrained Flynn in a painful looking hold, making him unable to do much other than wheeze and get dragged down the row of photographing prisoners toward the outer perimeter. Joining the others, we moved as quickly as we could, following Aye'Sayuh to one of the unmarked doors on the other side of the chamber.

As we shuffled along, there came the now-familiar steam-like hiss, and I whirled around painfully—Bradley's limp body still hoisted over my shoulders—to see two Imi guards step through a newly revealed door and into the room. The guards were both dressed in those Tron-looking grey bodysuits covered in circuit board patterns, like futuristic space dinosaurs. Both Imi were armed with some kind of alien gun; a rifle-shaped, bright orange canon that, for all their advanced technology, looked as though it was assembled with vacuum cleaner parts.

Barrett charged the guards, landing a painful looking punch in the first Imi's ribs, then guiding the momentum of his fall into the second guard, who stumbled, dropping his weapon. The orange gun slid across the slick white floor, slowing to a stop at Jade's feet. Jade looked to the gun, then to Barrett—who was now working to keep his two much larger opponents subdued. Jade retrieved the weapon from the floor, and after examining it for a moment, took aim at the guard furthest from Barrett and activated the weapon. The gun made a deep rumbling sound then kicked Jade backward. Nothing visible emitted from the weapon, but the Imi at which Jade had aimed suddenly erupted into a fine red mist and a hail of spattering gore moments afterward. All that was left was a pair of legs, a tail, and the smoldering stump of the lower abdomen. The half of the guard left behind remained upright for a moment, then tumbled over, kicking itself in a little circle, streaking the white floor with gushing torrents of dark red and chunks of pink debris. The walls around us looked like a Jackson Pollock painting.

"Guys," Jade said, slow and loud. "I think I killed one on accident."

Barrett stood just feet from the slaughter, still shielding himself and now caked with Imi blood and guts. The remaining guard was standing next to Barrett with his hands up, horrified.

"What kind of hard evidence do you need to confirm death?" Barrett shouted.

"I'm going to be sick," Becky groaned.

The other guard suddenly rushed toward the wall, where it went to work entering a code into the previously invisible control panel. Barrett moved toward the guard but slipped in the lake of blood swirling at his feet.

"Stop him!" Aye'Sayuh screamed at Jade.

Jade lifted the gun again, cringing. "But I don't want to turn this one into Ragu!"

Before anyone else could act, the air erupted with another deep boom, and Jade went stumbling backward. The wall next to the surviving guard exploded in a blast of sparks and flying debris. An electronic-sounding groan moved through the room, the light emitting from the wall panels flickering.

"What did you shoot?" Conner shouted.

"Who knows?" Jade answered. "Every surface in this place is a freaking computer!"

"Oh no," Emma said. Everyone turned to face her and found her staring out at the crowd of prisoners, who, little by little seemed to become frustrated with their NARS-Slates. "What are they doing?"

"Well great," Barrett sighed, the remaining Imi guard fleeing down the walkway.

What began as a stirring grumble from the prisoners quickly crescendoed into full-blown rage. They stabbed at their Slates with rigid index fingers shouting things like, "did I lose Apep?" and "mine froze up! Did yours freeze up?" and "I better not have lost that picture!"

"We've got to get to the harbor," Aye'Sayuh reminded us, pointing to the other side of the room. As we ran along the outer perimeter, the prisoners finally noticed us, not to mention the carnage we'd left behind.

"Who are they?" a prisoner screamed.

"This place is *invite-only*!" screamed another. "They're wrecking our community! They aren't being positive!"

The mob began closing in on us. Becky snatched the black baton from her waist, flicked it once to extend the blade, and a second time to release the chain. With the rest of us crouching out of the danger zone, she began spinning the chain and creating a defensive shield around us as we moved.

"What is that?" one of the prisoners whined.

"My Slate is still frozen," another said, charging at us while looking down at the device in his hands.

Two prisoners lunged at Paul and Jade, who were just outside of the swinging chain's protection.

"Don't blow them up!" Paul said to Jade, who was reflexively aiming the alien blaster at their attackers. Paul began to dispense the spazzing NARS zombies one by one with some ease, doing his best to keep the group moving without losing anyone to the clamoring hoard. Our group came to a stop at some anonymous panel on the wall, and Aye'Sayuh began keying in a code that was rejected every time.

"Aye'Sayuh," I said slowly, my hand reaching up to the sword sheathed on my back. More and more prisoners were leaving their stations and lumbering toward us now. "Why does it seem a lot like whatever it is you're trying to do isn't working?

"Jade shot one of the control panels," Aye'Sayuh answered, clearly stressed. "I've got to bypass the broken security system."

"Can you do that?" Paul yelled, taking another prisoner to the ground and landing a blow in his ribs.

Aye'Sayuh didn't answer. He just went on keying in an endless combination of codes, none of which made any difference. One of the approaching prisoners grimaced, lifted his arms defensively, and ran deliberately into the reach of Becky's spinning chain. The iron weight at the chain's end struck his mouth with an awful cracking sound, and he tumbled over spitting blood. Becky flicked her black baton, and the chain was drawn back into the rod in an instant.

"Keep them back!" Aye'Sayuh said.

"They're too close!" Becky cried.

I drew my sword. Paul rolled one prisoner into two others, then moved back and drew his sai. Barrett retrieved the small black staff that was strapped to his back, gripped it, and it instantaneously extended to three times its previous length with a loud metallic click.

"There's a lot of them," Conner observed plainly.

With the encroaching prisoners moments away from overpowering us, Jade hoisted the orange canon up at his hips, leveled at the writhing throng of narcissists.

"You're going to *shoot* them?" I yelled in disbelief.

"No," Jade said defensively. "Why? *Should* I?"

317

"No!" several of us said in unison, inching back toward the wall, our weapons raised.

"Maybe shoot *one* of them," Barrett said.

All of us looked at him, scowling.

"To scare the rest of them back!" Barrett clarified.

Jade looked down at the canon, then to the mob, then to the gun again, and suddenly whirled around, the weapon now aimed where Aye'Sayuh was still punching keys into a panel on the wall. Before anyone could ask what the hell Jade was thinking, the gun fired a third time, sending a blindingly bright blue bolt of voltage snaking toward the wall where it met with a deafening explosion of sparks and debris. When the smoke cleared a moment later, the wall next to Aye'Sayuh was home to an enormous smoking crater through which we could see the chamber on the other side. Jade hurled the blaster around at the mob—who, having seen its awful destructive power, finally slowed in their rabid assault, the first wave of them stumbling backward and creating an awkward pileup.

"That's not even the right way," Aye'Sayuh said, pointing to the opening made by the alien gun.

"Come on," Jade said, waving everyone into the opening. "We'll shoot our way there!"

"Are you sure you're British?" Conner asked, climbing through the opening in the wall. "Because that was a very American-sounding thing to say."

The next chamber was, like the others, a wide and mostly empty white room. The immediately discernable difference was that in this room, one of the four walls was home to an awful looking overgrowth of red vine. Splintering out across the wall's surface like a complex system of blood vessels, the vine nearly covered the entire wall like ivy on an old castle. Crimson colored and wet looking, the vine glistened and pulsated, flickers of light emitting from small nodes in its intricate network of connections.

"This looks weird," said Paul.

"I don't like it," Becky announced emphatically. "At *all*."

"We need to get out of here," Aye'Sayuh told us. He sounded so panicked that a wave of visible dread moved through the group. The rabble of outraged prisoners had begun hissing and clawing at the small opening we'd made it the wall, but they were so worked up that they weren't taking the time to move neatly through the hole one by one.

"Good *grief* these guys want their Slates back," Barrett said, shaking his head at their pathetic attempts to get to us.

Dropping a now barely conscious Bradley Press to the ground, I stood up stretching to crack my back as Aye'Sayuh shoved Flynn Hardey against his compatriot.

"You two just stay behind us and keep your mouths shut," Aye'Sayuh threatened them. Bradley was rubbing his temples, whimpering, but the two said nothing.

Jade raised the gun at the wall that led into the chamber Aye'Sayuh had hoped to unlock in the first place.

"Hey, whoa, wait," Aye'Sayuh warned Jade, lifting a hand to keep him from firing. "Don't fire that thing in here. You could get us even more trapped than we already are if you debilitate the system any further."

"Can't I just shoot, like, the spot where the door should be?" Jade asked, seeming to me to make perfect sense.

Aye'Sayuh made a wide gesture at the space all around us. "Everything in the center is powered by Apep, meaning everything is connected. If you keep blowing things up, you could shut down the entire facility including the harbor. We'd be stuck here."

"Well can you get us through?" Jade asked.

Aye'Sayuh seemed to be preoccupied with the red vines fanning out along the wall. He shook his head, not taking his eyes off the red tangle of growth. "I don't think so. The codes have been reset. They must have known we were coming."

"That's not good news," I said.

"So we can't get around in here?" Emma asked.

"The only access we have is basic Imi biological entry points. I'd have to access the facility's Apep hub and reset the building's security protocol."

"Can you do that?" I asked.

"I think so."

"So how do we get to that hub place?" Becky asked.

"Just open the door, I guess," Aye'Sayuh said, looking off toward the wall opposite us.

The twisting network of wall nerves all seemed to be growing out of something just beyond that wall.

MOD LOG, 24
MEM'RAH RISING

The invisible door housed within the wall's seamless white surface whizzed open with what had become a familiar hum. Beyond the door, however, was nothing remotely familiar to the Imi architectural experience.

"It looks like the last level of *Contra* in here."

Conner was right; not unlike the conclusion of the two-player run-and-gun arcade game we'd often played together at Ground Kontrol, this room looked like the insides of an enormous alien beast. The long, narrow corridor was lined with a pink, fleshy substance. It felt like standing on a tongue. The veiny patchwork we'd seen in the previous room had clearly been an outgrowth of what began in here—the intricate network of ropey tissue covered the walls and ceiling with such density that it coated our surroundings with an uneven, organic lining that fluttered and pulsated as if every inch of it were alive.

Like swarming ants marching toward a felled lollipop, the throbbing nervous system converged at six small podiums lining the walls, three on each side and the only exposed white plastic surfaces in the room. At each podium, the vein network escaped the confines of the wall and ventured out to undulating brain-like nodes hoisted up on each respective column. The brains—glistening and gumball pink—bubbled and dripped viscous slime where they sat. Each node was fixed with a single yellow eye cracked with thrumming red arteries and a fiery red pupil as dark as a blood clot. As soon as Conner spoke, all six eyes were trained on us, and the nodes throbbed wildly at our presence. At the end of the corridor sat a single giant podium, and on it a giant brain creature.

Unlike the others, this creature boasted binocular vision. Its round, dome-like carapace was covered in a kind of armor—like a cage of bones—over the brain tissue. This brain even had something of a face, with a bulbous elephantine trunk between its two blazing yellow eyes—each of them as big as my face and with a hint of sadness in their baleful stare.

"Oh my God," I whispered. "It *is* basically Mother Brain from *Metroid*."

"What's *Metroid*?" Becky mumbled again to no one in particular.

And before the monstrous brain stood an Imi.

Garbed in an elaborate display of jewelry and gown, the Imi looked like a mix between a pimp and space Dracula.

"He looks like space Dracula," Conner whispered.

"I was *just* thinking the same thing," I whispered back. "But I was thinking, like, mixed with a pimp."

"Totally," Becky agreed, also whispering. "He totally does."

"Bah'gohd," the Imi said, his body to the giant brain but his head slowly craning toward us. "Your family will be happy to know that you're alive."

A silent series of confused shrugs moved through the group.

"Great," Aye'Sayuh said calmly, giving us all an awful start. "I guess I'll go back to Vancouver and let them know I'm okay then."

322

The mysterious Imi turned to the eight of us and with his hands clasped behind his back made several intimidating strides in our direction.

"No, no, no, no," he was saying, again and again to the point of becoming weird. "Absurd, Bah'gohd!"

"Dude, why is he calling you that weird name?" I whispered.

"Because he's a dick," Aye'Sayuh said. "It means 'little fool.'"

"You *wound* me, sir," the Imi said in mock horror. "It's a term of endearment, like, uh, what's that one the people of earth use all the time?"

"Honey?" Becky asked.

"Sweetie pie?" I offered.

"Knucklehead," the Imi declared. "It's sort of like knucklehead."

"We say that all the time?" I mumbled out of the side of my mouth to Barrett, who shrugged and shook his head.

"Look," the Imi said, flailing a limp wrist at the group and making us all stumble backward, "you guys can't be in here, y'know? It's a health risk, a safety risk, a security risk—really. It's just truly goddman risky, so we all need to skedaddle."

"We're not with them!" Flynn yelled abruptly, reminding us all of their unfortunate presence. "We were specially selected for the NARS-Slate development program, and these people have abducted—"

"Yeah, yeah," the Imi interrupted him. "We'll get you back to your fix in a second, junkie, just calm the hell down."

"We're leaving, Mem'Rah," Aye'Sayuh insisted. "Open the harbor doors."

Mem'Rah.

He looked like a reptilian buzzard that had plundered an Egyptian sarcophagus. He pulled his robe open as he spoke like a businessman opening his blazer, revealing a second set of vestigial limbs folded like little mantis arms against his ribs.

A nauseous feeling suddenly rose in my stomach. I felt clammy all over. My legs seemed to have gone wobbly.

"Sure, yeah, that's fine," Mem'Rah said. "But we don't need Apep for that, just come with me."

"*This* is Apep?" Barrett asked in disbelief, nodding at the massive brain monster in the distance.

"Who, *him*?" said Mem'Rah, looking back over his shoulder at the creature. "Well, sure. The Apep for *this* facility."

It was quiet for a moment. I was still trying to get a handle on the noxious sensation in my gut. Then Paul slowly admitted, "I sort of thought there was, like, *one* big Apep."

He made a gesture with his hands to indicate bigness.

Mem'Rah laughed. "Mother Apep is just an origin myth." He drew our attention to the brain creatures in the chamber. "Apep are just Gainian electrogenic animals that create and transmit a sophisticated network of data that we can tap into and exploit to our own personal ends. Sort of like those eels you have on Earth. Look, it's all very technical."

Jade lifted the gun. "Should I shoot the brain things?"

Aye'Sayuh pushed the gun away. "No! You'll shut down the entire system, and we'll be trapped."

"Don't be so dramatic, Bah'gohd," Mem'Rah sighed.

"He is *nothing* like he seems on TV," Becky mumbled.

"No one ever is," Mem'Rah confessed. "It's a projection. An avatar. A hologram. That's what NARS is all about! Why be *you* when you can be an entirely fictional but infinitely *better* you? All it takes is a slight embellishment here, a skewing of a few details there, and before you know it, NARS users no longer realize that the things they post online are entirely fabricated."

"Why is he going on about NARS?" Barrett asked.

"Because!" Mem'Rah shot back violently, his clawed finger in Barrett's face. "In your desperate attempt to make your lives into a Spielberg adventure movie, you children are doing your world a terrible disservice."

"By tampering with a social network?" I asked sarcastically.

"It's not the social network," Mem'Rah tisked. "Don't be an idiot. You know *that*. The people of earth had come to believe their developed civilizations were all en route to some glorious destiny—some sense of *more* behind the cruel randomness of the universe. Only, the *more* isn't coming. So, the human animal, in its eternal quest to *connect*, is scrambling for some meaning, some profound self-actualization to grab them by their shoulders and shout in their sagging faces, 'There *is* more! I swear! And that more is *you*.' Yes, you *are* going to become everything you've ever dreamed of, only not *you* exactly, but a sort of pseudo-you that you can create online!"

"Wow," said Conner. "Doesn't really sell the program, does it? So your Apep servers are just factory farms?" Conner pointed to the grotesque, unhappy looking animals caged within the narrow corridor.

"Oh God, man, come on," Mem'Rah chuckled, looking at Conner as if he'd just wet his pants. "Surely you've gathered from experiential knowledge that the further a species evolves the more proficient they become in exploiting natural resources."

"That's one way of putting it," Paul mumbled.

"The harbor," Aye'Sayuh said sternly. "We just want to get to the harbor."

"Which one?" Mem'Rah asked with exaggerated curiosity. "We've developed several in your absence, Bah'gohd. We now offer many exciting departure flights to popular destinations around the world!" He counted his long talons as he spoke. "Antarctica, the tropics, just about every major city in the civilized world. We can even whisk you away to an exciting subterranean SIAHD facility beneath the Nevada desert. I can't get into all the specifics," Mem'Rah contended, holding up his hands as if to keep us from inching forward. "It's classified stuff. I'm sure you understand."

I was hearing everything—the dialogue, I mean—but I wasn't there, not really. I was working at controlling my breathing, attempting to get some semblance of focus. I was thinking about what Hayes said about the visualization of inherent victory. My hand on the leather-wrapped handle of a long shuriken blade fixed to my belt, I breathed deep and imagined the blade leaving my hand, gliding through the air, then entering the exposed tissue of Mem'Rah's chest.

This guy killed my dad, I was thinking, over and over again. *This guy killed my dad.*

Without even a passing consideration of the mission and all that was at stake, I blinked slow, exhaled, and drew the shuriken, loosing it with perfect form as it made flight toward Mem'Rah's heart.

The only thing more impressive than the flawless technique with which I had thrown the weapon was how effortlessly Mem'Rah dodged it. Hearing nothing but the blood pounding in my ears, I watched as the thin, dagger-like shuriken flew past Mem'Rah and continued its impressive journey to the far end of the chamber where it bore its way into one of the great yellow eyes of the giant brain monster. The Apep creature seemed to howl—an awful, pained wail that could be "heard" on a telepathic level—and the entire fleshy web that covered the room pulsated wildly. The animal reared back on rows of insect-like legs and heaved its massive bulk from side to side, unable to free the offending blade from its impaled eye. Gobs of pus-like goo flowed from the wound like a burst zit. Violent palpitations seized the smaller creatures, their pink gummy bodies swelling with every beat.

"The hell," Barrett breathed out, clearly deflated.

Mem'Rah's game show host persona fell away in an instant. He took a step backward, reached into his robe, and drew what looked like a variation on Jade's alien rifle. Striped orange and white like a creamsicle, and also looking like a gun assembled from vacuum cleaner parts, the weapon hummed to life with gut-rattling sub-bass frequency.

"Guns?" Conner shouted. "Millions of years of evolution on us, and you guys still use this many guns?"

Mem'Rah shrugged. "If it ain't broke…" he chuckled, leveling the canon at us.

An immense bolt of blue conduction erupted from the gun's barrel. Not untrained ourselves, those of us in the danger zone executed effective evasive techniques, collapsing away from the blaster's reach. The massive electric tendril connected with the door through which we'd entered the chamber—the only white surface in the room—where it splintered out across the entire surface for a moment before the door detonated. No strategizing necessary, we fled through the makeshift exit.

"I'm sorry," I shouted to anyone listening as we charged through the opening.

"It sort of worked out," Aye'Sayuh said from somewhere in the fleeing squad. "I wasn't sure how we were getting out of there."

"But did he break that brain monster?" Paul asked. "Don't we need that thing to power the harbor?"

"No, look around," Emma said, "the facility still has power. Everything is connected here."

As if on cue, the lights flickered off, then slowly hummed back to life. "Uh," Aye'Sayuh said, "we'd better hurry."

We barreled into the next chamber, which had by now been overrun with prisoners, all of them lifting their NARS-Slates in the air and squinting at them as if they expected this might somehow power the devices back on.

"What's going on?" they whined.

"*Still* no Apep. Unbelievable."

"Are you getting anything?"

"I *need* to check my NARS."

"I had planned to upload really crucial content right now."

Behind us, Mem'Rah appeared like a movie villain through the curtain of grey smoke and showering sparks. He was pursuing us with little more than a slow stride.

"What is this guy, Jason Voorhees?" Paul asked. "He's totally going to catch us walking all slow like that, isn't he?"

"Probably," Aye'Sayuh admitted.

"So what do we do?" Becky yelled.

"Try to get to the harbor," Aye'Sayuh said, his eyes on the sea of prisoners before us. "Maybe Danny shorted out Apep enough to disable the security protocols."

Hearing our voices, the prisoners noted our presence, finding in us the only appropriate receptacle for their collective outrage.

"It's them!" one of the prisoners cried.

"They're jealous of our NARS connections! That's why they ruined the signal in here!"

With the prisoners before us and Mem'Rah rapidly encroaching, we drew our weapons and assumed fighting positions.

"What about these dick wads?" Barrett asked.

"Grease them," I said.

The scene that followed is hard to describe. When I recall the details of the fight, it honestly competes with some of the most badass moments in *Enter the Dragon*.

The eight of us moved through the army of prisoners with mesmerizing non-lethal proficiency. Using the chaotic instability of their tantrum against them, every opponent defeated was driven into the next wave of encircling prisoners like dominoes. A sort of mobile clearing was formed around us as we advanced, our wake closing in with battered but relentless NARS zombies slowly staggering back to their feet. By the time we'd made our way out into the main chamber, most of the prisoners had been cleared from our path. The stragglers were still fastened to their IV chairs, their thumbs drumming hopelessly on non-responsive NARS-Slates, their eyes glazed over.

Aye'Sayuh drove the butt of Emma's "sword-stick" into an assailing prisoner lunging toward us. The prisoner stumbled backward, and Aye'Sayuh used the long staff to sweep the prisoner's feet from beneath him. Diving through the air as the prisoner collapsed, Aye'Sayuh landed with a graceful roll and sprung up in front of the previously uncooperative entry panel. Rather than keying in elaborate combinations, Aye'Sayuh simply flattened his lizard-like hand on the panel's surface.

We all waited for what felt like an eternity, and the door finally opened before us. Inside was the harbor.

"Weapons and uniforms in the transport," Aye'Sayuh demanded, pointing at the tall, glass-like column alongside the giant aquarium of a harbor.

"Ah, geez," Jade complained, cramming his belt and satchel into the transport. "We've got to get naked again. I forgot."

I turned to the girls, prepared to compel them with life-or-death urgency, but discovered they were both moments away from being nude already.

"Danny!" Emma shouted. "Don't look!"

Embarrassed, I turned to the others to find them all more naked than myself. So I dropped my weapons and supplies into the transport, undressed in a matter of seconds, and ran naked toward the harbor with the rest of my friends.

There was the hiss of hot water, the head-splitting high frequency, and a feeling like you're about to explode from the inside out.

PART FOUR
ALL HELL BREAKS LOOSE

"Like, when I step outside myself kinda, and when I, when I look in at myself, you know? And I see me and I don't like what I see, I really don't."

–Brian
The Breakfast Club

MOD LOG, 25
MANDATORY ASSEMBLY

The second journey through the space-time continuum was only slightly less nauseating than the one before it. The first thing I remember was the music[36]. The second thing was the light. Stammering to my feet, I felt an initial sense of self-satisfaction that my ninja mastery afforded me not only fast recovery from interstellar travel but that my biological tendencies also seemed to be under control.

"Hey! No boner!" Conner coughed, wobbling where he stood. "Way to go."

"Is this Becky's tape or something?" I asked, blinking at the music, trying to force the fog to clear from my eyes.

"Ah, shit," Jade grumbled. "This is bad, you guys. Maybe the worst."

I squinted into the light needling its way into my constricting irises. Expecting to see the confined, sterile white space of the Vancouver SIAHD center, I was immediately taken aback by the vast openness of the surrounding area. There was another sound as well—something other than the DeBarge song that was playing. Was it... People? It sounded like the awkward frantic

---

[36] DeBarge, "Rhythm of the Night"

murmuring of a huge crowd. There were all sorts of colorful shapes coming into focus.

It *was* people.

Maybe hundreds of them. They were staggered in rows… bleachers, I think. Wait, are we in a gym? Is this a gym?

Oh no. We're at school.

The destination harbor that had accepted us was situated in the center of the Wesley High School gymnasium during what looked like a pep rally.

"No no no," Flynn and Bradley were both mumbling, their lips quivering. "This isn't happening."

The song went on playing around us:
When it feels like the world is on your shoulders
And all of the madness has got you going crazy
It's time to get out step out into the street
Where all of the action is right there at your feet

"You know that dream where you're standing in front of the entire school only to realize you're naked?" Barrett said.

"Shut up, and someone get our clothes from the transport," Emma pleaded, pointing to the receptacle column just outside the harbor.

Like someone running from the shower to answer the phone, I hopped awkwardly to the transport and, with the entire school watching, began unloading our clothes and supplies. As I set to work tossing everyone their outfits and using my own to keep my self as covered as possible, a singular shape stepped slowly into my clearing vision. It was Mr. Clanton, infamous drill sergeant principal of Wesley High.

"Mr. Thomas," Clanton said, pushing his black-rimmed glasses up the bridge of his nose. "Do you care to explain what *exactly* is going on?"

I squinted at Mr. Clanton's stupid buzz cut, the beaded sweat on his forehead and dark stains around his underarms.

"I think we made a wrong turn through a wormhole, sir," I said, doing my best to force my sluggish tongue to enunciate.

Clanton looked to me, then to the group of students dressing in the harbor. His eyes widened the moment he must have noticed Aye'Sayuh. Clanton leaned in and asked, "Is this part of the presentation?"

"Presentation?" I echoed, looking around again. The gym was festooned with green garlands, red bows, and string lights. "Rhythm of the Night" finally ended, and a new song began[37].

I pulled my combat outfit up over my body. "Is this, uh… Is this a Christmas dance or something, sir?"

"You're not part of the SIAHD presentation?" Clanton asked, gesturing at the others as they made their way out of the harbor, his gaze lingering on Aye'Sayuh. "We've been called to mandatory assembly so that the SIAHD can present the student body with some new groundbreaking technology."

"What's with the music?"

"The student council was told to 'steward an atmosphere of eager anticipation.'"

"I love Christmas music," I said.

Clanton nodded at the harbor. "The SIAHD installed this big vivarium thing earlier this week, but we weren't

---

[37] Wham!, "Last Christmas"

told exactly what time today anyone would be… showing up."

I nodded, looking through him and making a face like something smelled funny.

"I can tell you I'm more than a little disappointed to discover that yours is the presence we've been waiting for," Clanton snarled, his bewilderment now giving way to hostility.

"You and me both, sir," I agreed.

Just then, a hastily dressed Flynn Hardey and Bradley Press came barreling out from the harbor, buttoning their pants and nearly tripping on loose shoelaces.

"We've been kidnapped!" Flynn screamed, pointing at the others as they made their way into the gym.

"It's true!" Bradley agreed. "They were jealous of our influence and—"

An enormous set of jaws appeared above Bradley and suddenly snapped shut over his head with a loud wet crunch like someone breaking a bundle of sticks inside a wet towel. Blood sprayed out over my face like splatter paint. The massive Tarbosaurus—or *bata'ar*, as they're called on Gaina—lifted Bradley's spastic, flailing body and swung him violently from side to side like a ragdoll. With half of the animal's body still in the harbor from which it had just appeared, the Tarbosaurus, gulped down Bradley's body the way a crocodile chokes down a fish. A dismembered leg ending in a blood-streaked Reebok landed with a wet thud on the gym floor.

Before everyone went into mondo mass hysteria, I heard Barrett say, "Oh fuck, it ate his head."

Then there was panic. Absolute apocalyptic all-out riot end of days panic. Flynn abandoned his dying friend to flee into the madness. Students were screaming and clamoring over one another, tripping and stumbling down the bleachers, piling at the gymnasium doors until they burst open, and all the while the music[38] booming out over the PA. In a matter of seconds, the fire alarm had joined the cacophony.

"What are we supposed to do?" I shouted at Aye'Sayuh over the pandemonium. The Tarbosaurus was still devouring the few scraps that remained of Bradley, the rest of us cautiously inching backward away from the gruesome scene.

"The backup plan!" Aye'Sayuh said. "We have to complete the mission. We need to get back to Danny's attic."

Paul interrupted. "There's a goddamn T. rex in our school!"

"Technically," Jade said, "it's a Tarbosaurus."

"We really screwed up that Feed Camp," said Aye'Sayuh, gripping his naginata (or, sword-stick) with both hands. "With the holes we blew in everything and no security protocols I guess it got inside and, uh, into one of the harbors?"

The great, bulky dinosaur snapped up the last scrap of Bradley—just a bit of his leg and bloodied hi-top stuck between the beast's teeth. Standing upright, the Tarbosaur cocked its head like a bird, its beady eyes flicking in their sockets.

"Um, Aye'Sayuh," Paul began timidly. "I have a question about my ninja training. Am I supposed to fight this T. rex thing or what?"

"Dude," said Conner, "this thing would eat *Stephen Hayes*, man."

---

[38] The Waitresses, "Christmas Wrapping"

"No way," I said. "Hayes could totally kick a T. rex's ass."

"It's not a T. rex!" Aye'Sayuh shouted. "And even if it was, no one is kicking its ass." He looked to the gym's double door exits. "We'll trap it in here. Come on."

We turned to run and were immediately frozen by an ear-splitting rumble that sounded like both thunder and someone blowing bubbles in a milkshake. The giant harbor situated in the center of the gym was filled with billowing fog and flashes of purple light, and before we could wonder what was going on another Tarbosaurus lumbered out from inside.

Barrett readied a swear: "Ah…"

Before he could get the second word out, *another* Tarbosaurus lunged out from inside the murky harbor.

"…*shit*!" Barrett finished.

We ran, and the *three*—much bigger, much faster— dinosaurs followed. By the time we arrived at the gym exit we were creating a small hysterical pile-up of our own. With the galloping monsters only feet away, we fumbled frantically through the doors like a group of spazzoids who had forgotten their extensive black belt training. The double doors swung shut on one of the dinosaur's noses, all of us scrambling to our feet in the hallway, watching the massive jaws growl and snap. The hall was already a ghost town, the fire alarm and failed NARS-Slate presentation effectively emptying the panicked faculty and student body.

"Get bent!" Jade yelled, panting, and flung a small shuriken at the Tarbosaur's pinched muzzle.

The shuriken skewered the dinosaur's nose like a throwing dart, and the animal seized so violently upon impact that the gym door was ripped from the hinges. Struggling like a cat that doesn't want to be held, the immense lizard pried itself into the small frame until it became clear that it was indeed going to escape the gym in a matter of seconds.

"You stupid British idiot!" Paul yelled. "It was stuck!"

"I got prideful!" Jade screamed back.

We went barreling down the empty hallway, away from the Tarbosaurus and eventually screeching to a halt at two exit doors that we discovered were locked. Even so, Jade went on pulling the handle as if he expected some new result. Behind us, the first Tarbosaurus had made it through the door and was now steadying itself on its feet in what, to the dinosaur, was a very small hallway.

"Why do you keep trying?" Barrett screamed at Jade. "It's clearly locked.

"I thought maybe it was just stuck!" Jade answered. "That happens sometimes!"

"Completely shut school doors that are obviously locked are sometimes only just stuck?" asked Conner, exacerbated.

"I know some stuff!" Jade cried in his own defense, still pulling at the doors.

The dinosaurs' heavy feet were audibly plodding along the marble hallway behind us.

"Break the glass," Becky suggested, drawing her weapon.

"It's shatterproof," Paul said.

Becky struck the door's window several times until it clouded with a dense web of fine cracks, but made no signs of actually breaking open. I looked at Paul, surprised.

"What?" he said. "I know some stuff too."

In one unified motion, we all turned to face the pursuing monster, which was now officially charging toward us.

Barrett reached around to the satchel on his back, but rather than drawing a weapon, lifted his skateboard. I watched as Paul caught on and did the same before I finally dropped my skateboard as well. As I was about to step on, Aye'Sayuh appeared beside me with a piercing gaze.

"Let me," he said, gripping his naginata.

There wasn't any time to argue. As if acting on a previously devised plan for this ridiculous situation, Barrett and Paul pushed off toward the animal in a triangle formation, Aye'Sayuh following behind them with his weapon in hand.

"He can't eat all three of us, right?" Barrett said.

"Shut the hell up," Paul shot back.

"Brain Drain!" Conner kept shouting at them. "Brain drain brain drain brain drain!"

I cupped my hands over the sides of my mouth and shouted, "It doesn't work like that!"

With Aye'Sayuh in the middle, Barrett and Conner coasted to opposite sides of the hall and squatted down low. The Tarbosaurus focused in on Barrett, positioning itself to snatch this tasty morsel from its little vehicle as it passed.

"It's going to eat my head isn't it?" Barrett was yelling. "I'm going to die like Bradley Press! This is the worst!"

But whatever plan they had devised seemed to be working. Realizing there was *another* hors d'oeuvre on its other side, the Tarbosaurus considered lunging for Paul instead and found itself caught in the limbo of indecision. Looking back and forth like a dog that can't predict which way his master will throw a stick, the Tarbosaurus came away with neither Paul nor Barrett for a second entrée. Both of them compacted as low as they could go without falling, their hands over their heads as if this could protect them from a dinosaur's mouth, they went flying by in an instant before the big animal could open wide.

Aye'Sayuh went rocketing forward, straight into the jaws of the beast. Before the Tarbosaur had a moment to work out how to best turn around in the cramped space, Aye'Sayuh was seconds from impact. Squatting at the last possible moment, Aye'Sayuh ducked low and hoisted the sword-stick into the air above him. As Aye'Sayuh's skateboard carried him between the dinosaur's legs, the naginata moved through the Tarbosaur's belly propelled by Aye'Sayuh's momentum like a surgical scalpel. In another instant, Aye'Sayuh had passed through to the other side along with Barrett and Paul. The Tarbosaur shuffled on its feet awkwardly. For a moment, it seemed as though it might give pursuit once again, but with its first step forward the Tarbosaur's abdomen opened like an unzipping duffel bag. There was an immediate waterfall of blood, and the animal's gigantic bowels came dropping out from inside with a heavy, wet splat. Still standing, it teetered over the steaming purple and pale white tangle of its own innards and made a sad, low rumble in its throat.

Then it fell.

Aye'Sayuh spun the bloodied sword-stick like a baton, then sheathed it on his back.

"It smells like blood and shit," Jade said, gagging as we stepped over the eviscerated Tarbosaurus.

Still twitching, the lake of blood was moving down the hallway so quickly that there was no hope of avoiding it. We stepped carefully around the mostly dead animal, joining the other three at the other end of the hallway.

"Okay," Becky sighed, her hands on her hips. She looked at Aye'Sayuh and said, "*None* of this was in that first plan you gave us back in Danny's attic."

"Right," Aye'Sayuh said, determination on his face. "We have to get back there. To Danny's attic."

"My attic," I whispered, the rest of the plan coming to my brain.

"What? Why?" Conner asked. "The plan had to do with that heresy thing."

"The Final Heresies," Aye'Sayuh agreed. "They should be in Danny's attic by now."

MOD LOG, 26
THE HISTORIAN

Aside from the further addition of what had become ubiquitous Christmas decorations, the streets of Portland were mostly as we'd left them. It hardly seemed like there was any impending apocalypse at all. We made our way back home as quickly as we could make the trip on foot, and I began worrying about what my mom would say. Surely Aye'Sayuh's presence and our cool space-ninja outfits would lend *some* credibility to what I had to say, but I doubt that would be all it took to convince her that the reason we had left without a word was for the sake of the human race.

Moms can be unreasonable that way.

"Are you freaking out?" Emma asked, studying my worried expression.

"If my mom is home she might be upset."

"About what?" Conner interrupted. "How we all left the planet without telling anyone?"

"Yeah," I said.

My house was the only one on the block not decorated for Christmas, which was a bad sign.

"Dude," Paul said, as we slowed to a stop in front of my house. "How come your mom didn't deck your house out for the holidays like she always does?"

"Because her kid is missing," Barrett reminded us.

"Your parent's kid is missing too," I said defensively.

"All of ours are," Paul said.

Conner shrugged. "Mine don't care."

Becky stuck her lower lip out and rubbed Conner's back. "*We* care, Conner," she said.

"I'm not missing to *you*," said Conner.

"Exactly," Becky said, closing her eyes and nodding slowly.

"I don't see her car," I said. "Maybe she's not here."

Emma was the first to notice that it had begun snowing, and a moment later it was really coming down. By the time we'd made it to my front porch the snow was already gathering on the lawn.

Opening the door slowly, I called out to my mom.

"That's it?" Emma whispered. "You've been in space for days, and you waltz in like you've just come home from school?"

"*She* doesn't know I was in space," I whispered back.

I called out again, but no one answered. On the small table next to the door sat a small stack of MISSING posters with just about the worst possible picture of me available.

"Ah, geez, give me a break, mom," I said, looking down at the goofy looking grin staring back up at me from the page.

"Oh for Christ's sake," Barrett said, cuffing me on the back. "You're mad she didn't consult your NARS profile for a better headshot?"

"Well, no," I said, embarrassed. "But my eyes are barely open in this picture."

"Would you guys get a grip?" Aye'Sayuh grunted impatiently. "Come on. We don't have much time."

We headed into the silent house, up the stairs, and toward my pull-down attic ladder. Aye'Sayuh moved up into the attic first, and I followed behind him. It was a weird feeling, being home. Part of me was at such ease to find it as I'd left it that I'd secretly wished none of this insanity was going on and that we could all just head up to my room, order a pizza and watch a movie. We could even rent *Short Circuit* again. All these thoughts were swirling in my disoriented head as I ascended the ladder to my attic so that when I peered into the room, I was even more startled to discover a black man with a white beard hunched over my work table, typing furiously at my Atari ST computer.

Aye'Sayuh was approaching this strange man as if this all seemed perfectly ordinary to him.

"Did you finish?" Aye'Sayuh asked the bearded man.

"Almost," the man answered. "Your last transmission said you were heading for a harbor at the Feed Camps. I had no idea if you'd make it back alive."

"How close are you?"

"Close," the man rubbed his face. He looked exhausted. "Look I got in like you said. I haven't exactly been *relaxed* trying to stop a hostile alien takeover by breaking into the room of a missing teenager."

"Who is this guy?" Conner asked blankly.

"You're that guy from the Vancouver facility," Becky said as if it were coming back to her slowly. "The one who was locked up and forced to read from that killer scroll thing."

"Stewart Raffill," I said. "Why is he in my room?"

"It hit me before we left Gaina," Aye'Sayuh said, turning to us with fire in his eyes. "The missing piece of the plan."

"Dude, what are you talking about?" Jade asked.

"The Esk Hahr o' Mek is the proof we need to expose the plot against the lesser worlds, and Dr. Raffill is the only person to have read any of it and survived."

"We also stole it," Raffill added without looking up.

"That's true," Aye'Sayuh said with a single nod. "We did steal the available fragments of the document while we were there."

"Great," Barrett. "Why the hell is he lurking up in Danny's attic?"

Raffill shook his head. "Can you see why this would make for a difficult environment to concentrate in?"

"Dude, aren't you a scientist?" Conner asked. "Did you really just end a sentence with a preposition?"

"A difficult environment *in which* to concentrate," Raffill corrected himself. "Sheesh, what's with this one and grammar?"

"I have my moments," Conner reminded us.

"When we left Vancouver," Aye'Sayuh said, ignoring the squabble. "I armed Stewart and told him how to escape the facility and get to Danny's shed. I'd left a communication Scroll there that I knew I could contact him on."

Aye'Sayuh saw Conner shaking his head and quickly reworded his sentence. "On which to contact him, *dammit*."

Conner nodded and gave Aye'Sayuh a thumbs up.

"He's been working with Henson and Bowie at the rebel base to further decode the ancient text of the Esk Hahr o' Mek for the sake of legitimizing our claims and exposing the Imi conspiracy."

"Great," Barrett said again. "So you've had some old white-haired guy living in a shed behind Danny's mom's house without her knowing. Cool. Why is he in the attic?"

"And why not tell us any of this?" Emma asked.

"Because we didn't know if it would go anywhere. That was the missing piece," Aye'Sayuh said. "The *Historian*."

"This Historian?" I asked, feeling my throat tighten.

"We still don't know who the Historian is, and yet, he was one of the first to piece together the sinister plot of the SIAHD." Aye'Sayuh took a step toward the group and looked as though he were pleading. "We *need* the Historian to complete the plan. He knew first. He can guide us. Before his imprisonment, Stewart Raffill worked for the SIAHD to track the sources of transmissions and codes. Dr. Raffill can use the correspondence Danny received through NARS to track the location of the Historian and to communicate with him."

"Or her," Becky whispered.

"Uh, guys," I stuttered.

"There," Stewart Raffill shouted, clapping his hands together. "That's it. I've done it."

"Guys," I said again.

Raffill leaned forward, squinting at the Atari monitor as if something were wrong.

"What is it?" Aye'Sayuh asked urgently. "How far is he? How soon can we get a coded transmission to him?"

"Or her," Becky said a little louder.

"It shouldn't take long," Raffill said, still squinting at the screen. "Almost all of the Historian posts were made from this computer."

MOD LOG, 27
THE FINAL HERESY

Before anyone turned to look at me, I could feel that dense lump in my throat and the sting of threatening tears. I was taking deep breaths, desperate to keep my hands from shaking.

"The Historian posts were authored on *this* computer?" Aye'Sayuh repeated, his tone indicating the words made no sense at all.

"It's called an Internet Protocol Address," Raffill said, sitting back and leveling an open hand at the monitor as if to remind us this confusing turn of events wasn't his fault. "It's a numerical label assigned to a device that connects to the Internet. The Historian posts—well, four out of the five anyway—were uploaded from *this* computer's IP address."

Finally, the group turned to face me.

"I had been obsessing over the details," I stammered awkwardly, unable to keep my voice from quivering. "After… after my dad died, y'know? I didn't know what to do, I just, I kept studying his notebook and trying to figure out what happened."

It was silent for a moment as I worked to keep it together. Everyone stood there waiting, as confused as I was panicked.

"I was reading his notebook over and over again and tracking all this research, and I figured out how to poke around in secret corners of NARS and stuff. I found out the truth about what happened to my dad."

"Danny," Emma said in a fragile sounding voice that made me feel even more humiliated. "Did *you* write those posts?"

"I needed something," I said, unable to keep the tears back. "I couldn't just sit up here playing Nintendo and pretending nothing had happened. I needed to *do* something. I wanted to finish my dad's work. I started to write it all down—to journal everything. I was just, trying to keep up with everything at first but then I couldn't let it go, and I wanted you guys to understand. It didn't seem credible coming from me. I didn't think you'd believe my dad. When Aye'Sayuh showed up in my attic, I was scared at first, but then I thought that maybe everything was coming together for a reason. I thought that this *meant* something, that this was a way for us to matter."

"To *matter*?" Barrett said, his eyes narrowing. "You made all this up so you could *matter*? You sound just like one of those sad, pathetic NARS junkies."

"No," I said, "I didn't make it all up. I just—"

"So you *know* all that stuff is true?" Jade asked. "All that stuff about dinosaur evolution and class 3 civilizations and addiction slavery?"

"Well, no, not exactly. But I read my dad's journal, and I did research—"

"You *read stuff*?" Paul asked. "You made us all believe we were saving the world because you *read stuff*?"

"The letter we all got from the Historian on Gaina..." Barrett began.

"I sent it from my Slate," I admitted.

"But how did you know all of that stuff?"

350

"I read an archived document in Vancouver," I said. "In the room where the scroll was hidden while you guys weren't looking. I searched a name from my dad's notebook, and I found that document."

"Why send it then? In the middle of our training?" Paul asked.

"I had this dream… I was upset…"

"What about Aye'Sayuh?" Emma asked, welling with tears of her own. "He's a SIAHD scientist!"

Aye'Sayuh sighed. "I was given grunt work to make life easier for my superiors at the SIAHD center," he said, his voice monotone. "The SIAHD was looking for promising NARS users to induct into the Slate development program. My job was to move through the lower rungs of NARS and clean house by finding inactive NARS accounts—profiles with no connections and no smiles— and eliminating them from the database. One of the first profiles I found belonged to a user that called himself The Historian. No photos or connections, just four posts. I couldn't figure out who owned the account, so I ran a search for other accounts that had searched similar keywords. The only result was another low-level profile belonging to a one Danny Thomas. But I didn't know…"

"You're just some grunt technician?" Becky asked, sounding betrayed.

"I'm an intern," Aye'Sayuh confessed. "I *was* anyway."

"You said you were a scientist," Emma pointed out.

"No, I said I worked for the SIAHD, and I did. My parents got me the job. I'm just a kid."

"What about the rebel base?" Jade said as if he'd figured out a way to undo this awful conversation. "We met David Bowie and Jim Henson ourselves! You said there were others."

"They were both made to work at the SIAHD center, just like they told you. I knew they were suspicious of the Imi and I recruited them with the same information that brought me to Danny."

"Stephen Hayes?" Conner asked.

"I wrote to him," I shrugged. "The Historian wrote to him."

"Why would they all go to space and develop alien technology?" Barrett asked, his voice full of venom. "And where the hell did some tech grunt get that base anyway?"

"I learned of the neglected facility by digging through classified SIAHD documents. I knew that the station was derelict and that no one would monitor or bother us there. Henson and Bowie and Hayes—and Powersurf for that matter—all participated because they are convinced of the same evil plot that we are—the one Danny's father uncovered."

"*We?*" Becky snorted. "Zero times. I was convinced of a plot I thought had been identified by an anonymous expert and confirmed by a scientist from the inside."

"But it was!" I was crying now. Much as I'd tried to keep it back, the ugly, shaking sobs were coming. I'm pretty sure there was snot.

"I believed," I was trying to say. "I believed in what I said—in what the Historian said, I just... I didn't know how to convince you. I screwed up. Things got carried away."

Becky leaned in close to me, her cheeks wet with tears, and said, "I guess you're just full of secrets aren't you?" She turned to look at Emma, then left the attic. Emma looked back at me with a knowing face of heartbreak, turned, and left as well. There was nothing I could say.

When they'd left Stewart Raffill broke the silence. "I hate to interrupt this emotionally impacting scene from a John Hughes movie, but seeing as how it seems everyone has already forgotten, we *do* have a way of confirming our little conspiracy theory."

Aye'Sayuh and I looked to Raffill with desperation on our faces. Raffill reached beneath my gadget table and dragged an industrial case out from underneath it. After unlatching the many locks one by one, Raffill opened the case, revealing a glass container packed in grey foam. Inside the container was an ancient looking papyrus.

"Esk hahr o' mek," Aye'Sayuh whispered.

"Fuckin' A," said Stewart Raffill.

THOUGH Aye'Sayuh and Raffill were both capable of reading ancient Imi, neither one seemed all that enthusiastic about reading this particular document.

"I'm the actual scientist," Raffill said, the three of us crowded around the table in my attic. "If the world *does* need saving, I'm no good to it with an exploded brain."

"Is that what happens?" Jade asked nervously. "Your brain explodes?"

"I have a question," Conner said, raising his hand. "Will our brains explode just from *hearing* it, or do we have to be the ones reading it?"

"You're the only one we know to survive sustained periods of reading from the scroll," Aye'Sayuh insisted, looking at Raffill and sliding the document toward him.

"Why tempt fate?" Raffill asked, sliding it back to Aye'Sayuh.

"Is anyone listening to my question?" Conner asked.

"I'd also like an answer to Conner's question," I heard Paul say quietly behind me.

"Dude, did you not tidy up at all before we left?" Aye'Sayuh said, waving a hand at all the NES cartridges, He-Man action figures, and empty Ecto-Cooler boxes strewn everywhere.

"Oh, I'm sorry," I said. "I seem to remember leaving in a hurry because of some big dumb lizard's face all over the news."

"Everybody shut up!" Raffill shouted. "We don't have time for this!"

"Yeah!" Conner agreed. "And are our heads going to explode or what? It just seems important to me."

"I'm going to read it," Raffill said, ignoring Conner again. "You translate," he demanded, pointing to Aye'Sayuh. Then, looking at me, added, "and you write it down."

"On what?" I asked.

"On this," Raffill said, pointing to my Atari ST. "We're going to post what we find online."

"To who?" Barrett asked.

"To every single NARS user," Raffill smirked.

"Can you do that?" asked Barrett.

"I think so," Raffill said with a slight shrug, doing little to bolster anyone's confidence.

He took a deep breath, then reached into the glass case that housed the notorious artifact known as Esk Hahr o' Mek.

AT first, the process of documenting the translation seemed a tad uneventful. Raffill read slowly from the ancient looking scroll in a language that sounded like a mix between Hebrew, Swahili, and beatboxing. Aye'Sayuh offered the translation—a predictably biblical-sounding doomsday monologue—and I wrote it down.

Beware the lesser beast, the upright ape, the savage lizard.
Let them not breed in great number. Let them not make for
themselves homes of sophisticated design.

"Is this really it?" Jade asked. "They don't want us to
have houses?"

"Would you just shut up and let them read?" Conner
shot back.

"I'm just saying, what about homes of *crude* design?"

Ignoring Jade, they went on reading:

Let them not take for themselves mates and breed for
themselves families. Let them not walk the earth with the
bow and the spear. Let them not build for themselves
canons and weapons of fire. Drive them away from the
great city. Drive them far from the heart of Apep.

Pausing for a moment to crack my knuckles, I noticed
that Raffill's nose had begun to bleed.

"Dude," I said, "you okay?"

Raffill raised two fingers to the dark rivulet of blood,
eyed the results thoughtfully, then said, "let's keep going."

Hear not their cries for compassion nor their pleas for
mercy. As stili'savra spears the sari with his great snout, so
the Imi subdue the lesser beast, the upright ape, the savage
lizard.

"It's starting to get weird," Paul said.

"What's a *stili'savra*?" I asked.

"A great predator," Aye'Sayuh said. "You guys call it a Spinosaurus. Your paleontologists don't know this, but it mostly eats fish—or, *sari*, in Imi."

Beside me, Raffill's breathing was sounding belabored, and he had broken a sweat.

"Dude," I said, "are you sure you're okay?"

"We have to finish," Raffill insisted.

Take from them their homes, for they know not how to live. Take from them their families, for they know not how to thrive. Take from them their world, for they know not what it means.

Raffill, now shaking uncontrollably, set the scroll down on the table.

"Are you alright?" Paul asked.

"Is it his brain?" Conner whispered.

"Dude, shut up," Jade hissed.

"My brain is fine," Raffill panted. "That's it. That's the whole scroll." He moved over to the Atari ST and began typing.

"Wait. What?" I asked, staring at a measly couple of paragraphs on my computer monitor. "That was *it*?"

Barrett sighed. "What are we doing? We can't send that to every NARS user. It sounds like a damn poem from the Dungeons & Dragons handbook."

Just as Barrett had finished his sentence, Raffill shot bolt upright, his eyes rolling back in his head. A voice came from somewhere in his throat, but it wasn't his. It sounded almost like someone was manipulating his vocal cords without his consent, issuing wet guttural vowels and burping consonants. At first, it was just some long numeric sequences, but then we began to realize that Stewart Raffill was reciting classified SIAHD information.

"Write it down!" Paul screamed.

"I am!" I shouted back, clearly freaked.

It was all there. Everything I had suspected. The SIAHD's efforts had nothing to do with a benevolent concern for advancing the human species and everything to do with slowly terraforming earth's technology to create Gainian colonies on what they referred to as "the lesser worlds." The plan was brilliant. Not only had humanity witnessed a strategic alien takeover, we had *welcomed* it. By the time the Imi were poised to present the world with their doomsday device—the NARS-Slate—humanity was begging them to activate it. By the time the Earth would be invaded, conquered, and colonized, we'd have no idea and would go on staring down at our little machines like tranquilized lab monkeys.

Raffill finished reciting the classified plot against the lesser worlds, then went limp, collapsing on the attic floor. We surrounded him, everyone shaking him and shouting his name. Barrett slapped him gently on the cheek in an effort to rouse him from his stupor and recoiled when Raffill's eyelids rolled open revealing two red, blood-soaked globes within. He started coughing then; sputtering up blood like one of those artificial volcanoes you build for a science fair project.

We tried to sit him up and pat him on his back. We went on calling his name and shaking him. None of us were quite sure what to do, and all of us were quite sure Stewart Raffill was dying. A minute later, his face and the area around him were both covered in blood, and Raffill was no longer coughing, moving, or breathing at all.

357

"It killed him," Jade said in a stunned voice. He touched his own head carefully. "Are... Are we..."

"It's not going to kill us," I said quickly, not sure if I believed it myself. "If it were we'd know by now."

"What the hell just happened?" Barrett asked.

"It's not Esk Hahr o' Mek itself," Aye'Sayuh whispered, gradually coming to some personal understanding. "The words activate *another* hidden message when read aloud in the original language."

"What?" Paul asked, baffled. "Can they do that?"

"Of course," Jade said. "It's like a message hidden inside a frequency or a barcode or something."

"You don't know," said Paul.

"I know some stuff," Jade insisted.

Still staring at Raffill's body, Aye'Sayuh said, "They coded the specific mission brief within the ancient creed that birthed it."

"So what the hell happened to him?" Barrett asked, pointing at the bloody mess before us.

"Self-destruct?" Jade wandered aloud.

"Self-destruct," Aye'Sayuh agreed, nodding. "A mission briefing this classified requires a sacrifice."

"How will anyone know what to do if they die every time they read it?" I asked.

"The expense keeps briefings tightly regulated," Aye'Sayuh said. "And prevents the spread of classified information via human communicators."

"*Human communicators?*" Conner repeated, incredulous. "Do you *hear* yourself? This guy's fucking *brain* just exploded you guys! Do you realize how screwed we are? Even if it would have done us any good, the one guy who knew how to send this to every NARS user is now dead in your attic, Danny. We're not a part of some great rebellion. We're a handful of teenagers and a couple of lone nuts taking on an entire alien race that's already won the war by brainwashing humanity!"

"Wait, maybe not," said Jade, peering down at the Atari ST monitor.

"Maybe not *what*?" I asked.

"I think he already did it."

I peered at the monitor over Jade's shoulder and saw the NARS interface, a message screen opened. In the recipient field was a string of code followed by the words ALL USERS.

"He already did it," I said.

"I just said that," Jade reminded me.

"You said you *thought* he already did it," I argued.

"Will you just *send* the damn thing?" Conner shouted.

I set to work copying the transcript into the NARS message. When the work was done, I clicked the SEND button without thinking, half expecting an error message of some kind. Instead, the Atari's cursor became an hourglass icon for a minute or two before the familiar message appeared on the glowing monitor.

MESSAGE SENT.

"Ah dammit," Conner said, looking down at his Slate. "I'm getting a message from Powersurf. The fiasco at Wesley High is all over the news. They're saying we engineered an attack on Portland."

"They mention us?" Jade asked, worried.

"Not by name," Paul answered, looking over Conner's shoulder. "They mention 'unidentified suspects.'"

"An attack on *Portland*?" said Barrett. "Because of one incident in a high school gym? That sounds pretty dramatic even for the news media."

"Apparently, things have gotten worse," Conner said, turning his Slate to us. The headline across the screen read, SAVAGE ANIMAL ATTACK IN DOWNTOWN PORTLAND, beneath it, a blurry photo of a Tarbosaurus charging through the panicked streets.

"Oh," Barrett said. "I guess we should do something."

Everyone was silent for a moment, encircling Raffill's bloody corpse as if it were a visual harbinger of our shared destiny.

I took a deep breath, looked up at my remaining friends. They stared back, eyes full of desperation.

"We can't win," Conner admitted.

Conner was right: Things looked bad. I realized at that moment that I had allowed myself to believe so strongly in my suspicions—compelled by my quest for significance—that I had not yet considered the ramifications of what it might mean to learn I was entirely correct. And now here we were; us versus them. The little guy versus the machine. The odds were hopeless, but what else was there to do? I'm not sure, but I think the guys knew this to be true as well. The weight of the moment bore down on us. Finally, I broke the silence by saying:

"Not with *that* attitude."

MOD LOG, 28
THE BATTLE FOR PORTLAND

When I heard the door open downstairs, I had this simultaneous sense of dread and joy knowing that my mom was home. Conner, Barrett, Paul, Jade, Aye'Sayuh, and I all shared a panicked look, knowing it was better for us to unite with my mom downstairs than for her to discover us surrounding a bloody mess of an old man in the attic. We hurried down the ladder and into the living room. The others waited as I walked cautiously into the kitchen where we could hear my mom rummaging around.

Dressed in her waitress uniform, my mom didn't see me watching her for a moment while she put away a skimpy haul of random groceries. She seemed to have aged in the time I was gone. Lines had worn deeper into her face, no makeup, her hair a mess. I felt a surge of guilt for leaving the way I had, and that guilt gave way to even more guilt when I thought of Emma and Becky and the way I had betrayed their trust. Unable to consider these things any longer, I stood up and cleared my throat.

Mom was startled. She turned around to find me standing there awkwardly wearing my space ninja outfit and a nervous smirk. The look on her face was hard to describe. It was a bit like the face I make when stifling tears at the end of *E.T.*, only more intense.

"Danny," she whispered, putting her hands over her mouth immediately after speaking as if saying my name might make me disappear.

"Hey, Mom," I said, stupidly.

Things unfolded the way they do in movies. My mom rushed to me, touching my face to ensure I was actually there. She wept, embracing me and scolding me, asking an endless parade of reasonable questions, each of which I had no time to answer before the next one supplanted it. I was lost in the emotion of the moment, fumbling for words to somehow explain the infinite complexity of our present circumstances with an insignificant window of time to do it. I had begun to cook up a heroic sounding sentence when I realized my mom's attention had been seized by something behind me. I spun around to find what, in that moment, was the most bizarre looking group of individuals to ever populate our living room: The guys in their astro-warrior getup, and our unlikely friend, the lizard alien. Suddenly my heroic sentence escaped me.

"Okay," I stammered. "See, I got these messages online—well, no, I mean, I *sent* these messages online—"

My mom looked through me, with both hands on my face, and asked in a quiet, controlled voice, "where have you *been*?"

I knew then how careless I had been. After all, everything I had been through over the last few years, my mom had been through as well. Then she'd lost her son under circumstances even *more* ambiguous than my dad's death. How could I have been so selfish? What was wrong with me? Did I care about *anyone* other than myself?

"I'm sorry," was all I could say. "I wanted to finish what Dad started. I *needed* too."

After we had embraced for a few moments, my mom whispered in my ear, "What is that thing in our living room?"

This was it, I thought. The moment where I look my mom in the eyes and declare with steely resolve that though I can not explain the stakes in full, she would have to trust that I was up to something bigger than any one of us. The fate of the world was in the hands of a few teenagers and that there was no time for fear or desperation or grief. My mom would then bite her lip, eye me knowingly, and release me into the world so that I could rescue it. Just like the movies.

Only it wasn't like that at all. My mom wept and clung to me like a desperate child. She pleaded for me to stay, even attempted to subdue me. None of the epic stakes I had described affected her whatsoever. In the end, our strange group was forced to flee my home with my mom clamoring for her only son, collapsed in our snow-covered front lawn, begging us not to go.

SKATING in the snow was out, and Barrett's Aerostar was still parked near the edge of the woods somewhere in Vancouver. The group sped on foot toward the distant sound of screams and sirens coming from the urban core of Portland.

"The girls aren't answering," Jade said, tapping furiously at his NARS-slate as we ran.

"They aren't answering me either," I said, immediately hating that I had indirectly brought up what happened back in my attic. "Their last tracked location was at Becky's house."

"What the hell did you do, man?" Barrett asked, sounding not at all sympathetic about it.

"I'm like an astonishing panorama of human fuck-up," I said. "I don't have much to say in my defense."

Understandably, no one spoke up to reassure me.

The audible chaos crescendoed as we made our way downtown, cars screeching past, headed in the other direction, careening out of control in the snowy streets. When we rounded the corner from 9th Avenue to Davis Street, we were nearly trampled by a panicked surge of patrons fleeing Fuller's Café, our old breakfast spot.

"Whoa," Paul gasped, dodging the small mob. "What the hell is their problem?"

"Dammit," Barrett sighed.

I looked at Barrett, who was staring down Davis Street. I turned to see whatever it was that had bummed him out just in time to behold a charging Tarbosaurus heading directly for us. Without time to discuss, the five of us all engaged evasive maneuvers, scattering around the street as the raging animal thrashed its way over the snow-covered concrete. Drawn to the clamoring escapees streaming from Fuller's open doors, the Tarbosaurus reared back and brought its massive head down on Fuller's glass entrance. Pulling its bulk from the shattered glass and debris, the Tarbosaur roared in pain and frustration, the music from within Fuller's[39] now filling the street.

"Do we try to kill it or what?" Barrett asked, drawing the small rod from his back and extending the staff.

"*Can* we?" Paul wondered, gripping both sai.

"I don't think so, dude," Conner shouted from the other side of the street. "Weren't there two of them earlier?"

---

[39] U2, "Christmas (Baby Please Come Home)"

As if on cue, the second Tarbosaurus turned the corner of 8th Avenue and stood growling at the end of Davis Street.

"Why the hell did we run down here?" Barrett screamed.

The first Tarbosaurus—glass fragments speckling its leathery muzzle—lunged at Paul with a loud snap of its menacing jaws. Paul leaped backward, rolling through the snow and springing back up into a readied stance.

"Okay, it almost ate me!" he announced. "We need a plan of some sort."

The second dinosaur rushed toward me. By diving backward into Fuller's demolished storefront, I was barely able to evade the monster's bite. I fumbled the landing and fell on a pile of broken glass. The suit mostly protected me from being shredded, but the fall had robbed me of my breath, and I was now trapped with a giant dinosaur blocking my only exit.

The Tarbosaurus made frantic attempts at fitting its oversized head into the café's unaccommodating entrance, snapping and snarling like a rabid dog. Wheezing, I rose to my feet and drew my short sword, not yet sure of how much good it would do me. The Tarbosaur withdrew its head, stood upright, preparing to ram the café. I wasn't sure the entrance would survive another blow. Gripping the sword with both hands, I readied the only line of defense available.

Before the animal could lunge, a long length of chain shot out from somewhere I couldn't see and went coiling around the dinosaur's maw like a snare. The Tarbosaur struggled against the restraint, inadvertently tightening the chain like a muzzle over its massive snout. With the dinosaur distracted by its awful fit, I launched into a mad dash between the animal's thrashing legs, diving into a somersault and springing up on the other side of Davis Street. I lost my sword in the process and watched it go skidding across the snow.

The chain that had bound the Tarbosaur was fastened to a nearby street sign where Becky was standing.

"Look out!" she screamed.

I turned around in time to see the second dinosaur towering over me with its mouth wide open. With time to do little more than brace myself for the chomp, I closed my eyes tight and instinctively shielded myself with my arms. The Tarbosaur brought its hungry maw down over me, but instead of a meaty teenage morsel, the animal got a mouthful of sword-stick. Emma had intervened seconds before I was snatched up, inserting her beloved naginata upright into the huge jaws so that the blade-end of the staff was driven into the roof of the Tarbosaur's mouth by its own bite.

The Tarbosaur wailed in pain, slinging his enormous head wildly, the naginata trapped in its open mouth. I lunged for my sword, snatching it from the snow and assuming a defensive posture. Before this absurd scene could unfold any further, an awful voice called out from behind us.

"This is the stupidest looking thing I've ever seen."

I turned to see Mem'Rah strolling up Davis Street flanked by a dozen or so heavily armed Imi dressed in those Tron-looking grey circuit board bodysuits.

"I mean seriously, guys. What the hell are you doing? You get some high schoolers killed, and now you're battling dinosaurs in the middle of downtown Portland?" he asked as he walked, his long crimson robes dragging in the snow behind him. "Whose idea was the Christmas theme music[40]?"

"I love Christmas music," I said to no one in particular.

Recognizing the orange blasters that some of the Tron Imi were carrying, all of us readily forfeited our defensive postures.

"The teenyboppers are relentless," Mem'Rah sighed.

Some of the armed Imi produced smaller handguns and fired shots at the two Tarbosaurs, bringing them down immediately with what turned out to be tranquilizer darts.

"After all this, what's about to happen is going to seem anticlimactic."

With their rifles trained on us, we were made to drop our weapons and stand silently as we were each restrained and led in a line away from the wreckage of Davis Street.

"Do you guys know what caused Atari to crumble?" Mem'Rah asked as we went.

"Like, the video game company?" Jade asked.

"Yeah, sure," Mem'Rah said. "Video games, computers, all that stuff. Know what did them in?"

"That crappy E.T. game?" Barrett asked.

"Ah! No!" Mem'Rah shouted, pointing a finger in Barrett's face. "Of course you'd say that because that's what everyone thinks. It's a great, simple story! Atari was on top of the world. With the approval of none other than Steven Spielberg himself, Atari tasks a single game engineer—Howard Scott Warshaw—to crank out a hit video game adaptation of *E.T.* in only a few weeks so that it can be released in time for the Christmas shopping season. Of course, Warshaw delivers the infamously shitty *E.T.* game, which was rapidly returned to retailers by frustrated

---

[40] John Lennon, "Happy Xmas (War is Over)"

gamers. Eventually, Atari itself was destroyed by the world's worst game."

"That story is bullshit," I grumbled.

"No duh," Mem'Rah agreed. "But boy is it interesting and easy to understand. That's the point. A simple answer that is clear and precise will always have more power in the world than a complex one that is true."

We arrived at an unmarked white van, the back doors open and awaiting us. Inside, the cabin was lined on either side with uncomfortable benches. Two of the Imi Tron guards shoved us in the van and onto the benches, five of us crammed on either side when you count the two guards and Mem'Rah, who sidled up next to me and smelled like a hospital.

"Scooch over a bit, will 'ya?" Mem'Rah grunted. "Some of us have tails."

I scooched over.

The guards outside the van slammed the doors on us, and the engine growled to life. The van rounded the corner of 9th Avenue as Mem'Rah continued with his generic and villainous monologue.

"That's the problem with complex conspiracy theories," he sighed. "Not only are you cutting against the grain of culture to convince people of something they so desperately don't want to believe, but we've already given them a yummy pill that's easier to swallow."

"A *yummy* pill?" Barrett repeated, his eyebrows lowered.

"Yeah," Mem'Rah said. "Or, like, just a pleasant and accommodating shape. Like a gel cap."

"No, you said yummy," Paul reminded Mem'Rah. "How can a pill be yummy?"

"Look, yummy was the wrong word," Mem'Rah conceded.

"Are you *chewing* this pill?" Jade asked. "Cause that's the only way I can see tasting it at all."

I was listening, but I wasn't there. I felt like my head was on fire. My back ached from my fall earlier, and Mem'Rah's presence was like a burning personification of everything twisted out of shape inside me. If this weren't enough, Becky and Emma sat side by side across from me, both of their eyes fixed on me, expressionless. Emma's hair was pulled back tight, but a single wispy lock had come loose and fallen over her forehead. Her lips had that pursed look she always made without realizing. Becky's arms were over her lap, her wrists tied.

I felt as though all of my great failures had converged on a single time and place, and this was it. I was a selfish, broken kid. I had failed my friends, failed my mom, failed at accomplishing anything that mattered, failed at saving the world.

And I had failed my dad.

"Where we going?" Jade asked, breaking the momentary silence.

"The Portland police department," Mem'Rah answered happily. "No big deal; some minor criminal charges. Typical teenage shenanigans."

"That seems dumb," said Conner. "A few rogue kids come close to sabotaging your plot for global domination, and you hit them with minor citations?"

"No offense, kid," Mem'Rah chuckled. "But you've got serious delusions of grandeur. You guys have got to stop talking like you're in a movie. The most you've done is necessitate a significant amount of expensive repair to Feed Camp Seven, which is really annoying, believe me."

369

"Yeah right," Conner said. "You're not letting us go knowing what we know."

"Shut up, Conner!" Becky yelled.

"We know so much!" Conner said defensively.

"Shut *up*!" Emma fired back.

"Oh Jesus, seriously," Mem'Rah whined. "*Knowing what you know*? The talk is exhausting. Look, no one is locking you guys up anywhere. Basic rule of dealing with wild untenable conspiracy theories is to treat them dismissively."

Mem'Rah began entertaining an imaginary conversation with a make-believe journalist. "What does the SIAHD have to say about recent string of strange events that transpired in Portland, Oregon?" Then, reverting to his normal voice, answered his own question. "The events in question were little more than the petty crimes of a few trouble-making teenagers."

"No way," Conner spoke up, interrupting the phony interview. "We'll tell everyone what really happened."

"Who would care?" Mem'Rah shrugged. "If you dorks uncovered a sinister plot, why would we just send you back home? Do government agencies *release* dangerous spies likely to leak classified intelligence?"

"Shit," Barrett grunted. "That makes sense."

"Of course, just between us," Mem'Rah said quietly. "If you guys don't calm down and mind your own goddamn business, we'll have to kill you and everyone you love. Like, even your pets."

"I don't have any pets," said Conner to no one in particular.

Suddenly there was a strange vibrating sensation coming from the pocket near my ribs where I'd stored my

370

Slate. I could see that everyone in our gang had experienced the same weird buzz.

"What was that?" Mem'Rah asked.

"My Slate," I answered.

"Give me that."

Reaching awkwardly into my collar, Mem'Rah withdrew the Slate and squinted at it. For the first time, he looked slightly panicked as he stared down at the message blinking on the screen.

"What the hell does *wind* mean?" Mem'Rah asked.

The van slowed.

"Why are we stopping?" Mem'Rah called up to the driver, clearly annoyed.

"Something in the road," the driver called back.

Mem'Rah looked bewildered. "Drive *around it*," he said.

"It's, uh, a little… A little robot, sir" the driver said, his voice trailing off. "It's doing circles in the middle of the street. Hang on."

"Robot?" Mem'rah echoed.

The driver's door opened. The inside of the van was silent for a moment, all of us listening to the sound of the driver's footsteps crunching in the snow outside. The steps sped up, then slowed down, then sped up again, then stopped.

"What the hell is going on out there!" Mem'Rah shouted.

"Um," the driver said slowly. "It's hard to say…"

Immediately, the sound of a piano riff[41] coming from lo-fi speakers filled the air outside the van.

"What the…" Mem'Rah whispered to himself.

---

[41] Chicago, "Hard to Say I'm Sorry / Get Away"

There was a gasp outside, the sound of a struggle in the snow, and two flat packing sounds in rapid succession.

Barrett immediately leaned forward, folded his arm, and drove his elbow into the throat of the armed guard sitting next to him. The orange rifle tumbled to the van floor and was instantly and awkwardly nabbed by Jade, who fixed the barrel on the other guard, gripping the weapon in his restraints.

Jade screamed, "Put it d—"

Before the rest of the word could make it out, the weapon went off and the second guard exploded into bits, covering the inside of the van with a chowder-like coat of red and green gore and again leaving nothing behind but the smoking remnants of the creature's bottom half.

"Oh God," Jade said. "Is it dead?"

Barrett, once again covered in the puréed insides of an alien, screamed at Jade. "It's *absolutely* dead, James Bond. Stop firing that thing!"

"I panicked!" said Jade, then spun the weapon around and aimed it at Mem'Rah.

"Dude," I said, scooting away from Mem'Rah. "Don't panic again, seriously."

"Seriously," Mem'Rah agreed.

The back doors of the van opened from the outside, and there stood three familiar figures.

"Wind," Stephen K. Hayes said, smiling and nodding at Barrett.

"Wind," Barrett nodded back.

"Hello, boss," David Bowie said sarcastically to Mem'Rah. "Terribly sorry to interrupt the road trip. You won't mind if we borrow your passengers, will you?"

Mem'Rah rolled his eyes. "Shouldn't you two be in a garage somewhere making puppets or something."

Jim Henson sighed. "As much as I'd like that, we've had to prioritize our lives a bit differently as of late." He reached out his hand and helped Emma and Becky down out of the van.

With the barrel of the gun in his back, Mem'Rah was led to the front of the van where four saddled gaulish stood in the snow.

"Is someone else here?" I asked, counting the animals and noting an extra.

A voice answered from a few feet away. "It wasn't at all necessary to involve this guy, but I thought it would be pretty funny," Powersurf said, pointing down at Rob, who was tracking his way slowly through the snow.

"Well, lads," Bowie said as he set to work removing our restraints. "You've done it."

"Not exactly how any of us thought you would," Jim Henson pointed out, "But you've uncovered the truth behind the Final Heresies and the plot against the lesser worlds."

Their praise made me nauseous. I didn't know whether to deflect it or to keep my mouth shut.

"Only... What now?" Jade asked, still holding Mem'Rah at gunpoint. "I'm not all that comfortable standing here like this."

In one fluid movement, Mem'Rah ducked low and used his massive tail to sweep Jade's legs out from underneath him. Jade fell on his back with an awful thud, and the orange rifle landed upright in the snow like a stake in the ground. Mem'Rah snatched the weapon and turned it on me, raising a warning hand to keep the rest of the group back.

"You guys are seriously so stupid," Mem'Rah said. "We're doing everything we can to let you off the hook, but all this dress-up is going to get you killed."

Walking more animal-like than before, Mem'Rah made several long strides toward me, extending a green arm toward my head. This lumbering vulture-like lizard creature, his lips peeling back over rows of long, sharp teeth. With his ornate robes dragging in the snow behind him, he skulked bird-like, his small fiery eyes burning me. With the gun trained on my head, I kept my hands in the air as Mem'Rah reached behind my ear, pinched my mo'ach implant, then tore it off.

I wailed in pain, my legs going wobbly before I collapsed in the snow. With my hands to the warm flow of blood pouring from the wound, I fought back a wave of dizziness and debilitating nausea. Suddenly I felt as though I was waking from a drug-induced sleep. Where I was and why I was there escaped me, there was only the fiery, knife-like pain in the side of my neck.

Mem'Rah pinched the mo'ach casing between a finger and thumb, the long screws still dripping blood. "I keep telling you to knock it off with this silly movie act, but you're determined to live it out."

Shaking, I managed to get to my feet. I attempted an awkward fighting position, but all I could remember of my comprehensive training were illustrations in a book I had read years ago. The snow was coming down in heavy sheets now. I could see only a few feet in front of me through the dense white. Mem'Rah hammered the butt of the rifle into my face. A blinding pain spread through my nose and cheekbones, a new flow of warmth running over my lips and chin. Why didn't I see the hit coming? Why

374

couldn't I dodge it? My mind had yet to comprehend the loss of the mo'ach.

Mem'Rah groaned and walked around to the front of the van toward the driver's seat. "I'd rather not have to kill everyone, but you guys are seriously making me wonder which option will be less annoying in the long run."

Propping an elbow on the van's open door, Mem'Rah leveled the gun at the group and sighed. "Now everyone is going to get inside the goddamn van and we're all going to—"

Appearing from the white fog behind him, the Tarbosaurus' teeth snapped shut on Mem'Rah so that only his flailing bird-like feet were left protruding from the dinosaur's clamped jaws.

"That's some seriously ineffective tranquilizer," Conner said.

"Take the van!" Hayes shouted, climbing atop his gaulish as his companions did likewise.

I stumbled over to grab Rob as the seven of us filed into the van, Barrett taking the driver's seat. The Tarbosaur lifted its head and choked Mem'Rah down in two loud gulps. As the van peeled off down the snowy street, tires spinning momentarily in the cold slush, the dinosaur grew smaller in the rearview mirror, then disappeared.

"Where the hell are we going now?" Conner asked.

Once again, all of us felt that simultaneous vibration from our NARS Slates and looked down to discover that David Bowie had uploaded a map leading into the rural wooded area of Vancouver.

"They're telling us to go back to the SIAHD facility?" Paul asked in disbelief.

"No, look," Jade said. "It's not the facility. It's the forest surrounding it. This is a map back to Barrett's Aerostar."

Crumpled on the bench in the back of the unmarked van, I was using one hand to pinch the bridge of my nose and the other to apply pressure where the mo'ach had been torn away. My head was spinning. I felt a soft, warm hand on my arm and opened my already swelling eyes to see through my mostly blurred vision that Emma was sitting next to me.

"Are you okay?" she asked gently.

"Yeah," I lied, then shaking my head, confessed, "no."

"I'm sorry I stormed out of your attic. I wasn't thinking things through," Emma told me.

Her apology was like a knife in my heart.

"Don't be sorry," I said. "I would have left too."

"Becky told me about what happened between you guys on Gaina," Emma said, the words twisting my stomach in knots.

My mind rushed toward some explanation that would smooth all of this over, but of course, nothing was there. Having given up on salvaging even a scrap of self-defense, I just said the only thing I could muster without any pretense to carry it.

"I haven't been thinking things through either. I've mostly been thinking about myself. I've made a horrible mess of things."

"Yeah," Emma sighed.

"I'm sorry," I said, meaning it very much.

"I know," she said.

"I'm sorry," I said again, this time looking at the others around me.

Conner took a deep breath. "Then Peter came to Jesus and asked, 'Lord, how many times shall I forgive my brother or sister who sins against me? Up to seven times?' Jesus answered, 'I tell you, not seven times, but seventy-seven times.'"

"Is that you or Jesus?" I asked.

"Both," Conner nodded with a little smile.

"I can see the Aerostar," Barrett said as the van began to slow. "What do we do with this van?"

"Leave it here," Paul said. "If the SIAHD comes for us, nothing we do to this van will change anything."

Barrett shifted to park, took a deep breath, then looked over his shoulder into the back of the van. "Where do we go now?" he asked.

"Home, I guess," Paul shrugged.

The Aerostar and the forest itself were both covered in a blanket of undisturbed snow. Either the blow I had taken to the face had affected my hearing, or everything was as quiet as any place I'd ever been. Aye'Sayuh, who hadn't said much since we'd escaped, looked around with a sad sort of expression.

"What is it?" Jade asked.

"I guess I should go back to Gaina," Aye'Sayuh said, nodding into the distance where we knew the SIAHD facility and the harbor transport were hidden. Aye'Sayuh looked to the small rabble of teenagers he had befriended under the world's weirdest circumstances.

"Come," he said to me.

Barely able to stand and covered in blood, I answered, "Stay."

Aye'Sayuh placed a hand over his chest and said, "ouch."

Copying his gesture, I agreed. "Ouch."

Aye'Sayuh nodded, saying, "I'll be right here."

"What the hell are you guys doing?" Becky interrupted.

"Are you seriously doing the end of *E.T.* right now?" Conner asked.

Aye'Sayuh and I both giggled like idiots.

"Righteous," said Conner.

MOD LOG, 29
ANTICLIMAX

The SIAHD had taken up temporary residence in my house under the guise of "concern for our safety in light of possible bacterial infection." Like the poor tripods in *War of the Worlds*, the human populace was allegedly at significant risk of falling to an alien sickness because of a few teenagers who had failed to follow proper sanity protocols while embarking on illegal interplanetary travel. Mom and I had both fully expected to be cut off from our home forever. Maybe some SIAHD goons would find us at our hotel in Vancouver and assassinate us or drag us away to the nearby lab. Before we could finalize plans for our new lives as fugitives, a friendly (human) SIAHD employee contacted our hotel room phone informing us that we were free to return to our house whenever we were ready.

Against our better judgment, we agreed to make one last journey home to gather supplies but were startled to find the house mostly as we'd left it. The only major difference was that every trace of Stewart Raffill's body (and blood) and had been completely removed from the attic. All my tech seemed to be as I had left it—not even my NARS account nor any of the files documenting the contents of the Esk Hahr o' Mek had been modified or deleted. Perplexed, my mom and I looked at one another, shrugged, then went to sleep in our own beds. The next day, we woke up, had coffee together, and both agreed we no longer saw any reason—nor had any energy—to run.

For several days I didn't leave the attic at all. I slept very little, focusing every bit of available time and energy to documenting everything that had happened in these last twenty-eight Mod Logs—including the Historian essays—posting our entire story in as much detail as I could muster for all of NARS to see. Well, at least the small number of people who pay any attention to my account anyway.

The messages began appearing in my inbox somewhere around Mod Log 04. Two posts later, there were too many messages for me to read. Dozens and dozens of letters drawing my attention to other NARS users who had made the same observations I had, only months before me, and with more detail and accuracy than my conspiracy theory had ever developed. Not only had I concocted the Historian to lend my story and my life some sense of credibility and significance, but I was also only one person in a long line of people who had come to the same conclusions. I hadn't even done it well.

I went on posting our story anyway. I'm not sure why. It was a bit like journaling some troubling dream—if I wrote it down, maybe my memories of what had happened would not escape me. Despite the pain of continuing, I became obsessed with finishing these logs. As the letters continued to pile up, I worried that even the incredible journey my friends and I had experienced was somehow illusory. I worried that any moment someone would pull back some veil of my own design and reveal I had fabricated every detail without even knowing, my lies so complex and expansive that even their designer was unable to wield them with efficiency.

I spoke to Paul and Jade, both of whom were understandably grounded. Conner's parents were also outraged, from what he'd told me, but I think he was secretly happy to have renewed their concern for him. Barrett's parents had spent more time together trying to find him than they had in years. This is the first Christmas they will spend with everyone under one roof since his parent's divorce. Though he hadn't said so himself, I could tell he was happy. I'd tried reaching out to Becky and Emma, but neither had given any indication they'd ever speak to me again.

After I'd finished writing and publishing the 28th mod log, I noticed a message in my inbox with the subject string THE FINAL HERESIES. The message linked to a NARS account called "Anticlimax." Whoever ran the account had brought every detail of the now robust and widely circulated Imi conspiracy theory together into a thorough and well-articulated timeline complete with photographs of newspaper clippings, recorded news broadcasts, even photos that some Israeli NARS users had taken from within a SIAHD laboratory. At the fulcrum point of the collected data was a strange message that had been delivered to every NARS account more than a week ago. Though the message had been largely dismissed as a prank, the Anticlimax account had tracked the IP address from which the message was sent and discovered both the time and location seemed to correspond with strange reports of animal attacks and increased SIAHD presence in Portland, Oregon.

Maybe—this Anticlimax person theorized—this mysterious NARS user really *had* stumbled upon what amounted to hard proof of the Imi conspiracy and the SIAHD had intervened. Of course, with hundreds of SIAHD officials flooding every corner of the city of

Portland, the news media chalked the debacle up to a few troubled teenagers who—in their impetuousness—were seized by wild and foolish conspiracy theories that gave way to a brief surge of criminal activity. Unlike the long line of conspiracy theorist before them, this Anticlimax character proposed a practical way forward: Abandon NARS.

In a strategic, concentrated gesture, any NARS users who had become wary of what the Imi were actually up to, should, on Christmas day, deactivate their NARS accounts. After all, this mysterious user pointed out, if there really *is* a conspiracy, is NARS worth it?

Thousands had flooded the Anticlimax profile with words of support as well as hostile disagreement. Countless users pledged their allegiance to what was being called "The Great Deactivation," while narcons and NARS loyalists went the typical route by hurling accusations of conspiracy paranoia and ridiculous fantasy logic.

I was caught in a debilitating recursive loop. I should have been thrilled to see my concerns validated and the incredible amount of people all over the world prepared to take a stand against the SIAHD. Instead, I felt painfully envious of this faceless Anticlimax person. I wanted credit for transcribing the document that had brought his or her theory together. I wanted to *lead* the rebellion against the Imi, not just follow along with it. Then came the inevitable shame I felt for my jealousy.

I wanted to matter.

ON the morning of Christmas Eve, 1987, Rebecca Burkley woke me up. Her long, red hair fell around her freckled face as she smiled gently, shaking me from sleep.

"Becky," I said groggily, sitting up and looking around the cold attic. She was dressed in a green sweater and black leggings, pink legwarmers drawn up over her high heels.

She gave me a gentle look. "Merry Christmas, Danny."

The grey light of morning filled the attic. Outside it was snowing again, the little flurries falling in slow patterns over the attic window. Unsure of what to say, I pointed out that I had tried several times to contact her. I wasn't sure why I was bringing this up. I felt flooded with emotion at the sight of her, our time apart creating a palpable barrier between us.

"I know," Becky sighed. "I'm sorry."

The sound of her apology filled me with shame.

"*I'm* sorry, Becky." I searched for the words to explain every foolish thing I had done over the last month but realized I was still caught up in the same nonsensical spiral that had compelled me to fabricate the Historian in the first place.

"Why aren't you listening to Christmas music?" she asked.

I shrugged, unable to look her in the eyes.

"Rob," Becky said. "Play Christmas music."

Rob whirred to life, music[42] issuing softly from his speakers.

"Danny Thomas," Becky said lovingly. "I don't know of another person who loves Christmas and Christmas music as much as you do. It seems wrong that your attic should be this quiet on Christmas Eve."

I lay back and put my hands over my face. Becky lay down beside me, both of us parallel, looking up at the ceiling from my uncomfortable twin bed.

---

[42] Stevie Wonder, "Someday at Christmas"

"Have you talked to Emma?" She asked.

I shook my head slowly. "I don't think she'll want to talk to me any time soon."

"Yes she will," Becky said. "You want her to, don't you?"

"Yes," I said quietly. There was a brief silence before I went on. "I feel as though I've been infatuated with her, but I'm only now learning to know her. To *see* her." I turned my head to face Becky. "And you," I added. "I wish I hadn't made such a mess."

Becky smiled. "She'll forgive you. You'll see."

I think we both relinquished something in that moment.

Becky sighed, "I don't think we know how to grieve," she said.

"I don't either," I agreed.

"You know, I've thought a lot about it these past few days—everything we've been through. I think maybe we were all trying to deal with the things we've lost. For me, part of this crazy adventure to save the world was about proving that my mom had made a mistake by leaving me."

"I don't understand," I said.

Becky sighed. "Well, if I could do something that really mattered and prove how entirely worthwhile I am, well then I'd know that my mom was wrong to leave me."

"*You* would know?" I asked. "I thought this was about your mom."

Becky shrugged beside me. "Sometimes," she said. "But a lot of the time I'm trying to convince myself." She turned to face me, her eyes only inches from mine. "Ever since my mom left, there's a part of me that's always a little afraid that the people I love will leave me."

"I am too," I said.

Becky, whispering now, continued slowly. "When we found out that you had written those Historian posts, I felt like the secret you had kept from me was a reminder that I don't deserve your honesty. Because, of course, the people I love will always reject me and then leave me behind."

Becky's eyes were honest and calm. I wasn't sure what to say. "I didn't know how to make sense of anything," was the best I could do. "Sometimes I feel like my dad is dying all over again."

"I know," Becky said as she took my hand and squeezed it.

We both looked up at the ceiling again.

"Are you finished writing our story?" she asked eventually.

I took a deep breath. "I'm not sure. Maybe I'll write about this." We both laughed.

"What about tomorrow? Will you erase your account?"

"I think I have to," I said aloud with a deep breath. "I think I have to give this up finally."

"Give what up?"

"Grasping at significance this way. I don't know why I feel this need to *matter*. I'm ashamed."

"Do you think that maybe if you had mattered more, your dad wouldn't have left you?" Becky asked quietly.

Her words cut through me. "My dad didn't *leave* me," I said. "He died."

Becky propped her elbow on the mattress and rested her chin in her hand. "Oh Danny," she said with a loving smile. "If only I could convince you to believe yourself when you say that."

And so I started to cry.

We stayed that way for a while—me weeping quietly with Becky beside me, squeezing my hand.

Eventually, Becky spoke again. "Your dad didn't leave you, Danny. He died. It isn't fair, and it isn't right, but that's what happened."

The tears finally let up, and I nodded silently.

She went on. "My mom didn't leave because I'm unlovable. I don't think my mom could *see* me, y'know? Not really anyway."

"I do know," I told her.

"Do you remember that poem that Conner mentioned that last night in your attic before we left?" Becky asked.

"Psalm 148," I nodded.

"Yeah," she said. "I dreamt of it once, on Gaina. I dreamed I saw the universe unfolding in indescribable beauty and wonder. We were there, all of us. And we mattered. Maybe not the way we thought we might, but we mattered to each other."

"I had the same dream," I confessed. "Was ALF in your dream too?"

"Matthew Broderick," Becky sighed.

Outside, the snow went on falling. Inside, the attic was warm, the music filling the silence.

"I'm going to erase my NARS account," I said after a while.

"Me too," Becky said.

A few feet away, unburdened by the weight of the world, Rob went on singing his Christmas carol.

Sleep in heavenly peace
Sleep in heavenly peace

FINAL MOD LOG
A SMALL BOY

The attic that I have made my bedroom was once just an attic. In those days, I had a bedroom not unlike most kids my age. Just an ordinary room. Before my dad died, he would often step into that bedroom in the mornings before he left for work. When I was a small boy, he'd remind me to make the most of my day, to do my best to be kind to the people around me, to stay out of trouble. When I was a little older, he'd reassure me that the season of alienation and frustration I was enduring in high school was ordinary but not permanent. "You're my favorite person," he'd tell me in the half-light of my old bedroom. "Things are hard sometimes, but we can get through them."

I believed him, of course.

Above our heads was a silent, unoccupied attic. Lonely and cold, visited just a few times a year. In one corner, boxes of Star Wars and He-Man action figures, in another, tiny t-shirts for a toddler with goofy, colorful text that read things like, "Dad's Dude." But in another corner still sat an old leather trunk packed with a Super 8 camera, a small projector, and dozens of reels of film. Documented on these reels were summers at the Oregon coast, birthdays with dinosaur-shaped cakes, and so many Christmas mornings. My favorite reel wore a strip of masking tape as a makeshift label, my dad's handwriting had left a single word there: *Dancing*. If you spool the reel on the small projector, extend the tripod that blooms in a cheap foldout screen, and dim the lights, you'll see my family dancing.

There will be my mom and dad, the Super 8 mounted on a shelf as they dance to Eric Clapton and Elton John together in a tiny studio apartment years before I ever came along. You'll see my mom, her belly swollen with expectation, swaying to Jim Croce records as my dad asks, "you excited to meet this little dude?" My mom goes on dancing, cradling me through her distended abdomen the way pregnant women often do. Then, there will be my dad and me. He'll place the camera on a shelf or tabletop, and he'll set Queen's *A Night at the Opera* or the soundtrack to *Footloose* down on the turntable, and he'll shout over the loud thump of the music, "Dance, Danny boy! Shake your booty!"

"Shake bwoodee," I'll echo back in standard toddler-speak. "Shake bwoodee, Dada!"

And we'll go on dancing.

I've since wondered why my dad so loved to film these instances of music and motion that they'd go on to uniquely populate their own reel of film. It's not like we often revisited the footage. I can think of only one or two such times. And yet, if ever an evening gave way to dance, my dad would say, "I should go get the camera." And so the dancing lives on in the film. It sits there even now.

After he died, it no longer made sense to me that I would sit in that old bedroom, my gaze to the door, waking every morning to the jarring disruption of my father's absence. Learning every morning, again and again, that he wasn't coming. I packed my things and stripped that haunted place bare, hauling box after box down out of the attic and then filling it with new things until a transfusion had been completed. My old bedroom no longer reminds me of those days. It is just four walls enveloping a collection of dusty boxes. My new room knows only new memories, none of them able to wander far from the dull ache of loss my mom and I carry with us every day. Of course, it is a happy place too. It is a room that has known friends and laughter and, as you know, even romance.

When these two rooms exchanged identities, I left only one box—one memory—in the attic. The box of film reels. In this very same box, I'd discovered my dad's notebook. While emptying the attic, I'd leaned over to lift the box several times, paused thoughtfully, then moved on to other boxes instead. Soon the entire attic was barren except that single box, sitting lonesome in its corner, knowing it could not be stirred. Moving the final box felt like the burial of those memories, and I wasn't prepared to commit them to rest. And so the box sits there to this day.

Inside, my family goes on dancing; My mom and my dad, young and in love. A young family about to change forever. A small boy dancing with his great hero.

I'm still there, dancing with my dad.

AKNOWLEDGEMETNTS[43]

Abigail Porter, Bethany Allen, Tyler Hanns, Matt Hughes, and Patrick Porter all read early drafts of this book and offered commentary and critique that shaped the story in tremendous ways.

Tyler was also kind enough to work out the design and layout when he was already swamped with other things. This is not the first time he's done such a thing for me.

I went through some stuff while writing this book several years prior to its publication. I am especially grateful to my wife, Abi, who went with me, and to my son Beck and daughter Isla, who smothered my sorrow with joy.

---

[43] Orchestral Manoeuvres in the Dark, "Enola Gay"

ABOUT THE AUTHOR

Joshua S. Porter is the author of four previous novels and a memoir. He lives in the Pacific Northwest with his wife and kids where he is the pastor of a small church. He is not ashamed to confess that he enjoys every song mentioned in this book and disagrees that this somehow compromises his punk rock credibility, as some have suggested.

www.ingramcontent.com/pod-product-compliance
Lightning Source LLC
Chambersburg PA
CBHW030622250626
47154CB00006B/1878